THE PRICE OF PLEASURE

High Passion Meets High Crime

Leighton Francis

Published by Central Park South Publishing 2023
www.centralparksouthpublishing.com

Typesetting and e-book formatting services by Victor Marcos

ISBN:
978-1-956452-40-2 (pbk)
978-1-956452-41-9 (hbk)
978-1-956452-42-6 (ebk)

To the GAGAs

and the greyhounds

who have inspired this

incredible journey.

66

Passion is the bridge that takes you from pain to change.

—FRIDA KAHLO

Love is comprised of a single soul inhabiting two bodies.

—ARISTOTLE

CONTENTS

PRELUDE

The black BMW glistened in the moonlight as it eased its way into the shadow of an Astor Street brownstone. Brownstone, of course a generic term commonly used for any of the mansions on this luxurious street in the Gold Coast section of Chicago. This version was grey stone with ebony trimmed windows and ironwork. It sat elegantly at the end of a street of like buildings, where a few of the mansions were even made of brown stone.

The BMW stopped and the engine fell silent. Dr. Preston Jacoby emerged from the vehicle with a confident gait. He walked up the short concrete stairs purposefully.

Without a knock, the black high gloss doors opened for him and once inside he handed the car keys to an obedient valet.

He didn't waste a step as he walked across the marbled foyer toward a grand winding staircase. While he was in midstride, a beautiful raven-haired server dressed in tight black ankle pants, patent leather stilettos, ruffled blouse, bow tie and a black vest that accentuated her proportioned cleavage offered him his favorite nightcap, 26-year-old Kentucky bourbon neat, off a silver tray. He smiled, took the glass with familiarity and pressed on to the staircase.

There was no hesitation at the top of the staircase as he walked to the third white lacquered door to his left. The door opened as he was a step away from its threshold and she was there, breathtaking. To say Gabrielle had a model's looks would be a disservice. Her brown hair highlighted with golden shades, her camisole short enough to accentuate her exceptional legs, yet long enough to just peak at the thigh highs that draped those legs. The sheer lingerie revealed the silhouette of a flawless body. She greeted him with her own cocktail, a clear liquor on the rocks, and they clicked glasses and politely kissed as their greeting.

With one hand, he undid the bowtie of his tux and slowly lowered himself onto the black suede couch in her room. She walked over to the small bar in the left corner of the spacious bedroom and pretended to freshen her drink, but the real purpose was to allow him to feast his eyes on her as she moved gracefully in her heels. The height of her heels accentuated her perfectly proportioned legs. She could feel his excitement from across the room. Pirouetting on the ball of one foot she turned after filling her drink and walked a slow runway walk toward him. In that situation and with her grace, the exaggerated walk seemed exceptionally sensual. Her sheer camisole bounced off the top of her thigh highs and she could feel his mesmerizing stare at her visual foreplay.

The rise in the superb fabric of his black Armani tuxedo pants broadcast his excitement for her as he followed her walking toward him. In like fashion, her eyes fixated on the prominent bulge in his pants. She stopped inches from his knees and he immediately spread his legs open, inviting her closer. Invitation accepted and she shuffled nearer until her silky legs touched the couch. She bent over at the waist, opened her mouth slightly and her face merged with his in a kiss that had an energy of its own. His hands roamed along her stockings as they kissed and their tongues danced. Her hands ran through his thick salt and pepper hair occasionally tugging at a handful of his locks passionately.

After their long kiss, she pulled away from his mouth, looked directly into his eyes and pulled his tux jacket off his shoulders. He spread his arms wide across the back of the couch, his chest pumping from excitement and breathlessness.

She ran the nail of her index finger across the lump in his pants and he throbbed with the tease. With her other hand, she undid each of the studs of his tux shirt. They both smiled as she held one of the studs up eye level. It was platinum with the head of a Greyhound sculpted on its tip and its shaft the dog's paw. With a delicate touch, she carefully placed each stud on the stainless-steel end table at the side of the couch. With the studs removed the tan skin of his chest beckoned her caress and her tongue flicked against a nipple. His back arched and his eyes widened at the concentration to one of his most sensitive erogenous zones. His hand instinctively found its way between her legs and he fondled her thong. The movement of her pelvis into his gentle strokes spoke loudly of how welcome his touch was to her.

Still teasing his chest with her manic tongue, she lifted his shirt out of his pants, tossed it aside as if it was a nuisance. She paused in her mission and returned her mouth to his lips and they furiously kissed as she unbuckled his pants that seemed to burst open because of the intensity of the excitement in his manhood. Her hand instantly went to the underside of his fully exposed erection that was not hindered by an undergarment. Still locked in one of their intense kisses, he slithered off his pants, socks, and shoes with the dexterity of a man burning with the mission of desire.

With her hand traveling slowly and softly the entire length of his manhood and his middle finger inside her womanhood, their passion was exploding. She was now pushing herself into his hand plunging his finger deeper. They both delighted at the sound of her extreme wetness creating a slapping sound as he pleasured her.

"I want to taste you," she said. They were the first words either had spoken since he entered the room.

"I'll explode. I want that inside you," he pleaded.

Without hesitation, she lifted her legs, pulled her thong to the side and straddled him. He entered her automatically, her softness soaked in the wet excitement of pleasure. Her womanhood consumed all of him with a lustful hunger. He felt glorious inside her, his hot throbbing erection stimulating every millimeter of her. She pumped him and shuddered as he moved in and out of her at her desire. She thrust faster as she felt her orgasm building and she could feel his happening as well because the tip of his erection was now uncontrollably throbbing as if being pumped like a balloon on its way to busting.

It took several deep thrusts, grinding into his pelvis at the end of one of those thrusts and they came together. Once their orgasms began they pushed their bodies into each other as if they couldn't get deep enough that most stimulating of moments. At the apex of their pleasure, they both shook from the aftershock of excitement, kissed and hugged and then held each other tight in silence, merged in affection.

After that long tight embrace, she pulled away, rolled onto the couch next to him, kissed him on the forehead and reached for their drinks. She handed him his while sipping hers and said, "I missed you."

"God, I missed you..." he answered.

He lifted his glass in position to toast and declared, "La Levrier!"

CHAPTER ONE

Cat & Mouse

Sipping a glass of chilled Sauvignon Blanc at the Drake Hotel Coq d'Or lounge bar, she delicately crossed her ankles under her tapered Chanel pencil skirt and tucked the loose blonde tendril that had strayed from her French twist behind her ear.

"Ms. Bernardin, may I offer you a refill?" Ivan, the bartender inquired, diligently poising the bottle just above Claire's wine glass. "Thanks, Doll," she smiled. "Just a touch."

The Coq d'Or, French for Golden Cockerel or "young rooster," was a nostalgic fixture in Chicago history since the repeal of Prohibition in 1933, and welcomed solo patrons like Claire who frequented it as a familiar outpost.

When Jon Fenwick confidently strode up to the heavily varnished mahogany bar and plopped himself two seats away from Claire, she straightened her back and adjusted her burgundy silk wrap blouse to reveal the slightest hint of cleavage. She tried to casually observe Jon out of the corner of her eye as he tossed back his first swig of Ketel One and grabbed a handful of cashews from a tumbler situated between Claire and him.

"Ivan, it looks like this place finally got a new assortment of nuts," she whispered.

"Yes. Management decided to replace the old mix. These are saltier. Makes patrons order more cocktails," Ivan winked.

"May I try your nuts?" Claire turned to Jon with a coquettish grin, as he mindlessly gripped the dish. "You mean these?" Jon shot back casually, dangling the glass between them to reveal the embroidered monogram on the cuff of his crisp white shirt, although not legible under the dim bar lights.

Claire slowly nodded as she reached for the bar mix. He pulled it back suddenly with a smirk.

"Did you miss out on Sharing 101 in kindergarten?" she said with an exaggerated gasp.

"I must have been napping on the floor mat," he grinned and popped another cashew in his mouth, demonstratively chewing it in front of her.

"And you obviously slept through Introduction to Etiquette as well," she added.

"Oh, hardly," he corrected. "I learned the fine art of saying 'please,' which I have yet to hear from Miss Manners herself."

"Oh, puleaaaase," Claire sighed and rolled her eyes, which flickered with a hint of mischief.

"Oh, finnnnalllly," Jon mimicked. "Now I believe the lady deserves a reward… something nice and salty."

Claire again reached for the dish, and this time Jon obliged.

He observed in amusement as she dipped her perfectly manicured fingers into the glass and lifted a cashew. She paused and then deliberately slid it between her polished red lips.

"It appears your appetite must be ravenous, but I'd be very grateful if you'd leave a couple for me," Jon pleaded as Claire savored more cashews.

"Seems that you might need them, so I'll be happy to spare a pair for you after I've devoured my share," she purred, then licked her lips ever so subtly.

Ivan could barely contain a chuckle. Ms. Claire was at it again, and tonight was an especially entertaining performance.

Jon opened this mouth to retort but was interrupted by his buzzing cell phone. He glanced at the number and, knowing that he couldn't ignore it, excused himself and left his stool to take the call out of earshot. With his back to her as he strode from the bar, Claire's well-trained eye took in his impressive height, slim physique and especially the way he wore his suit. Expensively. Even from a distance, Claire's well-trained eye could see the hallmark of a bespoke suit. Fine Italian wool/silk blend. No puckered seams. Tailored fit in the shoulders and tapered at the torso.

As soon as he was in the hallway, he barked, "Yeah, I'm at the Drake. Yep, she's here. Working it right now. Gotta go, but I need you to call me in 10 minutes and be my decoy, okay?" He could barely mask his disdain for his boss, Mac Owen, and even more for this bogus assignment—child's play compared to the high-profile cases he had been awarded in the past. But he had no choice.

When Jon returned to the lounge, Claire's bar stool was naked. Ivan quickly piped up, "She'll be back. Just took a trip to the ladies' room." Jon sighed to himself and stole a vacant stool next to him that had previously divided the two strangers.

He didn't have to wait long before Claire sauntered back to the bar, her perfectly coiffed head held high with an air of confidence that mirrored the female version of himself. Her hips swung in a graceful rhythm as her strappy black stilettos clicked across the hardwood, turning heads—including Jon's.

She assumed the stool next to him, pretending not to notice that he was a seat closer than before, as if she expected it. Jon slipped her a newly filled tumbler of cashews as a peace offering.

"I apologize for my boorish behavior before. I've just had a really exhausting day of travel and this damn place lost my reservation," he explained.

Claire dangled a nut between her fingertips as she considered his apology and deliberately let the silence linger.

"I'm sorry to hear that," she purred. "But there's no shortage of hotels in Chicago. I'm sure you'll find something if The Drake can't accommodate you."

"Not likely," Jon grumbled. "There's a huge convention in town and all the five-star hotels are booked solid. Not a single room to spare on such last-minute notice. I'm waiting to find out if The Drake has a cancellation. They're sold out, as well."

Before Claire could respond, Jon's cell phone buzzed again. He feigned annoyance as he answered the call.

"Fenwick here. Do exactly as I told you. That's what we promised the Board, and that's what we need to deliver. Look, I get it. The re-org fucked everything up, but we need to get Dubai to see things our way. I can't afford to expose any more weak links in our supply chain," Jon insisted. He rubbed his brow and pretended to listen intently before continuing his dialogue. "Damn it, Sayer. You know as well as I do what's at stake here. I'm counting on you to close the deal. Do what it takes and call me back when you've got answers. Meanwhile, I've got business to tend to here—that is, if this lame excuse for a hotel ever finds my lost reservation."

With that, Jon hung up and sighed. Out of the corner of his eye, he noted that he had successfully reeled in his alluring eavesdropper and patiently waited.

"Hmmmm…" Claire smiled, turning her attention fully to Jon at last. "Seems like you're really in a bind. You know, I might be able to help with your accommodations."

Jon leaned in, eager to hear her proposal. "Really? How?"

"I know the owner of a very quaint, first-class boutique hotel on Chicago's Gold Coast," she drawled. "It's a charming little gem that really captures the historic spirit of the city. I find it a rather intimate alternative to these mega-franchise hotels. But then again, if you're used to scratchy sheets, fickle Wi-Fi and temperamental thermostats, it may not be to your liking."

"Well, I do have a passion for fickle, temperamental hot things, but I could do without the scratchy sheets," he chuckled. "I'm in… that is if there's a vacancy."

"Let me check for you…" Claire offered. Jon waited for her to retrieve her phone from her purse, but she made no motions to do so. In fact, she just sat in silence, staring ahead. The minutes dragged and Jon didn't know what to say.

"Yes," Claire finally said. "There is a room available for you."

"What, are you psychic or something? How do you know?" Jon joked.

"I am the owner," she stated with a deadpan expression.

"Wow," Jon feigned surprise. "The owner AND an angel. Here I thought I might have to settle for some roach infested roadside motel near O'Hare."

"Despite your coarse manners, I simply couldn't allow that, Mister…?"

"Fenwick. Jon Fenwick. And may I know the pleasure of your name, Miss uh…?"

"You can just call me Claire," she smiled. "Now, if you'll collect your luggage, I'll call for my car."

"But I didn't even ask about your room rates or amenities," he mused, trying hard to suppress his eagerness.

"Our amenities are like nothing you've ever experienced before. As for the price, I'm sure we can work out something that accommodates your needs," she assured him.

"Well, I can't overextend myself," he replied. "If you wait here, I'll grab my bag from the concierge."

Claire nodded, taking another sip of her Sauvignon Blanc.

Meanwhile, Jon exited Coq d'Or and headed straight for the men's restroom to kill time. He stared at his reflection in the bathroom mirror. At 6'3 and 184 pounds, the benefits of his daily workouts kept the lines of his suit straight and his buckle taut. He combed his fingers through his brown wavy hair, happy to still boast a full head unlike many of his male counterparts.

Claire was waiting for him at Coq d'Or once he had retrieved his bag from the hotel bellhop. As he approached her, she teased, "Did they lose your luggage in addition to your reservation? I was going to call the FBI to issue an APB."

"Nope. Just an unbearably long line and an insufferable shortage of help," he quipped, nearly choking on the irony of Claire's last statement. "I hope I didn't keep you waiting long."

"Not me," Claire smiled. "But my chauffer might not be so forgiving. You may have to find a way to reward my driver's patience."

With that, she palmed Ivan a hundred-dollar bill and they exchanged a familiar glance.

"May I…?" Jon stumbled, reaching for his wallet.

"No, you may not," Claire cut him off. He knew better than to argue with the sassy blonde, but followed her swift, crisp steps as she beelined to the lobby.

A matte black Tesla beckoned their arrival at the Drake's front entrance. The valet loaded Jon's bag into the trunk while he whistled under his breath and then slid next to Claire on the heated black leather rear seat, close enough but respectfully distant.

The luxury sedan swiftly maneuvered down Michigan Avenue, dodging cars under the confident command of the driver. Jon was mesmerized by the prominent dashboard touchscreen that displayed the Tesla's anatomy and all of its vital signs. The control monitor flickered in the dark, adjusting the routing to accommodate real-time traffic conditions, automatically change the cabin climate and scan the radio for preferred music.

"We're here," the chauffer announced in a much silkier voice than Jon had anticipated. His gaze caught the delicate hand on the wheel encased in Italian leather driving gloves that matched the cap perched on the head of… a female. It was so dark in the backseat that he now saw the trail of long, straight black Asian hair spilling down her back from under the hat that blended in perfectly with her fitted black leather jacket. As she exited the car to get their luggage from the trunk, her tight black leggings and over-the-knee boots accentuated her slender legs.

A majestic Greystone looming before them, tucked discretely between the others crowded onto Astor Street. The light stone curled around two stories of tall bay windows trimmed in ebony, which matched a black pitched black roof that framed the third level. Its crowning jewel was a turret tower that popped like a witch's hat but was softened by sheer ivory swags skirting the windows. A black wrought iron fence snaked around the perimeter of the estate, flaunting both elegance and protection.

The driver lifted Jon's suitcase from the trunk, and he and Claire followed her down a paved walkway and up five steps to an arched entryway boasting a heavy wooden double front door. She clapped the doorknocker—the slender head of a greyhound dog. As she raised her hand, her right wrist exposed a tan leather bracelet with two gold greyhound heads interlocking. The dogs' eyes sparkled with emeralds—a stunning contrast to her black leather uniform.

"Thank you, Camilla," Claire smiled at her driver. "I just received word that Dr. Thornton needs a ride back from Spiaggia. I'll see to our newest guest from here."

No sooner had Claire uttered her last sentence then Camilla tipped her hat and hurried back to the Tesla.

"Welcome to La Levrier," Claire announced proudly.

A petite redhead in her early 20s opened the front door to a circular grand foyer boasting an airy opulence. Beyond another arched doorway framed by Grecian pillars, the floor gleamed with white Italian marble decoratively tiled in concentric circles of grey, tan and black. The walls were bathed in white, framed with paneled inset detailing and crown molding that stretched up to an 18-foot ceiling bearing a stunning chandelier that rained crystal teardrops. Two backlit alcoves embedded in the wall on opposing sides boasted large statue greyhounds carved from onyx, facing each other like sentinels. But the most impressive masterpiece was the magnificent staircase that curled around to the left, framed by a black banister with a gilded handrail. The ironwork of the railing wound into an exquisite pattern of flowing waves, and the steps cloaked in an ivory and gold tapestry runner.

"Jesus," Jon gasped. "You clearly run a fine establishment here, Claire. I'm not sure I'm deserving of such a place."

"Oh, trust me, you are," Claire smiled.

"One question," Jon asked. "What's with all the hounds?"

"You mean my GREYhounds? La Levrier means 'the greyhound' in French. In my opinion, it's the most majestic of canines. You'll meet my friends, Marius and Javert, in a bit. But first, I'd like the pleasure of giving you a tour before we show you to your room, if I may," Claire offered.

Jon nodded, speechless, as the redheaded beauty reappeared with a sterling platter holding two crystal flutes. "Sir, may I offer you a Veuve Clicquot?"

As Jon lifted his glass from the tray and handed the second flute to Claire, the young lady promptly snatched his rolling bag and disappeared down the hallway.

"To your stay with us, Jon," Claire announced, clinking glasses and slipping her arm under his.

Claire was right—these amenities were unlike anything Jon had ever experienced. And unlike any assignment he had ever received.

CHAPTER TWO

Bitch Slapped

Two months previous

"Hey, Jon Fenwick," Alisha McBride angled her path toward Fenwick as they both entered the regional headquarters of the FBI from different revolving doors.

"Hey, back. You heading upstairs?" Fenwick smiled and threw his right arm around her shoulders in a walking semi-hug.

"Yep, on duty," she said as they approached the security checkpoint. "Another day of admin'ing the hell outta you division six agents," she laughed.

"And, we love ya for it." They passed through security and resumed walking together through the sunny atrium lobby of the new building that resembled the foyer of a Fortune 100 company rather than a law enforcement hub.

"You know I never asked you this, probably because you're always in and out of here so much, but you don't come in through the entrance closest to the parking lot. How come?" She asked.

"Ahh, I don't know. I guess walking through the lobby makes me feel more professional. Like leaving all the grit outside," he said.

"Hmmm, I get it. That why you always dress so nice too?" She asked.

"Huh?"

"I mean, compared to a lot of the other agents, you are always sharp."

"Ahh, thanks, but…"

"Oh come on, like that suit you have on. That from New York?"

He stopped walking as they neared the elevator bank. She stopped with him. "Lisha, it's from Milan, just don't spread it around."

"Niiice, why something so nice for work?"

"Nosey one aren't you today?" He asked, flattered and enjoying the enquiry.

"Nope, not nosey, just curious. I've only been in your area for a year and you stand out." She paused, "In a good way, ya know." A bit on the spot, she looked at him wide-eyed, "I'm not hitt'n on ya or nothing, I'm…"

Smiling, Fenwick interrupted, "I didn't take it that way, no worries. I like talking clothes." He paused. "This isn't one of my best suits. I save those for occasions. These are my work duds."

"You always look so nice, so put together." She stared at the white burlap pocket square, peeking out like flower pedals from his royal blue suit.

"This is from a designer in Milan, but not a household name yet. It's not one of my custom ones."

"Well, it looks great on you and I like the way your shoes and belt always coordinate. Your shirt? What kind of collar is that?"

"It's a tab collar."

"Very cool, I see you in them a lot. I'd love to get one for my boyfriend. Where do you get them? Saks?"

"They're custom made, I'm afraid. I like them, they keep my tie neat."

"Damn, very, very cool. I mean everybody else is in dark, drab things. But why make the effort?" They started walking again toward the elevators.

"Be honest, it makes me feel good. Just like walking through the front doors. It seems to fumigate me from all the crap in the field. Besides, a couple of other reasons. The bad guys can spot some of the other people a mile away wearing their dad's dark gray baggy suit. They mistake me for a lot of things other than bureau. Another thing, I learned when I first started fifteen years ago, you look put together and they respect you out there."

"Geez, that makes sense. Thanks."

"For?"

"Details, come on, all us admins read your reports. We see the stuff you all go through—disgusting, animalistic garbage. We get immune to it like all of you, but it's good to hear how you cope with it, that's all."

As they stood in front of the elevators waiting for a car to arrive, Fenwick lowered his 6'3" frame down to near her ear and he whispered, "Besides, what else is a single guy going to spend his money on?"

They entered the elevator car together, but soon Alisha was off exiting on a lower floor. She smiled and mouthed a "thank you" as she brushed past him toward the door.

Fenwick exited at the top floor and he chuckled as he caught a male agent he just walked past adjust his tie that dangled carelessly from his button-down shirt. *Football.*

He thought as the agent walked past him. His walk wasn't too unusual, as most of the male agents and many of the female agents had the strut of an athlete. But, Jon would sometimes play a game in his mind to guess the sport an agent played in college by the way they walked. An old coach pointed this out to him once that the athletes in every sport have a way of walking that is unique. You could even break it down further into the position that a person played.

As Jon walked into the director's suite on the top floor, it was clear that Mac (Mackenzie) Owens's office was one of the best in the building, fitting for the regional director of the FBI. Its location was expertly chosen occupying the northeast corner of the north tower. There was no need for wall decorations when the Willis Tower, the Hancock Building and the other iconic skyscrapers were prominent through her huge windows. In fact, the wall-to-ceiling windows and corner location preempted her from having the typical government bureaucrat's wall of fame with awards, diplomas and selfies with politicos. Jon remembered her last office had such a wall and it she crammed it with plaques given by any organization imaginable from the Cub Scouts to Washington. The other walls in that office were just as cluttered with all kinds of African art that she claimed was from her ancestor's village, but to Jon, it had flea market ordinariness about it.

"Jon, I hope on your administrative leave you were able to reflect," Mac snapped looking down at her desk and the file she opened as he took a seat in front of her desk.

"Yes," he answered emotionless.

"Washington and I conferenced long and hard on what to do with you given we have to continue your employment. I believe we came up with something that is suitable," she emphasized the word, "to your demeanor." She looked up and gave his suit a once over and then his eyes a 'fuck you' stare.

"Ok." He returned the glare.

"So, here's what we got for you." Mac read the file. "There is a bordello in the Gold Coast here that has quite a slick operation…"

Jon gave a 'you HAVE to be kidding' sigh.

"Don't give me that shit. You should be glad you have a job after that last fuck up. Did I turn my slush pile of investigations upside down and take the first one on the bottom? To quote a woman, I admire 'You betcha'!"

Mac was waiting for that moment.

"You takes what you get." She joked, offensively mugging some urban speak with which she was totally unfamiliar. Jon so wanted to call her out on such a silly phrase, but he held his tongue and his expression. Mac continued grinding away at him, enjoying the domination. "On Astor Street, there is this madam who has been preying off an elite clientele for years. We don't even know the name she calls her business—that's how good she is. Our researchers wrote in their case log that she makes the Everleigh sisters look like toothless streetwalkers. I had to look up who they were, but it's all in here." She held up a blue folder and tossed it at Jon. He left it there without a look.

"Quite frankly, we're not for sure that they are doing anything illegal. We couldn't trace any money trail and we can't get a solid bead on who exactly is this woman. We have a couple of aliases, but every one of them has their taxes and every other piece of paper in order. That's where you come in. We've never put eyes on her or this business. Welcome to the gumshoe business Agent Fenwick. You'll collect a paycheck from the FBI, but your assignment is one step up from some scumbag private dick following a cheating husband."

Jon sat there stoically. This was no time for him to be a smart-ass, but he so wanted to lash back at this career bureaucrat who had never been in the field, shot at or compromised.

On a roll, Mac continued, "Speaking of dick, you should be thanking me because any one of the horndog males under me would love to be assigned a whore house as a theatre of operation. You're welcome." She stuck the dagger deeper and twisted a bit with that false politeness.

Jon picked up the file, and without so much as eye contact with it or with her, he asked, "Will that be all?"

"And, speaking of 'all,' yes, it's ALL in there. The CPD (Chicago Police Department) reports have done a good deal of preliminary grunt work. This is an easy assignment agent, so I expect a plan of operation and a budget on my desk in a week. And, don't give me some bullshit budget. You're putting this place under surveillance, not doing quality control."

Jon stood up to leave. As he stepped away from her desk, he turned and asked, "Mac, I have no training in numbers. I assume I can coordinate with financial if I need a consult?" He knew he shouldn't try and get out of the assignment. "Isn't this an assignment for vice?"

As if she was waiting for a chance to explode, "Put it in the Goddamn plan and budget. We don't waver from thought out, carefully scripted plans, right? You look, listen, write and we close this file. That's it! Then I'll flip my slush pile over again and get you your next horseshit assignment and then the next and the next until I retire."

Jon knew this meeting was coming and all he could do was take it and move on. As the meeting came to an end, he reflected on past meetings with her. Meetings were always 'yes/no' affairs with Mac in the past but this was the first time she had something to grind him into the ground with, as she was famous for with other field agents. He had stayed above her self-serving rages by always delivering results in every case except the last one. Their typical meetings were role reversals from this one. Jon summarized in monotone a detailed report he gave on a completed case. Mac sat there half listening to what he said and she would end with an 'Ok,' and he left. She was relishing the first opportunity to lay into this previously untouchable agent.

"Ok," Jon said opening her door and he left her office.

Jon went a few floors down to an area where field agents were assigned a cubical to serve as an office. It was bare bones because most of the agents at his level were out in the field on assignment. They did not need anything elaborate at headquarters. The field agents quipped it was the IBM model of administration; no agent had their own private office and they all preferred it that way. At the center of the floor, Alisha McBride had her desk. It was the largest and most elaborately equipped. Surprisingly, before this central headquarters was completed in 2008, the FBI in Chicago didn't have a centralized office building. Several small office spaces were scattered around the Chicago area and served very specific purposes. Offices for field agents were housed in one building, labs in another and even mainframes in yet another.

The cube assigned to Jon looked as though it had never been used. Grey padded mobile walls, an industrial desk, a monitor, and keyboard. As he entered his private hell for the next few weeks, he threw the file on the desk and lifted the keyboard that happened to be to the right of the monitor. He raised his eyebrows once he saw a dozen condoms in all kinds of colors that someone planted under the keyboard. As if psychic, heads popped up from many of the other cubes and Jon received a rousing snark from his fellow field agents.

"I hope yer packing, big fella!" One chipped.

"Make sure Mac gets what she wants!" teased another.

"How'd you score THAT assignment cowboy?"

"The fox gets to guard the hen house, Fenwick!"

The teasing lasted what seemed like hours but was only minutes, but even as the other agents sat back into their cubes to work, colleagues regaled Fenwick with occasional catcalls and quips. Mostly Jon smiled and didn't answer back, but after one last round of teasing as an agent anonymously threw a thong into his cube and yelled, "You need a bit of practice before you go back out in the field?" Upon that joke, the agents again stood up and had a hearty laugh. With that Jon stood up and with a smile, "Ok, ok… are we all done here kids? Can we get some work done?" He spread his arms wide and joked himself, "Hey, I don't pick 'em; I just follow orders. Besides, who else could Mac send on such a delicious case?" There were final muffled giggles, a loud licking sound and exaggerated deep breathing but the agents settled down and the office resumed working with the normal din.

Jon settled in and opened the thin file, riddled with Chicago police reports. The reports were repetitive.

Officer stopping in at an Astor Street address for domestic disturbance called in by a neighbor reporting suspicious behavior at the mansion. But each report was closed with a determination of 'unfounded.' There were no loud noises or other evidence of parties going on. There were several complaints that the private home was running a business out of a residential address, but again, a CPD officer went to the address and found no evidence to support the complaint. The CPD even assigned a detective team to conduct surveillance on the building at the request of a well-connected resident owning one of the other houses on the same block. The detectives observed visitors come and go from the house more frequently than the norm for that neighborhood and well-dressed, good-looking males and females that seemed to live at the house, but that wasn't against the law. The ownership records showed that the house belonged to a Claire Bernardin, and a CPD detective interviewed her and again found no laws broken. The report vaguely stated that Ms. Bernardin had an acceptable explanation of who resided there and their activities. But the, 'acceptable explanation' wasn't detailed in the report. The CPD closed the investigation. The CPD filed seven reports in all and all were closed because the Chicago police could find no evidence against Ms. Bernardin.

The last few pages in the file detailed a final complaint by the well-connected neighbor, and it contained photos of the silhouettes a couple kissing near a window at the house and several luxury automobiles with out-of-state license plates parked outside of the house. The neighbor insisted that the case should be turned over to the FBI because of the possibility of illegal interstate activity going on in the house. Analyzing the quick sign-offs and cop-speak in the file, Jon interpreted that the CPD was more than happy to accommodate the neighbor's insistence that this was the FBI's jurisdiction and that's how the case was turned over to the FBI's Chicago regional headquarters. The CPD was happy to have it off their lap and pass the buck to the FBI. In reality, the CPD figured this file would end up where it did—at the bottom of the FBI's priority—and it would have stayed there if not for Jon's current status with the bureau.

Jon scribbled notes on a legal pad as he read through the file to eventually formulate the plan that Mac wanted. He thought whatever they were doing in that mansion, there was no reason to sit outside and stare at it for hours. The CPD had already done that. Whatever was going on, they covered it up well. The same with interviewing Ms. Bernardin, done and done. In big bold letters, he wrote: HAVE TO GET INSIDE.

The first step was to find this Ms. Bernardin, tail her, get to know her movement and then possibly befriend her or at least get a casual conversation going. Based on the CPD interview of her, she was way too smart to get anything out of another interview. Besides, interviewing was not Jon's forte; action was.

He went into the FBI files on Ms. Claire Bernardin, probably an alias as the CPD suggested in the file, and there was predictably nothing there. Then he went into the public domain and he simply Googled her. Voila—four pages of tidbits popped up. They were all fluff pieces on society appearances; her charity work (she gave a lot of money to homeless and battered women) and several awards received. Nothing useful to him except there were several pictures of her and Geezus; she was a stunning woman!

He pictured in his mind a matronly heavyset madam or at least some rode hard and put away wet younger woman looking decades older than her years. Those are the typical profiles of the owners of these places. But, Claire Bernardin was fantasy quality pretty with a slim, attractive body and flawless features. He went back and looked at her picture several times while he continued his Internet cyberstalking.

Back to a plan. She attended and hosted society events, but Mac was never going to allow that in the budget. You go to such an event and in addition to the ticket to get in, they expect you to donate thousands to the charity or host organization and you were not there because you're friendly. Meeting her at event was out.

As far as he could dig up, Ms. Bernardin lived at the Astor Street mansion. He was not going to sit outside like the gumshoe Mac referred to and tail her that way, but some old-fashioned police detective work may reveal her comings and goings. She had to dine out, take in entertainment, or grab a cocktail now and then. Astor Street was a stone's throw from all the high-end places in Chicago. He was going to have to hit the pavement and ask around. It would get him back in the field, out of the cubicle and away from his colleagues' razzing. Done. He would print out her picture and canvas the Astor Street area and the downtown venues of the socialites. Not a bad way to collect your paycheck and the venues were not unfamiliar to Jon.

He did just that. He spent his work hours and freely donated some off-hour time hoofing it through the Gold Coast area, spending time in one place after another and then back through the list again. After weeks of hitting the streets to get a bead on Ms. Bernardin, several places struck gold for Jon. They were the Cape Cod Room, an old-school restaurant and the Coq d' Or lounge both in the classic Drake Hotel on Michigan Avenue. The other was the RL Restaurant where she would frequently lunch alone. Restaurants were difficult places to meet someone, but the lounge could be perfect. So, the initial "chance encounter" would have to be at the Coq d' Or. But, the puzzle would be how to know when she was there. Then he figured that puzzle out. He had become friendly with the cute hostess at RL, but she didn't know his name or anything about him. He left an envelope with the hostess for her to hand to Claire Bernardin on her next visit. He would use RL to keep his anonymity. He had a plan on how he was going to get close to Claire as a potential client, and he couldn't have an overly accommodating maître d' to spoil his cover to Claire as the person who sent this note. The note served a very separate function in his plan.

The elegant parchment stationery, embossed with a fictitious monogram, suggested it was from a highbrow acquaintance so there was a good chance she would open it and that's all he would need. The FBI had a filament composed of microchips that, upon contact, embedded in the skin permanently. These microchips could then be picked up via a simple tracking device software on Jon's cell phone so he would know exactly where Claire was anytime. He set an alert on his phone to notify him when she would be at the Coq D' Or. Next, he coated the entire note stationery with the filament, paying particular attention to the top of the paper where most people were inclined to grasp. Like microscopic needles, the microchips would immediately embed into her fingertips when she touched the stationery. Permanent and trackable, bam! He would be able to know exactly when she would be visiting the Coq d' Or.

Hello Ms. Claire Bernardin!

CHAPTER THREE

A Day in the Life

Jon could barely suppress his grin. The ever-elusive Claire Bernardin was finally all his. She, of course, hadn't the slightest idea of the weeks of careful planning and surveillance that had led to this evening... or the fake suitcase he had planted at The Drake as he feigned his way through his "lost reservation"... or his fictitious persona as a high-powered CEO barking commands over the phone to convince Claire that he was desirable La Levrier clientele caliber. Now, she was draped over his arm—the mouse leading the cat to the den.

He sipped his Veuve Clicquot and allowed her to escort him deeper into La Levrier's private operations.

An arched doorway edged in detailed white crown molding beckoned their path through a long hallway painted in light dove grey. As they strode down a crimson tapestry runner that covered the gleaming marble floor, every detail boasted tasteful opulence—right down to a small carved credenza holding a delicate potted orchid.

"Here's our main parlor, where our members can relax and enjoy a movie, cocktail... and each other, if they so choose," Claire announced, turning to watch Jon's reaction.

His eyes scanned the circular room with its huge bay window of three floor-to-ceiling panels hung with sheer fawn-colored swags, a cluster of loveseats and chairs upholstered in ivory suede and black leather throw pillows, a fireplace inset in an ornately paneled mantel and the centerpiece—an art deco chaise lounge cloaked in silver and black damask. A unique juxtaposition to the elegance of the room was a zebra-patterned rug—a touch of contemporary levity to the elegant glamour.

"Eclectic, isn't it?" Claire persisted, awaiting Jon's reaction.

"It certainly is… eclectic, beautiful and stylish," he finally uttered, returning her gaze.

"At La Levrier, we cater to a variety of eclectic tastes, and beauty is inherent in our style. Would you care to see more?" she ventured.

"Of course," he nodded. "Please continue."

No others were present, and the silence was almost oppressive until a distinct a series of clicks peppered the marble hallway. They were faint at first, but the taps turned into patters that grew louder and closer. Claire unlinked her arm from his and then broke into a beaming smile.

"Oh, there you are!" she cried. "Come here, Babies."

Jon whirled around to where the clicks emanated and gasped as he spotted two creatures making a beeline toward Claire.

"Jon, meet Marius and Javert," Claire boasted as her greyhounds scampered toward her. She bent down to scoop them into a hug, as they licked each side of her face in unison. Marius was a beautiful brindle greyhound and Javert was jet black with distinct white markings on his chest and hind paws.

Above the fireplace, Jon spotted an ink drawing of a black silhouette of the backside of a statuesque woman wearing a long, off-the-shoulder gown and pillbox hat. Her long arms gracefully reached down to pet the heads of two majestic greyhounds. The images starkly contrasted each other in pure black and white—simple yet striking.

Claire stood up and her greyhounds mimicked her dignity and strength. The similarity of the portrait to Claire, Marius, and Javert was not lost on Jon.

"They're stunning, Claire," Jon whistled. Javert blinked, as if he knew exactly what Jon said.

"They're obviously quite fond of you, too, or else they would have growled by now. They have quite a sixth sense, you know," Claire grinned.

"Well, I'm honored," Jon chuckled as he reached down to pat Javert's head and scratch Marius under the chin.

"They're my patrons and my protectors," Claire continued. "La Levrier does not permit those on the premises who do not pass their inspection, and neither do I."

"Again, I'm honored," he repeated. "Thank you for putting me up for the night in your lavish quarters. I'm actually glad that The Drake messed up my reservation."

"So am I," she purred. "Shall I show you your suite now?"

"By all means," he replied with a slight smile.

With Marius and Javert on either side, Claire led Jon back down the hallway to the foyer where the grand circular staircase was rooted. She gave her pooches a final pat and ordered, "Time for bed." Both dogs instinctively obeyed and trotted back down the hallway.

"They're not allowed upstairs," Claire explained. "For obvious reasons."

As Claire mounted the stairs, Jon's eyes followed her hips, perfectly encased in her trim black Chanel skirt, swung alluringly with each step. Her tiny waist was accentuated by her curvaceous, yet firm, behind.

"Your suite is on the far end of the hallway," she announced. "I thought for your first stay with us you might prefer quieter, more private accommodations this time."

"This time?" Jon questioned teasingly.

"Well, over time, many of our members develop preferences for certain rooms and..." she dangled, looking Jon squarely in the eye.

"And?" he raised an eyebrow, testing her.

"And for those with whom they choose to associate," she replied.

"I see," Jon mused. "I have yet to visit a hotel where the guests are so friendly with one another."

"We don't have guests, we have members," Claire corrected politely. "And we do our very best to accommodate every member's individual tastes regardless of age, gender, race or sexual orientation. That's why they always come back to La Levrier."

"Your member satisfaction rate must be very high," Jon mused.

"Oh, it is. It HAS to be," she insisted.

While Jon followed her thread perfectly, he enjoyed the challenge of 'playing dumb' to extract more information. They continued their journey down the hall, and all of the doors were closed, except for one.

Behind a slightly ajar door, a woman whimpered in ecstasy. There was no mistaking that those were cries of joy, followed by deep moans of equal pleasure that obviously belonged to a male.

"Those are two of our happiest members," Claire informed Jon, studying his reaction. His eyes met hers, urging her to continue. "Henrik is a regular at La Levrier. He visits from Brussels to meet Lorelei at least once a month, if not more. They fell in love about five years ago, and he has never missed an opportunity to be with her whenever his business travels bring him to the States."

"Wow, five years, you say? She must be one very patient lady. None of my exes would have lasted that long," Jon chuckled.

"Ah, but Jon, their arrangement works perfectly for them. Lorelei lives here at La Levrier, is finishing her MBA at Kellogg and has to stay locally to care for her ailing grandmother. Henrik has commitments back home in Brussels. He runs a very successful startup venture, has two children under the age of 10 and a wife with multiple sclerosis who's confined to a wheelchair. Unfortunately, her condition progressed rapidly and they are unable to enjoy a passionate relationship."

"So, he's cheating on his dying wife?" Jon questioned, feigning a tone of morality.

"You can't look at it that way," Claire said. "For Henrik, Lorelei has given him a new lease on life. When he first came to La Levrier, he was so depressed and downtrodden. It wasn't just his wife's health that had started to deteriorate; their marriage had been crumbling even before her diagnosis. He felt trapped and knew he couldn't leave her in her current condition, especially with two toddlers at that time. Lorelei was not only here when he needed her, she was a positive, steady and supportive influence in his life when he was at his worst. Henrik is a completely different man today than he was when he first walked through these doors years ago, unsure if he should even be here. His guilt was so strong; it was palpable. But he now realizes that meeting Lorelei was the best thing that ever happened to him."

"Well, that's quite a touching story," Jon added. "But, given that they only see each other once a month, don't you think they'd want a little... privacy?" His last word ironically was met with a loud shriek from Lorelei two doors away.

"Au contraire," Claire laughed. "They like being watched. Their lovemaking is an open invitation for others to experience and celebrate their bliss vicariously."

"Kind of a voyeuristic fetish, huh?" Jon commented.

"In a way..." Claire hesitated. "But that makes it sound a bit cheesy, Jon. Nothing that happens under this roof, behind doors or between the sheets of La Levrier occurs without a mutual attraction, consensual passion or shared feelings between two individuals. Be it between male and female. Female and female. Male and male."

"I see you have an open-door policy," Jon observed.

"You could definitely say that," Claire mused. "And, speaking of, would you care to peek inside of Henrik's and Lorelei's open door? I'm sure they would enjoy it very much."

At that point, Jon knew Claire was clearly challenging him. Waiting to see how far out of his comfort zone he was willing to venture. And, in the end, if he would be considered worthy of membership to La Levrier as a client. He also knew he couldn't refuse. He had accomplished his initial goal of meeting Claire. Now he fulfilled his next quest: to get inside. It was time to see the innermost workings of La Levrier. Not just the marble floors and the tapestry rugs, the ornate sconces and the fancy wall art, but the deepest secrets of this successful clandestine operation—including the people who owned, ran and served its manifesto.

"Yes, of course," Jon agreed. "Show me the way."

Claire placed an open palm on the outside of the door, gently pushing it to reveal the view to Lorelei's and Henrik's suite. A king-sized canopy bed draped in long folds of beige velvet flowed from black iron posts and met a plush cream textured carpet below. At the foot of the bed was a deep red settee casually adorned by a woman's black lacy garter belt and bustier. Mahogany nightstands guarded each side of the bed, holding art deco pewter lamps that cast illuminating shadows across the chocolate-colored walls. But the central light source was a small, yet raging, fireplace tucked on the far side of the room. It flickered fervently, matching the mood of the couple splayed on the bed.

Claire silently motioned Jon inside, welcoming him to take in a broader view. In all of his FBI days, Jon had had come nose to nose with knife-wielding gangbangers, kingpin drug lords, and even brutal serial murderers, but his assignments had never called upon his talents to watch a couple fucking like wild rabbits. Lovemaking, as Claire delicately put it. For the first time on duty, Jon felt a little self-conscious. Embarrassed even.

Claire urged him into the room. "Relax, Jon. Remember, they welcome an audience. They want us here." Jon obeyed and followed Claire until they were standing no less than 10 feet from the bed.

From this distance, he could make out Lorelei's extremely fit frame and chic, angled bob haircut that gave her an artistic flare. She wasn't a young girl, but a confident and carefree woman in her late 20s who took obvious pleasure in straddling her man. Lorelei bent down and grazed her tongue down Henrik's hairy chest and well-endowed cock. She took his erection between her lips and gently licked the tip of his manhood, then slid her open mouth down his shaft. Her head bobbed softly, slowly taking him in inch by inch. Her caress wasn't rushed but relished. His hands cupped her head lovingly and he raised his legs so she could maneuver even deeper. She kissed his balls and tenderly sucked them.

"Oh, Love, you always know exactly how to please me," he whispered, running his fingers through her glossy hair. She eagerly sought to make her happiness his, returning to his cock and pleasuring him with long strokes of her tongue before taking his entire length back into her mouth. As the intensity of her sucking grew, low moans of ecstasy filled the room. Jon felt his own cock twitch and harden. He was never one to consume pornography; certainly not when he could get the genuine article in his own bed. He could sense Claire staring at him, but he was more surprised when Lorelei lifted her head, turned to them and winked at Jon.

She softly caressed Henrik's cock, almost as if to show Jon what pleasure he was missing, until Henrik cried out and exploded. The dude was a geyser, Jon chuckled to himself. Torrents of cum showered Lorelei's bare tummy, and she encouraged him to continue.

"More, Baby, more! Make me all wet," she coaxed.

Henrik obeyed, and Lorelei lovingly rubbed her slick body against his as she pressed her mouth to his in a passionate kiss. This was nothing like what Jon would have expected to witness in a typical GFE.

"As you can see," Claire pointed out, "Lorelei enjoys her femininity and sexuality tremendously. What she and Henrik share is a beautiful thing."

"Yes," Jon agreed as she escorted him out of the bedroom.

"You can have that, too, Jon... if you'll allow me to help you," Claire said softly.

He didn't respond immediately, but let her continue walking down the hall, past the closed doorways that held other secrets... secrets that other members weren't so openly willing to reveal to strangers.

Finally, they reached Jon's room and Claire pulled out a silver skeleton key bearing the head of a greyhound, of course. She slid the key into the hole and turned the knob. "I hope you'll be satisfied with your accommodations," she announced as the door swung into a huge master suite.

In the same eclectic spirit as the rest of the mansion, his space was exquisitely appointed in grey and mocha. The dark wood floor was cloaked with an ivory pile rug that sat underneath a king bed with a white bedspread, taupe throw, and black-and-white striped tubular-shaped pillows. Above a black leather padded headboard were three sepia-toned photos of greyhounds... one motion shot of Javert running, another of Marius on his back with his graceful legs crossed, and the third of the two dogs profiled side-by-side like proud sentinels. A modern black leather reading chair and matching ottoman graced the suite, and there was even a mahogany desk fully equipped with outlets and a mounted digital screen. But what drew Jon's eye in the far corner was a glass cabinet holding a selection of liquor and a built-in wine cooler, along with a glass café table that had two all-glass bar stools. The suite was simple, with its clean, contemporary lines and open, inviting layout, that accommodated both business and pleasure.

"We have complimentary Wi-Fi, reliable temperature control, and 1,000 thread count Egyptian sheets. AND, I'll even have a bowl of cashews delivered to your room," she smirked as a throwback to their conversation earlier at Coq d'Or.

"Will that cost extra?" Jon joked, once again enjoying their banter.

"For YOU, the nuts and the entire room are on the house," Claire chuckled. "Consider it a trial stay in hopes that will join our family here at La Levrier."

"Hmmmmm," Jon mused. "That's awfully generous of you, Claire. But what makes you think I want to become a member?" By posing the question, he knew he was rolling the dice. He had to play it cool, not appear too eager. Jon was a master when it came to preserving his cover, and he certainly couldn't afford to blow it now. Not in his current precarious position with the FBI.

"Let me share something about myself, Jon," Claire spoke softly, yet firmly. "I have a rare gift for reading people, very well, in fact. My intuition tells me that we met for a reason—not as two casual strangers hooking up at a bar. You are searching for something you need in your life, and I'm here to guide you. My invitation goes beyond basic room and board. The decision is yours; take it or leave it."

"And if I take it… will it come with you, Claire?" Jon inquired, rolling the dice a second time.

Claire paused and collected her words carefully. "La Levrier is not just my business, but my passion, Jon. I will always strive to ensure that your membership with us is to your utmost satisfaction. That means a room that suits your fancy. A woman that meets your most discriminating tastes. And an experience that you will never ever forget, long after you leave these doors and every time you return."

"That all sounds very tempting, but I will have to sleep on it. Care to join me?"

"I will be happy to have you join me in my office tomorrow at a time most convenient for you. Just take the elevator to the top floor," she smiled. "In the meantime, I'll send up your turn-down service, a nightcap… and some cashews. Goodnight, Jon."

"Nite, Claire," he returned as she slipped out the door… the essence of her lingering behind in his luxurious, yet starkly empty, room. Little did he know that Claire had taken careful mental note and was already making plans for Jon. Plans that would unfold imminently.

CHAPTER FOUR

Mouse & Cat

About a half hour, after Claire left Jon to settle into his suite, there was a delicate rap on his door. Thinking it his turndown service or cashew delivery courtesy of Claire, Jon opened it without a glance into the door viewer. Instead she was quite the view herself. Tall, raven-haired with small facial features and a dancer's body that her crisp white blouse, silky knee-length skirt, and four-inch pumps displayed perfectly.

"May I come in? Claire suggested we might have some things in common and could perhaps enjoy a nightcap together," she purred.

"Sure, come on in." John opened the door wide, and she walked past with a stride between runway model and a CEO.

"May I offer you something?" Jon asked.

"A Bellini, up."

Jon picked up the house phone, "May I have a Bellini straight up and Ketel One on the rocks brought up?"

His visitor politely took the phone from his hand, "And a bottle of Veuve Clicquot." She looked him in the eyes, "For later."

Within an impressively short time, the service bell to his room rang, and a server carrying a silver tray brought the beverages into the room. As if invisible, the server arranged the drinks on the wet bar and left without a sound.

Jon handed her the Bellini, "What is your name?"

"Justianne."

He touched her glass with his, "To Justianne," he said.

"That is an incredible name, please let's sit." He pointed to his glass café table with two glass bar stools.

"Thank you. My parents were artists and…"

"I should say so, you are quite the work of art," Jon said sincerely.

"Again, thank you." She bowed her head toward her drink.

"Claire spoke very highly of you," Justianne said as the tip her tongue touched the rim of her glass.

"I'll be sure to thank Claire when I next see her. So, besides the fact that you are a strikingly beautiful woman, what did Claire think we might have in common?" Jon stared at her dark brown eyes.

"Quite a bit, actually. She described you as very attractive, a keen eye for beauty and fine things, intelligent, discerning and intuitive. And, with a very private side."

"Well, aren't we all private here?"

They sat close enough that when she slipped her foot from her pump, it immediately stroked his calf. The silkiness of her hose against his slacks shot electricity up his spine, and he tried to hide his arousal. She persisted and outlined his bulging calf muscle with her toe. Her touch was slow and precise. She knew a man's body.

"Oh Monsieur, you would be surprised how short-lived privacy becomes behind these closed doors. There is something about carnal knowledge that crumbles the walls people put up in their real world." The tip of Justianne's index finger played with the rim of her glass. The deep red polish of her fingernail popped out in contrast to the peach color of her drink. "Claire describes you, mon cher, as having some of the stiffest walls ever to enter here. Are your walls stiff?" Her foot rose higher up his leg, just above his knee and along his inner thigh.

"I can see one reason why Claire sent you. You're very articulate and expressive, I might add." Referring to her leg stroking his.

"You can thank my parents for my right and left-brain skills and Brown for my vocabulary."

"Brown, hmmm…, from what I hear it's a rather unstructured education there?"

"Well, it does give you a lot of freedom, but let's not talk schools, Mr. Yale. You didn't come to La Levrier to pick up a cheerleader at a twenty-something kid's bar." She leaned in closer to his face. As she did, her foot glided nearer to his crotch, and the nail of her middle finger fondled the back of his hand with a touch so light his hairs stood on end.

Jon smiled, "Ah, so you read my background before you walked through that door?" He let out a little laugh and nodded his head slightly. "You're armed with all the right phrases to press my buttons."

"And to press more than buttons." She smiled back and winked.

Her foot found his erect manhood, and she lingered on the tip with soft, slow circles. She could feel him pulsate, and her eyes widened each time she felt him throb.

"As I said before," he quickly glanced down at his crotch, "you are quite expressive." His speech was breathy.

"My writing professors always were emphatic—show, don't tell." She unbuttoned her blouse. "Could we move to a more comfortable spot?" She withdrew her foot and looked in the direction of the sofa a few feet away.

"Sure." He sipped his drink and watched as she stood, her breasts bursting from the open blouse. She walked over to the light gray modern sofa and sat. With some imperceptible move, her skirt rose high as she sat teasing him with a hint of the lace top of her thigh highs.

Jon stayed on the bar stool, a small smile on his face and he breathed deep taking in her image like a connoisseur.

Justianne smiled back patiently, then after minutes of the mutual admiration, "Are you coming over?" She delicately patted the cushion next to her.

"I'm admiring the view from here."

"Oh, voyeur was not in your dossier, Mr. Fenwick, but…" She arched her back, pulled her blouse out from her skirt and placed it on the side of the sofa. Her sheer black bra bulged with her breasts. She sipped her drink and stood. With a graceful tug, the zipper on the back of her skirt opened, and it fell to the floor. She bent at the knees knowing she was posing for him and made an excuse to pick up her skirt and place it too on the side of the sofa. As she bent over to give him a view of her backside, her black thong framed her like artwork.

She stood and faced him, now in her hose, heels, and lingerie. She reached for her drink bending at the waist and accentuating her cleavage.

"Do you like what you see, Mr. Fenwick?" She sipped.

"Oh, very much. You move with such seduction, like performance art."

"Then come closer for the climactic performance."

"Ah, but that's just it. I didn't check in here for a performance." He walked over to her, picked up her blouse and skirt, draped them over his arm waiter style and leaned in and kissed her on both cheeks then handed her the clothes. "Please tell Claire thank you, but this is a bit staged for my desires. I came to La Levrier for a more genuine experience."

Justianne returned his kisses with one of her own. She kissed him on his lips, a quick kiss of understanding. She stroked his face. "La Levrier is about mutuality and freedom. I like you, so maybe we can chat again."

"Maybe. You are charming and sweet, but please tell Claire what I said." He smiled and showed her the door.

"Enjoy the champagne!" She said as she walked out of the suite holding her clothes just as he did.

The next morning, Jon chose to have breakfast in the dining area of La Levrier. As he began his second cup of coffee and glanced at the New York Times, a blonde woman in athletic clothing approached his table. "Good morning, may I?"

"Absolutely, please..." he stood and pulled a chair.

"I'm Jennie, and you are?"

"Oh, you didn't read my file?"

"Huh?"

"My file, my dossier. Who I am and what I like, etc."

She chuckled, "Oh, I'm a member here. Are you?"

"My bad. I forgot. The members are both sexes here," he said.

"And all interests."

"So, we can match up with other members as well?" he asked.

"Sure, it's about your pleasure." She was poured a cup of coffee and, without asking, a server topped it with cream.

"So, you came here for?" Jon asked.

"Slow down; I came here for breakfast." They both laughed.

"Sorry, I'm still getting the lay of the land. Ooops, bad turn of a phrase there." They laughed again.

"No problem, this place is about passion and indulgence. Why shouldn't we have that on our mind, right?" She took a hearty sip of coffee.

"It's a fascinating place. I'd like to learn as much as I can about it," Jon probed, trying to get intel from any source.

"I think part of the sexiness of being here is that atmosphere of desire. We can strip away all the pretense, and we're here for the purpose of..."

"Yes, it is a very sensual place."

"Yep, I mean if I want to sit with a very good looking, sexy guy at breakfast, bam! I just ask to sit. I wouldn't do that outside of here. Never know what can happen," she remarked.

A waiter came and took their order. By this time, Jon gave up his paper and thought he would question her some more, possibly helping his investigation.

"So, Jennie, what draws you to La Levrier?" Jon asked.

"I like the experimentation and the adventure. Outside of here, sex is vanilla. Here it is romantic, a fantasy. I feel sexy twenty-four seven. Look, I sat down with you, and my initial pleasure was just having breakfast with a handsome guy, but as I sit here I am wet, and I admit I pictured in my mind your cock between my legs. I like that sex here can be that free and raw one minute then tonight I can dress up in my sexiest dress and have a seduction fantasy. But, right now, hell, I would love to fuck you. Raw, no foreplay, rip our clothes off, take you inside me and use each other to cum."

"Well, that's a very nice compliment, but my agenda was breakfast, which is coming right now, and the New York Times. Oh, and a good deal of coffee," Jon said kindly.

"Hmmmm… what would it take to change your mind?" She paused. Jon just smiled.

"I have an idea. I have a great body, but so many of the women here have great bodies, but I have something a bit different than most. Maybe a little peek would tip you over the edge?"

"Really Jennie, you're lovely but, to be blunt, I didn't wake up with a morning hard-on. Actually, I'm not a morning lover."

Seemingly without hearing what he said and without discretion toward anyone else in the dining room, Jennie walked over and stood next to Jon. "Are you at least curious?" She tugged at the waistband of her running tights. "It's a bit of a throwback to the nineties."

"Ah, if it is a penis, I really don't want to see that. I apologize, I'm a transgender activist, but I'm not into that." Jon was now straining to hold up his chivalry.

"Well, no, it's not a cock. It's more exciting than that. Here, I'll give you a little tease." She pulled her tights lower. As she lowered them near her pubic mound there was a colorful, detailed tattoo of the face of a beautiful woman with a hat and veil over her face; and exquisite eyes made up with lush blue eyeshadow and sharp dark eyebrows. The top lip of the woman had a ruby gloss that seemed iridescent even in the daylight. The tattoo's mouth stopped there giving the illusion that the face's bottom lip was her vagina. No one else in the dining room paid attention to Jennie's seduction. "Maybe if you don't want to kiss me this morning you would give my mistress a morning kiss. She loves French kissing, by the way."

Jon gave the artistic tattoo a thorough examination. "That IS amazingly sexy and incredible art. Had you just described it I would have imagined it silly or slutty, but it is alluring."

"You want to see more…" She began to tug her tights down lower, but Jon gently grabbed her hand and led it upward to return her running tights to her hips.

"I'm sure I'll be fantasizing about your mistress for some time, but no, please, I'll take a pass at present," Jon politely begged.

"I thought that was just what I was doing, giving you a pass!" She laughed, bent over and kissed him on his lips slipping her tongue into his mouth. "She'll be waiting for that mouth of yours anytime you're ready." She sat back down on her chair. Let out a sigh, "Ahhhh, let's see how they did with this avocado omelet." Her lips surrounded the first forkful, and she winked at him before delicately taking in the food. They filled the rest of their breakfast with light conversation and, much to Jon's dismay, it was uninformative on any of the details of La Levrier.

Several hours after his tempting breakfast, Jon had a note delivered to his door. While the staff person waited by the open door, Jon read the parchment letter. It requested him to meet with Claire in her office at his convenience, and it required he write down a time best for him. He wrote a time with the Mont Blanc fountain pen on the silver tray and thanked the delivery girl who was resplendent in a bellhop's uniform complete with bellboy's oval brimless cap. The black ankle pants, stiletto heels, and white bellman's jacket would fulfill many a man's fantasies.

After he closed the door, he chuckled, *Damn I missed a great line, I should have asked her if she wanted a tip!*

Two hours later, Jon took the elevator to the top floor of La Levrier. From the outside, the top floor looked like an 'A' frame attic room. Claire's office took up the fourth floor of the one hundred thirty-year-old mansion. Jon knocked firmly on the massive oak door. Claire welcomed him in with a dutiful smile. Her royal blue skirt rose high on her waist and hugged her body with its custom fit. A matching short, one-button bolero jacket covered a crisp light blue blouse with a pleated front. Her blouse was open enough that hints of a pale pink bra peeked through the last open button. Her six-inch heeled pumps were such a deep blue that they could have passed for black. The skin of Claire's legs had just enough color to forgo hose. She was stunning.

"Please, come in Jon." She opened the door wide.

"Thank you." He said with a warm smile.

The open door revealed a spectacular office space. Claire's office paid tribute to the age of the brownstone with its 1800s Steampunk vibe. Her desk was a slab of white Calcutta marble with subtle brown veining. An intricate lattice of rusted industrial pipes supported the marble. The desktop was remarkably clear of clutter; only an Apple laptop sat prominently on the marble. Her desk chair was padded with red velvet and mushroomed at the top in Queen Anne Victorian style. Its actual mechanics were ergonomic; distinctly it was handcrafted for the décor. A stand in the corner of the room displayed a gold mechanical contraption encased in a glass dome. There was a gold telescope on an oak stand that peered out the ornamental lead muntin of the south window and a large gold working fireplace that dominated one wall. A chandelier of faded copper hung prominently from the center of the ceiling and contained a multitude of lights that resembled real candles. A huge clock dominated another wall, its outside metal frame the same brown tarnished copper of the chandelier, but the clock face behind the round glass was all gold and showed the clock movements in great detail. A slight ticking marked the seconds. The parquet wood floor had several tones of brown and tan crisscrossing throughout. Marius and Javert were curled up next to the wall by Claire's desk. Each lay on their own black velvet pillow. The room was so tastefully ornate that Jon fell silent and just stared once he set foot through the door.

After his head swiveled slowly from side to side and up and down, he remarked, "What an amazing space!"

"You like?" she asked wanting a sincere answer.

"Very much. It is such a contrast to the modern, contemporary look of the rest of the mansion."

"Yes, I wanted my inner sanctum here to not only pay homage to the age of the house but to take me away from the business so to speak. Don't get me wrong, I love what I do. But, this is a refuge," she revealed.

"I wanted to re-create the 1800s feel of the house. Nikola Tesla lived here and worked in this very space when he invented the Tesla coil. He came to Chicago because he worked for Thomas Edison in one of his facilities here." Looking around the office, she smiled. "I don't know if it was his style of interior design, but this is my tribute to him."

"Thus, the Teslas you use as the house cars?"

"Precisely."

"And, you know all this, because?"

"Double major at MIT. Electrical Engineering and business. I've always been a fangirl of inventors and scientists."

"That says it all." He nodded as he paced around the office examining the details.

"Speaking of business, I don't invite just anyone up here. You are an exception."

"And to what do I owe the honor?"

"Jon, La Levrier has presented you with three women to fulfill your desires. Each was carefully chosen, by myself in fact, for your pleasure, yet you have not matched with any of these remarkable women." Her lips pursed and brow furrowed. "I'm concerned, do you really want to be here?"

"Three? I don't think our arithmetic is the same," he chuckled.

"Justianne, Jennie and the bellhop."

"Jennie was a plant?" He slipped and let his FBI jargon out.

"Well, not entirely, but she is a member. But you fit her profile needs. I went out on a bit of a limb seeing if you would bite, excuse the pun." They both laughed.

"And the bellhop?" he asked.

"Well, the bellhop I threw at you as a wildcard because the other women didn't compel you. A sexy woman in uniform and a take on the maid fantasy. But, alas, no deal."

"Or match..."

"Exactly."

"And you forgot that amazing woman who I met at Coq D' Or who brought me here. That's four," he winked.

Claire ignored the reference.

"So, Jon Fenwick, how can La Levrier fulfill your needs? Have you had a chance to 'sleep on' the idea of becoming a member or is this conversation entirely moot?"

Both still standing, he moved closer to Claire. He took her hand. She didn't protest. He looked into her eyes with a look as if he was consuming her.

"Have we made any mistakes? Are we missing anything?" Her voice lowered.

"I guess you could say that."

Claire's eyes widened, and she stepped back. "So, what are we missing here?"

Jon pulled her back in toward him.

"You made a big mistake on my desires."

"Don't hold back. We aim to please you. "

"Do you now." He pulled her even closer if that was possible. His tone lowered to match hers.

"I've always been one to admire the best. My whole life I coveted the rare, the one of a kind. The most exclusive." With each phrase, his lips drew closer to hers.

Claire pulled back with a strong yet respectful push. "Jon, I don't enter into the experience here. It is just not how I run La Levrier."

Jon's face dropped, and his smile disappeared. "I'm sorry, but..."

Claire's voice resumed a more businesslike cadence, "You've told me a great deal in this meeting. I have a better direction for your satisfaction with us."

"So, there is hope?"

"Not at all. But, you will be pleased with La Levrier. I assure you."

Jon moved away. His gaze at her returned to the lustful stare he initiated earlier.

"Jon, our meeting is over here. If there are any immediate needs you have… don't hesitate…"

"You now know my needs."

"Good afternoon, Jon, and enjoy your stay here. We will do our best."

It took Jon some time to begin to leave the office. He tried his best not to have his manner betray the feelings he had inside of rejection and tail between his legs embarrassment.

CHAPTER FIVE

Recruitment

As Jon exited Claire's office, he didn't glance back at her, nor would she have expected him to do so after their awkward conversation. It wasn't the first time that Claire had needed to make her boundaries clear to a man visiting La Levrier. And it likely would not be her last. There was an odd longing that Jon had stirred in the 24 hours since they first met at the Coq D'Or. And, now that he was gone, that longing was quickly replaced by emptiness that felt foreign to Claire… almost enough to cause her to call after him before he reached the elevator. But she restrained herself. Besides, she had an appointment waiting for her and prided herself on being prompt.

Claire sat back at her desk and, within minutes, heard another knock on her door. It was Bianca escorting a new La Levrier candidate, Danielle, to her office for a screening interview. She warmly welcomed both ladies into her quarters and dismissed Bianca with a nod as she invited Danielle to take a seat.

"I'm so glad you could join me here today," Claire calmly smiled at Danielle to make the young woman feel at ease. She poured herself and Danielle glasses of iced tea from a crystal carafe and, instead of seating herself behind her desk, made a point to sit next to her.

Danielle wrung her hands in her lap and smiled at Claire with large hazel eyes framed by strong, arched eyebrows and long lashes. Her light brown hair, streaked with golden highlights, was pulled tightly off her face in a high ponytail that swung down to her shoulders like a glossy mane. Danielle was stunning in her simplicity, wearing classic gold hoop earrings, a peach A-line '60s vintage dress and a pair of white wedge sandals with a matching clutch. Claire admired how this woman in her early 20s pulled herself together so elegantly on a modest budget.

Claire knew her circumstances, having met Danielle last week at RL. As Claire strolled into one of her favorite luncheon spots on Chicago Avenue, Philip, the maître d', greeted her with a deep bow. He was decked out in his usual tuxedo, white shirt and bow tie and his hair was meticulously slicked back with what appeared to be a fresh coat of black shoe polish.

"Oh, Ms. Claire," he clapped his hands theatrically as she entered. "Always such a pleasure! Shall I take you to your usual table today?" Claire nodded as Philip waddled down the aisles of like a proud Emperor penguin and led her to the far corner. He pulled out Claire's chair and draped the cloth napkin over her lap, knowing that she didn't require a menu.

"Thank you, Philip," Claire said. With another sweeping bow, he left her to solace.

Danielle was assigned to tend Claire's table, and it was obvious this was her first waiting job. The young woman's hands were shaking so hard she could barely serve Claire's

French onion soup without it sloshing down the sides of the cup and onto the white linen tablecloth.

"Ms. Bernardin is one our regular patrons!" Philip hissed at Danielle back in the kitchen area after serving her. "She comes here expecting the best experience and what do you do? Fuck it up! I don't care if you're Shelley's cousin or not. I don't give a shit if you've got a kid to support. I don't even give a rat's ass about YOU. Period. All I know is that if we lose Ms. Bernardin as a customer, there goes about a thousand bucks a month of business, not to mention the referrals she sends our way. She's well-connected, that lady. We get tons of out-of-town businessmen in here because of her. So, Missy, you either shape up your act, or I have a nice long talk with our manager. GOT IT?"

Danielle crept back to Claire's table wearing an unmistakable mask of humiliation. Claire knew that look well. She also knew how smeared mascara looked beneath a girl's eyes. How blush looked after being dabbed with tear-stained tissue. How posture sunk when one's pride was smacked in the gut.

"You okay?" Claire asked Danielle softly when she returned to refill her coffee.

"Sure, Ms. Bernardin," Danielle tried to shrug off with a manufactured smile. "I'm fine. Why do you ask?"

"Well, to tell you the truth, I couldn't help but overhear what I assume was supposed to be a private chastising," Claire confessed. "It wasn't pleasant for me, and I'm sure it was far less pleasant for you."

Danielle winced. "You heard all that?"

Claire nodded. "Unfortunately, so."

"Oh, please, Ms. Bernardin. Please don't let that upset you. We value your patronage at RL and don't want to lose you!"

"Don't worry," Claire smiled. "I enjoy dining at RL too much to let that happen. Besides, if Philip thinks that he's going to have a 'long talk' with your manager, he doesn't know what's coming. I'm capable of having an even longer talk with Robert. He and I go way back. In fact, I wouldn't count on seeing Philip the next time you report here."

"You wouldn't!" Danielle cried. "I'm sorry, Ms. Bernardin, but please don't have Philip fired because of me. I've only been here for three days!"

"Philip has been an obsequious pain-in-the-ass since Day One," Claire smiled. "But the last thing I want is to get you in trouble. In fact, I sense you already might have some troubles in your life, if I may be so bold."

"It's okay," Danielle replied, lowering her eyes. "I do. It's complicated."

"Care to share? I'm a pretty good listener..." Claire offered, motioning to the seat across from her. There was no one else in RL at this time, since it was too late for the usual lunch crowd, and too early for dinner. Danielle hesitated, but Claire said, "I insist."

No sooner did Danielle assume the chair across from Claire than Philip rushed to the table out of nowhere. "Oh, my goodness!" he gasped. "Ms. Bernardin, I deeply apologize that Danielle is disturbing you. She is new to RL and is still learning proper protocol..."

Before he could utter another word, Claire flicked him away with a ladylike, yet firm, back of the hand.

"Now," Claire stated, giving Danielle her undivided attention, "before we were so rudely interrupted, you were going to tell me what has been troubling you."

"Well..." Danielle began. "I'm pretty new to Chicago. Grew up in Des Moines and moved here with my boyfriend about a year-and-a-half ago, after I learned I was pregnant. He got a job in Chicago, and I thought we'd be married someday. Well, THAT didn't happen. After Clayton was born, Jed took off. Said he couldn't deal with being a dad... and POOF. I was stuck with diapers, rent, bills and a student loan which I'm still paying off from the University of Iowa. My cousin, Shelley, found me this job. She used to work here and knows Robert. That sums it up; I'm broke, stuck with a baby and need this job."

"I get it," Claire reassured. "But what you don't need is a jerk like Philip making you feel even worse about yourself."

"Guys are ALL jerks, as far as I'm concerned," Danielle sighed.

"Not true," smiled Claire. "There are plenty of decent men in this world who are seeking a beautiful, caring, intelligent and responsible woman just like you."

"Really? Show me!" Danielle scoffed.

"I would love to," Claire offered. "In fact, I have a business proposition I'd like to discuss with you. Not here, but at your convenience next week. Something that will allow you to pay off your debts, give your son the upbringing he deserves and affords you the happiness and life YOU deserve. You don't have to settle, Danielle. For a job, a man or anything other than what you decide is right for you."

Claire gave Danielle her private number and set up a meeting. Danielle recognized an excellent opportunity, especially one offered to her from such an accomplished woman as Ms. Bernardin. Surely she could trust her, and found herself seated next to her in her office the following week, sipping an iced tea and eager to learn more.

"Danielle," Claire began, "When I first met you last week at RL, I instinctively knew that you had potential. That's why I invited you here today. I was very serious when I told you that I had a proposition, and I'd like you to hear me out." Danielle nodded, urging Claire to continue.

"I was once in your shoes," Claire confided. "While I didn't have a child, there was a point in my life when I knew I had to do something to achieve my full potential—BUT, most importantly, to help other young women to realize theirs, to make a decent living and even to find love."

"Wow, it almost sounds too good to be true!" Danielle laughed.

Claire smiled, and Danielle leaned closer. "It is true, Danielle. La Levrier offers women something that brings them closer to their dreams without the demands and inflexibility of a typical job. If you were to work for me, I would respect and honor your needs. You would tell ME how many hours you wish to work, how you need to structure your days and nights, and the type of experience that best suits your desires. I, in turn, would do my very best to accommodate your preferred work schedule and to match your preferences, talents, and strengths to the needs of La Levrier's membership."

"Membership?" Danielle inquired. "Is this a club?"

"Yes, you could say that. La Levrier is an exclusive club open to those who want to enrich their lives with passion, intimacy, and adventure. Our members are seeking to fill what they're missing in their daily lives. Maybe that's a new thrill, a new partner or a new fantasy that they never thought possible. And, it works both ways. Our employees—otherwise known as Levriettes—are stimulated by this experience as much as our members.

We are equally discriminating on both sides. It all comes down to mutual satisfaction."

Danielle weighed what Claire was describing and finally spoke. "Okay, Ms. Bernardin, so forgive me… but are you saying that this place, La Levrier, is um… like, you know, like a brothel? And you want ME to be like… ah… a call girl? A prostitute?"

"Danielle, I wouldn't even put La Levrier in the same category… or you, for that matter," Claire defended. "We're not your typical escort service, but rather a Girlfriend/Boyfriend Experience. Both Levriettes and members are motivated to be with each other based on mutual attraction and chemistry. I personally am involved in selecting every Levrier based on potential and, quite frankly, caliber. They are the epitome of style, looks and intelligence. By the same token, I'm also very selective about allowing only certain members into La Levrier. They have to meet specific standards and criteria. We don't just take anyone, Danielle. That's why I'm having this conversation with you. I think you're special. You fit the ideal profile as a match for many of our members. Men who are successful in their profession, smart, attractive and gentlemanly. Men who would be an equally good match for you, in fact. That's where the synergy comes in."

"So, you're like a modern-day matchmaker?" Danielle probed.

Claire grinned at the analogy.

"Well… I just don't know. I've never done this kind of thing before. How do I know it's safe? What if I catch an STD? What if someone recognizes me?"

"Slow down, Danielle," Claire reassured. "Let me explain how this works, and then I'd like you to give it some serious thought." Danielle nodded.

"First, your safety is my number one priority. When we screen new members, I require proof of a physical examination, which includes a sexual wellness check. They must be DDF—Drug and Disease Free. On the rare occasion, if you were ever to feel unsafe or one of our members became inappropriate, we have security here 24/7. A guard is on duty around the clock. You probably noticed the high-security measures we have taken around the property on the outside. On the inside, there are surveillance cameras in every room. Every Levrier wears a bracelet with a built-in button that she can press, which sends an immediate signal to our guard."

Danielle let out a sigh of relief and took a sip of iced tea.

Claire continued. "As for being recognized, that's very unlikely. Everything that happens at La Levrier stays at La Levrier. We don't expect Levriettes to leave the premises with members unless it's by mutual consent and I am personally made aware of this arrangement. Our members are also asked to sign a strict code of confidentiality to protect the privacy of La Levrier, our Levriettes, and other members. Several of our members, in fact, are in the public spotlight as political figures, world leaders, celebrities, television personalities, high powered business executives and the like. Their privacy, as you can imagine, is non-negotiable, so confidentiality works both ways."

"Speaking of negotiation," Danielle ventured. "What are the terms of compensation?"

"Ah, but you haven't even decided whether you're interested in the position yet, have you?" Claire half-teased.

"Based on what you've shared to address my concerns, I could be interested, Ms. Bernardin. But, please understand, I have obligations. Significant financial obligations. I can't afford to take any risks."

"And neither can we, Danielle," Claire returned. "One bad hire could cost me my business, my reputation and not only my income but those of the other Levriettes. If this place shuts down, the consequences have grave impact on all involved. I won't lie to you. This is a risky business. That's why I take such cautious measures screening new hires and compensating them very handsomely."

"I understand," Danielle nodded.

"I'd venture to say that you could easily bring home quadruple what you currently make waiting tables at RL. And that's just for starters. In fact, I already have a match in mind for you."

"A match? You mean a man? How do you know he and I would be right for each other?" Danielle pressed.

"Yes, a man," Claire laughed. "The tall, dark and handsome variety. He likes elegant, refined and smart women. He's a business executive. Great sense of humor. A gentleman who admires beauty."

"I'm not sure he'd like me then," Danielle joked.

"Danielle, don't underestimate your femininity," Claire scolded with humor. "You are a beautiful young lady with charm, wit and intelligence. That's a rare combination and one of the most elusive, sought-after and desirable types of woman that a man wants. A fantasy, if you will."

"Thank you, Ms. Bernardin. You're too kind," Danielle said, blushing.

"Please call me Claire," she responded. "I'm not just being kind. I'm being honest. Look, give my proposal some thought... and be honest with yourself. La Levrier is not for everyone, BUT it is an opportunity to improve your circumstances and create a better, more stable life for you and your son. If you were to work for me, I would take care of you, not just financially, but treat you to everything to ensure your success as a Levrier. We'll even have fun together. Go shopping for evening gowns, beautiful lingerie, perfumes, jewelry… you name it. I have connections with some of the best makeup artists and hairdressers in the city. You will blossom from being a lovely young lady into a sophisticated young woman under my tutelage."

"I have one last question, if I may?" Danielle gently asked.

"Of course." Claire responded.

"Why me… I mean… how do you know I will be good at this?"

Claire thought for a moment as if hesitating to make the next statement. "Quite frankly, I'm a very good judge of people. In order for La Levrier to survive I can't make any mistakes on both the clients we accept and the staff. I have great confidence in you, Danielle."

Danielle's eyes brightened as she looked at Claire as the epitome of grace and style. To be Claire's protégé would be an honor, Danielle thought. Still, she had to consider her options carefully. Danielle thanked Claire and promised to be in touch in a couple of days with her decision.

After Danielle left, Claire felt a similar tug of emptiness inside as she did when Jon departed. Given that Claire interviewed at least a dozen Danielles a week and met with a dozen more Jons, this was unusual. She had denied, and suppressed, those feelings long ago. There was no room in her schedule, no room in her ambitions and no room in her heart for any significant attachments. That was that.

Claire wandered over to gaze at the gold mechanical contraption encased in a glass dome in the corner of her office. Peering down into the glass lifted her spirits, as she eyed the nostalgic relic that had once been a prominent centerpiece in her grandmother's living room of this very same home when Claire was a child. Its cogs, gears, and wheels tightly interlocked to create a three-dimensional sculpture. At first glance, the contraption looked like some type of mechanical instrument, but upon closer inspection, the discerning eye could see that it was a dog. A greyhound.

Claire's affection for greyhounds was rooted in her childhood years, thanks to Grandma Jaclyn. Claire owed her tribute to the breed to Percy, who was her grandmother's prized greyhound and, some joked, ruled the Greystone on Astor Street.

Percy relentlessly greeted Claire and her brother, Ted (who Claire affectionately dubbed "Teddy"), during their trips to Grandma's house. Those visits from Chicago's Pilsen neighborhood on the Lower West Side were always a childhood treat. To Claire, Grandma's "mansion" was a fairytale castle… an open invitation to feel like a princess for a day as she explored the labyrinth of rooms and experienced the refinements of life as a proper lady. To return to her modest flat with its heavy drapes pulled perpetually closed and Mama's alcohol-fueled belligerence was a pill that got harder and harder to swallow as Claire grew up. But she was the only parent Claire had, as her father had passed from emphysema when she was only six and Teddy was four. Claire barely remembered her dad, except for his passion for cigars that filled the house with pungent tobacco fumes.

She distinctly recalled visiting Grandma Jaclyn's home for the first time in awe. There was no mask of darkness, no blanket of haze and no veil of sickness. Jaclyn had done her best to support her son and his family, but she couldn't save him from his disease and, ultimately, his demise. Following his untimely death at 36, Rosemarie Bernardin befriended the bottle and started down her own path to self-destruction. After Theodore senior's life insurance dried up, Claire was forced to support the family at the age of 14. She held various odd jobs to make ends meet after school, but her favorite was assisting Sophia behind the counter at a third-generation owned local Czech bakery.

Seventeen-year-old Sophia was the owner's daughter—tall, slim and statuesque, blonde with hazel eyes and an extraordinarily wide and inviting smile. In fact, Sophia was the magnet that attracted most of the male teenage neighbors to the bakery to buy a dozen kolachky or a loaf of rye bread for their "mothers."

After they left the pastry shop, Sophia would jokingly elbow Claire and whisper, "there goes, Jimmy. Sweet guy but stupid as sheeeet!" or "How many times do you think Tony twiddles his diddle?" Claire would bust out giggling, but perhaps the funniest incident was when Raymond, proudly sporting his varsity letterman's jacket, swaggered into the shop and plopped down a pile of loose coins. "I'll have a loaf of houska, cinnamon strudel, and the trdelnik," he requested, winking at Sophia.

"Let's see here, Ray," she commented, eying his change. "You don't have enough money to be able to buy all three. I count $11.63. You'll need $18.60 for everything, including tax."

"I'm sure I have more than $11.63," he insisted. "You didn't even count my change!" Claire noticed that Sophia had not touched a single coin.

"I did indeed. Count it yourself," Sophia smiled sweetly. Ray acted surprised to be challenged and asked that Claire do it instead. Claire obliged and, sure enough, the change came to exactly $11.63. Ray huffed and stormed out of the shop from embarrassment.

"How did you DO that?" Claire gasped.

"With great pleasure," Sophia smirked. "That boy thinks his sheeeet don't stink, and he had it coming."

Claire laughed. "I'm sure he did. But I meant... how did you know exactly how much change he had without even counting it? You did that in less than a minute!"

Sophia tapped the side of her head. "Up here. Call it a gift."

It was then that Claire realized that Sophia was not just another beautiful girl, but a smart one as well. As the friends became closer, Sophia confided to Claire that she had been offered a scholarship to MIT, one of the best engineering schools in the country. Claire was speechless and applauded her new best friend.

"But I am not going," Sophia countered. "My family needs me too much here to run the bakery."

"You can't turn a once-in-a-lifetime opportunity like that down!" Claire insisted.

"Tell that to my father," Sophia sighed.

And Claire did. Still, Mr. Novotny would not budge. "No daughter of mine will go to a man's school!" he refused. He apparently did not recognize the depth of her intelligence or the expanse of her potential, and Claire was unable to reason with the irrational.

Claire and Sophia discovered they had so much in common—a hard work ethic driven by family needs, a shared passion for math and science, and a rare beauty that made men swoon and return to the shop for more—all desirable qualities for business, of course. They became inseparable as Claire worked overtime to help her friend manage the pastry shop by baking, serving customers and cleaning well into the late evening hours.

That Spring, when Sophia had graduated from high school, Claire talked her into standing up to her dad and explaining to him that a good college education at MIT could help her run the bakery even better... expand it into a powerful enterprise... open even more shops across the country... and make a fortune for the Novotnys. The two girls rehearsed as Claire role-played Sophia's dad, and Sophia perfected her presentation, finally confident that she could convince him to let her attend MIT.

The day after Sophia was supposed to speak to her father the previous evening, Claire reported to the bakery. Sophia was not in her spot behind the counter with her friendly grin awaiting her arrival. Mr. Novotny was.

"Where is Sophia?" Claire asked him.

"You are not welcome here," he spat in broken English. "Take your things and go. I never want to see your face in my shop again."

Claire was stunned, yet relieved when she spotted Sophia in the distance, arranging freshly-baked kolachky on a serving platter. They met eyes, and Claire called to her. Sophia quickly looked down and refused to acknowledge her presence. But Claire would not accept her best friend's dismissal that easily.

"Sophia," she called again. "What's going on here? Is what your father saying true? Do YOU want me gone?"

"Yes," Sophia nodded. "You are not my friend."

"What about MIT? Did you talk to your dad about college last night like we discussed?" Claire challenged.

"You are a bad influence on this family," Mr. Novotny yelled. "There is, and never was, college in my daughter's future. Stay out of our business… and GET THE HELL OUT!"

Claire stared at Sophia in disbelief and then tried to walk behind the counter to approach her friend, but Mr. Novotny blocked her.

"Go away, Claire. For your own good. That's just how it has to be," Sophia hissed.

Claire took her cue and finally left. She never saw or spoke with Sophia ever again. Every day, she ached for her best friend. Her heart was raw from the burn. Sophia's absence plunged deeper than even her father's death. Claire was not only stung by the betrayal, but by the devastating loss of potential that this young lady possessed. It seemed so unfair that Sophia should be robbed of her gift—and her right—to realize her dreams.

Meanwhile, Claire had her own family issues to combat. As her mother spiraled deeper into drunken desperation, her and Teddy's visits to Grandma Jaclyn became more frequent, until finally it was deemed necessary by the Department of Children and Family Services that both children maintain permanent residence at the house on Astor Street. So, as Claire entered her first year of high school, she and her brother lived with their grandmother and Percy in the stately Greystone. Unlike Sophia, she was able to have the good fortune of attending MIT, also on a full scholarship. Claire excelled in her studies. Not a day passed when she didn't think of her dear friend, and one of these days she promised herself that she would help others in need to achieve their life goals. Young women like Danielle, Camilla, Lorelei, Justianne, Bianca and many, many others.

Within months after Claire graduated from MIT, her mother passed away, and Grandma Jaclyn became seriously ill. Claire served as her caretaker until the day she died three years later, leaving her entire estate to her two grandchildren as she had no other heirs. Claire graciously accepted her good fortune and, now free from family obligations, knew it was time to pursue her calling. She just didn't know exactly how.

One day as she was sorting and packing her grandmother's possessions, she stumbled across a hope chest in the far recesses of the attic. During their childhood, this space had been off limits and uninhabitable. Ted continued to live at the residence and, while there were plenty of rooms for both, Claire had the vision to convert the attic into something spectacular in her plans to renovate and redecorate.

Prying open the latch of the trunk triggered a puff of dust. Claire coughed as she waved it away with one hand and peeled the lid back with the other. What she saw among the well-preserved treasures was a variety of items that appeared to belong to a woman at least a generation older than her grandmother. She lifted out a sepia-toned photo of a stunning brunette with loose curls pinned into an upswept hairdo, dangling pearl earrings, and a matching choker necklace. Her floor-length, form-fitting silk gown bedecked with rhinestones, beads, and ruffles that accentuated her tiny waist and feminine curves. She was not just another turn-of-the-century girl with a pretty face and figure; she had to be quite a show-stopper in her day, Claire surmised.

She rummaged deeper in the chest and pulled out a fur stole, an ivory lace corset with garter belt, a long black plume, a silver etched hairbrush and a tiny clutch purse embroidered with cherry blossoms. These were precisely the assets of a well-heeled woman who lived in the lap of luxury, or so it would seem. She turned over the photo and scrawled on the back was written "Margaret 'Marge' Bernardin, Everleigh Club, 1903."

The Everleigh Club? It rang a distant bell. Claire swept through the possessions and lifted a small mahogany-colored leather notebook, entitled "Everleigh Club Rules." A standards manual? For whom, Claire wondered. She opened the first page and read the faded print:

To our Everleigh Butterflies,

Each girl must be in perfect health and must look well in evening clothes. The Everleigh Club will provide training. Be polite and forget what you are here for. Gentlemen are only gentlemen when properly introduced. The Everleigh Club is not for the rough element, the clerk on a holiday or a man without a checkbook.

—Ada and Minna Everleigh

The Everleigh Club... Claire recalled that it was a legendary Chicago bordello in the Levee District run by two sisters in the early 1900s. The Everleigh madams, Ada and Minna, operated their social club as a mecca of elegance and extravagance. Claire spotted some additional photos in the trunk and gathered that these were pictures of the rooms. Silk curtains, damask easy chairs, oriental rugs, mahogany tables, fountains, a gold-leafed piano and even mirrored ceilings graced the premises. Dripping in opulence, it appeared no expense was spared.

That was it—Claire deduced that her great-grandmother was an Everleigh Butterfly... a product of the sisters who must have taken her under their wing when she came to Chicago from a small village outside of Normandy seeking to build a life for herself. Did this mean that Marge Bernardin was a high-class prostitute? Grandma Jaclyn had never spoken much of her mother, so the family history was pretty fragmented.

Intrigued, Claire ventured to the Chicago Public Library the following day and devoured the archives to research everything she could find on the Everleigh Club. What she discovered was even more fascinating. The Everleigh quickly gained a reputation as an upscale gentlemen's club, so much so that the two sisters carefully selected only that clientele deemed "worthy" of admission. Their standards made the club extremely exclusive, indulging the desires of only the wealthiest and most influential men. It grew to have such cachet that prospective clients had to provide a letter of recommendation from an existing member, an engraved card or enter the club through a formal introduction by Minna or Ada.

By the same token, Ada took equally great care in recruiting and interviewing prospective Everleigh Club girls face-to-face. Once hired, Minna was responsible for carrying out lessons to teach the new "butterflies" charm and culture. Her sass and social savviness welcomed clients through the doors, and it was she who handled all of the personal interactions to ensure that their visits were stellar. The club so was highly profitable given the caliber of patrons that, once the Everleigh sisters retired, they had amassed a net profit of $1 million which would be equivalent to $20.5 million today.

Claire had not only opened a Pandora's Box on her great-grandmother but lifted the lid on another idea. An idea that ultimately led her to where she was today, reflecting on her recent interview with Danielle and even more so on the imprint that her meeting with Jon had etched on her typically impassive demeanor.

CHAPTER SIX

Reporting In

"She's all yours, playboy," Agent Mike Gorski smiled from ear-to-ear as he walked out of Mac Owen's office.

"Right here, Gorski." Jon rubbed his nose with his middle finger; stopped, smiled, and then offered his fist to the fellow agent he had been in the trenches with on many occasions. They fist bumped and smiled.

"You warm her up for me?" Jon's face moaned, and he dipped his head toward the ground at his bad pun.

"What they teaching on that boudoir assignment you're on?" Gorski quipped.

"It's boutique, not boudoir, ass," Jon chuckled.

"Boutique, boudoir, bordello… I say tomato…" Gorski sang.

"Did I call you an ass already?" Jon smiled, and the two bumped chests in a guys' hug.

"I better get in there. Be safe," Jon said.

"You too," Gorski added.

Jon knocked firmly on Mac Owen's door.

"Come in." Mac's voice was loud and firm.

"Agent Fenwick, come on in. I appreciate you being on time." She made a notation in a folder. "Of course, looking here, you're always on time. It is one of your fine qualities."

"Thank you," Jon said as he took a chair in front of her desk.

"I read your initial reports on this case we are now labeling as L-L." She looked up at him. "I didn't appreciate your initial code name of La La." He smiled, she didn't. "We have uncovered the name of this organization, 'LE LEEvar.' Good, that's progress."

"Excuse me, but you pronounce it 'La LevREE-A, La Levrier. It means The Greyhound," Jon interrupted.

"Right," Mac shot back. "Good, we have the name, we've confirmed the owner, and it appears to be a high-class prostitute scam of some sort. But, in your report, you describe it so far as more of a dating site, like these Internet matching websites. And, you haven't seen or uncovered any money being exchanged. You've secured a room there, good."

"A suite, it's a suite," Jon added.

"Ok, a suite, but they haven't charged you for the ROOM," Mac emphasized.

"I think it might be how they market to new clients." He didn't reveal to her or put in his report that he had heard the term 'member' on several occasions. He wasn't holding anything back to Mac or his report; it was just that he didn't understand the full details of 'member' yet and precision was part of the job. "It's like giving a free sample."

"I see. I do like how this is not showing up on expenses. But, speaking of free samples," Mac stood up from her chair thinking her near six-foot height and muscular physique was going to emphasize her point. "There will be no fucking. Do you understand? NO FUCKING! It would be all we would need if this case ever hit the media and a case like this is bound to hit the media, AND our agent was fucking his brains out while he was investigating this whorehouse. I think I'm clear on that point, correct?" She paused and watched as Jon nodded in affirmation. "In fact, now that I think about it, you having sex there would be disastrous for morale here, not to say what my superiors in Washington would do to me if they found out."

"I'd like to point out, as I put in my report, so far I haven't found any whores in this mansion. No one seems to be there against their will or there for the sole purpose of making money. Up until this point, it seems like a place where people go to have a sexual fantasy. I haven't found any laws broken yet."

"But, you haven't got into the finances yet. Let's be real, Jon. This is a multimillion-dollar Greystone in one of Chicago's most exclusive areas. It sounds like it is furnished well, it's kept up, and taxes paid. Somewhere money is flowing in. You have to find that money. That's your job. You follow that money, and you'll find the crime." Mac was preaching with a finger-pointing cadence.

"I'm on it."

Mac sat back down behind her desk. "Now, here's another bug being jammed up my butt. Washington, all of a sudden, is paying attention to this case. I got a call from Bill Weathers over at the Secret Service. He asked me if I knew of a club, he called it a sex club, operating in the Gold Coast. I think we scored some points when I immediately said, 'Know about it? We have a plant on the inside at this moment.'" Mac bragged.

Jon thought, *ain't no WE in any of that credit being taken.*

Mac continued, "So Bill goes on to say he'd like us to put a priority on this club and he was asked by the highest levels the government to shut this place down. Not harassed, not disrupted, but he was adamant, shut down. And, he gets all authoritarian on me and makes it clear that if we can't do the job, then their people will come in to do it. So, I went on to ask how quickly he would like the doors to close and all he says is YESTERDAY."

"What's got them all over La Levrier?" Jon looked puzzled. "This went from a bottom of the pile assignment to having the Secret Service involved."

"He didn't say, and quite frankly I didn't ask. All I know is that this will look good for us."

There's that US again, Jon smirked to himself.

"If I would throw out a theory, I would guess that somebody on the Secret Service's radar has been there or is involved there. Keep your eyes open for that as well," she added. "It would be nice to have one up on the Secret Service or at least they would owe us a favor."

Mac swiveled her chair and looked out of her windows at the city high rises. Jon looked at his watch and rolled his eyes. Both of his moves were out of her eyesight.

Mac continued, "So, my friend, you're back on an important case through no fault of your own. I thought about replacing you…"

"So, that's why Gorski walked out of her all chipper," Jon remarked.

"As I was saying, I thought of replacing you, but you bumbled your way inside…"

Jon jerked his head as if a wrench banged him on the forehead. "Ok, Mac, I've been sitting here through several meetings and taking your shit, but when you knock my work ethic, that's about enough. I've paid a consequence for my mistake in the past, but you read my report here. I got myself inside with hard work and long hours. There was no accident here, no bumble as you put it. And, now that I know you need me I think the eating shit part of my employment is over. I have one blemish on an outstanding record, and every time I come in here you're digging at me like a schoolyard wannabe bully. You weren't on that mission that fucked up; in fact, you've never been on ANY mission. School, master's degree, and political connections... those got you behind that desk. Well, we all have masters or law degrees here, but some of us put our lives on the line in the streets. Let's just stop the childish barbs and taunts, right now, right here," Jon unloaded.

Mac stood up, and Jon followed her lead. A yelling match was about to escalate. "You dare talk to a superior like that. I will write you up..." The veins in her neck were popping big time.

"Superior? Superior? How dare you call yourself SUPERIOR to anyone in this building let alone me? Want a revelation? They offered me your job before you came over from Boston after you kissed somebody in Washington's ass. Actually, tossed their salad is what I heard..."

Mac, furious, interrupted, "You motherfucker. How dare you."

"Oh, you want to trade little playground barbs? Shall we start with your juvenile—I'm going to reach down in my slush pile and pick the bottom file—that was laughable, you think that stung? You can't even hold your own in a verbal skirmish let alone being in a firefight in the street. Think I'm afraid of you? Bring it, sister." Jon was not nearly as angry as Mac appeared to be, but he kept going because it felt good to dump on her.

"God Dammit…" She picked up files on her desk raised them high and slammed them down hard.

"Actually, the minute I heard it was you taking this job, I regretted not taking it myself. Not for me, but for everyone else in this building. I knew what we were getting with you. A leader without any field experience, what a joke. You're a bureaucrat, go count the Goddamn light bulbs and let the agents do their work. You shouldn't be handling a SLUSH PILE of assignments. Obviously, Weather's call highlighted that you have no idea which ones are priorities or which are not. Talk about BUMBLING into something. You gave me the assignment on the bottom of your priorities, AND now Washington is all over it. Who's the bumbler now, lady?"

Screaming, "Don't you LADY me… Don't you LADY me." She walked to the front of her desk so she could stand toe-to-toe with him. "If I wouldn't be fired I would take you down right now. But, I won't give you that satisfaction…" She was collecting herself a bit. Threatening a veteran standing inches from her who was six-foot-three and had a body like a steel coil tended to make one think hard about how physical this argument was going to turn. Still yelling, but a few octaves lower, "Well something good has come out of this. Now I know the anger and resentment you always held for me."

Jon interrupted, "You just don't get it at all, and you know nothing at all. Your desk jockey ego is fully inflated to think I even considered you enough to resent. Until you had something you could grind into me, quite frankly you were insignificant. INSIGNIFICANT! I did my job; you read my report, you never acknowledged the work I did or what I had to go through to get the job done. You might as well be a filing cabinet for all the use I have for you. I never had resentment, anger or disappointment. You filed my reports in the right place, gave me my next assignment and that's it. You never added to any case I was working on or contributed in any way whatsoever. Even when you might have had the chance to be a boss to me like the time I was shot during the Pelligrino case you didn't come to the hospital, you didn't even send a card. No, you've been insignificant to me." Jon sat back down and stared out the window.

Mac walked back to behind her desk and leaned toward him. Her clenched fists planted on the desktop supported her weight. She contemplated her next words carefully knowing she was an executive losing control of a subordinate. She took her time, eyes fixated on Jon, her body taut. After several minutes she broke the silence, "All right, let's stop this. Yes, I need you to finish this up. You've gotten yourself deep inside. It would be foolish to have someone start all over and cost us a lot of money. Bill said he needs this shut down yesterday, so now we have a ticking clock. Your job has been changed as of today. This is no longer reconnaissance; this is an offensive. This La Levrier has to be shut down and shut down quickly. You go back in there, find out what you need to do that, come back here report in, and we will shut that operation down. We don't have to be friends or even like each other. Let's go back to how it was before. You do your job, give me a report and on to the next one."

"Fine, good to go now?" Jon stood up to leave.

"You've got two weeks. Yes, good to go."

CHAPTER SEVEN

Modus Operandi

Jon hunkered down at his desk in his research mode. Ear buds delivered classical instrumentals, not the music the teens labeled classical like The Beatles and such, but Mozart and others of his era. Listening to music helped him concentrate and it fostered the vigorous internal that was his "process." Jon didn't post pictures and diagrams on a white board like film agents were shown to do, nor did he bounce ideas off other agents. When Jon was agent in charge on an assignment he created an internal dialogue on the research and decisions about the operational details. He questioned every idea like he was brainstorming with a colleague. His own internal devil's advocate.

On the LL case he worked quickly and came up with two plans for shutting down La Levrier. Typical, as bureau procedure was to have a lead plan and a backup. In putting together both plans, he followed his usual procedure of breaking things down to simple elements after careful research. The simple elements were clear: La Levrier had to be shut down immediately and as Bogart might say, 'we could do this the easy way or the hard way.'

The lead plan or Plan A, was to get as close to Claire as he could, but as Mac admonished, no fucking. Jon had to agree with Mac here. He was confident in his ability to seduce women, but he was also honest with himself about Claire. She was possibly the most attractive woman he had ever met. Her looks, her style, her intelligence, sense of humor and total personality topped his list of ideal female qualities. It was tough to keep his mind on the assignment when he was near her. So, there was no way Plan A would be the James Bond movie plot of sleeping with her, and she easily becomes loose-lipped between the sheets.

How could he get close to Claire? That opportunity was presenting itself. Claire brought him into her office, her inner sanctum, because he was rejecting the women she set up for him. By continuing to be a potential member that just can't find the right girlfriend experience, Claire keeps calling him in and trying to figure him out, all the while he is interrogating Claire and possibly somehow getting access to some inside information. Now that he was brought into the lair and been vetted by Claire as a potential safe member, he figured she would do almost anything not to let him leave without being a part of La Levrier. The consequences of not getting Jon or anyone targeted for membership were too risky. A person who is brought inside to La Levrier gets hit on over and over; Claire couldn't just let him walk away from La Levrier. He or she would know too much. A potential member who walked away could start talking up his experiences or near experiences there, and soon enough knowledge of La Levrier would be out. La Levrier's existence depended on absolute secrecy by its membership, and this secrecy only came through the potential ruin that would come to these high-profile members, but this confidentiality worked both ways. No one who gets onto Claire's radar as a member could afford to let out that they fulfill their innermost romantic desires by going to La Levrier plus, the club could ill afford the chance of being discovered. Once caught in the web, the prey and the spider are committed to each other's fate.

Plan A had its drawbacks. Claire was an incredibly private person, and that extreme privacy kept La Levrier going for as long as it had been in operation. But, even if he could strike up a friendship close enough to get some information that would lead to closing La Levrier, it would probably be some tiny little financial or legal quirk she left unattended. He sucked at financial crimes. He wasn't trained for it and never had a case assigned to him that included it. The possibility of him picking up on such a nuisance would be remote.

Jon paused his music, scrolled down on his phone app and picked up the pace and momentum of the atmosphere in his head.

Claire was brilliant. Her intelligence was abundantly clear the instant they met. And the case file he was initially handed underlined that intelligence. Her elusiveness from the CPD, possibly the IRS and even his difficulties tracking her confirmed her brilliance and the dual degrees from MIT sealed the deal. She was smart, perceptive and intuitive. Cracking through her firewall would be very, very tough. He was a Yalie and top of his class at the FBI, but he was honest with himself that Claire's native brainpower intimidated him. He wasn't going toe-to-toe with that.

The deal breakers to Plan A might have been time and chance. He would have to be exceptionally lucky to come upon the needle in that haystack. In this case, that needle would have to be uncovering a crime that shuts down the business of La Levrier instantly. That would be the killer blow, and that kind of luck takes patience and time. And then there's time and the deadline. Integrating himself in this manner with Claire would take time and would have to be delicate. All of a sudden, he didn't have that time any longer. Mac was a consummate bureaucrat and completing assignments on time was a concrete measure of success. It had always been the FBI's policy to solve cases with a less intrusive approach first. It saves money, possible litigation, and avoids harm to anyone on either side of the case. But, the FBI may force his hand, and he may have to switch quickly to an aggressive approach.

But, he really felt as though he had to give this less aggressive approach a try first. The people involved in La Levrier didn't seem like they were hurting anyone, they weren't even freaky. They just were fulfilling parts of their lives that were missing. And, the encounters seemed to be ironically mutual. If this was prostitution, it was sure an unusual twist on mankind's oldest profession. The Levriettes seemed just as excited and into the encounters as the members. *Where was the one-sided transaction? Where was the exploitation?* It all made him wonder what was the Secret Service's need to have this shuttered. Hell, if Claire just called this place a church and people belonged as members, then any money given to the church would be considered a donation. She could get a 501(3)c and the members could write their La Levrier participation off their income taxes! Of course, try explaining those donations to your spouse when you sit down with the accountant.

Claire being Claire had gotten into him enough already that he considered the possibility of going back to Mac and reporting in that he failed. He had to admit he was struggling with the whole purpose this assignment now took—shut down La Levrier and ruin its owner. He simply didn't have a problem with what he saw at the mansion so far. There was no moralistic high ground for him to be on a vendetta against La Levrier just because it involved sex. In fact, Jon saw the sex as a by-product. La Levrier was about the emotion, the passion, excitement and the fantasy more than the sex. Unless he knew all the details of why this business had to be shut down and could argue a reason to stop his orders as is, then he had no choice but to be a good soldier and follow orders and proceed.

Okay, if the mansion couldn't be shut down passively he had to have a second plan—Plan B. Plan B would have to be able to be turned on immediately once Plan A failed.

Jon cranked the inspirational music louder, sat back in his chair, closed his eyes and began a new rumination.

Given his two-week ultimatum from Mac, Plan B had to be immediate and decisive. Even though this was his wheelhouse, he was puzzled. There were some obvious actions he could take and his mind kept coming back to the first thought he had. *If he shut the building down, he shut the operation down.* What struck him was hearing in the media about two years ago that two older houses on Chicago's South Side just suddenly blew up one day. The cause was a gas leak in the city's pipeline running into the homes. These two classic Chicago bungalows weren't even half the age of the mansion that housed La Levrier. It would be very believable that a century and a half old Astor mansion might suffer a similar fate. But, to execute such a plan, dozens of contingencies had to be worked out and coordinated very quickly. Everyone inside had to be completely evacuated well before the demolition, the houses next door had to be guaranteed safe from any damage, there couldn't be any actual damage to the city's infrastructure and there had to be coordination with the Chicago PD and Fire Departments without them knowing the exact nature of what the FBI was doing. Plus, Mac had to approve the entire plan. Oh, Mac wasn't a huge obstacle. She loved to order grand spectacles that got media saturation. It was sort of that vicarious living thing that desk jockeys do when they send the troops out to battle. As long as she didn't have to get her hands dirty, and of course as long as it didn't cost a lot of money, she would love the drama of rendering La Levrier physically inoperable. Besides, Jon could hear Mac going all cowboy to Weathers at Secret Service when she told him she solved his problem with a big bang. Plan B even had a positive side for Claire. She had to have the place and its furnishings insured, whereas, if he found some tax violation, prostitution, sex trafficking or illegal money—something other than physical damage to shut La Levrier down—Claire would lose everything without a chance for any recovery. Going straight to Plan B was extremely tempting and more in Jon's skill set. Still, both Jon's and the Bureau's code was to take the course of least resistance first before force was used. But, again, that deadline was killer.

Jon pulled the buds from his ears, shut down the phone app, leaned into his desk and began typing on his keyboard.

Within three days of his shouting match in Mac's office, Jon presented both plans to Mac in great detail through a series of emails. He made a convincing argument in the introduction to Plan A why this approach should be the first to be tried. He included all the right buzz words on the mission of the Federal Bureau of Investigation, the prevention of collateral damage in terms of both property and human life, and the existing data that thus far, no agency including Jon's own investigation turned up any crimes. Going straight into Plan B would be a violation of Claire's and the rights of all those involved. That kind of disregard for the rights of citizens was more the style of the CIA, Secret Service, not the FBI. Mac bought his arguments and approved him to initiate Plan A. She even extended the two-week deadline so that the clock began then and not from the date of their last meeting. Still, this was an impossible deadline, and Mac insisted that she prepare all the parameters to press the button for Plan B to strike the minute the clock struck twelve on the fourteenth day. Reading the tone in that email from Mac, Jon could picture the look on her face beaming in anticipation for that moment.

⚬⚬⚬

Preston was already starting his fourth perfect Manhattan when he heard a knock on his suite. Gabrielle greeted him at the door with a deep kiss.

"You've started without me," she purred.

"I've had a tense day my dear. I needed some relaxation, that's why I checked in," he slurred.

"I thought it was unusual you were here on a Tuesday." She kissed him again and finished her tender kiss with a caress near his ear, a favorite of his.

She walked past him and as she did, her peach boudoir robe fell to the floor with an effortless pull on the silk belt near her collarbone, another favorite of his was watching her walk from behind. Her round cheeks seemed to protrude with each step. He stared at her as she purposely bent from the waist and pulled back the comforter from the king bed.

Without warning, he put both palms on her cheeks that were now even more plumped up, a look he always liked and a tease she was expert in displaying. He shoved her hard into the bed and even against the soft layers of bed sheets the force of his push made her wince.

"Preston, what?" She turned her head to look at him, surprised by the force he used.

"So, you thought it unusual I came today. Why?" He held her body face first into the bed sheets with one hand spread wide on her upper back. His other hand ripped her thong off with a pull so hard the silk fabric left rope-like burns on her porcelain skin. Immediately after her thong was torn away that same hand went hard against her womanhood. Gabrielle jerked from his aggressiveness as he forced several fingers inside her. She was dry, and his fingers did nothing to take away the pain of his friction against her and inside her.

"Did you have another member to take care of?" He forced his fingers deeper inside her with each syllable of the word, 'member' his slurring became more pronounced.

"Presss…to…n." She mumbled as her face flattened into the bed. She clenched her butt cheeks hard trying to repel him from the pressure he was exerting on her womanhood.

"Come on, Gaby. You know what I like." He removed his hand from inside her and reaching his arm back he cracked her as hard as he could across both butt cheeks. Her skin immediately turned bright crimson, and she let out a yelp that was loud, even with her face into the bed.

She furiously wiggled and kicked to get free from him. But at the first movements of her legs, he knelt on them to control her. The digging of his knees into her hamstrings left instant bruises, and she stopped kicking.

Rocking her head back and forth wildly her mouth came free, and after a large gasp of breath, she yelled, "This is not you! This is not us!" She fought for air and shook him off again. "Stop…stop…now!" Lying on the bed her arms were free as Preston held her down with strong leverage on her upper back. Although this didn't give her the mobility to break free, it did give her the ability to bring her hands close enough together that she could press her Levrier bracelet sounding the silent alarm for security.

Preston shoved her head back into the bed, and his hand returned its rape of her womanhood.

He then became startled and turned his upper body to the door. He heard a key working the lock of his suite.

Ted, Claire's head of security let himself in without hesitation.

Preston straightened himself and stepped back from Gabrielle who lay limp on the bed sobbing. "What's going on here?" Preston insisted.

"What's going on here is that you need to get anything you brought into this room and meet Claire in the office on the second floor. I'll be escorting you there."

"You have to be kidding? But…" Preston slightly swayed as he faced Ted.

Ted didn't answer. Instead, he whispered into an imperceptible microphone somewhere on him. In what seemed like seconds, other staff charged through the door and went immediately to Gabrielle. They immediately laid hands gently on Gabrielle's back and comforted her.

"Gabrielle, we're here… you're safe… put your mind into a different place right now." The two females' tone were soft and comforting. With a light touch, one of the women applied aloe all over Gabrielle's skin from her hips down.

As they ministered to Gabrielle, Ted walked Preston out of his suite. Both men were silent as they left the room.

After minutes, Gabrielle pushed herself up into a sitting position, and one of the women hugged her and Gabrielle laid her head on the attendant's shoulder.

"Gabrielle, this is a terrible hurt and loss. I know you felt strongly for Preston," she said.

In tears, Gabrielle tried to understand what just happened to her. "He was never like this. I don't know what happened to him," she cried all the harder.

"And, it certainly wasn't you, dear." She held Gabrielle tight. The other attendant leaned in with a look of concern and placed a hand on Gabrielle's shoulder while her partner embraced her. "We'll be here for you. Did he hurt you anywhere we can't see?" the staff person asked.

Gabrielle slowly and delicately placed her hand across her vagina and lowered her head.

"Whenever you're ready we'll get you up to the nurse. Whenever you are ready. You're in charge here now Gabrielle," the attendant assured her.

⌇

Jon returned to La Levrier immediately after submitting his strategy to Mac. He reserved his suite with the usual email via the private app provided to him. When he arrived, a Levriette handed him his Veuve flute, and he asked the same staff person if he could get a meeting with Claire.

Moments after entering his suite the door chime rang, and he was handed a note with the usual La Levrier aplomb, parchment stationery, handwritten and personalized. It read:

I would be honored with your presence in the business office at your convenience and pleasure between 2:00 pm and until 4:30 pm today.

It was signed: *C~*.

Jon arrived at the reception area to the business office on the second floor at two-fifteen. He was thrilled that Claire picked the business office for this meeting given his need to probe into some records. Maybe he could meet the deadline after all.

The business office was not like any he had encountered previously. The anteroom had a clear Lucite desk. The desktop was in the shape of an ellipse; it looked like a clear, flattened reproduction of Chicago's famous Bean sculpture. Holding up the top the clear base was in the shape of a 'V.' The mix of geometric shapes was striking. A clear Ghost chair served as a desk chair for, of course, a female staff member who was as much a work of art as the furnishings. She didn't appear to be twenty-one quite yet, and the desk and chair showcased her long, bare mini-skirted legs as if the clear Lucite office furniture was purchased specifically with her in mind. In fact, Jon wouldn't put that past Claire. Three similar Ghost chairs served as guest chairs. Two of the chairs against one wall and another on the wall opposite. The wood floors were original although sanded and refinished to a light oak. Their genuineness betrayed by the telltale remnants of blackish lacquer build-up between many of the floorboards. Probably left there as much for the veining effect it gave the floor, as well as it would have to be impossible to dig out without ripping up the entire floor. Then what would be the point of restoration? The walls were a light gray, and several original looking architectural drawings of the mansion dotted the walls but were not overdone.

Margot, the receptionist for the office, rose as Jon entered the room. She walked in front of her desk and greeted him. "Mr. Fenwick, please come in. Claire is handling a bit of an immediate situation. You can have a seat if you like or I could call you when she is free?" Her voice was one of the softest Jon had ever heard, above a whisper yet crisp and precise.

"I'd be glad to wait. Will it take long?" Jon asked.

"I'm not sure. As you know, it is the staff's custom here to stay discrete." Margot stood straight in front of the desk with no apologies for her near six-foot height.

"I'll wait." With that Jon tapped the inside of his right ear with the fingernail of his right index finger. It activated a tiny hearing aid. He could now hear everything going on inside the office.

Claire's voice raised, "Dr. Jacoby, I will get right to the point. Your membership in La Levrier is terminated immediately. My apologies, I misspoke. Your membership and all the privileges were terminated a half-hour ago. You will also find that we withdrew your membership deposit and a penalty fee from your account."

Preston Jacoby interrupted her. His speech was now full-blown drunk talk. "No, no, no. This place is fantasyland... whaaa I do? Gaby and I are a couple. Isn't this place, anything goes?"

"First of all, Dr. Jacoby. You are too drunk to get into a discussion about our policies. You signed a contract to be a part of La Levrier, you were explained the boundaries, all activities are mutual, no one dominates the other, and no one gets hurt in any way. This is our golden rule. Are you cognizant enough to understand what I am saying to you right now?" Claire's voice was loud and firm.

"Why do you kreept saying that?" His slurred word was ironic.

"Ok, that's enough. Your contract says I get to determine your fine when there is physical harm involved. Your bank account on file will be charged $250,000.00 dollars and withdrawn immediately." Claire typed on her laptop and didn't look at Jacoby again. "Teddy, escort Dr. Jacoby out of the building."

"Claire… Ms. Bernardin…" Preston pleaded, but Ted put his body in front of Jacoby's chair blocking the view between Jacoby and Claire. Resigned, Jacoby stood, a bit off balance as Ted walked him out the door. They passed Jon waiting in the reception area.

Margot typed on her laptop and seconds later looked toward Jon, "Claire would be delighted to see you now. She had no idea you were waiting." Margot stood up and opened Claire's door for Jon.

Jon walked in and immediately offered a courtesy, "Sure you don't need a minute?" he asked.

Claire rose from her desk, a larger version of Margot's clear Lucite beauty, and greeted him. Her white crepe dress hugged her body perfectly. Her smile was wide, and her eyes grew at the sight of him. He did give her a pleasing sight to look at. His jeans fit just right, not too skinny to make him look as if he was copying the kids, but form fitting enough to accentuate his muscular legs. He had on a contrasting vest, button-down shirt and a tie just loosened from his neck. His suede oxford sneakers completed his bespoke casualness.

"Oh, you overheard all that?" Her smile morphed into a smirk but retained her delight in seeing him.

"Yes, you look no worse for wear," he chuckled.

"That is a moment when this pleasure turns into a business," she quipped. "I wish I could be all noble and say, he's a good man and that his indiscretion was an accident or some such thing, but I confess I never had a good feeling about him. I have always felt deep down he harbored short man's disease, and I guess the morning Manhattans brought it out today. Anyway, problem solved. My main concern is the woman he mistreated."

"I agree, who is it?" Jon asked.

"Oh Jon, you overheard too much already. Absolute discretion is a pillar of La Levrier. Now, let's leave that terrible situation and discuss why you wanted to see me."

"I wanted to discuss becoming a part of La Levrier, but after hearing that fine you levied I must admit I'm having some second thoughts." He made his smile look genuine.

"As I said, let's leave that situation. Now, how can I help?" Claire's smile disappeared, yet her face remained warm.

"Well, as long as I mentioned money, let's start with money. What are the dues? Is there an initiation fee?"

She laughed. "Jon this is not a gym. There are no dues or membership fee. A person wishing to become a part of La Levrier makes a one-time donation of 3 million dollars to our endowment. We do the rest. Your every need and desire is met. There is no invoicing, past due, limits on your spending, levels of membership or other nonsense. Everything is equal and mutual here. A potential member discloses the privacy and security of those funds; it's a rather extensive disclosure so that La Levrier is not involved in any third party, spouse, or partner dispute over the use of the funds and that is it. The money is gone. There is no back and forth to be discovered or traced. You want to roll around in ten pounds of Beluga on your sheets, your fees have covered it."

"So, what happens if I use up my donation?"

Claire laughed. "Jon, the average active participation of our members is 2.6 years. If you can spend 3 million dollars in two and half years on drug-free pleasure, I will personally call the Guinness Book of Records, and they will have a full-page entry on you."

"So, that fine you just levied? That comes out of the donation as well?"

"You will find in your agreement that you also have to give us access to an emergency fund. We don't touch it unless something like what you overheard occurs. It wouldn't be a fine if it came out of money you already spent, correct?" Claire explained.

Jon nodded, then launched into his next curiosity. "And the residents? How much are they paid?"

"Jon, not your concern and we don't disclose that to members. I assure you that our Levriettes are paid very, very well, and their perks are beyond anything corporate America is providing."

"And my stays so far?"

"Jon, you wouldn't have come back unless you were going to be a part of La Levrier. Your donation will more than cover the expenses you incurred while here. La Levrier's business model is very successful. Don't worry about our expenses. You just concentrate on your pleasure." Claire assured him. She handed him a black matte folder that had the slight texture reminiscent of fine sandpaper. On the cover was a rendering of the gold Greyhound bracelet that the Levriettes all wore. "Here, I've made up a member packet for you and everything is explained. Of course, if you have any questions…" she smiled.

"I must admit, I'm curious about something." Jon looked away from Claire, and his eyes squinted.

"What's on your mind?" Claire inquired.

"How do you know I even qualify?" he asked.

Claire beamed a broad smile. "That fellow who escorted the member out of my office. That's my brother Teddy. He's head of security. I shot him a picture of you when I stalked… er… met you at the Coq D'Or." A devilish smile grew on her face. "He ran a background check on you based on that picture. That's all he needed." Claire pressed a few keys on her laptop then turned it around for him to see. A picture of Jon exiting an Aston Martin Rapide. His full name appeared in gold under the picture.

Claire read off the screen as she scrolled down the pages in his file. "Jon Fenwick, just shy of a billionaire… how sad." She faux-frowned. "Owner of an international security firm, armored car company, four banks in Singapore and the inventor of the Mac Lock."

God bless that Jeremy in operations. Jon thought.

Jon gripped the folder with both hands and lifted with emphasis, "Let me carefully look this all over. Are there any time constraints on my decision?"

"You take all the time you need, and in the meantime, enjoy our hospitality. Once you make your decision, I am sure you will then need time to discretely arrange for your donation. La Levrier is not going anywhere."

Hmmmmmmm… Jon thought.

CHAPTER EIGHT

One More Shot

Jon took the elevator down to the lower level of the mansion. Every member staying at La Levrier that night received an invitation to a private concert by Stan Kenton, the renowned international jazz/funk virtuoso. In Jon's personal life he was a huge fan but never had the opportunity to attend one of his concerts let alone a private performance. This was not to be missed, assignment or not.

The elevator screamed of the La Levrier style. From the live elevator operator decked out in a dark blue bellman's uniform with black velvet striped slacks, waistcoat, white gloves and bellman's cap to the steel walls framed with wrought iron girders and the door cage that could only be worked by the operator.

"Lower level, Mr. Fenwick?" Kenneth assumed as Jon entered the elevator car. Jon was quite impressed that Kenneth knew his name, as Jon had never laid eyes on him before. More evidence of Claire's attention to detail.

"Of course, ...err... Kenneth." Jon leaned forward and read the operator's gold name badge on his chest. His name was in black calligraphy, and above his badge was embossed the profile of two greyhounds' heads facing nose-to-nose.

Kenneth pulled hard on the large steel lever and the cage door closed. He then yanked a brass throttle, and the elevator slowly descended toward the lower level.

After a short, fascinating ride (one doesn't get transported in that style any longer), Kenneth forced the throttle back into an upward position, and the elevator stopped. He pulled the cage lever back, and Jon arrived on the lower level. Kenneth popped off the oak stool he sat on inside the elevator car and stood at attention just outside the door. His gloved hand waved Jon a welcome to enter.

The lower level was a reproduction of an old speakeasy. The walls were wide vertical copper planks from floor to ceiling. The ceiling itself appeared to be a black velvet material dotted with tiny lights giving the effect of a starry sky. Small, but elaborate chandeliers hung close to the ceiling for more light when needed. Intimate café tables with white tablecloths where spread around the spacious room. There were four chairs at each table, and each had a white chair cover tied in the back with a black tulle tieback secured with a gold cuff with the two greyhound heads facing each other. The staff set the tables with small black china chargers and black smoked crystal for red wine, white wine, and champagne. A cylinder of four red roses completed the table setting.

A hostess who carried a tray with each of Jon's favorite drinks in the appropriate glass greeted him. There was a cocktail of Ketel One splashed with Bombay Sapphire on the rocks, a flute of Veuve Clicquot Champagne, and a Kelt cognac, neat, in a tall snifter.

Jon lifted the cognac off the tray, and the hostess remarked, "Excellent choice. Please sit wherever pleases you."

"Thank you ever so much," Jon answered, and he scoured the room that was half filled even though the performance was an hour away.

At one of the tables fronting a small stage, Claire sat alone. She had on a black sleeveless dress that fit tight to her body. She wore high-heeled black sandals with straps that crisscrossed around her ankles and feet. She sat, her dress rose high on her thighs, but its reveal was still appropriate for the matron of the mansion. Jon made a beeline for her table.

"Ah, the Kelt tonight," Claire observed.

"Yes, I'm in the mood for savoring tonight." Jon's eyes did just that as he admired the aesthetic of Claire in her little black dress.

"May I?" He pointed at an empty chair not assuming a welcome.

"I would enjoy that." Claire's voice departed from her professional veneer.

"Kelt, you really remember every customer's tastes? Isn't that the job of your staff?"

"First of all, 'customers' is never a word I use here…" She wasn't admonishing him as much as reassuring him. "Second, some members are more intriguing than others." She paused and took him in as he positioned his chair to sit. "Your choice of Kelt cognac is a prime example."

Jon smiled.

"Aged three months at sea in oak Limousin barrels at the finish process. And, you prefer the V.S.O.P. or the XO rather than the Petra or the Les Quatres Vents, which are pricier and a poser would order because of price and not familiarity. Your choice shows you are no stranger to this cognac. You prefer the blends you regularly drink rather than trying to impress. It says a great deal of your tastes and style. Impressive." Claire raised her glass of champagne, and they toasted.

"So, I am not a poser?" Jon said ironically.

"Hardly. You are a man who likes fine things but not for the show, but for their quality," she continued. "You seek things out because of the qualities they possess and not for their popularity or fashion. In fact, you seem to create your own personal fashion. Impressive." Claire was looking straight through him.

"So, is that why I am so intrigued by you? To use your word." It was easy for Jon to be honest in his admiration. An admiration like a hunter looking at his prey and being in awe of its physical beauty, still being a hunter.

"Jon, you are kind, but as I told you, I do not cross boundaries as the founder of La Levrier. Now let's change the subject. Do you want to discuss more of your tastes? As you know, I am still trying to match those tastes for your sensual pleasure."

"Why work so hard. Isn't it obvious what my desires are?" Jon sipped his cognac and let his eyes drift onto Claire's body.

"Again, I'm flattered, but that is not in the structure of La Levrier. I'm still sure we will be able to accommodate your sexual desires, but it will not be with me, Mr. Fenwick." Claire sipped her drink and let the rim of the flute linger on her lips. We have beautiful Levriettes here that I'm sure one you will be able to connect with. In fact, several that you have not met yet have expressed their attraction to you."

"And your attraction? What of your attraction? I know you like men and in each conversation we have, I pick up more of your tastes and quite frankly I don't see how I am not the one for you. Unless you have a lover already, then I certainly understand."

"I could easily lie to you and say, yes, I have a lover, a partner, all of the above, but I can't. No, I don't have a lover," she stated.

"Why not lie to me? You're attracted to me, correct?"

"If I were, I wouldn't reveal that to you, but I look forward to your company tonight as we enjoy this table and this performance." Claire looked at her glass; her index finger tapped at the stem.

"Claire, I hope you don't think I want to make love to you because you are the owner of La Levrier? I'm not attracted to you because you are forbidden fruit or because of some other psychoanalytic nonsense. Who can explain the chemistry that makes up attraction? The women you've been throwing at me are all worthy candidates for my desires, but you have something extra," Jon confided.

"Jon, you're sweet. And don't think your desire is falling on deaf ears."

Jon interrupted, "Am I not attractive to you?"

"Jon asked and answered. Well, sort of answered before... I'm not going there with you," she chuckled. "Excuse the pun, but I'm not throwing my cards on the table about anything personal between us. Even if I could maintain my boundaries and do so, I cannot let my guard down in that manner."

A server approached the table and refreshed both of their drinks. Claire looked up at the server, a young woman resplendent in a copper cocktail dress just like all the servers in the lounge. "Is the performance on time tonight?" Claire asked.

"Yes ma'am, you still have plenty of time before Mr. Kenton comes out," the server dutifully responded.

Claire threw a mock frown in Jon's direction.

Jon responded to her body language, "Oh, come on, you're enjoying this conversation," he insisted.

"Any woman would enjoy the attention and flattery from a handsome, well-groomed, athletic and sophisticated man."

"So, you've checked out my body?"

Claire rolled her eyes. "Geez, I let out a tidbit, and you pounce on it like an entertainer starving for applause."

Jon lowered his voice and talked out of the side of his mouth like a comedian, "The only thing I'm starving for is you, honey!" They both laughed and clinked glasses again.

"So why do you think this direct, lay it all out there, approach is going to work on me, Mr. Fenwick? If I'm this diva that you're painting me to be, why not make me jealous by bedding one of my most beautiful Levriettes? Or, impress me with your masculine prowess, play hard to get, or any other of those standard games?"

"Don't think all of those things crossed my mind when I first saw you. And that's the key. When I first saw you, I desired you and wanted to fuck you, but as I came to know you and that also meant getting to know La Levrier, I desired you in a different way. I want to make love to you. I want to slowly and delicately undrape you from your dress…" He looked down at her dress. "Caress your skin, smell you as I kiss your neck, touch you to know how you feel. Explore your body, be connected with you in such intimacy that being inside you is a spiritual act as much as a physical act. Yes, the Levriettes are beautiful women, some of the most beautiful I have seen in person I have to admit, but there is an art about you. I can't explain it. It is what strikes me. Isn't that the essence of La Levrier? Bringing two people together to experience the pleasure of life?"

"Jon, you are either Casanova reincarnated or you have a great scriptwriter, but your approach is getting better by the minute," Claire blushed.

"This mansion oozes who you are. The walls, the furnishings, even this performance tonight speak to me on a level I haven't ever connected on with a woman. It's hard to throw myself at these other women, when all I think about is you when I'm here and, by the way, when I'm not here as well."

Claire's eyes looked down at her glass. A small smile spread across her lips. She was silent. She looked back up and into Jon's eyes then down again. She thought about what he said.

A beautiful Levrier dressed in a black tuxedo with tails, top hat, ankle pant tuxedo striped trousers, six-inch patent leather heels and white gloves strutted onto the stage. "Gentlemen and ladies, Mr. Kenton will be out in a few minutes. Please be comfortable, order your next cocktail and please keep any distractions away from us all enjoying this amazing performance tonight. Flirt, tickle and tease your partners all you want..." She struck a pose that would make the best cabaret master of ceremonies jealous as she emphasized, "But let's keep that under the table, shall we?" She bowed to the waist and spread her arms wide letting the audience delight in the full view of her perfectly shaped breasts. The audience greeted her public service announcement with hearty yet polite applause and generous laughs.

Jon leaned in closer to Claire, "Before the no flirting light goes on I just want to remind you of one thing, Ms. Bernardin. As opposed to the other members here, YOU seduced me into coming to La Levrier. There must be something to that."

Claire waited for Jon to finish then she leaned into him, her lips an inch from his, and she whispered back, "She didn't say no flirting, she just said keep it under the table." He moved his lips closer to hers as if ready to kiss, but she retreated into her chair. He pursed his lips to the right and squinted his eyes.

The cocktail waitress approached the table and without asking refreshed both Claire and Jon's drinks. "Will there be anything else before the performance begins?" she asked. Both Jon and Claire smiled and shook their heads courteously.

They looked into each other's eyes and both connected into the passion that was building between them. Nothing had to be said, and nothing could be said at that moment. They didn't break their connection even as the Kenton Band took the stage and adjusted their instruments, positioned microphones, raised stools, stationed water bottles, and arranged cocktail glasses. Even though all the activity was just a few feet from their table neither attended to it. Both wondered to themselves if the other was reading their thoughts and both were comfortable if, in fact, that could be a possibility.

Stan Kenton walked on stage, and the applause was more exuberant than that the MC generated, yet it was still polite and devoid of catcalls, whistles or other nonsense.

Kenton's long white duster style suit coat, white matching pants, black scarf cinched with a gold ring with the Greyhounds' heads facing each other and white fez befitted the grand master of funk.

Once Kenton entered the stage Claire and Jon smiled, then broke their eye contact and looked at the performer. Jon moved his chair next to Claire's. His body language conveyed the excuse of a better view. Claire did not protest his closeness.

Kenton was masterful. His jazz piano playing and his funk lyrics ranged from sorrowful to angry to sexual. His voice was full of emotion and energy. It was clear that this small venue brought him back to his roots as a performer. The connection between him and this audience was magnetic. It indeed was a once in a lifetime experience to be in this room witnessing this legend at his best.

Kenton played for an hour and a half without a break. Although he didn't break a sweat while he played, several of the band members were cascading perspiration throughout the set. Kenton's stamina was quite an accomplishment for a man in his late sixties.

After his last song, he sat at the piano, smiled, nodded his head to the applause, and basked in the standing ovation that seemed to last forever and then he walked into the crowd. For the next two hours, Kenton and the guests in the La Levrier lounge stood around and talked, laughed and drank as if they were old friends gathered at one of their houses. The conversations ranged from serious to funny to instructional, and everyone seemed to be in the discussion.

Kenton announced: "Well this old man has got to get his rest. Playing the United Center tomorrow." And that marked the end of the evening.

"Jon, I want to escort Mr. Kenton to his suite and thank him for this magic tonight. Would you excuse me?"

Claire started to walk away from Jon's side where she had been the entire evening.

"Of course." Jon offered his right hand to her and nodded slightly. "But, I hope we can continue this communication soon?" He asked.

Claire grinned, placed a finger to his lips and turned to be with Stan Kenton. Jon watched as she offered Kenton her arm and walked with him toward the elevator. All of the guests deferred to Claire and Kenton and let them take the elevator alone up to the suites. Jon just watched her walk into the elevator and as she turned to face the closing cage door, they made eye contact once again.

CHAPTER NINE

Substitute Teacher

After their meeting at La Levrier the previous week, Danielle had followed through as promised and considered Claire's proposal. While Claire's offer was beyond tempting, Danielle considered herself a woman of ethics. That is until her last encounter with Philip at RL prompted her to think otherwise. All it took was for him to frame her by overloading a faulty tray with a slight crack.

"Oh my GAAAAAAAWD!!!!" Philip shrieked from the sidelines as the last RL meal Danielle served ended up in the laps of a family of five. Looking out of the corner of her eye, she caught Philip smirking while she dabbled Crab Cakes Benedict off the father's Polo shirt.

Philip scurried to the scene with a stack of napkins and profuse apologies for the newbie's uncouth behavior, but the patriarch seemed not to mind too much that Danielle was fawning over him, judging by the stiffening bulge in his khakis. If Danielle could provoke this type of reaction from a man wearing Hollandaise sauce, she imagined what she might be able summon by rubbing something more tantalizing over a naked torso.

As Philip clucked at her awkwardness in front of the entire crew, Danielle promptly took the stained napkin and stuffed it in Philip's face. "There," she smiled. "Now look who has egg all over his face!" She spun on her heel, tore off her apron and the last sound she ever heard from RL was Philip's lingering gasp as she headed out the door onto Chicago Avenue.

The next day she found herself sitting outside of Claire's office ready to accept her first assignment. When she and Claire had spoken by phone, Claire indicated that she already had someone very special in mind for Danielle...a brand-new member who was sophisticated, worldly and very attractive. She had enticed her further by sharing that he was 6'3 with an athletic build—qualities that sent Danielle swooning as she revealed her penchant for tall men.

"Claire will see you now," the young receptionist purred. Danielle rose from the Ghost chair and prepared to meet her new boss.

Claire greeted her with a warm, knowing smile as if she always knew that Danielle would be back. She hugged her like a daughter and motioned for her to take a seat. Instead of sitting down next to her immediately, Claire walked to a closet in her office and pulled out a garment bag. She presented it to Danielle like an award and encouraged her to unzip it.

Danielle's shaking hands nervously tugged at the zipper, and Claire's smile grew broader as she offered some assistance. Danielle was usually not at a loss for words, but this afternoon was a rare exception. The delicate sheath of pale pink chiffon dripped with elegance as the garment bag fell away. From the front, the dress was simple: a halter-style, sleeveless pink sheath embroidered with a grey ribbon trim studded with pearls around the neckline and armholes. The collar was cinched with a single pearl, revealing a large, triangular cut-out that exposed the entire back. The backless gown funneled into a rose made of the same grey ribbon with clusters of pearls that sat perfectly in the center of the waistline. The dress was form-fitting across the hips and hung a few inches above the knee.

Danielle's hand flew to her mouth, as she eyed the meticulous detailing. This dress was no TJ Maxx special on a waitressing budget.

"I hope you like Christian Dior?" Claire asked. "Size two should fit you perfectly. Of course, I'll have our tailor, hair stylist and make-up artist visit your suite this afternoon around 3 p.m. for the finishing touches."

"I don't… know… what to say…" Danielle stammered, trying to formulate her next question.

Claire laughed, having witnessed this reaction time and time again from every new Levrier when presented with her first dress. "I'm sure you're wondering what the special occasion is…"

"The Red Carpet? Am I going to the Oscars?" Danielle giggled, growing more relaxed.

"Well, I wish I could say I had an 'Oscar' for you, but no one here answers to that name," Claire joked. "Actually, I think you'll fancy Jon even more. We have a very nice evening arranged for the two of you to get acquainted."

Danielle gulped, struck by her new reality.

"No, I don't expect you to immediately jump his bones," Claire winked, putting Danielle at ease. "In fact, Jon is not even aware that he is going to be set up tonight. You will just happen to be attending a private gathering and book signing hosted at La Levrier with one of Jon's favorite mystery writers, Lionel Edwards."

"Lionel Edwards! Are you serious?" Danielle cried. "I just finished his last best-seller, Dark Soldier. And, before that, I read his other thriller, Forced Intentions. You mean, he—Lionel Edwards—is going to actually be HERE?"

"Yes ma'am," Claire grinned. "Of course, it's no coincidence that I found you and Jon had this in common. You two should have quite a bit to chat about. I've also talked Lionel into bringing advance copies of his latest book manuscript, which hasn't even been leaked to the reviewers yet."

"WOW!" Danielle's eyes widened. "What is it?"

"I can't tell you," Claire's teased. "Lionel has sworn me to secrecy."

"How do you know Lionel?" Danielle probed, still blown away,

"That, too, my dear is a secret. Let's just say that you will likely be seeing Lionel more than once here at La Levrier. I expect you to keep that in the strictest of confidence. In fact, after you and I finish our meeting here, Mari will be meeting with you over tea to review the La Levrier policy handbook in detail. For now, let's focus our conversation back on Jon."

"Aside from tall, dark and handsome, what is he like?" Danielle pressed.

Claire couldn't help smiling as she tried to describe Jon to Danielle. "Jon is…" she searched for the right words. "Special. He needs to be handled with the utmost care, which is why I choose you, Danielle. He is not one to tolerate fools lightly. He admires a woman with femininity, poise, and style. She must be clever to match his quick wit. Alluring to sustain his interest. Confident enough to assert herself, yet still allow him to take the lead. Don't mistake his reserved nature for being aloof. He will warm up to you once you prove yourself worthy of his attention. Let your conversation flow naturally, engage him in an intelligent dialogue and discuss your mutual admiration of Lionel Edwards. Once he sees that you are a woman of substance, you can move on from there."

"Move on... as in?" Danielle leaned in.

"As in, YES," Claire nodded. "One thing you must absolutely know about Jon is that he enjoys the dance... the subtle art of seduction... the cat-and-mouse chase. Tease, flirt, use your feminine charm. It's all about the allure when it comes to this man."

"Sounds like you know him quite well," Danielle observed.

Blushing, Claire brushed off Danielle's comment. "Well, yes, as I take the time to carefully know all of our members' likes and dislikes... what makes them tick and, likewise, what ticks them off."

"So, Claire, do you honestly... think Jon will... like me?" Danielle ventured shyly.

"Danielle, I have confidence in you. I see great potential. Jon will enjoy not only your beauty but your enthusiasm. He needs someone positive and passionate in his life. A woman who is authentic and sure of herself. The rest will follow."

"I hope so. I don't want to disappoint you on my, um, first assignment."

"Danielle, I'll be honest," Claire sighed. "Jon is not easy to match. He's a new member, and so far, has been rather discerning. Frustratingly so. If he doesn't respond as planned, don't be discouraged. I'm still trying to figure him out myself."

"Okay, then," Danielle smiled. "I will do my very best."

"I know you will," Claire agreed. "Now, I believe that my next appointment is waiting. Mari will see you to your suite, give you time to settle in and relax and then take you to tea. At 6 p.m. this evening, you will report to The Fountain Room on the second floor to join Jon and three other couples for a meet-and-greet and private reception with Lionel. There will be seating arrangements, and I expect that you will engage Jon without making your intentions overt. Any questions?"

"No, none that I can think of at the moment," Danielle shook her head. "Will I see you at all tonight?"

"Yes, I will be making an appearance this evening, and then you and I will chat again tomorrow morning before you have to head home to your little one. I trust that you were comfortable with the sitter arrangements we made for Clayton this evening?"

"Oh, very much so, thank you!" Danielle beamed. "Giovanni seemed just delightful, and Clayton took to her right away. I'm sure he'll be in good hands."

"I never want you to have to worry," Claire assured her. "You are part of La Levrier family now, Danielle, and we will take the best care of you and your son." Danielle nodded in gratitude. Not only was Giovanni an experienced nanny with excellent references, but he came compliments of Claire.

"I have one last gift before I let you go," Claire smiled as she presented Danielle with a slender, rectangular black velvet box.

Danielle accepted it, still stunned by Claire's outpouring of generosity. Upon prying the lid, a beautiful bracelet of two interlocking gold Greyhound heads with sapphire eyes bound by a tan leather band twinkled up at her.

"You are to wear this at all times whenever you are on La Levrier grounds," Claire instructed. "Every Levrier has one, and she wears it not only for fashion but for protection. Mari will show you exactly how it works. As you grow with La Levrier, the gemstone eyes will be replaced by rubies, by emeralds and eventually diamonds, based on your tenure here."

"It's gorgeous," Danielle gasped. "I don't know what to say, except thank you!"

"The pleasure is all mine," Claire answered as she led Danielle to the door, pondering just how much pleasure Danielle would bring to Jon. Would she be an adequate substitute, at least enough to divert Jon's attention? A wave of a foreign emotion suddenly swept over her. Was it jealousy? Claire scoffed silently to herself and straightened her suit jacket for her next meeting with a prospective member. She did, after all, have a business to run.

Later, at 5:55 p.m.

At five minutes to the hour, Danielle twirled in her full-length mirror. Vanity was not one of her traits, but tonight it was impossible not to notice the transformation of a pretty girl into a graceful woman. With just a few minor nips and tucks, the seamstress tailored the blush cocktail dress to flatter every curve. It was equally matched by Danielle's chignon that was fashioned into a rose at the nape of her neck, mirroring the design on the back of her gown. A pair of dangling rose gold earrings with a single pearl echoed the pearl beads along the cut-outs of her dress. The artistry of the La Levrier on-staff cosmetologist enhanced Danielle's natural beauty—simple, yet sophisticated. The Levrier bracelet adorned her wrist and sparkled as she slid on her strappy ivory sandals with four-inch heels. Danielle was statuesque at 5'7, but the added boost would make her even closer to Jon's height and accentuate her long, slender legs.

Given her high heels, Danielle opted to take the elevator to the second floor so she could arrive punctually at the six o'clock hour. Kenneth, the bellman, was there to greet her as the elevator car approached her floor and beckoned Danielle inside.

"Second floor, Miss Danielle?" he queried. Danielle smiled and nodded as he closed the door cage, tapped the button and offered his arm to escort her when the elevator landed.

"Here we are, The Fountain Room," Kenneth announced. "Enjoy your evening and your company." With that, he disappeared, and it wasn't long before another staff member took his place to lead Danielle deeper into the room.

She now understood the connection, and the significance, of the rose on the back of her dress and spun into the design of her hair. The Fountain Room was a breath-taking atrium filled with freshly cut roses of every variety, color and species imaginable and imported just for the occasion. American Beauties... Cornelias... Hermosas... White Dawns... countless blooms, tastefully displayed as bouquets tied in tulle, clustered in crystal vases and even placed as single buds on end tables. At the center of the room was a three-tier bubbling water fountain with a gilded greyhound sculpture as the spout.

Ivory rose petals floated on the top layer, coral petals on the second and fuchsia petals on the third. This certainly was not your average garden-variety cocktail party, and the members looked to be equally as colorful and exotic as the flora.

Danielle's pulse quickened, and her cheeks tingled. She inhaled the aroma of roses and tried to calm herself from the thought that she was only a handshake away from meeting the famous Lionel Edwards and from encountering the enigmatic Jon. Her eyes searched the room for him based on Claire's description, but to no avail.

"So, what do you think is up with all the roses?" She stirred from a deep voice resonating behind her. Danielle didn't even have to look up to know who it was, as she caught a whiff of his Mont Blanc cologne, Jon's signature scent per Claire.

Danielle turned to meet Jon's gaze and quipped sheepishly "Maybe La Levrier is trying to test our allergy threshold."

"I wouldn't put it past that Ms. Bernardin," Jon chuckled, amused by this stunning woman's creative banter. Danielle appeared to be at first glance a younger, taller version of Claire herself, which is why Jon was drawn to her the instant he entered The Fountain Room.

Danielle returned his smile and summoned a phony sneeze, to which Jon responded with a friendly "gesundheit."

"Danke," Danielle said in her best German accent. "I think I need a kerchief. May I?" she flirted, reaching for the pocket square neatly folded in Jon's suit jacket. She was surprised that is was made of burlap—an interesting juxtaposition to the backdrop of his fine silk suit.

"You might scratch your nose on that, my dear," he warned and pretended to swat her hand away, but then surprisingly kissed the back of it. "I suggest we might seek softer pastures. Care to take a seat with me?"

He led an obliging Danielle to the intimate ensemble of lounges clustered on the far side of the room. The staff meticulously arranged every flower, every petal, and every thorn for the elegant soiree. Each chair was draped in silk damask and held a different variety of rose. Jon pulled out a chair for Danielle and handed her a Tiffany Blue as if formally presenting it to her. She accepted the rare blossom graciously.

No sooner had they both seated themselves than a hostess appeared with a tray of cocktails. Jon's favorite three were part of the display, and this time he chose a flute of the Veuve Clicquot. He offered the same to Danielle. Never had she been afforded the opportunity to sip such an expensive brand of champagne, let alone to be in the presence of an equally distinguished gentleman. They clinked classes and slowly swallowed their first sip. As they awaited the arrival of their favorite guest author, a single glass turned into two, and then into three.

The bubbles euphorically rose to Danielle's head. Even Jon was becoming giddy—an unusual departure from his typically guarded reserve. He felt strangely at ease with this stunning stranger and draped his arm around the back of her chair. She eyed him coyly and, hearing Claire's advice in her head, did not immediately respond. He took the initiative to move his chair closer until their thighs almost touched. She crossed her leg, allowing the drape of her dress to fall away from her thigh closest to Jon. The gesture was subtle... an invitation but not an ovation.

The ovation was saved for the entry of Lionel Edwards, who strolled into the room accompanied by Claire. While Lionel appeared much shorter in real life and had packed on a few pounds since his last book jacket author's photo, it was Claire who took the audience's breath away. She was swathed in a scarlet, sarong-style sleeveless wrap dress exposing one bare shoulder. The satin gleamed against her pale, flawless complexion like a second skin and gathered at her tiny waist to accentuate her feminine silhouette. Claire pinned back her hair into a neat twist interwoven with a braid that held a tiny row of miniature roses.

"My dear friends," Claire beamed as she approached the small, seated group, "I am honored to welcome my favorite author, Lionel Edwards, who has undoubtedly touched many of your lives with his page-turners. His passion for the pen… his compelling story-telling… and his presence here tonight are to be as much treasured as some of the rarest blooms in this room."

"Oh, Claire, if you keep going, you'll have to raise this roof to accommodate my swelling ego," Lionel rasped, jokingly waving her off. Claire winked back at him, and everyone clapped as Lionel sat at the head of the circle among his fans.

"You may wonder…" he began mysteriously, leaning into the group, "what's the fucking deal with all the roses. Are we at my funeral?" Snickers filled the room.

"Hell, no," he said. "We're here to celebrate the birth of my latest murder mystery which is hitting the shelves in three months: Rose from the Dead."

This smart play on words was not lost on Jon or Danielle, who listened intently to Lionel's description of the book, excerpts he read aloud and lively Q&A to follow. He gifted his fans with signed hardbound copies of his last best-seller. While the lecture was fascinating, Jon's eyes were glued to Claire the entire time. He was frozen by her beauty—a rose in full bloom. Jon was in awe. He yearned to admire her, to gently touch her, to make love to her... but she was completely distracted by her hostess duties. He tried to make eye contact, but it seemed the harder he pursued her, the more she avoided him. In fact, Claire made sure to give all the other male members hugs except for him.

Being snubbed was not something Jon was accustomed to experiencing, and the champagne he consumed only fueled his desire for Claire all the more. His cock became a rock in his pants. He had to have her, but her professional boundaries were carved in stone, and that was that. Well, screw her, he thought, and laughed at his own choice of words. He deserved better. There was another beautiful woman at his side who seemed far more receptive to his advances than Claire would ever allow herself to be.

Danielle welcomed Jon's warm palm on her bare back as he gently steered her past Claire and out of The Fountain Room, down the hall and to the elevator up to his private suite. Her legendary legs were framed on top by the hem of her dress which fell above her knee, and on the bottom of the frame, by her high-heeled strappy sandals. Feeling ultra-confident after three flutes of Veuve Clicquot, Danielle sat on the edge of Jon's bed.

Her thighs parted ever slow slightly to invite Jon's caresses. He removed his suit jacket, loosened his tie and joined her. He took his time, treasuring her body like a delicacy. His lips brushed hers and lingered in a tender kiss. As Jon's fingertips approached her womanhood, Danielle guided him to touch her... to feel the wetness that welcomed him… to experience the swelling of her lips that yearned to take him in. His cock throbbed as he touched the swelling of her clit. She arched her hips and inched up her hem, while Jon's thumb moved aside the lace of her white thong and then lowered his mouth to her. Danielle moaned softly when the first flicks of his tongue caressed and tasted her irresistibly sweet nectar.

She quivered and thrust her pelvis higher. "Please, please," she cried. "Take me… I want you. All of you."

Jon's tongue continued to tease her, its tip now slowing to consume her in tender circles. Now and then, he would pause, enjoying the thrill of controlling her maddening desire. She squirmed and wiggled, begging him not to stop, but to continue to fill her with his passion. Jon obliged and returned to kissing Danielle on the mouth as he moved on top of her, now fully reclined. Their hips touched while Jon led this dance of intimacy, gently grinding his pelvis into hers. Danielle craved the ever-growing bulge in his pants. She fingered the outline of his penis, which stood erect under his fly, aching for freedom. She undid Jon's belt and reached for his zipper.

Jon hungered to enter Danielle as he felt her delicate fingers touch him. She pleaded for more as she thrust her hips closer. Every ounce of her femininity screamed out for him, their sexual tension mounting by the minute.

As the minutes passed, something overcame Jon. He could sense Danielle's growing frustration, yet he did nothing to satisfy it. He tried to placate her with kisses, but she was beyond the fervent foreplay.

"Jon?" she whispered. He gently removed her hand from his cock and sat up, taking a minute to collect himself. "Is something wrong?" Danielle asked.

"No," Jon stated simply. "You are perfect."

"Then what? What is it?" she implored, her voice cracking ever so slightly to betray the hurt.

"I can't. I just… can't," Jon confessed, brushing her cheek with the back of his hand.

"It's okay. You know there are… pills for this type of thing," Danielle assured him.

"I'm afraid that no pill is going to cure me, my dear," Jon said. He knew deep in his heart that this wasn't a performance issue. He closed his eyes and gave Danielle a long, slow kiss, allowing his mind to drift selfishly to the real object of his passion. In his thoughts, Claire's lips hungrily returned his affection. As his hand moved through Danielle's hair, Jon felt Claire's silky strands under his fingers. He yearned to loosen every aspect of her, including the tightly wound coif, and whip her hair into a wild, untamed mane. But the moment was gone.

"It's someone else, isn't it?" she asked, more as a statement than a question.

All Jon could do was nod as he watched Danielle stand, smooth her dress and slip her heels back on. She mustered a smile and thanked him for the evening. "No hard feelings, I hope," she said graciously, catching her pun. She did just as she had been instructed by Mari. Every Levrier had to end an encounter on a positive note, despite the outcome.

"Not at all, Danielle," he muttered. "You are lovely and all that a man could want. I'm sorry I can't be the one for you."

Jon watched as she turned and headed to the door, leaving him behind in his bed, alone to be with the fantasy of a woman he could never have.

CHAPTER TEN

Close but no Cigar

Danielle awoke the next morning in her La Levrier suite, taking a few minutes to absorb the unfamiliarity of her surroundings. To not hear Clayton rustle and squeal, hungry for breakfast, was disorienting. All of the Levriettes slept on the fourth floor and shared rooms, depending on who was going to be spending the night on any given assignment. Some of the single Levriettes had established permanent residence at the mansion, but those like Danielle with children or other obligations elected otherwise. In meeting with Mari to review the Levrier handbook yesterday, Danielle discovered another revelation: not all of the Levriettes were women. Claire maintained a very open LGBTQ policy, and her philosophy was liberally based on equal enjoyment of passion irrespective of gender identity or preference. There were Levriettes who were female, male, bisexual and gay.

She peeled back her ivory velveteen duvet and rose from her queen bed with its diamond-tufted grey leather headboard. Although not as large as the master suites reserved for members, every element of the room was exquisitely appointed—another reflection of Claire's impeccable taste. As Danielle's feet touched the cream faux fur throw rug on the dark wood, she spotted a parchment paper envelope on the floor by the door. She hurried to retrieve and open it. On matching parchment stationery, she read the feminine scrawl: "Danielle, I hope you enjoyed your first evening with us at La Levrier. I am most eager to hear how it progressed with Jon last night. Please join me at 10:00 a.m. for tea in my business office this morning.— Claire"

Danielle had set her phone alarm to 8:30 a.m., so she had ample time to take a shower in her private bathroom and prepare for the meeting. Although Danielle had tried her best and Claire had warned her of the obstacles, Danielle dreaded reporting her failure to seduce him thoroughly. It was, after all, her first assignment, and she wanted to make a good impression on her new boss. Unlike her brief stint at RL, Danielle was committed to making this arrangement work.

9:59 a.m. Saturday

Danielle, freshly showered and again wearing her street clothes—a black mini skirt and oxford blue J. Crew button-down blouse—entered the reception area of Claire's office. She was surprised to find that the girl seated at the desk was not at her usual post and Claire's office door was ajar.

"Please come in, Danielle," she heard Claire's voice beckon from the room, fully expecting her arrival. "I gave Jessica the day off, so I'm here alone."

Danielle entered her office, as Claire rose from behind her desk to greet her. In contrast to her show-stopping red gown last evening, she sported a sleeveless white linen sheath dress. A gold statement necklace popped at Claire's neckline—the heads of two interlocking Greyhounds linked on either side by a band of tan leather. Even from a distance, Danielle could see diamonds glinting in the dogs' eyes. On Claire's feet were white kid leather Jimmy Choo pumps with skinny ankle straps. She stepped out from behind her desk and motioned Danielle to the coffee table where they had sat the day before to discuss the details of her first date with Jon. Claire poured Danielle a cup of tea, and her hand swept over a tray of freshly baked croissants, assorted jams, and whipped butter.

"My weakness," Claire smiled, encouraging Danielle to indulge. Danielle grinned in return as she politely helped herself to the pastry.

"Irresistible, wouldn't you say?" Claire pressed as she also lifted the buttery croissant to her lips and took a bite.

Danielle followed her cue. "Absolutely delicious," she concurred.

"Is he?" Claire winked at Danielle.

Danielle's heart leapt to her throat, unprepared for Claire to so quickly jump to the topic at hand. Jon. Last night. Her success, or lack thereof. She struggled to find the right words to explain the turn of events and set her croissant down, then reached for her teacup with a slight tremor.

"I know, Danielle," Claire said with a slight sigh. "I'm disappointed, not with you, but with Jon."

"What?" Danielle gasped. "How did you...?"

"One of my staff members saw you leaving Jon's suite not long after you and he retired from the gathering. She said you were fully dressed and very composed—not a hair out of place," Claire explained.

Danielle looked down at her hands, not quite sure how to respond.

"Look, it's an observation, not an accusation," Claire added softly.

"But the fact is, I let you down…" Danielle began.

"No, no," Claire shook her head. "We both knew that Jon was not going to be easy. Admittedly, this was a challenging first assignment. Yet, when I saw you both together last evening, I had high hopes. There seemed to be a spark between you two. Jon looked the most relaxed I have ever seen him. You did your job. You flirted beautifully, engaged him in colorful conversation and seduced him enough to return to his suite together. That was exactly as I asked you to do."

"But, still, I… we… didn't…" Danielle countered.

"Have sex?" Claire interrupted gently. Danielle nodded.

"We almost did," Danielle shared. "In fact, Jon seemed at first like he was receptive. We were both loosened up; we kissed, we touched… you know, all the signs were there that he wanted to go further, but…"

"But?" Claire questioned.

"All of a sudden, it was like, something stopped him. It was really strange, Claire. I don't know how to explain it," Danielle said. "I thought maybe he was just having a case of performance anxiety… something like that."

Claire nodded, encouraging Danielle to continue.

"I even told him there were, you know, pills for that…"

Claire's eyes widened, as did her lips into a smile. "You did?"

"Well, I mean, I was trying to reassure him that it was okay if he was having issues in that department…" Danielle explained.

"Hmmmm," Claire surmised. "I wonder if that may be the case, Danielle. ED is so common among men Jon's age, which is why we are fully stocked with Viagra. It's in the top drawer of every member's nightstand, along with condoms, lubricant, and other supplies. Did Mari cover that with you yesterday?"

"Yes, she sure did," Danielle said. "I could have offered Viagra to Jon, but he basically told me that there was no pill that could 'cure' him."

"I see," Claire returned. "Was he defensive? Offended?"

"No, not at all," Danielle said. "He was a real gentleman. But then, he… well, he got this kind of faraway look in his eye like he was somewhere else, or wanted to be with someone else."

"Go on…" Claire urged.

"I just felt awkward, like I had overstayed my welcome at that point. That's when I asked him if there WAS someone else," Danielle said. "I'm sorry if I got too personal, but I was a little buzzed and…"

"It's okay," Claire dismissed. "What did Jon say when you asked him?"

"He didn't say anything. He just nodded. Yeah, he nodded, like he couldn't or didn't want to say it in so many words, you know?"

"Yes, I know," Claire sighed. "It explains a lot of things."

"Should I have pursued it? Stayed longer?" Danielle questioned.

"No, you did the right thing, Danielle. Your instincts told you to leave at that point, and you followed them correctly."

Danielle took another sip of tea and debated whether she should share with Claire what she wanted to say next.

"My instincts have always guided me," she began. "They've never failed to be right. I knew when I took that job at RL that Philip had it in for me since Day One. I knew after I had Clayton that my ex was going to leave. Maybe it's a gift and a curse to have such strong instincts, but one thing I've learned is that I should never doubt them. I have a strong instinct about Jon, too…" she hesitated, watching Claire's body language. Claire leaned in and tilted her head, giving Danielle permission to continue.

"Forgive me if I'm overstepping my bounds… but, I caught Jon staring at you last night as Lionel Edwards was talking about his new book. He didn't take his eyes off you. He was… like… really into you."

Claire waved her hand dismissively and scoffed with a smile. "Well, I'm sure that wasn't the case. You are much younger and far prettier," Claire joked.

"Younger, true, but not prettier, Claire. You are gorgeous. I aspire to be like you someday. You're kind, graceful, confident, successful and yet so down to earth. Truly beautiful inside and out. Not like one of those snobby rich bitches—excuse me—with one too many facelifts, tummy tucks and hair extensions strolling down Oak Street trying to act half her age. That's why, in my humble opinion and own observations, Jon is attracted to you. He's not into fake."

On rare occasion, Claire found herself blushing. This morning with Danielle was one of them.

"You've shared with me that no Levrier match has ever worked for Jon," Danielle continued. "Even I couldn't get him to cross the finish line last night when the opportunity presented itself. What does that tell me? He's a good guy.

He wasn't going to use me just to get his rocks off. The truth is: no one else will do BUT you. I was close, but no cigar."

Finally, Claire summoned her words and chose them carefully. "I'm flattered, really, Danielle. I don't deserve your praise, so thank you. I haven't spoken with Jon yet because I wanted to get your take on the situation first. Even if Jon wanted me, I can't break my own rules. I don't associate with La Levrier members. Simple as that. But, I so appreciate your insights and your instincts. I hope last night didn't temper your appetite for La Levrier and that you'll be receptive to future assignments."

"You're welcome. And, no, I am not easily deterred. I don't ever want to disappoint you..." Danielle said.

"Take 'disappoint' out of your vocabulary," Claire interrupted. "When you run a business that involves intimate interactions between two human beings, the outcome is never predictable. While I do my best to profile and engineer successful matches between Levriettes and members thoroughly, the system isn't fool-proof. It happens, so don't take it personally, as I told you yesterday. Jon was only your first, and there will be others. I will be meeting with him next, so I'll get his perspective on last night. I'm sure Jon will have nothing but nice things to say about you."

"Thank you, Claire," Danielle said, rising, "I look forward to hearing from you about my next assignment."

"You will, Danielle. I look forward to it as well," Claire responded, and the two women hugged.

After Danielle left, Claire took a moment to collect herself before seeing Jon, who was due to arrive in her office at 11:00 a.m. Sitting on her loveseat instead of at her desk, she sipped the rest of her tea, stretched her shapely legs and pondered Danielle's revelations. Claire and Danielle both shared the gift of reading people, and Claire couldn't deny that Danielle's instincts about Jon were right on. The real problem now was that this no longer existed solely in Claire's head; Danielle had verified precisely how she, herself, was feeling.

There had been several occasions when La Levrier members had developed what Claire termed "puppy crushes" on her, but these were fleeting infatuations when Claire made it clear that her boundaries could not be crossed. If the prince of Andorra, the heir to the world's largest diamond empire, Asia's top piano prodigy and even Lionel Edwards himself could cease and desist their advances, why couldn't Jon?

It wasn't as if Claire had been shy about communicating her limitations to him, yet he persisted. Jon's words, "I want to make love to you… to caress your skin… be connected with you in such intimacy…" rang through her thoughts. Not only did her recollections of Jon's deep, soothing voice and how distinctly dashing he looked, echo in her mind, but her body also softened. Her fingertips lightly stroked her bare arm, as she closed her eyes and envisioned Jon's tender touch. She could almost smell the faint trace of the Mont Blanc cologne he always wore. She could sense his lips inches away in the "almost kiss" they shared two nights ago during the Stan Kenton concert.

Claire tried to thrust these images aside. While she had allowed herself to admire especially attractive, charming La Levrier members, she always kept her professional distance. One false move, impulsive miscalculation or vulnerable moment could spell disaster for her operation.

She would never allow such foolishness to destroy an empire she worked so hard to build.

Finding and having sex was easy. Any time Claire wished, she merely had to go on a fishing expedition at Coq d'Or. Once baited, each lover was strictly catch-and-release for her. No one had ever broken through the net to penetrate her public persona and probe the private Claire. She had meticulously guarded every aspect of her life, and her heart was no exception. It had to be protected at all costs, even if that meant denying herself the human need to love and to be loved.

Jon could not be an exception, she decided. It was time to find a new match and, in the minutes before their meeting, she returned to her desk and she typed her password to unlock the digital archives of suitable Levrier prospects she had on special reserve. This time she would find for him the "cigar"—not just someone close.

CHAPTER ELEVEN

Down to the Principal's Office

"Come in, Jon," Claire ordered a little too curtly, when she heard his footsteps in the reception area.

"Nice to know my arrival was anticipated. I hope the coffee is as warm as you are," Jon quipped as he entered her office.

"Help yourself," Claire commanded and motioned to the coffee service arranged on her table by the couch and chairs.

"I'm used to it, thanks," he smiled, trying to ease her out of business mode. He drank in her vision as she gathered papers from her printer and stuffed them into Jon's file. Claire was an odd blend of soft purity and stiff professionalism wrapped in a crisp, white linen sheath dress. So outwardly put together, yet so subliminally sensual. After filling his coffee mug, Jon plopped into the loveseat, making a space for her beside him.

She promptly sat back down at her desk across the room. Cat and mouse all over again. Jon sighed and played along, rising to sit in the chair opposite her desk. Just like Mac made him do every time she needed her fucking ego stroked. Sir Submissive sank to the occasion again but met Claire's eyes with conviction.

"What can I do for you?" Jon grinned, delighting in how he was turning the tables on this conversation by taking charge.

"It's not what you can do for me, but what you can do for yourself, Jon," Claire snapped.

"As John F. Kennedy once said..." Jon began.

"Let me get right to the point," Claire interrupted stiffly. "Why are you here?"

"Well, I do believe you invited me to your office this morning, Ms. Bernardin," Jon answered in his usual unflappable manner. "Oh, and I forgot... would you care for some coffee? How rude of me not to offer as I was pouring a cup for myself."

"No, thank you," Claire shook her head. "And that's not what I meant. My question was why are you here... at La Levrier, Mr. Fenwick?"

"Again, Ms. Bernardin, I was invited. By you, in fact. Isn't that noted in your Jon Fenwick file along with my full bio, photos, favorite cocktails, conversation topics, sexual desires and the like?"

"Of course," Claire responded. "And, truthfully, your file would have found a home by now in my cabinet, safely tucked away with a high satisfaction rating based on the fact that we would have connected you with your ideal match. But, here it is, on my desk, wide open and begging questions."

Jon simply smirked.

"What are you smiling about?" she frowned. "This is no laughing matter. La Levrier has failed you. There is a flaw in my formula."

"There's no such thing as failure when it comes to your business and, when it comes to you, there is no flaw. You are flawless," Jon responded evenly.

"So was Danielle. Or so I thought." Claire flicked her wrist dismissively, skirting his compliment, yet betrayed by a small curve of her lip as she tried to suppress a smile. "But what I thought doesn't matter. What matters is what you think, Jon. And you're not satisfied. Not with Danielle and not with any of the others before her. I've presented you with beautiful, intelligent and interesting women, Jon. Yet, they're not enough…"

"No, they aren't," Jon interrupted this time.

"Why?" Claire persisted.

Sensing her impatience, Jon leaned back in his chair and laced his fingers. Claire waited, and waited and waited.

"WHY!" she finally burst out when she could take his silence no longer.

"Why, Ms. Bernardin, do you always yell at your members?" Jon questioned, feigning a look of shock.

"I… am… not… yelling," Claire whispered, punctuating every word as she tried to compose herself.

Jon rose from his chair.

"Where are you going? Are you leaving?" Claire panicked.

"No," Jon returned calmly. "I am going to pour you a cup of coffee."

"I don't…" Claire stammered.

"Yes, you do," Jon stated matter-of-factly. "Cream? Sugar? Arsenic?"

"What?" Claire gasped.

"Okay, I'll spare the latter," Jon smiled. "Now, drink this. It will calm you," he said, handing her a steaming mug as he re-seated himself at her desk.

"Thank you," Claire responded, accepting the coffee. "Back to the point, Jon. Maybe I should have asked the obvious question. Do you have a sexual preference other than women?"

"No," Jon replied. "You can mark that one off your checklist. I believe that's question number four on your form, correct?"

"Hmmmm, why yes, it is," Claire cocked her head. How did Jon know that? Usually La Levrier profiling questionnaires were not visible to members.

"Why do I feel like I've been a bad boy and sent to the principal's office for a scolding?" Jon mused.

"I'm not trying to punish you. I'm trying to understand you," Claire clarified.

"Well, you might be the first," Jon quipped.

"Okay, then, if you're straight, you like attractive women, you have no significant relationship distracting you from your endeavors here, then let me present you with another candidate. She is not a regular Levrier but asked for me to alert her when I found the right match. Allow me to tell you about Courtney. She is 39, 5-foot-9, 123 pounds, strawberry blonde, a former Olympic swimmer and a very successful interior designer. In fact, she was the visionary behind La Levrier's décor. Not only is she stunning, but witty, creative, fun, outgoing and incredibly smart. I've had Courtney on special reserve for just the right man."

"Wow, Claire, she sounds like a bottle of fine wine," Jon joked. "Is she looking to have her cork popped?"

"No, Jon, she is looking for an equally special man who will appreciate all of her fine assets," Claire corrected, not indulging his humor. "La Levrier is about more than sex. It's about romance, love, passion and connecting two people who share a mutual desire to be together on all levels."

"There's only one level I want to be on right now," Jon smiled.

"And that is?" Claire asked, puzzled.

"Your desk," he dared.

"So, Courtney doesn't interest you?" Claire pressed. But the flush of red that developed on her neck belied that her body hadn't missed Jon's last comment.

"If you truly want me to be a satisfied member of La Levrier, you know exactly what is required to make me happy," Jon responded.

"Jon, I…" Claire began.

"Yes… you… do," he whispered, mimicking her tone from their earlier conversation.

Jon stood, lifted his file from her desk and threw it in her wastebasket. This time, it was Claire's turn to remain silent. Never in all of her years of operating La Levrier had a member ever made such a bold advance.

He moved closer to her, making them inches apart. She didn't protest.

"Now, then, shall we start over? Allow me to introduce myself. I am Jon Fenwick. Forty-six, 6-foot-three, straight, single and am desiring a beautiful, successful, intelligent, elegant, highly feminine, fashionable, classy and alluring woman who answers to the name of Claire Bernardin. I'll accept nothing less, otherwise I will be forced to withdraw considering my membership in La Levrier."

Claire froze at the thought of Jon leaving. His ultimatum was clear. Still, she couldn't summon a single word as the silence hung uncomfortably between them.

"I'll tell you what," Jon reasoned. "You can pass along one message to your interior design friend."

Claire relaxed, hoping Jon might finally take the bait and give Courtney a try.

"Tell her that she needs to find you a bigger desk. Given all the activity of your daily business operations, I'm afraid this one just won't do. It doesn't meet your needs… or mine." With that, Jon's arm swept across the desktop and swiftly knocked all of its contents on the floor. Files went flying. Pens went leaping. And papers went fluttering.

Before she could rebel, Jon took Claire in his arms and lowered his lips to hers. He gently kissed her in a full, passionate embrace, not wanting to frighten her with too much force. She returned his kiss, giving into his vigor. He tenderly cupped her face and stroked her with his fingertips as their eyes locked. Hers softened, permitting him to continue, and he lifted her by the hips onto the bare desktop, laying her down flat. Claire let out a tiny yelp, but he continued to cover her with kisses to calm and soothe her. She responded eagerly, and his breathing grew deeper as he slowly unbuckled the ankle straps of her pumps and slid his hand up her calf. He inched up her thigh, lightly brushing the delicate skin as his hand pushed her white linen dress up higher around her waist. She had on no hose—only a sheer nude lacy thong.

Jon's fingertips barely touched the band of her panties when he felt his cock spring to life, begging for release. His hardness filled the fabric of his blue slacks, and he led Claire's hand to his fly. Just the slightest touch of her palm made him throb. Instinctively, she unclasped his waistband, pulled down his zipper and eased his pants down until they fell to the floor. The head of Jon's cock pushed its way past his starched white shirt tails with a mind of its own. He unfastened his tie and buttons from the top, while Claire undid the bottom. Soon, he was completely naked, towering over her as she reclined on the desk.

Jon pulled her dress over her head and admired Claire's slim, shapely figure adorned in a matching bra and panties set. Her hard nipples stretched the sheer fabric of her bra, and he brushed them with his thumb. His touch was delicate and he attended to her breasts with a tenderness unusual of a man. Claire slightly moaned as she arched her back and raised her knees. Jon removed her thong with one hand and unhooked her bra with the other until she was also nude.

"God, you're so beautiful," he sighed, admiring the vision before him. Seeing Claire naked surpassed his innermost images of her. Even in his fantasies, he hadn't even expected to see her pussy so cleanly shaven and glistening with anticipation.

Claire likewise admired Jon's strong and well-toned physique. He was the epitome of masculinity, with broad shoulders and a narrow torso that showcased his love of athletics and disciplined workout regimen. His manhood was pressing against her thigh as he lowered to kiss her, this time more vigorously as their tongues danced in extended foreplay.

Claire's body opened under him, beckoning his strong, stiff cock to slide deeper and deeper. He started to move, oh so slowly and deliberately, with magnificent control. She angled her pelvis so that he brushed up against the rise of her sex, teasing her clit with every stroke, the lightest touch of his skin against hers… so arousing, so intoxicating, so intimate.

Jon's breath was ragged and shallow, and Claire was as close to the edge as he was. He pushed deeper and she moved with him, her body responding, arching up to meet his. And then, just as she felt the first white-hot ripples of orgasm, he looked into her eyes. His were dark with hunger and desire… and things that have no words, only feelings, as she began falling over the edge into the void. Finally, she let go, relishing the release of pure ecstasy.

As she began to orgasm, the first mesmerizing pulse of his climax started, too. Waves of passion rolled through them both, driving on and on until they became totally spent. They collapsed in unison, breathing hard, all tension gone. He slid out and, after a moment or two, cuddled her, curling up with her back to his belly and his arms wrapped securely around her. Claire shivered from the remnants of excitement, utterly drained and yet blissfully content. Unlike any experience she had before, this transcended sex. This was…

She made a mental note to ask Courtney for a larger desk as she turned and kissed Jon.

CHAPTER TWELVE

Jericho

Claire sipped her morning coffee in her suite and, uncharacteristically, she wasn't scrolling around the Internet news, checking emails or the other flood of information that dominated a typical morning. She just sat and replayed over and over in her mind the scenes of sexual passion that consumed her and Jon the day before.

Javert and Marius lay in their puffy beds on the floor to the right of Claire's four-poster king. Each of the circular beds was dominated by the initial of their name: J. and M. Claire smiled when they slept on top the other's initialed bed, even though remarkably they most often slept in their own bed.

Her thoughts on their exquisite lovemaking were overpowering the negative turmoil that competed with such ecstasy. How could she let her boundaries down? How could she not allow her boundaries down? Was La Levrier still viable? Sustainable? Did she have to be stone-hearted? Could having a lover of her own be good for La Levrier? Would this take away her edge of objectivity? Would it give her an edge of empathy? There was nothing typed into the business plan that would exclude her from having a lover. Of course La Levrier would survive. Oh, of course she would survive.

Being human, her rationalizations were heading in the direction of giving Claire the answer she wanted. Why was it was okay for her to take a lover in a business that paired lovers? Why shouldn't she have a lover? How would he take away from La Levrier? Would taking a lover be any different from any other personal interests that she had and should have? She deserved a personal life; considering the people she helped become fulfilled through La Levrier. What was the downside? Was there any? Hold on, was this just a one-time thing or something more? What would Jon desire? Was Jon pleased with her?

But, their lovemaking! Every nuance of their passion had no downside, no negatives. Before Jon, her other sexual encounters seemed like mutual masturbation next to the sharing and connectedness of their lovemaking. She couldn't even use the word 'fucking' in her thoughts of last night. Oh, there were moments of fucking, but the experience was of making love. And there would be more fucking in the future, but it would be moments of lust fueled by the passionate energy to please and be pleased. She instinctively knew this about Jon. They seemed so in sync in so many aspects of their lives.

Hmmm... what if she denied Jon a membership? Banned him from La Levier? That would solve any conflict of interest if he were interested in being her lover. That was an option worth thinking through completely. But, would he come back? Would he take that as her rejecting him altogether? Would he understand?

Both the hours separating her from that time with Jon and her second cup of coffee assured Claire that she was analyzing last night with a clear head. She was going to follow her heart and let that be the organ that determined the next steps in her feelings for Jon. Let the intellectual walls come down and allow the emotional floodwaters free.

Jon slept in that morning at La Levrier. In fact, he enjoyed his first cup of coffee in bed. To add to his luxury, he grabbed the remote for his comfort-controlled king and raised his mattress to the zero-gravity position to bask in the ecstasy of his feelings from last night and his thoughts. Claire had crashed through his conflict between being a target in an investigation versus the dreams of a woman who could fulfill every essence of what drove him to be the best man he could be. He had been with women in the past and each was exceptional in their own right. But, they were puzzle pieces in a matrix of an ideal that Jon was accepting as pure fantasy. The intellectual equals weren't sexy. The sexy weren't intellectual, the sexy and intellectual weren't passionate, the passionate lacked bandwidth, and then there were the many who were just mechanical. All were pretty, many were beautiful, some were stylish and others were natural. Claire put it all together. How could this be possible? Was this real? How real could a romance be given she was a suspect? How could he let his boundaries down with a woman that he may have to arrest? Could he arrest her even though she was so fulfilling to him? Why now? Why her? Why? Did Claire have the same feelings for him? What if this was just a one-time thing? What if she banished him from La Levrier? That might solve his conflict. If La Levier kicked him out, he would be off the case. If he was off the case he could pursue Claire as a lover. Conflict of interest over.

Claire dressed with the usual attention to detail, yet this morning she had the added delight of the possibility that Jon would see her at some point. How fun to anticipate what would impress and excite Jon with what she was wearing.

Slow down here, Claire; I'm not going to do anything different to impress Jon. He was attracted to you as you are. She thought to herself.

Her 'nothing different' was quite good. She paired a gunmetal Tracy Feith pencil-skirted suit with a Max Gengos pale pink blouse and Miu Miu heels matching her blouse. Her choices reflected perfectly who she was-sexy, smart, beautiful and a CEO.

She gave herself a final once over in the platinum free-standing, full-length mirror and unlocked the door between her private residence and her office. The day began.

Jon took his time assembling himself for the day. He was due to report to Mac on his progress and, by the coded texts that she fired off to him, Mac was full of piss and vinegar, and—herself. Jon was in no hurry to be dressed down by his boss today after the heavenly dressing down he enjoyed last night. But duty called, no matter how long he could delay climbing off that cloud.

His morning repose basking in his feelings for Claire accomplished its purpose. He couldn't get the images of making love to Claire out of his head. But, the relaxation also served to free his tightly woven boundaries as a professional and this free association brought a flood of conflict. Who was he? How could he let personal feelings get in the way of his work? Could he continue to work for the Bureau now that he has compromised his ethics? Why couldn't he have love in his life? Why shouldn't he have love in his life? Is this woman a criminal? Is she safe? Is he safe? What would he do if he couldn't be an agent any longer?

He thought a shower and dressing would help calm the battle in his mind. After all, his mother always said that men do their best thinking in the bathroom. He smiled, as always, to the thought of one of her brilliant momisms from a woman with only an eighth-grade education. His cover dictated Jon's choices of attire more than his meeting with Mac. He had to carry out his secret identity. If his existence at La Levrier was only to seduce Claire, he might have chosen differently, maybe.

He had thoughtfully packed on this visit to La Levrier one of his custom Seville Row John Murray suits, part of his wardrobe he typically kept hidden from work assignments, but this assignment was evolving into anything but typical. It was an unusual blue in a shade somewhere in the middle of a dark blue and a royal blue. The composition of the exclusive fabric brought out the uniqueness of the color. It fit Jon's physique perfectly with give in just the right places. He paired his suit with a starched white shirt and no tie. His tan cap-toe shoes and belt, both from John Murray, matched perfectly. His only jewelry was his A. Lange & SÖhne watch with a tan strap that complimented his other leathers. He completed his Jon Fenwick near billionaire look with a swatch of white Sultana burlap as a pocket square. He glanced at the full-length mirror in his bathroom before he walked out of his suite, excited that Claire might see him.

Jon lingered about the mansion. His delay intended to increase the chance that he would see Claire. He went down to the dining room, scanned it to see if Claire was about. She wasn't, but he still took a seat. The agent part of his brain said that the dining room gave him his best opportunity to run into Claire.

The dining room glistened in the morning sun. Each of the square tables was fully set at all times. The tables were picture book with white tablecloths, white china chargers rimmed with gold and carrying the gold Greyhound logo in the center of the plate. The eight-piece silver setting featured hand engraved figures of a Greyhound in elongated stride on each handle. The chairs were a bright white leather in Italianesque design. Jon turned up the coffee cup from its saucer and within seconds it was filled without a word. The dining room service was always haute cuisine. The servers did not engage the guests; in fact, their goal was invisibility. Each guest was informed of the dining etiquette and politely corrected if they strayed into the American dining banter with their server. The attention showered on the members was impressive. A stained napkin was replaced after use, plates and silverware were exchanged without notice, and guests, male or female, were escorted to the restroom and back. The only conversation between a member and the wait staff was if the guest asked a question or when the server explained a course, which they did in detail with every course offering. Jon was left in his thoughts of Claire while he waited to catch a glimpse of her.

Jon sipped at his coffee and gave an uninterested glance at the morning menu. He raised his right hand to summon a server and the waiter appeared immediately.

"Just the grill toasted croissant with the maple butter, please," Jon ordered.

"Very good sir," the server responded.

His attention focused on the door to the dining room perchance Claire would enter or even pass in the hall. His mind still tortured him. *Stop, just stop. What am I, a school kid? Waiting to see a glimpse of the little girl I have a crush on? Geezus, collect yourself... be a man here.* He thought to himself.

Claire sat at her desk and stared at her monitor while her breakfast was laid out on the right side of her desktop. She was thinking of Jon and wondered why he had not contacted her first thing this morning. Was his passion real or was she just a conquest? Why didn't he text? What's the game here? The rules?

Claire picked indifferently at her grapefruit and yogurt but sipped her coffee vigorously. She stared at the wall in front of her. The painting of a white Greyhound in full stride in a field of thick green grass served as a focal point for her meditation on Jon. She didn't feel like working and there was nothing wrong with that. She shook her head, took her eyes off the painting and forced her attention to her monitor. *Stop, what's wrong with me? It is a man. Okay, we made magical, sensual love but is it something or nothing at all?*

Jon shook his head slightly and looked at his watch. He couldn't delay heading over to the meeting with Mac any longer. He started to rise from his seat and a staff person pulled his chair for him. Jon nodded and smiled to acknowledge the service and exited the dining room and La Levrier.

Jon was so annoyed with these meetings with Mac. Since his suspension, he was on such a short leash it seemed like Mac was calling him in just to aggravate him. He approached her office from a distance. He saw Mac sitting at her desk, elbows spread wide and head looking down at some file. Jon chuckled at the image that flew into his mind of a raging bull in a pen, nostrils flared, puffs of smoke bellowing out ready to pounce on anything that dares to enter its lair.

Brrrraaa, time to wrestle the bull, he thought.

"Jon, sit," Mac commanded. "Now, status."

"I've just made a significant advance in getting very close to the head of La Levrier. I'm hopeful that in a short time I will get access to their records." Jon felt sick to his stomach at how his words belied his feelings for Claire.

"That's your Plan A… Ok… but that time has run out. I approved of two plans and as you stated in your proposal, which again I emphasized, I approved, if Plan A is not working quick enough we move into Plan B. Well, it's that time here Jon. I'm ordering you to put Plan B into play immediately. We are shutting 'La Loov-ray' down." Mac was firm.

She still can't get the name right, he thought.

"I thought we were to give Plan A a shot before moving into a more destructive option?" Jon kept his neutral veneer but his voice cracked of pleading.

"Jon, I thought you'd be chomping at the bit to blow something up. You like breaking things so much. Get moving on Plan B. Whatever you have to do to make that happen… make that happen." Mac didn't sway from her agenda.

"And, just to be clear here as I get Plan B going, if I do get enough data to shut La Levrier down, I can abort Plan B, correct?" Jon asked.

"You have 10 days. Shut it down, A or B, shut it down." Mac's voice was indifferent.

"You mind if I ask, why is Washington so hot on this place? Have you ever found that out?"

"I did find out, but I am not privy to reveal the specifics. Let me just give you the highlights. A very sensitive member of the administration is a customer of this 'Leev-Ray' and after repeated attempts to get this person to stop going there, all these efforts have been ignored. Had the person left 'Leev-Ray' alone we would leave it alone as well. You haven't revealed any convincing argument on what laws it is breaking. Oh, we could find or manufacture something to shut it down, but I don't have that kind of time. So, I'm ordering you to jump start Plan B. NO discussion. I'll be there on demolition day. Meeting over."

Jon stayed in his chair.

"You seem a bit distressed, Jon?" Mac added after a long pause.

Jon shook his head and snapped, "No, no… just thinking about planning the operation."

"Well, if you have any doubts about the direction this is taking, maybe you should have kept your junk in your pants and you wouldn't be so emotionally attached to these hookers," Mac quipped with a smirk.

Not much had gotten to Jon in his career, but his stomach felt like an acid pool as the meeting ended. He lingered around FBI headquarters to assemble requisitions for the materials he would need to bring down La Levrier. He avoided fellow agents and moved around the offices solemnly. He had to make arrangements for city services, safety concerns, arrange a support team and choreograph the demolition. His heart wasn't in his work and he flew through the necessary arrangements and then quietly left headquarters.

Jon returned to La Levrier in the early evening. He politely rejected the offer of a cocktail at the door but did head straight to the lounge. Claire was almost sure to walk in at some point and he longed to see her.

The floor to ceiling mahogany paneling of the main lounge had a medium rose color veining in the wood. The predominance of the rose hue gave the room an androgynous feel that screamed of Claire's touch. Usually, such floor-to-ceiling paneling would cry out 'men's club' but the softness of the wood toned that conveyance. The fifteen-foot gold bar top kept continuously polished by the bartender glowed as if it was backlit. The bar itself was made out of a unique natural black wood. The eight draft-beer tap handles were all gold Greyhound heads. Their shine complemented the gold in the bar top. A large mirror dominated the back of the bar. The mirror frame was the same black wood as the bar and contrasted perfectly against the rose mahogany wall it rested on. All along the margins of the mirror was painted a chain of gold Greyhounds running. Each dog's front paws were touching the back paws of the next, so delicately painted that from afar it looked like gold leaf surrounding the mirror. The other walls in the lounge were decorated sparingly with pictures of Greyhounds in action save the 10 that were of just the dogs' faces. On the wall opposite the bar hung an enormous painting of two black Greyhounds sitting majestically to the sides of a throne where an Egyptian pharaoh and his queen sat in full splendor. A shiny black Steinway waited to be played in the right corner next to the bar.

Jon sat at the bar and ordered a ginger ale. He bantered with the bartender and frequently looked in the mirror hoping for Claire's entrance.

"Drinking light tonight?" Claire took the seat next to his.

"Hello!" Jon smiled from ear-to-ear.

"Hi." Her smile more subdued, but her eyes taking him all in.

"I just thought it a bit early for an adult entertainment," he said.

"Hmmmm… isn't that what you come to La Levrier for?"

"Good one! I used to." His broad smile erupted again.

"And now?" she inquired.

"I have one main reason to come here."

"You have a funny way of showing it," she said without a smile.

"Huh?"

"Well, I thought you might say good morning or some sort of communication today after yesterday?" Her voice was hesitant and mindful if the bartender was within earshot.

"I'm sorry. I was trying to be a gentleman and give you some space. I know what an emotional explosion yesterday might have been for you. I never want to come across and demanding, needy or pushy."

"It was an explosion of many of my senses. But, didn't you think I might need some reassurance? Some contact? A hello?"

"I ahhh…"

"Jon, don't try and think for me. I am perfectly capable of doing that for myself. Beneath this enterprise, my position, my staff relations, I am a woman and I need to know where you stand. I don't give myself easily. I need communication." She was firm, but not angry or hurt.

"Well, this is a good start. I understand. I so wanted to see you and have some contact with you all day today. I looked for you this morning; then I had to take a meeting and even being here… as you can see." He held up his glass of ginger ale. "Was just taking the chance that I would run into you. I should not have danced around."

"Do you want to continue this?" She interrupted.

"Absolutely! I haven't felt this intensity before." He said as enthusiastically as he could without the bartender overhearing.

"Then don't leave me hanging. I need to know you are alive and thinking of us."

"May I say that goes both ways? Don't feel afraid to reach out to me. I think it is important that we both let down the lifetime of walls we have put up."

"Yes, but slow down cowboy. We've had one amazing time together. I think we need to see where this may go."

The bartender came near, so they paused in their personal conversation and discussed some innocuous topics about the architecture of the lounge. Then Jon whispered, "Could we take this conversation elsewhere?"

"Absolutely, you have a lovely suite," she agreed.

"Let's go over your membership again, Jon," Claire said loud enough for the bartender to hear as they lifted off their stools.

As soon as Jon closed the door to his suite, he took Claire by the hand and turned her to face him. He kissed her passionately. She returned his kisses with just as much lust as she received. Their bodies pressed together and they were on the wall next to the door. Jon raised Claire's arms over her head as they kissed and he caressed her ears and neck affectionately. Claire purred while he covered her with his emotion. His mouth moved down onto her neck and shoulders. Her body arched with each kiss.

"I have so much passion for you," he said, his voice low and breathy.

"I know… I feel the same," she responded, finding it hard to speak through the sensations she was experiencing.

Jon returned to kiss her lips, as he did, he unzipped her skirt and it fell to the floor. Her skirt bundled in a circle around her ankles and Claire instinctively stepped out of it. They kissed more aggressively and Jon unbuttoned her blouse and it slipped off her body with ease and slinked to the floor. She withered against the wall clad in a pale pink thong, matching sheer bra and her heels. Her panties soaked with her nectar even before Jon's hand reached her womanhood.

Claire pulled his suit jacket off him and undid his tie in a frenzy. She then unbuttoned his shirt and pulled it off his arms then threw it to the side. Their kissing consumed them with their hands roaming all over their bodies. Claire could feel his rock-hard erection against her pelvis and she was compelled to release it from his pants. His pants fell to his ankles and in one motion she ripped off his underwear. His erection exploded from its confinements. Claire looked down at it and her excitement escalated. Jon's fingers on her clit helped that excitement immensely. He touched it with such a delicate pressure unlike any man before. Most men were rough and hurried in their touch; Jon was tender and caring. His touch made it about her and not about him. Claire held Jon's manhood in her hand as she climaxed. With each shudder of her orgasm, she could feel Jon's cock throb with lust. After she enjoyed the full measure of her orgasm, she lifted her leg high up onto Jon's back. Her heel digging into the small of his back so that the lips of her womanhood could spread wide to take him inside. Her hand guided his cock inside her and for minutes they just kissed, erotically united with their bodies. Claire felt her next orgasm building and she began to thrust her pelvis into Jon and he responded in kind. Soon, they were making love lustfully... their lust became fucking. Jon climaxed and Claire followed immediately.

"I'm weak-kneed in ecstasy. Can we move to my bed?" he pleaded, breathing hard between words.

They held each other in bed. Jon gently stroked her face and hair while he placed tender kisses on her eyelids and face. Their bodies were intertwined so close that a single piece of paper couldn't have been slipped between them.

"Do you think we'll ever make love in a bed?" Jon whispered in her ear with a smile.

"Next," was all Claire had to say.

CHAPTER THIRTEEN

The Fuck Up

Jon essentially glided into this office at FBI headquarters and at first glance toward the bare gray walls of his cubical, his mind flared into the association: *Wall-Claire's wall-lovemaking-Claire.* He sat, forced himself to collect his thoughts and focus. The images of Claire and their last encounter continued to blanket his mind, but out of the conflict of trying to stop thinking of Claire and start concentrating on work, the memories of what put him in the position to get the La Levrier case exploded in his mind like a slap to the back of the head. His grand 'Fuck-Up.'

One year ago. 8:45 a.m. Monday

With the meeting minutes away, Jon Fenwick sat at the head of the conference table with seven agents of the 26 that would be attending.

"Fenwick, what the hell are you driving lately?" Agent Don Colona bantered.

"Same old thing you rode in with me when we went on the Cindy Case," Jon smirked.

"That was a hellava ride," Colona remarked.

"My car?" Fenwick shook his head.

"No, the case," Colona shot back.

The other agents sipped their coffee and enjoyed the back and forth between Jon and Colona.

"That was the last year that the Infinity was a great car, "Fenwick mused.

"Fenwick is more into clothes than he is cars," Agent Sharon Giles quipped.

The agents chuckled together as a five more of the attendees of the meeting entered the room.

8:52 a.m.

Eight more agents walked into the room. One large male agent banged Jon on his shoulder with his fist as he entered the conference room. Jon looked over his shoulder, smiled, but didn't flinch at the playful but hard punch.

Folders opened, and papers shuffled as agents settled into their seats around the conference table.

Agent Lamar Allen, a muscular African-American ex-college football lineman, rolled his eyes and cracked, "What's that rag doin' hanging from your coat jacket?"

Jon glanced down at his lapel pocket. "It's burlap. You never saw burlap before?"

"You know, it's what they bag potatoes in. Fenwick's a big potato fan," Agent Dan Jenkins chimed in and got a laugh from the assemblage.

"It's called style, baby, style… look and learn." Fenwick played along.

Allen shook his head, "You got a tiny spud in that pocket?" He looked around the room and waited for his affirmation. Some of the group smiled, others winked, and one or two laughed at the big man's tease.

"Fenwick's gotta eat every few hours or he gets jittery. He keeps that spud in his pocket in case there are no Big Macs around!" Allen emphasized the words 'big' and 'mac.'

That comment got the biggest laugh of the morning. One agent struggled to keep their coffee from spitting out onto the table. Others repeated BIG MAC loudly. Some had tears in their eyes they were laughing so hard.

8:55 am

The remaining six agents expected at that meeting walked in. They took places around the table and most adopted the jovial look of the group.

9:00 am

Jon stood up and pressed a button on his cell phone to open the video screen on the wall behind him. A photo of a four-story house appeared. The architecture of the house was a very ordinary tan brick, rectangular building with medium-sized windows on all sides. The windows all had security bars over them.

"Ok, everyone. Let the record show that this is our tenth and final meeting on Operation Viking. Just to recap here for a minute. The Knarr (code for the building on the screen) is the Macy's of crime in Chicago. The basement is the armory where the Vice Kings run guns. The first floor is their drug operation; the second floor is their prostitution business, third floor is where they house the illegals they use as sex slaves, and the fourth floor are the offices, a huge safe, communications center, computers, etc."

The screen displayed the building at different angles, and Jon paused. "You all have these images and, as you know, we have only fuzzy pictures from telescopic cameras on the inside. So, once we are inside, we have no idea what to expect. In your files, you have renderings of the inside of buildings that are from the same construction firm. We are only guessing that the floor layouts will be the same but, given the use of the Knarr, walls have probably been put up or removed and the room configurations have changed and so forth. We cannot be sure of navigation once inside there. We've all been in crack houses and such, and you know the physical chaos to expect. The Knarr will be no different."

"Remember, our main goal is the fourth floor. Securing all the records and data is the goal. We need to navigate those lower floors quickly to get to the top before they have a chance to destroy anything. This is where Viking is different from other raids of this nature. The activities you will confront on the lower floors will demand you intervene. There will be confrontations immediately to stop you, but we are getting to the fourth floor as quickly as possible. As we have practiced, there is only one way to do that. We have to go from the first-floor entrance and up the stairs. We can expect firefight all the way up, and each of you know your roles as we choreographed in our role-play. Just to review and finalize as we rehearsed: Lamar, you and your team will hit the basement hard. Entering through this basement door, you need to cut-off the armory immediately. Last thing we need is to have them load up on additional firepower.

"Allen, you gonna fit through that tiny door?" An agent quipped, and the group chuckled again.

Allen shot back, "That's why I'm goin' in last. Ain't no way I'm getting stuck in that doorway and hold'n us up." A big smile grew on his face.

Jon continued, "I'm leading Sharon, Mark and Don's teams through this front door. Note that this front door like all the doors is solid steel. Our material engineers' analysis determined that these doors are all three to four-inch-thick composite steel. We will use the same procedure on each door. Ed has trained his high explosive crew to blow the doors in ten seconds upon our arrival to maximize the element of surprise. I don't need to tell you to stand your teams clear from the blasts. Based on our modeling there is a staircase that leads to the fourth floor immediately inside the front door. That is why our full assault is taking place through the front door. The back entrance has an empty space before the staircase, and we could be trapped on that landing if it is well defended by Vice Kings. They will probably expect any assault through the back anyway. A frontal assault increases our chances of surprise and less resistance." With a laser pointer he highlighted areas of the mansion on the large screen monitor at the front of the room. "A team of 10 grunts will remain at the main street entrance and the back entrance here and here securing anyone who is running from the building. I doubt anyone will be doing that given the nature of the bad guys we are dealing with, but we will have the grunts doing that. As you see the grunts are not here in this meeting as they have limited tactical duty. They will strictly follow team leader's orders. "

"Don splits off immediately and secures the first floor. Remember Don, there could be civilian customers on that floor, yet these civilians could be armed as well. Based on how the Vice Kings do business our best recon says they don't allow civilians into the Knarr to buy drugs as most of their drug transactions are street deals, but we need to be prepared for civilians to be there. Sharon, you have the second floor. Sharon, here we suspect that civilians will be present. Be extra alert. Our intel says this is a very profitable business for them, 24-hour trade, so a high probability that civilians will be there. But again, these civilians could be armed. Be vigilant. "

"Mark, you have the third floor with Juan and the INS team. On the third floor, we anticipate the least Vice King presence, but, whoever is there, especially female, are all innocents. Human life is the highest priority here."

"That brings me to the fourth floor. At zero six-minutes we will be ideally on the fourth floor with my team. Our first action is to immobilize any Vice King presence on this floor. There will be no civilian presence on this floor-NONE! Any persons on that floor are V.K. (Vice Kings). Their apprehension is second priority. Everything, everything is about locking down any paper, computers and electronics in that room. If any V.K. gets in the way of that objective, immobilize them immediately. We are authorized to use deadly force is necessary. To repeat, Viking is about data, not arrests. We will secure the area and once the Knarr is buttoned down, the grunts will stand guard over the moving teams that will clean out everything in that room and load it into the storage trucks."

A young male agent asked a question, "Jon, I asked at the second rehearsal about the need for overhead support such as a chopper or two. Have you revisited that need?"

"Darnell, I didn't forget your idea, but this isn't Hollywood..."

Light chuckles erupt in the room.

"As dramatic and costly as a couple of copters would add to this operation, I don't see a need. The only advantage they would have would be to film the operation, and I have that covered." Jon tapped his phone again. "At this fifteen-story building two lots away I have a film crew taking footage of Viking. And, as you all were prepped, each team with have two agents with lapel cameras filming the inside action."

"Will those lapel cameras be covered in Burrrr… Lap?" Lamar Allen chirped.

A roaring laugh burst from the group.

"Smart ass…" Jon answered. "I'll make sure all my groomsmen on this mission get a complimentary burlap pocket square at the end of all this as a gift for standing up."

"Ok, I'm not taking any questions here today. We've been over this operation several times and we are well prepared. Today is the final overview and conformation. V-Day is this Thursday at 1:00 pm. Everything administratively is in order. Legal approved 'go' last Monday. Last Wednesday we assembled the personnel and equipment allocation. The green light is on and I will meet you all on the dock at seven a.m. Thursday. That's it. Get some rest and come ready on Thursday."

The agents stood and began to exit the conference room. Several agents lingered to chitchat as others bantered with Jon.

Thursday 12:58 p.m. Thursday V-Day

At a fast jog, all of the agents ran to the Knarr from all directions. Each team leader was at the front of their teams with the demolition crews right behind them. When they were paces from the doors that needed blasting, Ed and his men raced ahead and slapped the plastic explosives at predetermined spots all over the doors. The explosives whacked onto the doors with a splat, and then the agents ran as fast as they could away from the door. Ed and his assistants crouched on the lawn of a nearby building. The teams of agents lay on the ground a few feet behind the demo teams. After each of the men returned to the group, the demolition leader pressed down on an ignition, and the doors blew open as planned.

The teams of agents popped up from the ground and ran hard toward the building. Bill Allen and his group single filed through the basement door without hesitation. They immediately heard shots from the basement as Allen and his men met resistance.

Jon and the other teams raced to the front door. As they did, FBI marked vehicles pulled up onto the streets around the building. Three unmarked dark blue panel trucks parked behind the marked vehicles.

Once Jon arrived at the front door, he and two of his team raised their handguns and peeked their heads inside the Knarr. A flurry of shots rang out toward the front door impeding the assault's progress.

"High-low, high-low entrance," Jon shouted. With that command, several agents raised their guns over their shoulders and fired cover rounds into the building. As they did, Jon and four agents slid on their bellies like seals and entered the building.

Once inside the building, Jon and the four agents with him popped up to their feet and fired furiously at the guards in the staircase. Their deadly accuracy eliminated the stairwell guards. Jon peeked out of the door jam and waved the remainder of the agent teams to enter as planned. Soon after their arrival, the teams crowded into the staircase poised to climb to the upper floors.

Don and his team broke down the first-floor door and braced for a fight. A vicious battle ensued. Automatic gunfire exploded out toward the invading agents, and a drawn-out gun battle began.

In the stairwell, more V. K. mercenaries entered the stairwell between the second and first floor and delayed Jon and the other teams. Jon and three agents inched up the stairs exchanging fire with the guards on the upper stairs. The FBI ironically had the upper hand as they were trained for such assaults in close quarters, whereas the gang members would flash themselves into the hallway opening and wildly spray bullets from their automatic weapons. Each time a V.K. sprang into the open hallway, the three agents fired with deadly accuracy. For the agents, it was nothing more than a target shoot at a carnival, and they inched up and up the stairs to the next floor.

At the second floor, Sharon and her team crowded around the door as Jon and the remaining teams continued to inch up the stairwell.

A loud boom sounded after an agent broke the second-floor door down with a ramrod. More gunfire erupted and the battle for the second floor began between Sharon's team and the V. K. that were on that floor.

Jon, leading his team and Mark's team, continued to inch up the stairs. The pounding of feet running on the upper floors could be heard above along with screams from what sounded like female voices. Below, Jon could hear gunfire, grunts and yelling. Chaos was all around.

Added to the bedlam, sirens from the streets could be heard. Coordinated fire trunks and ambulances circled the Knarr and corded off the scene from the public while they awaited casualties. All in Jon's plan.

With the same methodical procedure, eliminating V. K. soldiers each time they showed themselves in the hallway, Jon and the agents worked their way to the third floor. Mark and the INS group followed the same precision as Sharon and they split off to break into the third floor to rescue the captive women. So far none of the agents near Jon had been harmed, but he had no way of knowing what had happened in the action that took place on each of the floors.

As if the V. K. had finally communicated among themselves, they changed their tactic in the hallway as Jon and his team moved upward toward the fourth floor. Instead of a single gang member stepping into the hallway to fire at the agents, at a bend in the staircase six V. K. jumped down onto the wood landing and opened fire on Jon and his group. The sound of bullets hitting Kevlar vests and helmets pounded through the hallway. Again, the trained FBI agents had a remedy. All of the agents laid belly first on the stairs giving the appearance of a human ramp as their bodies completely covered the stairs. As if anticipating such a maneuver by the gang, while the majority of the agents dropped down, two agents with automatic weapons stood up. With marksman-like efficiency they sprayed the landing with accurate firepower and all of the V. K. defenders were killed in seconds. But, the defenders' strategy did wound three of Jon's team. As the wounded agents stayed on the stairs, Jon and the rest of the group used this opportunity to run up as many stairs as they could before they hit the next round of hallway defenders. To Jon's surprise or by the speed by which he and the agents could race up the remaining stairs, they did not encounter any V. K.

Jon and his team stopped three stairs from the fourth-floor door and paused to prepare a ramrod. But, the door cracked open and a head looked out. Several of the agents fired through the wood door and a thump of a body was heard even against the noise of the battle that raged inside the building. Jon and two of his team sprung toward the slightly open door and put their bodies on either side of the door jamb to ready themselves for a room invasion. This was a procedure they trained for and one these veteran agents had executed many times in their careers. The V. K. defenders and workers on the fourth floor had little chance of stopping the agents no matter how well armed they were on that floor.

Within minutes Jon and his team had entered the fourth floor in full force. They eliminated any resistance they met, and the remaining gang members gave themselves up. Jon's team gathered the gang members into a corner of the room, disarmed them and held guard over them while they were cuffed with standard plastic cable ties and ordered to sit.

Jon relaxed his hand holding his gun and pointed it to the floor while he surveyed the situation in the room. There were four desks each with several computer screens and a hard drive near each stationed near windows. A wall of file cabinets filled one wall, and an enormous antique looking safe dominated another wall. The entire floor was open and approximately twelve hundred square feet of space. Unlike the model they used for rehearsal, there were no walls dividing this space into rooms. There were four closed doors that upon a quick glance Jon guessed were closets, maybe a bathroom or kitchen break room. Jon didn't attend to them at that moment assuming they were storage and there didn't appear to be any activity coming from them. They would inspect them during clean up.

Jon stood in the center of the room, took a deep breath, looked around, holstered his gun and took out his cell phone to check in with the other floors. As he began to press a key on the phone, one of the closed doors opened and banged against the adjoining wall. A large young man, near six feet-seven inches and well over three hundred pounds ran toward Jon like a wild animal. He had a vicious looking knife in one hand. The lunging young man took a wild swipe at Jon and missed with the knife. That move gave Jon a wide opening to rear back with his arm and he put a fierce elbow onto the young man's face. The young man's movement toward Jon gave the blow double the impact that Jon could deliver. The loud crack of bones caught everyone's attention in the room. The man fell to the floor and held his face with both hands. Jon towered over him and as the man removed his hands and he looked up at Jon, he gave Jon an angry look and began to brace himself up with his elbows. Jon instinctively took out his weapon and as the man sneered at Jon, Jon took his pistol and smashed the man hard across his face with the weapon. The man grabbed his face again with both hands and while he did, with great effort Jon pushed the man on his stomach and cuffed both his legs and hands in three places. Because of his size and apparent strength, Jon tightened all the cable ties extra tight. The man withered in pain.

Jon collected himself and resumed making his calls to his team leaders on the other floors. They each reported that their floors were secured and Operation Viking was ready to be handed over to the clean-up team.

Friday 8:00 am

Jon was ordered into Mac Owen's office the next morning. It seemed a bit unusual that Mac would want to see him so soon after an operation was tied up in the field. Typically, Jon would get the paperwork completed after the clean-up, and the final numbers available. But, Jon had no reason to be concerned since Operation Viking was a success. He thought that Mac wanted to discuss the press conference or some other publicity appearance.

Mac's door was open so Jon walked in right on time.

"So, Jon what do you have against Governor Ritter?" Mac was yelling as soon as Jon walked pass the door threshold. "Sit!" She commanded.

"What are you talking about?" Jon stopped halfway into the office. His brow squinted and he hesitated to go any further.

"You know Goddamn well what I am talking about, now take a seat." Mac pointed at one of the side chairs in front of her desk.

Jon reluctantly took the seat she indicated. "What's going on?"

"Viking... Viking is a disaster," Mac insisted.

"What? I haven't filed my report yet, but by all appearances, this was a huge home run. We shut down..."

"Stop, stop! The Governor's son, Quinn, a high school football star is in critical condition at Northwestern. And if the boy lives, he's at best going to look like Quasimodo the rest of his life and at worst he will have brain damage and be a vegetable."

"Who's this Quinn? There was no Quinn on any one of our teams or in the grunts. I don't know of any Quinn." Jon looked puzzled.

"Don't fuck with me, Jon. Quinn Ritter has been on the front page of the media as much as his father. A senior in high school, all-American football lineman, good student, scholarship to Florida University for football. How could you not know who you tortured and beat to near death?"

"Mac, what are you talking about? The raid on the building was an intense gunfight all the way up four floors. The only hand-to-hand that took place was when some young man came rushing me from nowhere after we had the fourth floor secure and the records protected." Jon's look turned thoughtful.

"That MAN was a minor and his name is Quinn Ritter, the Governor of Illinois' eldest child. An all-American kid with an impeccable record and an unlimited future."

"Jesus Mac, anyone there will tell you that that kid came out of a closet with a knife, a hunting knife and came at me like the devil," Jon insisted.

"Stop… stop right there. He is a high school kid. You, big bad Jon Fenwick couldn't control a high school kid?"

"Wait a second here. We just survived a fierce firefight up a hallway in a criminal hellhole, exhausted, post traumatic, and this man, ok kid, probably high on something comes at me full bore. What am I supposed to do… ask him for an ID? Get a DNA sample?"

Mac's volume raised another few octaves. "Don't give me that cutesy, smart fucking ass remarks. You crippled the Governor's son. His Goddamn son! Are you fucking insane? His face is caved in… Goddamnit, his face is caved in. Did you look online this morning? It's all over the national news. FBI tortures Governor's son."

"Where is this torture coming from?"

"You took your pistol out and smashed his face in when he was down and helpless. What the hell is wrong with you?" Saliva spewed from her mouth as she yelled.

"He was getting ready to bounce up and come back at me. I reacted. The kid was almost twice my size for God sake. I could've shot him, but I took the route of immobilizing him. That's not torture, that's self-defense." Jon's anger was building back at Mac.

"The kid had circular half-inch wounds in six places from the cable ties you used to cuff him. That's excessive force right there. You cut through his skin with the cable ties. Unnecessary and excessive… I call that torture. What did you have against the kid? This doesn't smell like normal restraint."

Jon thought quickly, "Come on Mac. I've cuffed hundreds of suspects. I know what I'm doing. Put two and two together. Footballer, excessively big for a teenager, looks like a man, he's in a known drug den? The kid probably used steroids to the max. You know that makes your skin incredibly brittle. The cables cut right through his skin. Not my fault." Jon was firm. "What was he doing there?"

"Look, the media are salivating over that kid's fall from grace like rabid hounds. It's in every headline, but none of that matters. Don't you fucking get it? All the Governor cares about is his precious baby boy, and he'll do what it takes to protect his reputation. Who cares if that jock was in a crime scene... if he was there for drugs... if he charged you first? Your actions shifted the focus away from all that. The FBI is in the hot seat now. Thanks to you, we're at the forefront of the media lynching of law enforcement. This is not the day and age for that kind of brutality and you know that. YOU WERE WRONG." Mac pounded both her index fingers on her desk in rage.

Jon fell silent and looked beyond her out Mac's windows into the city view.

"The Governor is talking about criminal charges against you. Are you hearing me? Criminal charges!"

Mac stopped her tirade. Moved to her chair and slammed into her desk chair with a thud. "You're immediately suspended while a full investigation takes place. Your second will complete the report on Viking. Now, get the fuck out of here and I don't want to see or hear from you unless I contact you. Done."

CHAPTER FOURTEEN

The Heat

The three black Chevy Impalas were unremarkable other than they were showroom polished and their extra dark tinted windows were illegal in the city of Chicago. They pulled into La Levrier's covered carport to the east of the mansion. The middle car stopped precisely in front of the side entrance.

A buff young man in a blue suit tapped at the microphone in his ear as he bounced out of the driver's seat to open the rear passenger door. Four more secret service agents burst out of the other cars. They immediately fanned out in a protective perimeter and looked into the distance. An attractive, shapely, middle-aged woman alighted from the vehicle. Not a single aspect of her body language signaled any urgency. She led the way into the mansion and, although the driver and another female secret service agent walked with her up the four concrete steps to the side door, these two agents stopped from going inside.

Once inside she received the La Levrier greeting. A beautiful Levrier held a silver tray in her left hand with three personalized choices of libation: a Manhattan, a Krug vintage champagne, and a Hendrick's and tonic.

She lifted the Manhattan off the tray and smiled at the server.

"Welcome, Madam Vice-President," the Levrier proudly advanced.

"Thank you. You don't know how glad I am to be here," the Vice-President responded.

"Madelene has been eager to see you. Where would you like her to meet you?" the Levrier asked.

Bette Gordon, the first female vice-president of the United States, sipped her Manhattan, cupped the glass with both hands, closed her eyes and smiled. "Please ask her to meet me in our suite. It has been a hard few weeks and I could use peace, quiet and intimacy."

As Bette walked up the glossy white stairs of La Levrier's central staircase, her heart pounded. But, this time it wasn't from the pressures of her job; these beats thumped in anticipation of being with her lover once again.

Once Bette opened the door to her suite, the vice-president veneer dropped off her as easily as her form-fitting, grey knit dress which swooped stylishly just above the knee. Without a care, she stepped out of it as it piled to the floor. Her sheer pink boy shorts and matching bra accentuated a lean, toned body. Out of her dress, she looked instantly ten years younger than her 47 years.

"How delicious you look," purred Madelene, lying on top the anvil grey comforter, Bette's signature color. "Oh, if the country knew what was beneath those suits of yours!"

Madelene laid on the bed with her right leg bent at the knee and her shoulders propped up with three fluffy pillows. Her long feminine legs were accentuated by black pumps that made her calves plump with just the right seduction. She wasn't about to miss the entrance of her lover to their suite, so she faced the door. She wore her raven hair down so that her thick rolling curls fell well below her neckline. Her broad, welcome smile delicately outlined with a flaming red lipstick that contrasted well with her dark features. A thin black line of lace hinted at the V-string panty that was barely visible at the angle of her hips on the bed. Her chest showcased her erect nipples that appeared on fire under the matching bra.

"I save what's underneath for you my dear," Bette's smile was wide and inviting as she walked toward the bed. "Only, for you..." Bette stopped at the head of the bed and bent over and kissed Madelene's lips. The first touch of their lips was soft and gentle, so different from the sensation of any man's lips. Madelene's mouth widened during that tender kiss and Bette's lips parted to welcome more of Madelene inside her. The tips of their tongues touched as delicately as their lips. The sensation of that slightest touch between the most sensitive erogenous area conveyed the intense passion they held for each other. Their oral stimulation lasted long and, when one of them lost contact with the other, they reconnected without hesitation. Such care and connection was not primal; it was a communication beyond words. It was pure emotion.

As they spoke to each other with their kiss, Madelene's fingernails softly stroked Bette's lingerie, moving between the sheer lace of her panty to her skin and back again. They luxuriated in each other in erotic bliss. Bette's hand ran along Madelene's left leg with a touch of her fingers as soft and delicate as Madelene's. They could have basked for hours in that tantric expression if the needs of their bodies didn't crave attention as much as their lips and hands that already engaged with such delicate, controlled affection.

As their tongues danced with more vigor, their bodies screamed for their own attention. They both could sense the wetness between the legs of the other and the throbbing of the swollen lips of their womanhood. Their pelvises pulsated in longing for each other in a more raw, lustful way, and Bette moved onto the bed so more of their bodies could join the excitement. Their kisses became more aggressive and consuming. They intertwined their legs and hips in such a way that the hoods of their womanhood pressed against the other, now feeling the full measure of their passion toward each other. They then experienced the wetness of each other's excitement, and it escalated the passion that already seemed majestic.

With their bodies entangled, skin touching skin in every possible way, their clits blossoming hard and swollen with each lingering thrust of their pelvises, their hands roamed seeking their own pleasure. They brushed skin, slipped beneath lingerie, found the most intimate parts of each other and, with each touch, shared the same loving, tender stimulation that defined their lovemaking. With their hips tilted so that their clits pressed together in unison, their fingers caressed the other's swollen pussy lips with a gentle flutter that increased the stimulation.

Bette's breathing became fast and deep, and Madelene instinctively knew to press even harder with her pelvis into Bette. Bette pushed back against Madelene and the exquisite feel of clit against clit was heightened by their hips gyrating against each other through the lace of their lingerie. Now, their passion took on a primal lust. Madelene held a thrust and ground it into Bette's throbbing clit, Madelene's clit pushing and grinding into Bette's. Bette climaxed with a gasp of air and a huge shudder of her body, a moan involuntarily released. "Oh, yes. I love that, just like that," Bette cried out.

Madelene was close behind and, with a symbiotic expression, climaxed with the same reaction. They held each other very tight and their bodies couldn't get enough of each other. Legs, hands, and every part of their skin yearning to touch and explore the other. They kissed furiously and, as they did, both ran their fingers through the other's hair, then onto their faces. They rolled on the bed with their bodies crying out for each other. Madelene fell onto her stomach, and Bette caressed the back of her body. She undid Madelene's black bra and kissed her back and neck with affection. Bette's mouth moved down Madelene's torso and she lifted Madelene's panty down her legs slowly. She kissed each part of Madelene's skin as the panty eased its way to her ankles and then off. Bette's mouth lingered on Madelene's anklebone before it began its journey upward. Bette kissed Madelene's calves, the back of her knees and the back of her legs using her lips and her tongue generously. Madelene arched her butt up and spread her legs as she felt Bette's mouth nearer to her pussy, still swollen and throbbing in ecstasy. Bette obliged with kisses on Madelene's womanhood and delighted in the thrust of her backside toward her mouth. Madelene's body language told Bette exactly how welcome that affection was.

Bette took her hand and gracefully stroked her own pussy while she continued her oral pleasure of her lover. Bette licked the lips of Madelene's pussy with the same tender, light stroking that her tongue lavished on Madelene's mouth. Bette knew just the right pressure and the right spots that would send her lover into Nirvana.

And it came. The delicate flick of Bette's tongue over and over, concentrated on Madelene's clit, sent her right over the edge.

"Right there, right there... don't stop. That's it," Madelene begged. And Bette obliged.

"Ahhhhh... Oooooh," Madelene exploded. Her autonomic body spasms highlighted the intensity of her orgasm. The sweet nectar of her climax dripped from her pussy, and Bette welcomed the taste of her lover's ecstasy. Bette felt such fulfillment in sharing every ounce of intimacy with Madelene.

Bette put her head on the small of Madelene's back and hugged her tight. She smiled and closed her eyes, sharing in Madelene's complete surrender to pleasure.

Admiral's House-Vice-President's residence—Washington, D.C.—Six months earlier

The office inside the residence of the Vice-President of the United States had the look and feel of the Oval Office of the President. The well-lacquered oak chair rail and baseboard seemed to sparkle against the white walls of the office. The prominent oak desk was positioned to face the two entry doors almost hidden to the inside of the office. A small sofa and two cushioned side chairs faced each other with a long coffee table between them. The carpet prominently displayed a blue crest that was the seal of the Vice-President of the United States. Every aspect of the room stated important and serious.

Protocol dictated the location of a meeting. If the Vice-President wanted to convey authority, she sat at her desk and her guests sat at the desk side chairs across from her. If she was being diplomatic or deal-making, she assumed her seat in the sofa arrangement. On this day, Miguel Contador, a 20-year veteran of the Secret Service and the current head of that agency and his second assistant, Bill Weathers, in charge of the Vice-President's security detail, sat across from the Vice-President at her desk.

"Madam Vice-President, we have a delicate matter concerning your security to discuss today," Miguel began.

"I didn't receive any advance briefing reports on this meeting, Miguel," Bette Gordon stated.

"As I said, Madam Vice-President, this is a delicate matter and one that is personally difficult to discuss with you," Miguel smiled, but otherwise his face was stern.

"Give it to me straight, Miguel. Just lay it out for me. But, are we on the record here?" Bette declared.

"I would prefer if this meeting were off the record, Madam Vice-President," Miguel stated.

"I agree, especially when I am blindsided without a briefing report on the nature of the meeting. So, let's get right to it, shall we?" she said sternly.

"Madam Vice-President, let me put this carefully. My staff and I are very concerned about your visits to a mansion in Chicago."

"So, that's what this is about," she sighed to herself, not shifting her position in her chair or taking her direct eye contact away from the two agents.

"Let me finish please," Miguel insisted.

"You will not allow my people to escort you inside the mansion, and this is a serious breach of security procedure for the Vice-President of the United States."

"Have I not egressed from that building several times during my term, and have I not been completely safe?" she insisted.

"Madam, please let me continue," he paused.

"Procedure calls for us to inspect a residence that you will be visiting at least four days in advance of your visit and each time you visit. You are fully aware of those procedures. As an example, when you visit your father's home in Indianapolis, we routinely inspect his residence, the neighborhood and any other buildings you will be visiting on each visit and before EACH visit. My people have never set foot inside this mansion, at your insistence."

"That's correct," she agreed.

If this conversation made Bette uneasy, her unchanged position at her desk, the unwavering eye contact and her steady tone of voice did not belie it. She kept firm, with her eyes locked on the speaker.

"Madam, we have been very understanding and patient with this situation and, quite frankly, up until a few weeks ago, we had assumed that these visits were to an old boyfriend or some such thing."

"Well at least I don't have to open any closets in this conversation," Bette thought.

"And?" she asked.

"We've stood our ground at your request. We secure the perimeter, the air space and the neighborhood each and every time you visit there. But, at your command, you have requested no security inside from your Secret Service team. That request moves up the chain of command each time, and I am fully aware of it each time, as is Bill. We note it as a security breach and these incidents are piling up."

The men looked at each other, and Bill gave a slight nod to Miguel.

"Several weeks ago, we discovered information from a leak, and found out that this mansion is a place where men and women go to have discrete encounters," Miguel paused and searched Bette's face for a reaction. He was disappointed.

"*Good… they have no idea…*" she thought.

"Miguel, you and I have had a great working relationship, and Bill, here, he and I go back to my Senate days. We have been cordial, I have always respected your work… by God, you are protecting my life every minute of every day," Bette began.

"That's all true Madam Vice-President," Miguel interjected.

"That's my point, Gentlemen. I respect your work. I always have and always will," she paused, sat back in her chair and glanced out the window. "Miguel, Bill, let me put it this way. Do you think I am a fool?"

Both men shook their heads. "Quite the contrary," Bill Weathers added.

"Well then, good, because I don't consider myself foolish either. I will not, and do not, risk this office, my duties or my country. Quite frankly, Gentlemen, you are just going to have to trust me on that." Bette moved her eye contact back and forth between them.

"But, Madam, I am afraid this is bigger than just us taking your word. I must insist that we have access to this mansion, inspect it as is procedure, and have an agenda with 15-minute time intervals delineated as we do with all your comings and goings," Miguel was firm but respectful.

"Men, President Truman snuck out of the White House and would take his Packard for a drive at night just to get away. President Reagan rode his horse on his ranch alone…"

Miguel interrupted, "Yes, Madam Vice-President, but these didn't have the extra component of intimate relations."

Bette interrupted, "Come on, Gentlemen. President JFK had starlets brought into the White House to have sex. President Johnson was known to be an active philanderer. And, the granddaddy of them all, President Clinton, was getting blowjobs under his desk!" She put both her hands up signaling them for silence. "I hesitate to go here, but… is this because I am a woman?" Her hands went up again. "No, wait. Would we be having this conversation if I were a man?" She pumped her hands toward them signaling silence once more. "You don't need to answer that because I already know the automatic answer that is going to shoot out of your mouths with complete indignation. But, I will maintain that, in fact, we wouldn't be having this conversation if I were a man… you both and your PEOPLE would shake your heads at my little dalliances, maybe even make sly jokes about it at the water cooler and you all would protect me as vigorously as your duty calls. BUT, you would not be interfering with a MAN'S privacy. I guarantee you," Bette insisted.

"Madam, Ms. Vice-President, we're not implying anything about this place. We just want a chance to secure it. Maybe know a little more of what is going on," Miguel repeated.

"Madam Vice-President, we, my team, your security team, we just want to protect you to the best of our ability. What you do there is and will remain your business, I assure you. Just like the examples you brought up," Bill Weathers offered. "We obviously weren't part of those teams protecting the former Presidents, but did they know the comings and goings of their bosses? I would bet they did," he added.

"The answer is still no. No, you cannot enter that mansion. Keep doing what you are doing and that is final," Bette insisted.

"Madam Vice-President, then I must implore you to stop going there. This is not just a matter of your security but it is for national security as well," Miguel turned his sternness up a notch.

"And, the answer is still NO," she stated one octave just below yelling.

"Madam Vice-President, if you keep insisting, I am duty-bound to bring this matter to a higher level," Miguel tried to play his trump card, and maybe too soon.

"Higher than me?" Bette chuckled.

"We have a new Middle East crisis every minute, a psychotic Russian Premier, GNP issues and sundry domestic issues and you are going to bring this matter to the President? Come on now, Gentlemen, come on now," she chuckled.

"With all due respect Madam, there are Senate and House committees that we report to and other bodies that we can appeal to if we want to play 'draw a line in the sand' here." Miguel courageously held his ground.

"For the last time, the answer is NO. Now, this meeting is over. I have real work to do. And, as we declared at the beginning of this meeting, our discussion here never took place," Bette paused, stood up and added, "I truly thank you for your service and protection. Please have a good day."

The two men took their cue and stood. "Thank you for your time Madam Vice-President," they both said in unison and walked out of the room.

Mac Owen's Office—FBI Headquarters Chicago—Five Months Later

7:00 am Central Time

Mac Owen's phone rang at the precise time the conference call with Bill Weathers of the Secret Service arranged.

"This is Midwest Region Chief Owens," Mac gave her full title knowing that her assistant and Weather's assistant exchanged data about their bosses in preparation for the call.

"Makenzie…" Bill Weathers started.

"Please call me Mac. May I call you Bill?" Mac interrupted.

"Please," Bill answered.

"Mac, we have a situation here and discovered that you are on this, so we didn't want to trample over something you have in the works," Bill began. "In fact, because you are already on this helps us a great deal because we have an urgency here on this matter."

"I understand it's about the whore house on Astor Street?" Mac had to revert to being Mac.

"Whoa! Let's slow down here and hope this isn't a bordello," Bill shot back.

"I don't understand," Mac commented.

"My assistant informed you that this conversation is classified and anything I tell you is for your ears only, correct?" Bill requested. "I do not have to add that your job depends on this confidentiality, correct?"

"Yes," a subdued Owens replied.

"We have a major security problem with this mansion that you have under surveillance. A very high-ranking member of the White House is visiting this address on a regular basis and will not let our people inside during those visits. Obviously, we are in charge of security for that person and this presents a vexing problem. Do you understand?"

"I understand completely. Let me tell you that just a few months ago, I assigned one of our best people to infiltrate this place in order to uncover exactly what kind of business they are conducting there. The Chicago PD received complaints about this mansion, but CPD was not able to gather any intel on the activity in this building, so we were given the assignment. I saw right away that it had potential for disaster written all over it, so I made it high priority from the moment it hit my desk and assigned it to one of our top field agents." Mac didn't quiver as she spewed facts directly opposite of her priority in this case that was at the 'bottom of her slush pile.' It was as if she believed her own lie.

"That's damn good work, Mac. So, you are getting intel that something sexual is going on there? Is that why you called it what you did? Is that what your agent is bringing back?"

"That's our operational theory. We're just at the beginning stages of an investigation. In fact, our agent only recently got inside undercover," Mac cautioned.

"What are you finding out?" Bill's voice was eager.

"We don't have anything substantial yet. It seems like some type of high-class sex business along with entertainment and amenities. We don't know if it is primarily entertainment and the sexual activity is just secondary or if the entertainment is secondary and the sex is the purpose of the place."

Mac flipped through a file as she talked with Weathers. Her eyes were intent on the pages in the folder indicating her need to refresh herself on this previously frivolous case on her agenda.

"Ah huh, just want we feared," Bill's voice was troubled. He paused. "What have you done to shut it down?"

"We've been trying to gather financial data, but it runs as tight as a drum. We haven't come up with anything solid yet," Mac stated.

"How long has your agent been on the premises?" Bill interrogated.

Mac quickly scanned the file, "Sixteen days."

"How much longer until you get something substantial?"

"I've ordered my agent to put a fire under his pants," Mac chuckled, but Weathers showed no appreciation of her humor. He didn't respond.

"Chief Owens, we need that place shut down yesterday. The presence of our person there is a compromise of national security."

"You can't derail this person on your end?" Mac inquired. "We'll shut it down all right, but I'm not sure we can meet your timetable."

"Owens, the specifics of what we have done on our end are on a need-to-know basis. We have appealed to our person, we have ordered them to stay away, we have even gone around their back and loaded up their schedule to make it impossible to be in Chicago, but all these efforts have failed. There must be some powerful attraction there," Bill insisted defensively. He carefully used gender-neutral references as not to reveal the identity of whom they were guarding.

"I'm assuming it isn't the President you are talking about, so why haven't you gone over their head to their boss?" Mac's tone was as if she was talking to one of her subordinates. She pushed herself away from the file and leaned back in her chair.

Bill took offense to her question, "We're doing our job here Chief Owens. It's not that simple. This is more than I should be informing you of, but we haven't gone over their head because that would broadcast that we're not doing our job. Our people cannot give out any impression, even in the slightest, that we are not carrying out our duty. Can you imagine how you would feel if your security team put any doubt in your mind? How the President would feel about his protection?" Weathers paused the silence underling the absurdity of her questions.

"We have to take a stronger, more direct route now. One that doesn't put to question that we are fulfilling our responsibility here. When I found out that you were on this operation, it was the best of both worlds for us; the FBI takes it down and solves our problem without us needing to take this matter higher," He stopped again as if letting his statements sink in.

"Whatever that mansion has, it has to stop and stop now. We don't care what it takes to do so. Do you understand?" Bill was terse. "How long will it take to shut that operation down?"

"So, who has our back here if we take down this place?" Mac kept her authoritative tone. "We do your dirty work and, if this goes south, it is the Bureau that looks like we stepped outta line."

"Owens, I'm not going to argue semantics here. That place closes -whatever it takes- or we take the whole job over and how does that look on your record when you couldn't accomplish some simple stalk and kill?"

"We'll get it done," Mac spat back at him folding her hands in front of her and leaning into the speakerphone.

"How long, Owens?"

"Give me ten days."

"I give you yesterday," Weathers' voice raised. "I want daily updates, and let me remind you that YOUR boss's office is just down the hall."

"I'll get it done," Mac barked.

"Yesterday," Weathers hung up.

Mac sat in silence for a moment and then paged her admin. "Jessie, get Fenwick into my office, stat!"

CHAPTER FIFTEEN

The Greeting

Claire recalled Jon's parting words to her during their last encounter, "Do you think we'll ever make love in a bed?" It has been three full days since they'd unleashed their passion and had confessed their true feelings. Since then, they'd texted a few times, but their demanding schedules kept them apart. That was fine with Claire. And it wasn't. Not really.

She had tried her hardest to stave off Jon's advances, but they were more than that. He had managed to uncover what lay hidden in the impenetrable fortress Claire had erected to survive in a man's world—quite literally. Now that he held the key in his hands, there was no turning back. She could not deny the vulnerability that vexed her, as she was torn between her feelings toward Jon and her duty to La Levrier. Could they be mutually exclusive? She wasn't sure.

Claire's response to Jon's question about making love in a bed was simply, "next." But she didn't know if there would be a next time. Maybe it was just a fleeting fancy or, more accurately, a fantasy. She'd best abandon it in her mind, but her heart told her otherwise. So did her gut, which churned in anxious waves, wondering and waiting if she would ever see Jon again. With each passing day, the chances grew slimmer.

Claire resolved, once again, that Jon was just another commitment-phobic man in a sea of thousands. When the stakes grew higher along with the emotional investment, the alarms sounded and it was time to abort mission. On the other hand, who was Claire to judge? The same could be said of her. But arguably, she had made an exception for Jon. This would be her last, she resolved, as she briskly threw a Hermes scarf over her shoulders in a makeshift shawl and prepared for her next task: a visit to Agent Provocateur.

She marched to the exclusive intimate apparel boutique on Chicago's famous Oak Street, dotted with a row of tiny, high-end shops. Tucked away on the garden level a brownstone, Agent Provocateur (AP), with its seductively clad window mannequins, beckoned the arrival of a very familiar face who made scheduled monthly visits to inspect the latest lines imported from France and Italy.

"Good afternoon, Ms. Bernardin," Pauline Brunswell smiled warmly as Claire entered. Cloaked in her pink, body-skimming waffle weave AP uniform reminiscent of a '50s housecoat and black lacy thigh-high stockings, Pauline immediately greeted Claire with a glass of champagne and offered to take her wrap. "We've been expecting you."

Claire thanked Pauline, who led her through the one-room boutique, past the row of dressing rooms and to a private room at the back of the store. "We just unpacked this shipment this morning, and I think you're really going to love the new fall line!" she said excitedly. "Of course, Ms. Bernardin, we haven't put any of these items on display yet until you've had first choice."

Pauline, the store manager, had been at Claire's service for the past three years, and she was loyal to their arrangement. As AP's top client, Claire had established an ongoing monthly retainer so well-funded that it gave her exclusive rights to have first pick of each shipment of fresh inventory before it went on the floor.

Claire entered the cozy room as Pauline instinctively refilled her champagne flute with Veuve Clicquot, the store's signature bubbly. Gold damask silk covered the walls, and the contrast from the glossy black ceiling and crown molding gave a regal effect. The vibe was elegant and inviting. Scattered around the room were shiny gold racks, black velvet benches and high-backed stools draped with countless displays of garter belts, panties, teddies, bras, stockings, chemises and robes in a rich assortment of fabrics—embroidered satin, sheer silk and delicately woven lace inlaid with gemstones, ribbons, and other notions.

Claire's eyes swept the room, attempting to take it all in. But that was impossible, given that each item called for personal inspection and the attention it was due. "Of course, Ms. Bernardin, I will be happy to set aside the items you've selected for Sunniva to model for you, as always."

Claire smiled. The drill was always the same. She would take her time combing through the individual garments, making her selections and then sitting back to see how they flattered a live model in a one-person fashion show. Claire knew all too well that a camisole on the tabletop could look very different when displayed on the curves of a woman. She insisted on ensuring that every article would suit each Levrier perfectly. Pauline kept a careful running list of all Levriettes by size, height, weight and specific measurements, and Claire had allotted a budget in her monthly retainer for all of her girls. In fact, one of the first onboarding tasks of a new Levrier was to visit Pauline to get measured. Every month, Claire bestowed each Levrier with a gift from AP—a ritual all anticipated with the expectation that it would be put to good use.

"Shall I give you and your new assistant the next half hour to look over our beautiful new collection?" Pauline inquired politely.

Claire was puzzled. "My new assistant?"

This time, Pauline looked perplexed. "Yes. I believe they're using the restroom now and will join you in a minute…"

"I'm here, Pauline, thank you very much for escorting Ms. Bernardin in. I'll take it from here."

"Jon!" Claire gasped, nearly choking on her champagne, as he strode into the private chambers with his usual confident stride and a slight smirk outlining his lips.

"I thought you'd appreciate a man's opinion this time," he offered, unflappable. "After all, La Levrier's members know best what flatters a woman, turns us on and makes us want to ravish her in unimaginable ways…"

Claire smiled coyly and just shook her head in silence.

"How did I find you?" he asked. "Simple. Your secretary graciously offered her help when I inquired about your schedule. She informed me that you already had plans for lunch. She must have detected my grave disappointment because she volunteered the location of your hot date. Too bad it wasn't with me," he said, feigning a frown.

"Too bad you hadn't asked me for that so-called 'hot date' first," Claire said coolly.

Jon clucked teasingly. "You know me. I'm not a planner."

"Obviously," Claire returned.

"You know what your problem is, Ms. Bernardin?" Jon continued. "Trust. Lack thereof. Oh, and I might add patience to the list. Lack thereof on that one, too."

"So, let me get this straight," Claire sighed. "You stalk me and then insult me after three days of cryptic communication. Then you expect me to push the reset button and fall madly into your arms?"

"Exactly," Jon grinned as he lifted the champagne flute from her fingers and set it on an end table. He took her in his arms in a tight embrace, lifted her chin and kissed her gently on the lips.

"Baby, I've missed you," he whispered. "I've been buried at work, but today I stole away to be with you. And, if here is where you are, here is where I am. I can think of worse places." A smirk filled his face as he scanned the room.

Claire returned his kiss but slithered out of his arms. She wasn't about to let Jon off the hook that easily.

"Isn't this a lovely basque!" Claire gasped, holding up a sheer black lacy garment with floral French embroidery and bows.

"So, that's a basque?" Jon chuckled. "Delicious."

She progressed in her pursuit of the perfect lingerie to suit her Levriettes, flipping through the racks and occasionally lifting an item for closer inspection. Claire pretended not to notice, or care, what Jon thought as he eyed her choices.

"Now THAT is what I call sexy," he interjected while Claire fingered a white lacy garter strung with tiny seed pearls.

"Hmmmm," Claire pondered. "It looks awfully close to the doilies my servers use on our buffet table at high tea. I'm not sure…"

"Then what about this?" Jon held up a sheer net tulle bra edged in a satin scallop piping. "You, in fact, would rock this little number."

"Your taste is improving." Claire managed a half a smile.

"I know," he smirked. "In lingerie and in women."

"Here's the ultimate test," Claire quizzed, as she showed Jon a high-waisted leopard faux fur thong playsuit with a gaping hole in the back to accommodate a set of ripe buttocks.

"Grrrrrrrr," he purred. "I'm really not into the animal print thing. It looks more like a Halloween costume unless you've got any members who are zookeepers."

"That I do not," Claire answered, "and, even if I did, this thing is hideous. I'm surprised it's even in AP's collection. Maybe Pauline threw it in to humor me."

"Pauline has a sense of humor?" Jon ribbed.

"She let YOU in this store, didn't she?" Claire grinned.

"Oh, she let me do more than that," Jon winked.

"You didn't try to seduce her, did you?" Claire asked, amused.

"Now who has the sense of humor?" Jon laughed. "No, I'm afraid that I've got my eyes on only one enchantress. Which is why I asked her to let Sunniva off early this afternoon."

"WHAT?" Claire demanded. "WHY? I don't buy a thing until I've seen her model it first. Pauline knows that. Who are you to make those decisions?"

"I am your dutiful assistant now, Madame Claire. Trust me; I made it worth Sunni's time. She left with a full bra and a full purse," Jon stated, bypassing Claire's accusatory tone.

"Then you tell me who is going to try these on to ensure they're going to flatter my Levriettes?" she demanded.

Jon scanned the room and he looked over his shoulder, pretending to seek a replacement model. His eyes then fell squarely on Claire and he smiled with a slight nod.

"Oh, no!" she stammered.

Jon assumed a seat in a toile-upholstered, high back armchair and casually crossed his legs. "Show time," he responded calmly.

"NO time," Claire retorted.

"Too bad," Jon smirked. "Looks like Pauline will have to put all of these sumptuous items on the floor today. Your Levriettes will be so disappointed. So will I."

Claire narrowed her eyes at Jon, stuffed her arms with garments and then huffed off.

Jon wasn't sure exactly where she went. The minutes marched on while he slowly sipped his champagne, closed his eyes and sank further into the cushions.

"Feeling tipsy yet?" Claire inquired. Startled by her voice, Jon's eyes jolted open as he took in the vision before him.

Claire stood ten feet in front of him on a small wooden platform surrounded by a triple mirror, where he could easily consume every angle that reflected her slim, shapely silhouette. He worked his way up, starting with the black satin mule slippers on her feet. The slender heels were patent leather, and a fluff of flirtatious marabou feathers trimmed her toes, making her lean calves appear even longer. As his eyes wandered upwards, they took in a floor-sweeping emerald gown with a slit that exposed one bare leg all the way up to her waist. The rich green silk was accentuated by black French Leavers lace, which trailed across the shimmering fabric at an angle that accentuated the curve of Claire's waistline and bust. The lace was completely sheer in places, creating a subtle peekaboo effect along the hem, backs of her thighs and areolas. With Claire's hair still in an elegant updo, she was '50s movie star breathless… Grace Kelly reprised.

"Not bad for your first runway look," Jon encouraged. "A tad conservative for me personally, yet still very feminine. It's a keeper. Now, show me what else you got."

Claire shook her head at him, yet he detected a slight smile purse her lips. She was indignant, yet game, which pleased Jon as he clasped his hands and calmly waited for her next number.

About 10 minutes later, she reappeared, this time sporting a short kimono robe crafted from layered lace in rust red and gold. Burgundy fringe hung from the bell-shaped sleeves and edges of the front of the robe, which she left open just enough to tease Jon with a matching bra and bikini panty underneath. The bra fastened in the front with a tiny red bow, flattering Claire's cleavage. But the panty was even more revealing, as it plunged several inches below her navel and rested barely just on top of her pubic bone. Jon motioned for Claire to walk toward him and spin around. She obliged, showing the outline of a thong visible through the lace of the kimono.

"Hmmmm… Geisha suits you," Jon smiled, not giving away too much as he felt his cock twitch and begin to stiffen under his fly. The desire was nearly killing him, but he played it cool. "Add this to your basket. Next?"

Claire obliged, disappearing once again to the dressing room around the corner of the wall. Jon was growing increasingly amused and aroused by the little fashion show he invented, and he could barely wait for Claire to model her next number. Eventually, she reappeared.

What Jon saw next nearly sucked the breath out of him. Claire appeared wearing nothing but a leather spider web bodysuit. All of the straps were connected by a circle in the front just above her navel. They stretched across her abdomen, hips, bodice, breasts, and shoulders in an intricate pattern. The bodysuit concealed her nipples with red leather pasties in the shape of flowers. He was speechless.

"Well?" Claire inquired, waiting for his prolonged response as she stood shivering on the platform, clearly out of her element but willing to rise to the challenge.

"Um," he searched for the right words, shrugged his shoulders and then blurted, "I didn't know you were auditioning for an act in Cirque de Soleil..."

Claire took her cue and exited stage left without a word.

Jon was excited to see the other fashions as he refilled his Veuve Clicquot brut and hers as well. She took a long sip and waited for her to indulge him with another ensemble, this time hopefully more tasteful than the last. That number, although playful and displaying her body magnificently, was the antithesis of what Claire represented in all her sultry splendor. He anticipated that the other items that would showcase the alluring glamour he admired so much about her.

He checked he watch. It had been 15 minutes since Claire's last appearance. "Need some help in there?" Jon shouted toward her dressing room.

His question was met with silence. He waited another five minutes and then grabbed both glasses and headed toward her changing quarters. The door was closed, and he gave it a light knock. No response. Jon tapped again. "I brought you some champagne," he offered. Still nothing.

"Gee, I hope you're still breathing," Jon ribbed. Silence. He was growing a bit concerned, so he rattled the knob of the door. Surprisingly, it opened without just a slight nudge. Inside, he saw Claire, standing expressionless and to his surprise, naked.

"That is by far the BEST item I've seen on you yet!" Jon smiled broadly, handing Claire the flute of bubbly. "But why the hide 'n seek? I was anxiously awaiting your next runway appearance."

"Really?" Claire gasped. "Judging how disappointed you were with the last, I gathered the show was over."

"What are you talking about?" Jon was stunned. "With a body like yours, you can make anything look amazing. If you're referring to that last circus costume that looked like you were wearing a tightrope rather than walking on one, I was just joking. It wasn't really AP's finest. Put that and the leopard suit together, and we've got quite an act."

He took a step closer to her. "But, truth is, I'd rather be the one taming the pussy."

Claire didn't smile. "Is that all you want, Jon? Pussy?"

"Is that really what you think, Claire?" he matched her tone.

She just stared at him, giving him room to continue. The pause was uncomfortable, but the floor was clearly his. "I've certainly been presented with enough opportunities to get pussy anytime I wanted, from a variety of beautiful women, thanks to your persistent match-making attempts. Have I taken anyone up on the offer? Have I, Claire?" he pressed.

"Well, no…" she stammered.

"Then your question is answered," he concluded.

"I just don't know what you want from me," Claire murmured. "You're hard to read. On one hand, you're passionate, funny and attentive… on the other, you can be distant, reserved and sometimes even cutting. Your lack of consistency is confusing. I don't know which Jon I'm getting from day to day, or if you'll just decide to disappear altogether."

Jon paused to collect his thoughts. This was not the conversation he was expecting behind closed doors. "Claire, I don't know what to say, except to turn around and look at yourself in the mirror. What you just said of me could be the same of you. This reflection works both ways. Don't think for a second that this relationship is a one-sided risk. You're not the only one putting skin into this game, you know."

Claire could not help catch the pun as she stared at her naked reflection. Exposed. Vulnerable. Completely bare and void of any fashionable, yet protective, armor. Jon stared at her reflection from behind without uttering a word. He simply loosened his tie, unbuttoned his shirt, unhooked his belt and neatly stepped out of his clothes until he was completely naked.

"Now, we are one in the same," he whispered. "Defenseless. Naked. Scared."

Claire felt his arms wrap around her waist as he drew closer and tenderly kissed the top of her head. "I'm not going anywhere. The man you met at Coque d'Or is the same man who stands with you now. Except for one major difference…"

Claire waited for him to continue.

"I've fallen in love with you, Claire. All of you. Not just your body."

Now Jon waited for Claire to respond. She searched for the right words, but she lost her usual composure. Instead of words tumbling from her lips, tears escaped her lids. Jon stood patiently and dabbed her wet cheeks with his fingertips.

"Jon," Claire sniffed. "I can't…"

"You can't?" Jon repeated, feeling like a boulder had just crushed his heart. He longed to hear Claire validate his own feelings with her own. The depth of emotion he felt toward her had caught him equally by surprise, and clearly not what he had envisioned when Mac handed him his marching orders. Now, for the first time in his life, the smug FBI agent faced the toughest assignment yet, and she was standing right before him.

"I can't… hold back any longer. I feel the same about you," she said, turning to face him.

Inwardly, Jon breathed a sigh of relief. The last thing he wanted to do was lose her. Despite her tear-stained cheeks and softening of the typically well-coiffed, polished Claire, she had never looked more beautiful to him than now. Her raw vulnerability made her even more attractive from the inside out. A real woman.

"How about we CAN?" Jon smiled, pulling her in close. She didn't resist but fit perfectly into his form as his lips devoured hers fully, passionately. Claire was just as eager as they embraced in an inseparable kiss, both mad with desire. He tenderly cupped her breasts, feeling the swell of her taut nipples beneath his fingertips. His thumb slowly circled her areolas, sending a warm tingle rippling through her body as if it were hard-wired to her womanhood. Jon's fingers then trailed down Claire's torso, teasing her with light strokes that betrayed the depth of his kisses as their tongues intertwined.

Claire thrust her pelvis forward, pleading Jon to touch her in the most intimate of spots. He didn't immediately placate, but let their repartee build into prolonged anticipation of the pleasure that awaited them both. Meanwhile, his cock twitched as Claire pressed herself more insistently into Jon's hips, feeling the dew between her thighs.

Jon continued the kiss, but not the touch. Instead, he gently nudged her toward the long bench of the dressing room. He placed his hands on her shoulders but, instead of facing each other, he spun Claire around so that he faced her back. She felt his stiffness press into her buttocks as pulled her even closer from behind.

"Do you feel how hard I am?" he whispered in her ear. "That's what you do to me. My cock is so eager to explore every inch of you…"

Claire moaned as she ground her buttocks into Jon's shaft, rubbing up and down, enveloping him in the crevice of her cheeks. He silently urged her to recline face-down on the bench, which was covered with a black velvet cushion. Jon straddled Claire from that position, as she felt the warmth of his and caress her back with tender, loving touches. His lips followed, slowly easing down her neck and her spine. She tried to turn over, but to no avail.

"Don't move," he softly scolded. "I've thought of nothing but this moment all day… the pleasure of basking in your extreme femininity."

"Mmmmm…" Claire grinned ear to ear, so giddy with happiness that she could barely contain herself, which was a rarity.

Jon's presence filled her with sensual warmth, as he gently straddled Claire, covering her like an incredibly soft, comforting blanket… tickling her senses as he nibbled her ear and breathed deeply.

"I want to make love to you and show you all the affection I've built up for you," he whispered as his body completely eclipsed her.

"That's exactly how I feel about you. I have so much passion for you…" Claire agreed, succumbing to Jon's will.

He moaned softly in her ear as his hips thrust into her buttocks. "My cock is throbbing, ready to burst," he teased. He took pleasure in allowing just the tip to press into the entry of Claire's womanhood, but no further. He wanted to delay the gratification until neither one of them could stand another second. It required immense will-power, as his cock was raging in a state of full arousal.

"I want you…" Claire panted. "Please…"

"Not yet," he lightly reprimanded, pulling back just a bit to prolong the pleasure. "Raise your hips." Jon placed his forefinger lightly on her clit and, with the slightest of pressure, stroked Claire from behind.

Claire's pussy was drenched—a waterfall in Jon's hands. She arched her pelvis higher, like a cat. The lips of her naked pussy were pink, swollen and glistening. "FUCK ME!" she begged. "I can't take this much longer!"

"Can't take what?" Jon jested, and he stopped stroking her clit. There was a moment of silence. No words, no touching, and it felt like hours.

At just the right moment, Claire felt the head of Jon's cock glide across her clit. They lay down flat together as he pumped her from behind, his shaft sliding between her lips—not entering her fully just yet, but enjoying the welcome she had created.

They sunk into each other's warmth—a perfect fit— so incredibly close that they could merge into one being. Their intimacy and intensity melded, and their bodies melted as they gently rocked together. This time, Jon slid fully into Claire, thrusting into her full depths. They danced to their own rhythm, so smoothly and serenely, picking up the beat, then slowing down again, gliding into ecstasy.

They lost themselves in the sensual symphony of their lovemaking. Their bodies knew each other so innately, that one waited for the other without having to utter a word. At just the right time, Claire and Jon exploded in an all-consuming unison and drifted into another dimension made just for them in the seclusion of AP's private dressing room, without a single care in the world. And, once again, without a bed.

CHAPTER SIXTEEN

In Security

As Claire sauntered confidently back to the La Levrier from AP, she couldn't help but smile. The last thing she had ever expected to find during her trip to the boutique was Jon, and yet he had cleverly found her. He had proven to be quite the charming sleuth, not only with Margot, her secretary, but with Pauline, AP's manager. The day had indeed taken quite an unanticipated turn, and that and would just continue.

Claire became so absorbed in recounting every sensual detail with Jon in the dressing room that she almost didn't notice one major addition to her office as she slipped her shawl off and tossed it over the back of her loveseat.

"My God, you scared the Hell out of me!" Claire gasped while flicking on her Tiffany desk lamp.

"Hello to you, too," he grinned. "I didn't think I needed to schedule an appointment unless, of course, you're busy."

Wearing tight jeans, a black muscle T, tinted black-rimmed glasses and a short, cropped haircut with matching grey scruff, Ted Bernardin grinned mischievously as he uncrossed his right thigh and shifted legs.

"No, my next appointment isn't until another hour from now," Claire smiled at her younger brother. "You just surprised me showing up on a whim."

"Yeah, I know," he admitted. "But I got some intel that I thought you know about. It really can't wait."

"What, Teddy? You're getting married… to what's his name? Fazo?" Claire beamed.

"Oh, Gawd! Fazo is so yesterday. Come on, you know I've been seeing Jorge going on about eight months now. And, NO, we're not even close to talking rings."

"How is it that we live under the same roof here at La Levrier and even I can't keep track of your latest conquests?" Claire ribbed.

"Everything about me is top secret. You know that. That's what I do best," he said. "Which is why…" Ted continued, swinging Claire's office door shut with a single push from where he sat, "we need to talk."

Whenever Ted prefaced a conversation with a "we need to talk" statement, he meant business. He took his duties as chief security officer for La Levrier very seriously.

"Want some coffee?" Claire offered.

Ted shook his head. "I just had a venti frap. Your K-cup can't compete, Sis."

"Okay, the last time you came to me it was about that homophobe member… who, was it, that Doug Elzinga, who flipped out when discovered that La Levrier welcomed LGBT members? Remember, he insisted on having his sheets boiled and threatened to infest this place with rats to exterminate all the gays? You bounced him right out of here!" Claire chuckled.

"Don't remind me," Ted groaned. "That jagg-off wasn't exactly a lightweight. I was bruised and sore for days after our little tussle."

At 5'10 and 195 pounds of solid muscle, Ted was a built like a brick—the result of his stringent daily fitness and taekwondo regimen. Stealth and silent, he was a real undercover asset not only to Claire but to every member of La Levrier.

"And then there was that horrible incident recently with Preston and Gabrielle. I still don't think she has fully recovered. What an ass he turned out to be!" Claire said.

"Yep, agreed," Ted nodded. "Which is why I think you need to take tighter precautions when screening prospective new members. In fact, I highly recommend we do routine spot checks even on current members for added safety."

"Come on, Teddy, we already conduct extensive background investigations on all new applicants, and if anything pops up as a red flag, they're out of here!" Claire scoffed. "Our security policies have always worked, so where's all this coming from? Some new workshop you attended? I mean, occasionally someone slips through the cracks..."

"Claire, that's just it—we can't afford slip-ups! It's a different world now than when La Levrier first opened. Our security procedures need to change," Ted insisted.

Claire waved her hand dismissively. "I think you're overreacting, but if you feel so strongly about this, why don't you put your recommendations in a proposal and I'll review it next week?"

"No, Claire, we have an immediate concern here. Trust me on this one," Ted interrupted.

"Okay, what in the Hell is going on?" Claire demanded, whirling around from her Keurig with an empty mug.

"Look, I'm not trying to stress you out, so take this tidbit for what it's worth," Ted began. "My sources tell me that someone's been poking around in our business, and it's significant enough to hit my radar."

"Who? The CPD?" Claire looked only slightly concerned as if she was confident that La Levrier would pass the muster of any local inspection.

"No," Ted stated simply. "That would be child's play. God only knows we've maintained a pretty low profile with the Chicago police over the years."

"Well, then, WHO, Ted?" Claire demanded.

"Look, don't shoot the messenger," Ted held up his hands. "I'm not one hundred percent sure, but it looks like it might be the doings of some government agency."

"WHAT?" Claire blurted. "Are you kidding me?"

"Hey, I've still got to do my own investigation to validate this leak, but I just thought you ought to know sooner than later. In the meantime, I'm tightening security provisions and hiring some extra bodies to stroll around, especially at night. All with your permission, of course."

"Sure, that's fine. Do what you have to do, I guess..." Claire sighed.

"Geez, you don't seem to understand the gravity of this situation," Ted frowned.

"It's just... well, I don't know how after all this time, La Levrier would suddenly be the target of some government probe. Are we talking at the federal level?"

"That's a possibility," Ted admitted. "I'm not ruling anything out."

"But HOW..." Claire stammered.

"You know HOW, Claire," Ted countered firmly. "When you play with matches, you might start a fire."

Claire shook her head in disbelief. "I've always been incredibly careful."

"Careful enough to outsmart the intelligence of the U.S. government?" he challenged. "I've told you time and time again not to take on certain clients like Senator Cohn and Congressman Harding and above all, the Veep, for God's sake!"

"Ted, they're people just like us. They have needs. They have desires. They have…"

"They have a public profile, Claire! Don't you get it? La Levrier might as well be sporting a bullseye on our rooftop for national security target practice. The instant you let any dignitary or celebrity through these doors, we're fucking marked."

"But the whole reason that the elite come to La Levrier is that they feel safe and protected. Thanks to your airtight security operations, they have a safe haven where they can explore their private desires," Claire reassured her brother.

"Sure, that's a great selling point for La Levrier, but at what cost? Is the price of their membership and the cache of their position worth getting us busted? Not to mention what happens to their reputation in the spotlight once their cover is blown? Did you ever consider THAT little detail?" Ted challenged.

"But Teddy, that's why YOU'RE here," Claire retorted. "I wouldn't trust anyone but you at the helm of La Levrier's security. You've never once failed us, despite some pretty close encounters in the past."

"While I appreciate your vote of confidence, we can't be too cavalier. This might be even too big of a mess for me to clean up if it explodes," he said. "I'm not taking any chances. Going forward, we need to make some changes and be extra vigilant."

"But respectful of our members' privacy, of course," Claire added. "We can't sound off alarms or make them feel uncomfortable in any way."

"That's a given," Ted agreed. "Rest assured; I'll get to the bottom of this, no matter what it takes!"

CHAPTER SEVENTEEN

On the Job

If Jon Fenwick and Ted Bernardin had one thing in common, it was determination. No sooner did Ted tell Claire that he would get to the bottom of the security investigation than he bolted from her office on a mission. What troubled Ted more than anything was that Claire wasn't taking this matter seriously. At least not enough. Maybe that was because he had intentionally spared her the grim details from his informants. Never had Ted's undercover network steered him wrong but, as La Levrier's chief security officer, he was obligated to conduct his own due diligence to check out the validity of their claims. Any hidden bugs, cameras or plants on La Levrier property had to be immediately exposed and destroyed. But this wouldn't be easy when he was dealing with the caliber of a classified agency he had never before encountered in his security career. While Ted was no amateur, he was no match for the Federal Bureau of Investigation. Until he could verify all the facts, he had avoided naming the FBI in his chat with Claire, as he didn't want to sound like an alarmist.

Jon, on the other hand, had already begun to set out on his own mission. As Mac reminded him during every encounter, the clock was ticking as D-Day, or Day 14, drew nearer. His attempt to enact Plan A had failed miserably in Mac's eyes. It seemed that unless he uncovered any earth-shattering evidence over the next 24 hours to put Plan A back on the table, Plan B would be inevitable. That meant that leveling La Levrier was the only option to kill the operation with the fool-proof finality that the FBI demanded. Any hesitation or hint of Jon's ability to follow through would spell his own death sentence with the agency. While Jon's long-standing loathing of Mac was a deterrent, he never let it stand in the way of his pride. If anything, it propelled him with even greater vigor to prove her wrong and maintain his standing with the FBI. He had invested way too much in his career to ever let anyone compromise his future and his loyalty to his profession.

Just as Jon's passion for the FBI could not be swayed, neither could the passion he felt for Claire. After their last encounter at AP, his feelings for her were undeniable. That is, undeniably real. He could no longer rationalize that he was drawn only to her femininity, her sophistication, and her style. She was the embodiment of every woman he had envisioned as his equal, partner and soulmate. He could tolerate a thousand Macs on the job, but losing one Claire off the job would be an irreplaceable loss. As much as he hesitated to admit it, he couldn't envision life without her. At the same time, he couldn't envision life without the FBI.

To do his job would destroy Claire, yet to not do his job would destroy him, his career and his future. If Plan B was inevitable, maybe there was a way that Jon could do both and everyone could escape unharmed. He rationalized that Claire was so resilient that she could always rebuild her business. She would never need to know that Jon was behind the mayhem. As long as the explosion looked like an accident and Jon executed an escape plan, he could get Claire and everyone safely out of the Astor Street mansion. La Levrier would someday rise from the ashes and, at that point, Mac would be long gone—hopefully reassigned to another post at the FBI. Meanwhile, his success with this case would elevate Jon to excellent standing, and he could move back to the high-profile assignments for which he was destined. What happened with Operation Viking was ancient history, and Jon vowed that he would never set sail on those seas again to the point of drowning in misjudgment. He had learned to tame his ego, as Claire had mellowed him considerably.

Claire. He simply had to see her again. Recalling her frosty reaction to the lapse of time after their first lovemaking encounter, he did not want to do anything to upset their delicate state of affairs. Time was of the essence, both because he wanted—and needed—to be with Claire and because of Mac's mandate. Like it or not, these were the official orders of the FBI, and he had to act, which meant stepping up his sleuthing or risk losing his job. First, Jon decided to make a stop at RL for an Angus burger, then head to La Levrier where he could put the wheels of his mission in motion.

7:00 p.m. that evening

7:45 p.m.

Jon headed back down the hall after his brush with Ted, cussing silently to himself. He knew exactly who Ted was, having witnessed Claire's brother escort a rather intoxicated and surly member out of Claire's office a couple of weeks earlier.

A little deeper digging had turned up the stats of Theodore Andrew Bernardin. Age 38, single and active member of the LGBT community. He frequented the East Bank Club daily for regular workouts with his personal trainer and lover Jorge Bruns, drank only craft beer and got his humble start in a security-related career working as a bouncer at She-nannigans on Chicago's famous Division Street at the age of 19. He then pursued an education in private investigation from St. Xavier University and earned his Illinois PI license. Of course, there was no mention of Ted's position at La Levrier in any public documentation, but one could assume he had been Claire's chief security officer and right-hand since Day One.

Jon replayed the scene of his run-in with Ted earlier that night. It clearly didn't go well and, in retrospect, Jon wished he would have forgone the attitude. Jon now feared that Ted would dash straight to Claire and tell her of their encounter. Claire would question why Jon was prowling around her office, but he could easily pass it off as though he were looking for her. That indeed wouldn't be a lie. He desperately wanted to see her, even though it had only been a few hours since they were together in the early afternoon.

In fact, now would be a good time for a nightcap. Jon headed to the main lounge, where he was confident Claire might be, mingling with other members in the mahogany-paneled room with its signature gold-topped bar. He assumed a stool and ordered a Ketel One on the rocks with a splash of Bombay Sapphire. The room was alive tonight with members making small talk over the tunes of the Steinway whose keys were tinkling under the strokes of the talented pianist.

"It's Open Night," commented Barron, the bartender on duty, as if reading Jon's thoughts. "Looks like you're kinda new here. Once a month, La Levrier hosts a social gathering for members to meet other members, if they so choose. Some of our members are attached, while others enjoy more flexibility and variety, shall we say. How about you?"

"I'm… uh… one of the attached ones," Jon responded, not telling a total lie. He now considered himself attached to a certain Claire Bernardin. A woman whom he was growing increasingly impatient to see.

"Well, you're perfectly welcome here in the lounge at any time. The festivities just began about 10 minutes ago. I expect that Ms. Bernardin will be arriving shortly to welcome our guests and say a few words."

Jon's heart jolted at the mere mention of her name. He could not have timed his visit to the bar any better. He only hoped that Ted had not gotten to her first. Jon found himself glancing at the large mirror at the back of the bar, just as he did on the night he awaited her arrival after their first rendezvous. In contrast, his heart was much heavier now with emotion as he anticipated seeing her reflection any second, floating into the rose mahogany paneled room in all her splendor. He wondered what gown she would wear… the shade of her lipstick… the style of her hair… the scent of her perfume… the first words she would say to him, hopefully, preceded by a smile. "God," he thought to himself, "I'm back to third grade with a crush on Melissa Stinson. Snap out of it, Jon!"

Fifteen minutes passed, and Jon found himself checking his A. Lange & SÖhne watch every five. "Barron, when is Claire, I mean, Ms. Bernardin, expected? I was really looking forward to seeing her tonight," he queried, trying to suppress the hint of anxiety in his voice.

Barron studied the large gilded clock on the opposite wall and furrowed his brow. "Hmmmm… she seems to be running a bit late this evening. She must have gotten detained, but I expect her soon. Ms. Bernardin never misses an Open Night."

Jon hoped that Barron was right, but his instincts told him otherwise. Claire was always punctual, and it would be unlike her not to properly host her guests as the mistress of ceremonies. With every minute that Claire didn't show, Jon's thoughts raced. What did Ted say to her? How would she take it? Would she confront Jon? Would she avoid him? Would this spell the end of their relationship?

Fuck Mac. If she hadn't tightened the screws on his back about busting "La Luuvray," he wouldn't have needed to take extreme measures and find himself in the tenuous position he just did. But, no, she was so insistent on that damn ticking clock that he had to prowl around like a Hardy Boy and get himself caught. He shouldn't have been so sloppy, either. That was his own fault. But Jon accomplished what he had to, and he hoped it would be enough to placate Mac. However, that was now the least of his concerns.

He swigged down the final sip of his cocktail and noticed that the pianist had stopped playing, most of the members had paired off and the crowd had thinned considerably since when he first took his seat at the bar. Still no sign of Claire. It was getting late, and he thought to text her but decided against it. Maybe it was just best to leave their day on the high note they had when parting from

AP earlier that afternoon, giddy after their lovemaking session. If Claire was upset, she would need time to digest any news Ted had shared. Now would not be the time to provoke her. It would do them both good to sleep on it tonight, and he would contact her tomorrow morning.

That next morning couldn't come soon enough. Jon wanted to be sure he was awake early to start the day on the right foot, and that meant getting a restful sleep—that is, if he could manage it. Tonight, he decided, would be spent at La Levrier. He ordered another Ketel One to go, slipped the key from his pocket and headed to his suite, hoping it was still available to him.

CHAPTER EIGHTEEN

The Mark

"Mr. Fenwick, Sir..." Jon heard a familiar voice echo down the corridor on the way to his private quarters from his trip to the lounge downstairs. Jon looked over his shoulder to see Kenneth scampering behind him, eager to catch up. Jon was prepared to hear the inevitable—that he was no longer welcome here and that his membership was terminated. He summoned a half smile and turned his weary eyes toward Kenneth to acknowledge his presence. At least it wasn't Ted, he sighed with relief.

"May I show you to your suite?" Kenneth offered enthusiastically. He seemed eager to assist, so Jon allowed him to escort him the rest of the way. As the key turned in the lock, Jon instantly felt great relief as the door readily swung open. Kenneth waved his hand to motion Jon into the room and took a slight bow. Jon nodded in gratitude—a silent signal that Kenneth was dismissed.

As Jon entered his room, he realized it had been way too long since he had stayed overnight at La Levrier. His suite was spotless and much attention to customize the amenities to his personal preferences showed in the great care taken to make it perfect. Jon's private bar boasted his favorite elixirs, the glass café table with two glass bar stools was gleaming and the pillows on his modern grey sofa were fluffed as if anticipating an evening of entertainment.

In fact, Jon's private quarters were exactly as he had left them except for one new addition hanging on the wall above his loveseat. Perhaps he had never noticed it previously, or perhaps the impact of the sketch had previously not registered its uncanny resemblance to the woman he adored. But there it was—a vintage Erte print of a statuesque dame parading her greyhound on a leash as she sported a flowing white gown, matching turban and fur stole twirled around her arm. The stark white silhouette of the woman and dog contrasted sharply against a midnight black background in true art deco style. Funny how much the image now spoke to him as he envisioned Claire strolling down Astor Street with Javert and Marius, as if transcending the framed art.

Except for Kenneth's greeting and the familiarity of his suite, Jon felt like an unwelcome stranger at La Levrier, jaded by his encounter with Ted and unsure of what had kept Claire away from her guests tonight. His uncertainty twisted into anxiety as Jon took a final swig of his Ketel One from his earlier visit to the bar and tried to calm his thoughts.

"Maybe she just got caught up with another engagement..." Jon rationalized.

"She probably didn't show because she wasn't expecting me..." he told himself.

"I'll bet she just went to take a quick nap and fell asleep..." Jon sighed.

As these excuses swirled through his mind, Jon entered his bedroom. It was a well-appointed masculine ensemble with mahogany plank flooring, a hemp throw rug and a rustic teak chandelier inset in a tray ceiling. The walls were painted mocha and trimmed with white crown molding which matched the bed sheets, duvet cover and plump throw pillows in assorted patterns adorning Jon's king-sized sleigh bed. Above his headboard were four heavy black frames arranged in a square formation. They each contained smaller Erte prints boasting a goddess, a dancer, a flapper girl and a harpist. Despite all of its sophisticated splendor, the room felt hollow to Jon as it echoed his own aching void.

He sat on the edge of his bed and slowly untied and slipped off his oxfords, socks and rest of his attire, wishing it wasn't his own fingers unbuttoning his shirt and unfastening his pants. What a lonely sensation it was to be solo in an empty room of a house designed for passionate encounters, especially when Jon was so intimately involved with the owner.

The tranquilizing effects of his cocktail were starting to descend as Jon slid under the covers and sunk into his pillows after his nightly cleansing ritual. With face washed, teeth brushed and lights out, Jon succumbed to the fatigue he felt in his bones, but his mind went elsewhere. Back to Claire.

She was everywhere. She stared at him from the Erte artwork in the suite. Her essence filled Jon. He was there next to her, touching her, gazing at her, gliding his fingers across her tender skin. He was engulfed by the image and feeling of Claire and all the moments they had shared from their first encounter at Coq D'Or to their last afternoon at Agent Provacateur.

He could feel the softness of her feminine form as she curled next to his frame, filling his arms. She belonged to

Jon, and he to her, like two halves uniting after a lifetime apart. He could almost sense her breath on his face as her lips gently brushed his cheek, barely touching the stubble that had begun to form as nighttime descended. The silky strands of her loose hair tickled his neck erotically as her lips slid from his face to his chest. Her tiny kisses felt feather-light, almost ethereal, as he floated in the delicacy of her presence. As his breathing deepened, her tongue followed suit, flickering ever so tenderly right below his beltline.

The teasing continued, as Claire's tongue wandered lower. Jon's mind drifted to her beautiful face nestled in the privacy of his most intimate zone. His fully aroused cock twitched eagerly in anticipation of getting lost in this glorious moment when he could recapture the dream of his fantasies. His senses drank her in. Every pore of his being succumbed to the sensation of his cock sliding between her lips, being caressed by her tongue and inching deeper into the welcoming tunnel of her mouth.

Deliberately and slowly, she sucked until his shaft was throbbing. She rolled her tongue, toying with his tip until he felt like he was going to burst. Just as Jon was on the verge, Claire surprised him and withdrew her lips. At that point, he knew he must have awakened. That is, until she swung her thigh over, mounted his cock and straddled Jon with a force of passion. This was no dream. Claire was live, in the flesh and unleashing a fierce desire that exceeded his wildest imagination.

He could barely make out her silhouette in the dimly lit room, but Jon knew that this was Claire. No other woman felt, tasted and excited him the way she did. He took her face in his and brought his mouth to hers, expressing all the desire he felt in deep, endless kisses.

Their bodies were inseparable, gliding on the same plane as their mutual arousal heightened. Her hips thrust faster and more forcefully, riding him with a lustful pace that pushed Jon to a new plateau. He matched her stride, eager to please and ready to explode. It wasn't long before she yelped and released a low, guttural cry of ecstasy. As soon as Jon felt her pussy lips clench against his shaft, he wasn't too far behind. He pressed his pelvis closer and plunged with all his might, releasing a torrent of all the affection he had been holding back in her absence.

Wave after wave of passion flowed between them, as their bodies couldn't deny what their hearts felt. Overwhelmed and exhausted with emotion, Jon and Claire collapsed in each other's arms and he held her tight. He never wanted to let her out of his sight after such exquisite lovemaking. Not now. Not ever.

The night swept over them, seducing both into a peaceful slumber. The morning arrived all too early and Jon awoke to an emptiness in his gut. He noticed that Claire was not where he found her last night—beside him. He rubbed his eyes and peered through the dusky light filtering through the blinds. His room was empty and strangely quiet. "Claire?" he called out. No response.

Was it all a dream or had their encounter last night really happened? He looked to his left and saw that the pillow and bedsheets where she had slept were rumpled. Normally Jon was a sound sleeper—not a thrasher—so these would have been intact had he been alone. The question was why, after such an amazing night, would Claire leave his room? Then Jon spotted the note.

It was on his bed stand, tucked in an envelope with a single letter "J" on the outside. His heart thumped in his chest as he ran his fingernail on the underside of the flap and gingerly peeled it back, careful not to tear its contents. Inside was a single piece of Claire's signature stationary and, penned in her elegant handwriting, was the following:

J,

Last night's lovemaking was unparalleled—such depth and passion I've never before encountered. You me us there's so much more I want to experience. So much more of you I want to understand. But I'm afraid, Jon. I'm afraid that I cannot take this any further, knowing that there are still secrets between us.

Ted approached me yesterday with some news that left me feeling betrayed. I am baffled by your motives. Without trust, there cannot be an "us."

I know as you read this, you will be wondering why I came to see you last night. The time we shared was as real for me as it was for you. I wanted to see if my feelings for you were genuine, despite knowing what I know now. They were they are. Therein lies my problem, Jon.

Am I sleeping with the enemy? Giving myself to a man whose mission is suspect? Putting my heart and my business in the line of fire? I cannot afford to compromise all that I've worked so hard for my entire life. You, of all people, should understand my ethical dilemma. Either you tell me the truth or I will be forced to uncover it for myself.

I am giving you a final chance to explain yourself. Please meet me in my office at 9:30 a.m. this morning. I will be expecting you.

C

What choice did Jon have now? He was clearly marked—Ted's target. Jon's attempts at subterfuge had gone awry. It wasn't the first time his FBI investigation had backfired, but one thing was for certain: it was his worst. A surge of panic rose in his chest, and all the emotion he felt from last night's encounter sunk and gripped his heart.

Jon retreated to his bathroom, turned on the shower spigot, slipped behind the glass door and faced the hot water that pelted his skin like stones. Mac launched the first in a rapid-fire round of accusations. His skin has grown thick and impervious to her attacks over the years of knowing that was her style, so he had learned to weather her swipes. Then came Ted with a fresh pummeling. The rocks that Ted flung in his direction stung slightly deeper. Jon couldn't deny that a man he barely knew and whose PI experience was far inferior had outsmarted him and, worse, was the brother of the woman he loved. But, of course, the most painful of all was the single boulder that Claire had just hurled. It hit his stomach like a bomb. An interesting choice of words for a man who specialized in demolitions and had been planning to take down La Levrier.

The moment of truth was finally here. Just like his wet, naked skin fresh from the shower, Jon felt totally exposed. But it wasn't the vulnerability that bothered him or even what loomed in Claire's office in 30 minutes. It was the fact that the previous night—the first time that they had ever made love in a bed—would now be their last.

Jon shaved, brushed his teeth and selected his favorite navy-and-white checkered shirt, blue vest with subtle grey pinstripes and tan leather buttons and dark denim dress jeans. The ensemble worked—it was casually formal, but not over the top. He fixed a cup of coffee at his bar and allowed himself a few minutes of peace to collect himself. Just as his watch was about to hit 9:20, he heard a subtle scratch on his door. Thinking it might be the scraping of another note being slid under the frame, he went to open it.

Standing at attention was a familiar figure. Tall, statuesque and rather stately looking, his escort stood patiently.

"Marius, what a surprise to see you!" Jon smiled. The Greyhound looked Jon in the eye and subtly lowered his head. It was a cue that the time had arrived for Jon to leave for his meeting with Claire, and he followed Marius out the door, down the long hallway and to the bank of elevators that awaited his descent.

CHAPTER NINETEEN

Back to the Principal's Office

Jon followed Marius closely as the greyhound instinctively led him to the office of his mistress. La Levrier was atypically quiet this morning, which made Jon feel a tad uneasy. He quickly pushed aside any anxious thoughts. He mustered the skills he employed on the job, showing no physical display of the emotions that stirred inside him. Yet, his control shook when it was Danielle—not Claire's usual receptionist—who opened the door to the reception area and greeted him with an equal poker face.

"Mr. Fenwick is here," Danielle announced as she tapped the closed door to Claire's office.

"Please see him in," Claire responded. Danielle nudged open the door and held it for Jon to enter.

The instant he saw Claire, he wanted to melt. She looked impeccable in a Chanel woven ivory suit consisting of a short-tapered jacket with three-quarter length sleeves and gleaming gold buttons, a matching cream skirt with a mid-thigh hem and black silk cowl neck blouse that fell in soft folds around her collarbone. Her hair coiled into a neat French twist, just like the time he first laid eyes on her at Coq D'Or. She stood up from behind her desk to acknowledge his presence and when their eyes met, she offered a slight, knowing nod, trying to keep the tone strictly professional.

Perhaps that was because the proverbial elephant in the room was sitting in the chair just across from his sister. Not a surprise, of course. Jon as much suspected that Ted would be present and part of today's proceedings. Danielle offered Jon some coffee, but he politely refused. He was accustomed to Mac's blunt interrogation, and he felt a similar vibe in the room.

Claire cleared her throat as she invited Jon to take a seat across from her desk next to Ted, while Danielle assumed the loveseat by the coffee service.

"Jon," Claire began cordially, "thank you for joining us this morning. I think we know what this is about, so let's get right down to business, shall we? Ted informed me of last night's unexpected encounter, and I've invited Danielle to join us to document this discussion. In the event when there is ever an issue with a guest of La Levrier, our policy is to address such issues swiftly and fairly. There are always two sides to every story, and I'm hoping that this morning we can come to one version of the truth."

Ted's eyes bore into Jon as Claire opened the meeting, but Jon remained impervious to his old school intimidation technique.

"Of course, Ms. Bernardin," Jon replied with equal decorum and a twinge of sarcasm. "How can I help you today?"

"You can start by telling us exactly what you were doing in Ms. Bernardin's office after hours last night," Ted fired at him, launching his first missile.

"IN Ms. Bernardin's office?" Jon questioned calmly. "I recall that when you and I met, I was in the hallway outside of her office and I told you that I was looking for her."

Ted shifted in his seat and leaned closer to Jon, looking him straight in the eye. "I remember our encounter quite well, Mr. Fenwick," he stated. "But I have proof that you were actually inside her office."

"Ted, if you're referring to my opening the door of her office to see if Ms. Bernardin was inside working, you're correct. But as soon as I saw that she was not at her desk, I left," Jon explained.

"Did you consider knocking first to see if Ms. Bernardin was present?" Ted persisted. "Not only is it uncharacteristic for guests to be in this area after hours, but also common etiquette would dictate that a couple of knocks on the door would reveal whether she's available to receive anyone."

"I tapped a few times," Jon responded. "But got no answer. At that point, I pushed the door slightly, which was ajar, to see if she was there. It was an obvious breach of etiquette. My bad."

"Mr. Fenwick, not only did you 'push the door slightly,' you made a home for yourself right at her desk. The very desk we're sitting across from right now, in fact," Ted retorted, sweeping the desk with his hand.

"That's a pretty bold accusation, considering you just stopped me in the hallway. I'd like to know on what basis you have any proof," Jon challenged.

"Don't underestimate me," Ted warned. "I do my job, and I do it well, as I'm certain you do yours, Agent Fenwick."

Jon met Ted's gaze, unfazed. "*Agent* Fenwick?" he chuckled. "While I appreciate the accolade, I'm afraid you must have me confused with someone else, Sherlock."

"The only person who is confused around here is you… about your identity, it seems," Ted smirked.

"Teddy!" Claire interjected. "Show some respect. The purpose of this meeting is to discuss last night's incident, not to attack our guest."

"Last night's incident and our guest's identity are closely related," Ted defended. "There was a deliberate motive behind why Jon Fenwick was in your office after hours. And I have reason to believe that he was on a mission to uncover some intelligence."

"Yes, you could say that," Jon smiled to himself. *"I wanted to uncover one intelligent beauty."* Of course, he didn't say those words aloud, but they weren't far from the truth.

"Teddy...er, Ted," Jon responded. "I'm both flattered and offended by your perception of me. I obviously crossed a line last night by wandering into Ms. Bernardin's office area without an appointment. I said I was sorry, and it won't happen again. But my 'motives,' as you say, were well intended. I wanted to see her."

"You wanted to see Ms. Bernardin so badly that you moved an entire file cabinet in her office? Did you think she was under it or perhaps hiding in a drawer?" Ted badgered as he leaned even closer to Jon, almost in his face.

Jon didn't flinch in response to Ted's bullying. Instead, he replied calmly, "I don't know what you're talking about, and I resent the implication. As I said previously, I just wanted to see Ms. Bernardin."

"And what did you want to *see* her specifically about?" Ted pressed.

"With all due respect, Ted, that's really none of your business," Jon scoffed.

"When someone interferes with my sister's business, it's my business to protect *her* business. So, yes, it is *my* business," Ted spat.

At that point, Claire stepped back in. "What—and how—is this information relevant to your investigation, Ted? Where are you going with this?"

"Mr. Fenwick's motives are extremely relevant to my investigation. It seems unlikely that you would move your own heavy file cabinet and leave your desk light on when you're so eco-conscious. And, it seems even less likely that Mr. Fenwick was just paying you a social call after hours," Ted retorted.

Jon exchanged glances with Claire and then made a bold move.

"Okay, Ted, you busted me," he relented. "I was paying a social call to Ms. Bernardin—to whom I will now refer to as 'Claire'—after hours. And do you want to know why? Because I am in love with her."

Ted opened his mouth as if to object but remained speechless. Secretly, Jon delighted in his ability to throw such a curveball. An awkward pause hung in the air for a minute, and finally, Ted regained his composure.

"So, Mr. Fenwick, are you now telling me that you are a stalker?"

"No, I am not," Jon said smiled. "I'm telling you that I'm in love with your sister."

"You're kidding, right?" Ted chuckled sarcastically. "Claire, should I escort Mr. Fenwick off the property now?"

Claire looked up, blushing, from behind her reading glasses and scanned both faces—first Jon and then Ted. "No, Ted," she said softly. "Mr. Fenwick... Jon... is telling the truth."

"And the feeling is mutual? *Really?*" Ted pressed.

"Yes, quite," Claire stated. "But it's something that is very private and needs to be kept only in this room. Ted and

Danielle, I assume I have your word that this shall remain a personal manner, not to be shared with staff or members."

Danielle obliged with a nod, although she and other La Levrier staff members so much as suspected so, and the rumors were already swirling. Ted eyed Claire cynically and then he glared at Jon before speaking again. "Whatever game you two are playing is very dangerous, and one of you is going to get hurt. I just hope it's not my sister for your sake, Agent Fenwick."

"Ted, that's enough!" Claire insisted, rising from her seat. "We just told you our secret. If Jon said he wasn't snooping, he wasn't snooping. Give him the benefit of the doubt. And drop this 'agent' stuff, will you?"

"I'll drop this 'agent stuff' once your lover confesses why he's really here. They say love is blind, and I can see that you've lost all peripheral vision, Claire. You're too focused on your feelings to see your Peeping Jon for who he really is."

"And who is that, Ted? Because, so help me, if you're wrong, I'll have no qualms about dismissing you from La Levrier and from my life!" Claire asserted, losing her proverbial cool.

"Do you want to tell her or shall I do the honors?" Ted asked Jon, ignoring his sister's tirade.

Jon contemplated his next move carefully. Did Ted really know the truth about him? He decided to find out.

"Okay, okay," Jon began his confession. "Yes, I'm Agent Jon Fenwick. I still go by that sometimes. It kind of stuck after I left the FBI many years ago before I started my own consulting business. Yeah, like you, Ted, I know a thing or two about security. Might you have heard about the Mac Lock? I invented it. It's now in almost every financial services institution across the U.S. and in 27 countries worldwide. Lately, my firm has been running full speed ahead on international cybersecurity threat investigations. Wanna know more?"

"I've learned quite enough, Agent Fenwick," Ted smirked. "I can see that you and I have so much in common. Right down to our love of Lamborghini Aventadors. At least you have good taste in two things: women and cars."

"You got that right, Ted," Jon concurred. "No one surpasses Claire, and nothing handles better than a Lamborghini Aventador Roadster."

"Not even an Aston Martin. All hype and no torque. I drove a Rapide once and the steering was shit. You also have to be under 5 feet to squeeze inside the thing. I'd imagine you'd be too tall to even take it for a spin."

"Yeah, maybe," Jon agreed. "But I sure as hell wouldn't turn it down if given the opportunity."

"You mean you've never been behind the wheel of an Aston?" Ted inquired, surprised.

"Nope, but it's on my bucket list," Jon chuckled.

"Then please explain how this photo of you driving an Aston Martin Rapide appeared when we did a background check for your profile, Agent Fenwick." Ted slipped the photo out of manila file and slapped it on the desk like a royal poker flush.

"I see that St. Xavier University taught you well, Ted. Nice work. But that isn't me," Jon smiled in return.

"I so much as suspected it was falsified," Ted retorted. "In fact, most everything about you is a work of fiction. If you're going to create a fake profile, at least remember the model of car you claim to drive. Perhaps you missed that class in your FBI training."

"Ted, while I appreciate your due diligence, you still can't prove that Jon was inappropriately wandering the halls of my office by the car he does—or doesn't—drive. If Jon was a former FBI agent, so be it. Most of our La Levrier members held previous positions or have current careers they want to keep private. That's what we're all about; we protect their identity. They can feel safe here. How is Jon any different?"

"How is he different? Come on, Claire, Jon isn't even a member of La Levrier! He's obviously holding back joining for obvious reasons. Don't you get it?" Ted spat. "The facts are there. Either accept or deny them, but know that I'm only trying to protect the assets of La Levrier and most of all—you."

"And I appreciate that," Claire responded calmly. "Ted, was there any further evidence? Any fingerprints?"

"Nope, Agent Fenwick left no fingerprints. Looks he put his FBI learnings to good use on one front at least," Ted growled. Jon just shook his head. He could have easily gotten just as snarky but bit his tongue.

"Okay, I can see that his conversation isn't going anywhere at this point. It's one man's word against the other," Claire intervened. "So, thank you, Ted and Danielle for your time this morning. Jon, I'd like a private word with you."

"So, I'm being excused?" Ted shouted, quite upset. "I don't want you alone with this man. Not now. Not ever. He's bad news, Claire!"

"Ted, thank you, but I'm quite capable of deciding that for myself," Claire corrected with a tone that Ted knew was his cue to cease and desist. Danielle closed the laptop on which she had been typing notes to record the confidential session and handed it to Claire as she prepared to leave. Ted silently shook his head, gave Jon a parting glare and followed Danielle out of Claire's office.

Jon sat patiently, feeling just like he had in fourth grade when he got sent to the principal's office by Miss Navarro. He could barely remember why, but it had to do something with disrupting the class spelling bee by throwing the poster board with the hand-written rules out of the window. Never one to follow rules even at the age of 10, Miss Navarro didn't appreciate his open defiance, while the rest of his classmates giggled. His own laughter did nothing to help his cause, and soon he found himself squirming in the hard chair across the desk from the head principal, Mrs. Siegel. Little did he know that more than 30 years later, he would be sitting in the same spot, across the desk from more formidable female figures wielding their authority! First Mac, now Claire.

Claire followed Ted and Danielle to her office door and then closed it behind them, listening to ensure that they had indeed left. She then returned to her desk and finally spoke. "Jon," she began stiffly. "I'm at a loss for words here. I want so badly to believe that Ted is wrong about you, but..." she paused. He waited.

"What, Claire..." Jon interjected softly after the pause lingered longer than it should.

"Well, the thing is," she sighed, sinking into her chair just a bit. "Ted is rarely ever wrong. Not only is he a damn good PI, but his instincts are razor sharp. Whenever he sniffs trouble, I usually follow his advice. La Levrier has had its share of issues, but they're minimal because they were caught early, thanks to my brother."

"I understand," Jon nodded. "But you said two important words: *rarely* and *usually*. Nobody is 100 percent accurate 100 percent of the time. There's always a chance of error."

"What are you saying?" Claire questioned, narrowing her eyes.

"Giving credit where credit is due, Ted is right about my former FBI affiliation and the photo with the Aston Martin. Surely you can appreciate that in my position as the head of a top security company, I'm a prime target for ransom-seeking cyber hackers and malicious attackers. That's why I've deliberately kept a very low profile over the years. When Forbes wanted to interview me for a cover story and take a photo shoot, I declined. I don't appear on camera. Period. As for my past with the FBI, my enemies outnumber my friends. Any number of bad guys could come looking for me at any time. Exposing my identity is a huge risk, as I'm sure it is for a lot of your members here. You get that, don't you?" Jon explained.

"Of course I do," Claire agreed. "But what I don't understand is why you kept this such a big secret from me. I respect your privacy, as you do mine. So why not share, when we've shared so much already?"

Jon shrugged. "I didn't think this information was relevant to our relationship," he said.

"Seriously?" Claire pressed, looking offended. "Do I mean that little to you?"

"What does one have to do with the other?" Jon questioned. "My career and my feelings for you are separate."

Claire paused chose her words carefully. "Were you going to tell me… ever?"

"Perhaps in time. If the opportunity was right," Jon defended.

"Look," Claire lectured. "If this—we—are going to work, there can't be any secrets between us. It's a shame that I had to find out all this about you through my brother and not from you directly. That doesn't say a lot about your trust in me."

"This isn't about you, Claire," Jon said, lowering his voice to a whisper. "And it has nothing to do with my trust in you. It's more about protecting myself. Ted can make all the assumptions about me he wants, but the fact remains: I love you."

"Without trust, love can't exist," Claire shook her head.

Claire's words sunk like a lead weight on Jon's chest. If only she knew the truth about his undercover mission at La Levrier, it would clearly be the death of their relationship. For the first time in his FBI career, Jon resented leading a double life. He had come awfully close to losing her once before, and if she found out that he had actually hacked her computer files, they wouldn't even be having this conversation.

"So, where do we go from here?" Jon flipped the question, tired of being in the hot seat.

"I don't know…" Claire trailed. "Honestly, Jon, I don't know if we can go on. I have to think about it. If—and I mean a remote *if*—we do, you can't pull anything like this ever again."

Jon just nodded, unable to find the right words to reassure Claire. All he could do was listen to the sound of his own heart and, at that moment, sadness muted it. He stood up to leave, regretting what he had to do next.

CHAPTER TWENTY

The Veep

The ballroom at the Watergate Hotel in Washington, D.C. was decked out in all its splendor. Just remodeled after a 30 million-dollar facelift, image change and amenity upgrade, the Watergate put an extraordinary effort into erasing its infamous legacy in the public's eye.

Most spectacular of the remodeling was the first interior designed by famed architect Frank Gehry, and it was the grand ballroom of the Watergate. The ballroom's stage was signature Gehry. It was retractable and framed with stainless steel curved and bent giving it the effect of a shiny steel drape flowing horizontally above and below the stage opening. The stage itself constructed of azure glass walls and floor. The podium, the speaker's table and chairs also built of the same azure glass. When populated with the speakers the glass framed by the steel gave an eerily cool feel that those on stage were floating in some kind of hologram. The benefit was that no one could take their eyes off the speakers on stage, especially if it were your first time attending a function in the room.

Richard Larsen, CEO of Alliance Healthcare, the world's second-largest health insurer, had the honor of taking the podium first. His Swiss accent gave a delicate effect to his English.

"Good morning ladies and gentlemen. What an honor to be with you all here today at our annual board meeting. To me, this meeting is the state-of-the-union address for our company. We truly are a union as Alliance conducts business in every country in every continent on the globe."

He paused as raucous applause burst from the audience. The catcalls were a bit of a surprise given that the audience was exclusively made up of international business owners, top-level executives, millionaires, billionaires and international dignitaries. This board meeting had none of the mom and pop investors of an Apple or Google meeting and no one dressed in jeans and tees.

"Thank you, thank you," Larsen raised his arms and waved his hands down to quell the applause. "And, with the sixth largest GNP in the world, our state-of-the-union is as important as another one given annually in this city."

Again, applause exploded from the audience. This round was even louder than previously.

Larsen went on with his speech and the format followed a US president's annual address. He pumped up the accomplishments of the company, announced some new initiatives and frequently the audience interrupted him with a round of applause and 'here-here's.' Several times he received a standing ovation.

Larsen called out several prominent figures that were in the audience and at her turn, Bette Gordon did her best Miss America stand-up. She torqued her body in every direction without moving her feet, smiled, and waved with the fingers of her right hand closed together. For those six-seconds she received $30,000.00 for her next campaign fund.

This state-of-the-union differed from the President of the United States' version in that drinks and dessert was served to the 1,500 guests after the CEO concluded his remarks. Once these refreshments arrived, the event became a time to mingle and deal make.

Since Bette committed only to sit through the dinner and speech, she headed for the exit once the cocktail and dessert hour was announced. As she rose from her table, two secret service agents immediately appeared out of nowhere to escort her out of the ballroom and the hotel.

Given the expanse of the room and the many patrons that wanted to say hello, Vice-President Gordon's exit was slow, but her secret service escorts' job was to make sure it was steady more than even protect her from this previously screened and searched crowd.

An exception occurred to her determined progress. A rotund, red-faced man somehow wiggled through Gordon's bodyguards and confronted the vice-president face-to-face.

"There sure are some fine-looking women at this event, isn't there, Madam Vice-President?" The man remarked.

Bette smiled and feigned cordiality, "Yes, people tend to put a bit of extra effort in at events like this," she said politely.

"But, in particular, the ladies are looking very 'butch' as the British might say."

"I have never known that to be a common English idiom, sir… ah," Bette did not flinch at the innuendo, but it did make her curious as to the identity of this oaf.

"Jimmy Backus, CEO Texas Alliance Healthcare," he extended his right hand.

Bette shook his hand and looked him in the eye. "So, Mr. Backus, you didn't inch your way into my face to compliment the females in attendance here, did you?"

"Well, Madam Vice-President you're as perceptive as you are pretty." He smiled broadly and cleared his throat. "Normally, I would have underlings deliver you my message, but there are no unders or lings allowed in this event so I thought I would take this opportunity myself to have you consider a proposal from my colleagues." He seemed to get great glee from his perceived coded statements. He puffed his chest and droned on. "You see, a big investment for the Southwest Combined Business Council is our partnership with the Venezuelan National Oil Conglomerate or VNOC. And as you know, your administration is choking VNOC out of OPEC and thus their influence on oil revenues. This hurts our investments dramatically and our friends in VNOC are mighty angry with you and your president."

Showing no reaction to his rapid-fire statements, Bette responded, "With all due respect Mr. Backus. This is not the time or place to discuss this matter…"

Backus interrupted, "Oh, quite the contrary. Isn't this little soirée' for exactly that reason?"

"Not with the Vice-President, Mr. Backus. I'm not here for the wheel-and-deal portion of the program. I'm making an appearance for a friend. Now, I must insist you allow me to continue my exit with my friends here." She cleverly nodded in the direction of her secret service escorts without losing eye contact with her intruder. It was time to emphasize her muscle to rid herself of this rudeness, yet his remarks hinting at her sexuality had her a bit stunned. She did not let on her upset. "If you want to discuss or influence administration policy, please go through the traditional channels such as your elected officials, lobbyists, voting, etc."

"Maybe it would be more productive if we had this discussion in Chicago at a certain mansion you like to frequent? The security people from VNOC tell me and others that the female scenery there is quite something," He paused and stared at her to read her reaction. She offered none. "One particular female is supposed to be exceptionally stunning… at present." He thinly disguised his threat.

"Mr. Backus, you've got my attention with your witty repartee. How about we discuss this a bit more candidly outside the ballroom?" She sarcastically offered.

"It would be my pleasure, Madam Vice-President."

They walked out of the ballroom, she continued to be stopped several times by well-wishers, but Backus' size along with Gordon's secret service men presented a formidable wall that helped them move through the crowd quicker.

Once they were outside the massive doors of the ballroom, Bette scanned for a place to talk. Unsatisfied with the offerings, she turned to her guards. "Les, can you lead us back through where we entered the building… you know, squeaky wheel?"

'Squeaky Wheel' was a code signal that she requested security backup. Her men knew exactly what to do and unbeknownst to her or Backus they made that request via their earbuds.

They walked through a back route out of the conference area of the hotel, through a service corridor that was cleared from any staff and approached two large metal delivery doors with push handles. One of the secret service men pushed through the doors and held them for Gordon and Backus. The other guard stopped like a sentry behind the three.

As Gordon and Backus exited the building, Backus' eyes widened as he saw the scene in front of him. Six black SUVs were parked bumper-to-bumper and formed a semi-circle in front of the door like a wagon train under attack. A dozen secret service agents in bulletproof vests and guns drawn rushed right up to Backus. Two of the armed secret service men grabbed each of his arms. A secret service agent, clearly in charge, walked up to Backus and stopped inches from him.

"Sir, you are being charged with a threat to the Vice-President of the United States and arrested. We are taking you into custody. You have the right to…" The head agent finished stating Backus' Miranda warning and they took Backus into one of the SUVs.

Bette Gordon calmly walked away from this fracas the moment the doors opened. She stepped to her immediate left at the direction of her personal guards and entered her car that was one of four parked with their motors running a short distance down the alleyway from the doors they exited. She didn't look in the direction of the arrest.

Three days later–Bill Weathers Office–morning

Seated at the large conference table in Bill Weathers' office were 14 other agents that made up the core Washington security team for the Vice-President. Weathers stood at the head of the table and addressed the group. "People, we finally have something here that helps us on White Sox," he announced.

Operation White Sox was the code name given to the secret service's effort to keep Bette Gordon away from what they came to find out was La Levrier. They still did not know the nature of her business inside La Levrier but her exclusion of them inside festered enough for the secret service to make it an 'operation.'

"These La Levrier trips have always been a thorn in our side and more than that, a suspected vulnerability in our security of the Vice-President. Given the Vice-President's own report of the incident at The Watergate, which you all have read prior to this briefing, Walt and his team have been analyzing her own statement of facts from that report. Given the words exchanged between Ms. Gordon and one James, Jimmy, Backus, we now have proof certain that La Levrier can be leveraged..."

Many of the agents in the room chuckled at the unintended alliteration. Weathers didn't get his linguistic handiwork at first, then smiled, but quickly returned to his dead serious monotone.

"As I was saying... leveraged... as a way to blackmail Ms. Gordon. I believe Ms. Gordon will remain insistent on her ability to visit La Levrier. As a result, I intend to put even more pressure on the Chicago FBI office to get that place shut down. Now, in the meantime prior to that mansion being shuttered, we will continue to try and divert the Vice-President. If she makes a visit there, we have to be hyper-vigilant about these trips and her involvement with whatever goes on in that building. We will continue to insist that we have access to the interior of that mansion on her visit and I have developed a plan..." He passed out folders to each of the agents. "... by utilizing the Chicago Police and the local FBI in an unprecedented way to canvas the area immediately once we find out about a visit by the Vice-President to Chicago."

A hand went up with a question. "Bill, this really seems like a lot of machinations here. Why don't we just take this higher up the chain and let the President know what's going on and put a stop to this? It just seems like a lot of resources for what?"

"I know, I know... but I think everyone on this team will agree that Ms. Gordon has always been a tremendous friend of the secret service and of all of us personally. You all know I have been a part of her security her whole political career. As head of her security, I am making the call to give her this tiny bit of space one last time. Gosh, we all like her. Further, she is being given this same plan as you have in front of you, so she is either on board with this program, doesn't go there or lets us in on what the hell goes on in there. This is it, ninth-inning in operation White Sox. Game over." Bill was surprisingly effective in his analogy. "Ok, we have a job to do... that's all."

Chicago's Lakefront—ten days later- 11:16 pm

Three Blackhawk helicopters landed on an open grassy frontage park that sat next to Lake Michigan. Chicago Police Patrol cars blocked the entrance and exit ramps to Lake Shore Drive. Three black government SUVs parked with their motors running on the bike path that runs through the grass. A helicopter door opened and a secret service agent popped out, then the Vice-President walked down the four stairs of the helicopter's ramp. She went directly into the middle SUV and the small motorcade took off. Two Chicago police on motorcycles escorted the motorcade through the park and two patrol cars were parked strategically behind trees. They traveled through the lakefront park until they could exit onto Lake Shore Drive at that point, two police patrol cars joined them.

None of the vehicles had lights flashing or sirens blaring. The vehicles headed north toward the downtown area and Gold Coast neighborhood--the location of La Levrier.

The motorcade exited Lake Shore Drive at North Avenue and then proceed south on inner Lake Shore Drive toward Astor Street. At Division Street, two streets north from Astor Street and La Levrier, the lead police car took a sharp right turn and drove westbound. All of the other vehicles followed suit.

Inside Bette Gordon's SUV, she asked, "ah, what's going on here?"

The agent sitting in the passenger seat turned and answered, "Ma'am, we've profiled a potential threat one street away from your requested destination. Per our new protocol, we are aborting the destination."

"Can I get some details?" Bette asked respectfully.

"When we get them, Madam Vice-President," the agent responded.

Resigned to the agreed upon new procedures, Bette didn't press the agents. She consented to the new orders around her visits to La Levrier, as she knew that pushing hard against their procedures could ruin the possibility of future visit. She wasn't going to risk that no matter how badly she missed Madelene.

She took out her personal cell phone and texted Madelene:

> Hey Babe, some kind of security issue two
> blocks from L.L. Won't make our rendezvous
> tonight after all. Will make plans to see you
> soon. I miss you badly and need you even more.
> B~

A return text appeared immediately:

No worries my love. As much as I can't stand
being without you, I want you safe, so there is a
you! You are real, correct?
M~

WE are real, babe. That's all that matters. We'll
talk soon. When I get a secure line.
B~

Hey Lover, are you still going to make that
presentation at the U. of C.?
M~

Yes, still on my schedule.
B~

Mind if I sit in the audience?
M~

It would be a great treat. Just don't wear
something too sexy or I'll be incredibly
distracted! It would be great to get your critique.
B~

I'm going to tease the hell out of you. It will be
good practice. LoL
M~

For what? LoL
B~

You'll see.
M~

Damn you!
B~

Be safe-Miss You!
M~

You as well-Miss You!
B~

The motorcade drove on and took Bette to a secure hotel in the downtown area. After she became settled in her room at the Peninsula Hotel, she flipped on her official cell phone and the first email in her queue was a security alert report on the incident on the way to La Levrier.

The report detailed how three men had taken strategic positions in a perimeter outside of La Levrier.

The report was brief and straightforward. Four men were spotted by a security drone that was purposely flown overhead La Levrier the day of the Vice-President's planned visit. Although the drone was positioned over La Levrier for the 24 hours before Ms. Gordon's visit, it didn't detect any suspicious activity until two hours and eighteen minutes prior to the helicopter landing on the lakefront. The men approached La Levrier from different directions. One of the men positioned himself on a rooftop on the residence across the street from the Astor mansion. Another lay in the street level landscaping of that same building. The third man lay flat on top of the roof of a garage directly behind La Levrier. He had a direct view of the carport where Ms. Gordon was typically dropped off. This man had on a very intricate camouflage bodysuit that mimicked the roof shingles of the garage. The other two men wore black bodysuits, black running shoes and darkened their faces. Had the drone not seen them from the time they arrived at the area, there was a good chance that the drone's cameras wouldn't have picked these men up once they settled into their positions.

Secret service agents apprehended the three men without assistance or knowledge of the Chicago Police Department or the local FBI. It all happened fast and clean. Preliminary interrogation of the three men revealed that they were plotting an assassination of the Vice-President. They were of middle-eastern descent and armed with high power rifles that they assembled once positioned at their places. All three were to act independently to get the shot to take down the Vice-President. The men gave up the information that a fourth assassin was poised to deliver a suicide bomb that was powerful enough to level the entire building minutes after the failure of the three shooters if those attempts did fail. The men in custody gave up the name and location of the suicide bomber and that person was being apprehended.

Eleven days later–La Levrier

Bette gently knocked on the door of her suite at La Levrier. Madelene, dressed in a white form-fitting mini-dress, charcoal heels and black pearls answered the door in mid-knock. She flung the door open with the same abandon that was in her heart at the arrival of her lover. The wait between their visits was intolerable for both.

"How did you ever pull this off?" Madelene's smile was wide and within seconds she pulled Bette into her arms and held her tight.

"My love, all I can think of is pulling that exquisite dress off you. I am so starved for you." Bette held the back of Madelene's head in her hand as she drew it closer to her face to kiss her.

They kissed passionately at the door. Mouths open wide, tongues flirting, their bodies pressed against each other. Bette's fingers ran through Madelene's long, thick curls a sensation as pleasurable for Madelene as it was for Bette. They kissed long and intensely. Several times they paused their kissing to breathe each other in, their cheeks delicately pressing together. Madelene's fingers played in Bette's hair while her other hand roamed Bette's back.

They both felt that time stood still at that doorway and savored the moment. A man makes love as a slave to the primal urges that overpower him, and they rush their lovemaking. A woman makes love with her soul when she gives herself to another woman. She makes love to a woman to touch that soul. Madelene and Bette caressed each other as if their bodies were the messengers to that deeper union they shared.

They both separated from each other at the doorway at the same time. They walked toward the four poster with Bette slightly in front of Madelene. A few feet from the bed, Madelene stroked Bette's hair from behind and her hand ran down the nape of Bette's neck and found its way to the zipper of her dress. Madelene kissed Bette between her neck and shoulder as she gently eased the zipper down as far as it could go. As the dress peeled away, the fabric opened to reveal Bette's flawless skin. Madelene placed soft kisses on Bette's back as she slowly curled the dress over Bette's shoulders and the dress tumbled to the floor. Bette purred as Madelene continued to kiss Bette's exposed skin. Bette stood only in her pale pink bra tipped with ecru lace and matching thong and her heels. The image Bette created was statuesque. Her round butt cheeks puffed from the thong perfectly with not a blemish or mark on her skin. Bette's bra straps created the same effect on her upper body. The pink and ecru lace lying across her back and shoulders effortlessly as if its only purpose was this sensual display. Madelene admired Bette as she continued to lavish her skin with her lips.

As they stood in that sensual moment Madelene's hand found its way to the front of Bette's panty and she slipped her hand inside the thong. She stroked the shaved mound of Bette's womanhood with her fingers. When her soft touch reached the lips of Bette's womanhood, Madelene felt the wetness of Bette's arousal and she became moist herself. Madelene stroked Bette's clit with a touch that was so delicate that it barely made contact with that most sensitive skin. Bette became wetter at this loving touch and immediately her pussy was glistening with the nectar of her excitement.

Bette turned to face Madelene and remarked, "It's not fair I'm the only one undressed here." With that Bette reached around Madelene neck and unzipped her dress while she kissed her. As duty called, Bette dropped her arms to Madelene's side and lowered the zipper all the way. With a flick of the back of her hands, Bette opened the dress wide and it automatically slid to the floor in a move that mirrored her own undress. Madelene wore a push-up bra that accentuated her plump breasts perfectly in a full and feminine manner. Her round, firm breasts bulged in the bra, but not in a painful looking way. Her breasts looked full and feminine. Her nipples were hard and erect. She stepped out of her dress and pressed her nearly naked body against Bette's, stimulating another round of caressing and tender touching.

They tumbled onto the bed as their bodies locked passionately together. Their touching and kissing was affectionate and soft. Each of them had several mini-orgasms already, so their energy wasn't directed toward climax, but love.

At one moment Madelene looked at Bette and commented, "You're so expressive tonight. You're making love as if it is the first or last time." Madelene stroked Bette's cheek with the tips of her fingernails. "Is this the last time, my love?" Her look was taut. It was clear she was being strong for Bette, but underneath she wanted to sob.

Bette considered her question and returned Madelene's look with a similar one, but Bette's eyes welled up with tears. "I don't know, my sweet, they are making it impossible to get here. We may have to figure out a different venue. But, we will figure it out. I cannot be without you. You are my inspiration and my energy." Bette fell onto her back and contemplated. "I do know that in the next election I'm not going to be on the ticket and after a few months out of office I'm going to come out." She leaned up on her side and looked at Madelene, "We're going to come out, that is, if you'll have me?"

Madelene smiled, "I'll be there... Oh, I'll be there."

CHAPTER TWENTY-ONE

The Plot Thickens

"Mr. Fenwick, may I help you with your bags… err, bag?" Kenneth already reached down for the handle of Jon's Bric's overnighter.

"Thank you, Kenneth, but a bit of heavy lifting may be just the trick to get a bit of my manhood back right now." The smile on Jon's face barely hid the downcast body language as he headed for the front doors of La Levrier. His familiar, confident stride now displayed slumped shoulders and energy.

"Yes, the staff is a bit abuzz with the volume when you were in Ms. Claire's office a few hours ago," Kenneth whispered. "We all thought you and Ms. Claire were growing quite fond of each other until that meeting," Kenneth's head swiveled and assessed their privacy. "You're one of our favorites around here. We were hoping you'd become a member." He paused as if baiting Jon to reveal his intentions.

A bit taken back that Kenneth knew about the meeting in Claire's office, Kenneth's compliment slightly helped Jon's bruised emotions. "Thank you, Kenneth. The feeling is mutual." Jon didn't bite at the bait to reveal any more than Kenneth and staff already knew. The men held silent as they walked through the first-floor sitting room, its early morning polished elegance lost its uplifting effect on the melancholy Fenwick.

As the men approached the foyer, Kenneth, stopped and asked, "You didn't call for the car? May I summon it for you?"

"No need, but you can call me a cab."

"But, one of our Teslas is ready," Kenneth proudly offered.

"Kenneth, have you ever known me to take La Levrier's service?"

"No… not that I have known… why is that, sir?"

"Kenneth, you're fishing here today," Jon's Mona Lisa smile inched back. "You're wondering if I'm coming back. But, I imagine you're trained never to ask that question. Well done; you didn't break protocol." Jon's head, downcast the entire time lifted and he made direct eye contact with Kenneth. "You can call that cab now if you please."

Kenneth was emotionless as he pressed a few buttons on his cell phone, and then stood at the front doors to wait for the cab.

After a very short wait, Jon exited La Levrier, entered the cab and in a 'now I have to face the music' tone instructed the cab driver to drive to the address of the FBI headquarters building.

⸎

Mac was offering no waiting service that morning, as her door was wide open. Jon walked in with his usual aplomb and style. Untypical for the office was his form-fitting jeans, tan wingtips, double-breasted corduroy vest and contrasting blazer. Of course, his signature burlap pocket square peeked out of his breast pocket. He had dropped his overnighter in his cubical on the sixth floor and grabbed his files boldly labeled 'La Levrier' and 'Limited Access.'

"Fenwick, our resident John, I hope you're here with news that makes me smile more than that little play on words." Mac's sarcastic smile was lost on Jon.

"Little is the operative word," Jon said under his breath.

"I'm sorry?" Mac snapped.

"I was saying that I have a lot of data. I said 'lot of operative work.' Sorry, I have to speak up. I've been burning the candle for the last 48 hours."

"Right, okay, let's get right into it." There was an uncharacteristic demure manner about Mac that morning.

"As I've reported before, shutting down La Levrier can take two paths. I reported two plans for the shuttering of La Levrier. Last I reported, I was at a stalemate in shuttering this business through conventional means. I had labeled that Plan A."

"Yep, yep. I remember you couldn't give us leverage on a financial shutdown or seizure of assets." Mac's energy seemed drained.

"Correct. I now have intel after the covert investigation of their records that can lead to collapsing them financially." Jon shifted his chair closer to Mac's desk and spread open his largest file. The file was so thick it more accurately resembled a 1,000-page book.

"Good, good. We want to avoid risking any personnel or collateral damage. Go ahead..."

"La Levrier is owned and run by a sole proprietor. I've given you her name before, Claire Bernardin. She is a single woman and as far as I can determine no family members, close friends or anyone she is involved with romantically is entrusted with the financial dealings of the business. This is important in a seizure of assets and records. Everything focuses on Ms. Bernardin. This makes our work more efficient and surgical. We don't have a network of people to investigate or raid their offices or homes that would take up additional time and resources. Let me detail how La Levrier operates."

"Mmmm, hmmm, saving time is good," Mac, said as if to herself.

Jon cast his eyes down on the file ledger, more to avoid eye contact with Mac than to refresh his memory of the details. "Each member is required to pay three million US dollars up front…"

"This is not for the faint of heart, is it?" Mac interrupted.

"Oh, it gets better. The member must demonstrate the secrecy and security of the funds. The member's procedures for accomplishing this must be approved by La Levrier, specifically by Ms. Bernardin personally. La Levrier can assist by providing the potential member with several models of how to protect the money on the member's end, but the exact procedures are to be taken by the potential member. The initial sum that Ms. Bernardin interestingly terms, 'a donation,' is deposited in the Mirabaud Private Bank of Switzerland. From this point, the money becomes tracked by ID numbers only and no names. The name, La Levrier, is not even associated with the funds. The donation sits in an investment account that does quite well, to the tune of 12 percent interest per annum. This donation is totally non-refundable. Once secured, the member's initial funds become deposited into the Mirabaud account, then another deposit is required. This second installment is

$500,000.00 US dollars and acts as a security deposit. La Levrier exercises the right to levy fines on the member for rules violations, damage to the mansion, injury to a staff member and various other penalties."

Jon placed two original copies of the La Levrier Rules of the House in front of Mac. She raised her eyebrows at the fine leather-bound booklets with the heads of two Greyhounds embossed in the leather. Mac picked one up and turned it over, examining the front and back covers as if she had never seen such a luxury presentation for what was essentially a brochure.

"Hmmm…" buzzed Mac.

He noted her admiration and offered, "Everything that La Levrier does is first class."

"Plunking down that kind of money it should be first class." Mac smirked.

"I think we need to put this in perspective and, if you do, you will see why this business draws a substantial clientele. The average member actively visits and uses La Levrier's services for 2.6 years That boils down to $1,153,846.15 per year or $96,153.85 per month, and further, to $3,205.13 per day. The average member uses the club three times per month during their time belonging to La Levrier. There is nothing extra a member can buy or charge, so there is no paper trail. There is no tipping, no gifting. A member can request his or her lover receive a gift, but, La Levrier pays for it as well as procures it for the member.

Jon continued. "There is no garage and street parking is impossible in that area, and, again to avoid any lapse in secrecy, the staff arranges all transportation to and from La Levrier. A member can be dropped off from their own car and driver, but any paid transportation is paid for by La Levrier, so there is no trace to the member. Because it is impossible to drive and park your own vehicle, there is no way a spouse, detective or life partner could follow and see a member's car parked outside La Levrier. Few of the clientele of La Levrier drive themselves anyway. A complete 15-point tailoring measurement is required as well as an extensive questionnaire of likes and dislikes in every aspect of the member's life. So, all a member needs to do is ask and requests are fulfilled, perfectly and promptly."

Jon paused. "So, you see the fulfillment of a member's needs is comprehensive. Think about it. For the super wealthy, a hotel that provides this volume of amenities at $3,205.13 per day is like you or me staying at the Days Inn. It's a bargain. And, hiding such an expenditure is a non-issue," he added.

"You sound like a door-to-door salesman for a steak knife company. Breaking down the cost of buying the Goddamn knife based on each bite of steak." Mac chuckled. "But, I get your point. These people don't blink an eye at the cost." Mac swiveled in her chair to face out the large windows behind her. "I always wondered who is buying all these high-rise condos going up here. Have you ever priced them?" Jon didn't answer. "Most of them start at a million five, and it's up from there." She swiveled back to face Jon. "I guess she really has no shortage of customers in a city like this." She said pensively.

"Well, her client base is not just Chicago rich. She draws from all over the country and the world." Jon offered.

"I guess I knew that. We'll get back to that later." Mac thought about the Vice President's involvement and the reason for the urgent status put on his assignment.

"Let me continue. Back to what I was explaining about the security deposit. If it is not used, it is fully refundable. But, I've seen Ms. Bernardin give a fine and dismiss a member. The security deposit earns interest for La Levrier and not the member. Back to the deposits. The money stays in Mirabaud for a temporary period of time in an individual account. Think of it as a cooling off period. Then the real financial wizardry begins. These individual accounts are dissolved, the initial ID number is erased, and the money is transferred into larger accounts owned by La Levrier. These larger accounts are invested using a different numerical ID—again, no name associated—and in a different offshore country. The primary country that is used is the Cook Islands. The Cook Islands have a financial instrument called a Cook Islands Asset-Protection Trust. The brilliance of using the Cook Islands is that it is a self-governing state associated with New Zealand in the middle of the South Pacific-6,000 miles from Florida. By their laws to file a lawsuit against a Cook Islands trust, you have to appear in the Cook Islands to file in person. The Cook Islands does not recognize American Court orders nor does it cooperate in any way with American law enforcement. By the way, for some quick razzle-dazzle, she also uses the Cayman Islands, the Bahamas, and other small municipalities. But, the big money is all locked up in the Cook Islands. And the banks there invest these trusts in foreign real estate deals, heavy machinery leasing companies, a jet leasing business and many other diversified investments. These investments are placed all over the world."

Jon took two pages out of his files and placed them on Mac's desk.

"Here is a complete list of the banks and their respective countries that are used to invest the money. All investments are in foreign projects, and the money never returns to the US. The money sits effectively stateless, protected fiercely by the Cook Islands and the other temporary local governments she uses."

Jon let Mac study the papers for a minute then added, "My guesstimate is that this has made Claire as rich as any of her clients and maybe a few put together."

"So, how does Bernardin pay the bills for the operation? How does she draw her salary? Her expenses?" Mac questioned.

"Credit instruments are used, no cash, no US dollars per se. Not hard to do everything with a credit card and there is nothing that announces that your credit card is from a foreign country. If she needs petty cash, I'm sure she can draw from her AMEX Black."

"Let's move on here. I'm sure I can read the minutiae in that encyclopedia you brought in." Mac's hot and cold temperament started to percolate at that moment. "And, we shut this down, how?"

"Let me set the stage for just a few more facts here before I get to that." Jon's tone backed her bark off. "With all this money being floated around, I initially went directly to tax issues. I thought we could turn all this over to our tax guys in the Bureau, but Ms. Bernardin is paying taxes. She is filing her taxes as a recreational club. In fact, in another of her brilliant moves, she uses Greyhound dogs as her branding logo as it were. This adds to the club disguise both from a law enforcement standpoint, and if spouses, snoops or whatever would investigate and dig deep it could very well be a sporting club-greyhound racing club, etc.

She has a liquor license and an entertainment license, so no laws are broken there. A typical records seizure raid under the guise of some tax evasion cannot work in this case. In fact, I stumbled on security protocols she has in place that will immediately block such action at the very knock on her door. Such a raid would just waste time."

"I like hearing your concern about time. Now, let's go, Jon, give me a plan here," Mac insisted.

"We have no legal standing to raid the mansion, seize records and then turn this over for the IRS to prosecute." Jon started.

"Too long, too long. I told you before. This has to be closed yesterday." Mac was revving up for a full Mac tantrum.

"Here's the good news. There have been cases filed in the Cook Islands that have pierced this investment trust where she keeps her money. But, our boys will have to go there to file them. The IRS will take too long, even with their dedicated 'wealth squad' team. Even though that team is dedicated to go after such shelters and they have had success, they are so backlogged they only go after 200 cases each year. But, if a Bureau team goes down there immediately, like tomorrow, and files a lawsuit against La Levrier, then we can essentially freeze her whole operation. Our filing should include a lien on all her accounts, and her money will be frozen immediately. She will have to close up ASAP and, from a security viewpoint, she would know we are hot on her tail and would permanently close just because she is feeling our pressure. Or, we could strike some kind of settlement with her that would include closing La Levrier. Let her keep her money. She pays us a fine, and we both walk away. But, in the process, La Levrier is shuttered."

A look between anger and puzzlement exploded on Mac's face. Jon stared at her briefly, his look communicated, 'What are you not buying about all this?'

Jon broke the silence, "Why can't we get a team to the Cook Islands in the next few days? We're still within range of your time frame, and there is no possibility of collateral damage. Hell, to save time the legal team can work out the particulars while they travel down there."

"Jon, nice job. But, that's all you have? We fly a team to the Cook Islands to get her money frozen? I know financial investigations are not your forte, and you did a credible job here. The problem as I see it is that you are a day late and a dollar short. Actually, more like a month of days late and millions of dollars short." Mac smirked, holding in her quick temper for reasons only she knew.

"As a courtesy to the working hours you put in to come up with this goose chase of a plan, I heard you out. I am going to respond in a forthright and calm manner. Further, what I am going to share with you, I really don't have to share. But, I am going to tell you the reason why your little 'chase the money' plan cannot work. By the way, have you ever worked with an attorney? Nothing about them is quick unless it's creating invoices. I don't care if they work for us or outside the agency. There is no way a legal team can be assembled in, what did you call it, 'days… tomorrow?' Mac's usual rage began to break the contained veneer she wore throughout the meeting.

Jon sat stoically, hardly moving even a facial muscle. He knew he was grasping at straws to present a financial strategy at this late date, but he had to do this for Claire. Even at the cost of an infamous Mac tongue-lashing. A large part of his frozen body language was his surprise at Mac's restraint. She caught him off-guard with her subdued presentation. He couldn't remember the last time Mac wasn't bellowing in a meeting. Like every agent under her, you coped with Mac in the same way you braced yourself for barging into a crack house. You knew bad things were going to be thrown at you in an unpredictable, random way, but you had to keep your professional manner in spite of whatever you confronted.

"So, let me tie-up two conversations here. Just yesterday, I had to suffer through another call from Weathers at the Secret Service. He was furious that we haven't taken out this place yet. He was all full of threats, to this office and me. He said that maybe the next president needs to re-evaluate the costs of such a large building when no work gets done? Maybe the federal budget could be best served to convert the Chicago FBI headquarters into condos? He asked if there was a real need for our office space." Mac lifted her eyebrows and made piercing eye contact with Jon. "We don't have any time. We don't have one minute of time. One second of time. We don't have tomorrow, we have TODAY. That business needs to be non-existent... NOW!"

Here she is, Miss America... Jon clenched in his best defensive mode.

Outwardly Jon didn't flinch. Maybe it was Mac's return to her old self. Maybe it was his self-confidence. Maybe it was the fact that he was still agent in charge of this case. Maybe it was that he had a corollary to his original Plan B, but Mac didn't rattle him at the moment. Well, maybe it was just that Mac wasn't going to do the dirty work herself. That job was still his. The fate of Claire and La Levrier was still in his hands. There was no mention of, 'I'm taking you off this case' or 'I'm bringing in agent XYZ to take this case the rest of the way' or anything like that. As long as she didn't pull that TRUMP card, Jon still held out hope he could pull some rabbit out of his hat to help Claire.

What did cause a lump in his throat was the vice he now found himself in with Claire. He snooped around for more information in an attempt to save Claire and her business, but all it may have accomplished was cost him her love. He still vowed to keep her safe when things came down, no matter how La Levrier would be closed. It was just that Mac wasn't buying his way of doing that.

"Agent Fenwick, here's where we are at. I've heard you out here, but I'm ordering you to initiate Plan B and initiate immediately. I don't care how you get it done, but I'm talking in the next few days. Let me be clear. In the next few days, Ms. Bernardin and La Laveray will be closed. You will complete this assignment, and we file all this neat little data in the archives."

With a jerk, Mac slid all Jon's files and papers toward him. "So, go down to your cubicle on the sixth floor and solve any obstacles in the way of doing that. I expect that before the end of the business day you will have on my desk the final details of the strategic plan for the elimination of La Leveeer. Done, closed, next case. I am not going to suffer through another phone call from Weathers."

"On it," Jon responded.

"Yes, you are." With that comment, it was evident that the meeting was over. Mac just stared at him in silence, so Jon got up without another word and left her office.

Jon went back to the sixth floor. Interestingly, the catcalls and taunting from his colleagues were non-existent. Given how infrequently he made an appearance on the sixth floor, the 'bullpen' as the agents called it, he readied himself for some friendly taunts about his case. Given the state of his emotions, he needed to be Teflon as he walked through the bullpen. But, they didn't come. Either his fellow agents moved on to other peers to razz or somehow plugged into the anguish he was suffering over the duty that lay before him. Either way, the lack of teasing was very noticeable in light of how little he had been on the sixth floor in the past few weeks.

Jon traded a few hellos and quick banter with three fellow agents but extracted himself from these water cooler conversations by explaining the tight deadline he was under on an active case. He used terms such as, "I have to wrap up this case by this afternoon," and, "Mac, has me on a tight deadline on the case I'm in charge of," to extract himself from the water cooler conversations.

Once at his desk, he flipped open his laptop, flicked a few keys and a title in bold black letters with a blue background exploded across screen PLAN B FOR THE ELIMINATION OF LA LEVRIER. He opened the file and froze.

He went to pound his fists against his desktop but pulled them up millimeters from striking on the desk. He controlled himself because that attention would get noticed from the other agents in the bullpen and they would ask questions, or they would swoon over him with concern. He couldn't risk that any show of conflict over his duties would possibly get back to Mac. No, he had to deal with this alone. Not unfamiliar territory.

A flood of emotion came over him as he sat there looking at the computer screen. The screen filled with the details he wrote weeks ago of the destruction of his lover's livelihood. Staring at the screen stimulated the epiphany that Claire just didn't captivate him; he was totally in love with her. He never intentionally wanted to hurt her. Jon couldn't compartmentalize this into a neat little box somewhere between FBI agent and lover. How could he possibly destroy the business that Claire built with such passion and skill? This would crush her. How dare he! He was in an impossible position. To not follow through with his duties as an agent would probably end his career, especially since this assignment was on the heels of his last fuck-up. And, truth be told, what else did he know except being an FBI agent?

Fuck, fuck, fuck. His brain seemed to be banging back and forth inside his skull, concussing from the two pressures pressing on him. Claire must not be hurt. Banged his brain on one side of his head. I have to follow-through on what I proposed to the agency, and his brain banged against the other side of his head. He simply couldn't do what he must do for the agency. But, was this really for the FBI? What was all the Secret Service crap about? La Levrier was not hurting anyone, a threat to national security, illegal, not even immoral. Was this just the whim of some bureaucrat there? *I hate fucking bureaucrats. Fucking Mac! Fucking Weathers!*

He had to get control of his thoughts and concentrate on what he was going to hand into Mac. That was the immediate need. The task of putting together the details for Mac was not insurmountable by the end of the day; in fact, much of the skeleton of the plan he already worked out when he had first presented Plan B to Mac weeks ago. What he needed to do was to contact a few city services and get them on board with everything. An FBI agent calling the police and fire department for backup was routine and automatic. For Jon, it was just a matter of contacting any one of the department heads he worked with before and letting them know what was coming down on which day and they would take care of allocation of resources. No detailed explanation, just be there on the day and time the Bureau was going to do some dirty work.

Jon sent out emails via a secure server to his contacts at the Chicago Police Department, Fire Department, and Department of Streets and Sanitation. Within minutes he received confirmation that they would have backup at La Levrier at the date and time he requested.

Next, he opened up a spreadsheet template and began to plug in the confirmations from the Chicago departments in the appropriate rows and columns. As he finished putting those details into the master spreadsheet on Plan B, he had to stop.

Goddamnit, this is not right. She hasn't done anything wrong. Fuck'n government assess. I can't do this. Love or no love, this is an innocent woman, and we are going to destroy her?

Fuck this, I have to know what's up the Secret Service's ass that they are so hot on getting rid of La Levrier or Claire.

Jon called Mac. "Mac, I'm finalizing the details of Plan B and just was curious. Why is the Secret Service of all agencies so hell bent on getting this Chicago business out of the way? You've never explained this in any of our meetings."

True to her usual form, Mac snapped back, "Ah, Agent Fenwick, that is information way above your pay grade." She hung up on him.

Oh, really princess, there's more than one way to pick your brain.

Jon made another call. This one was to Hector Torres—one of the tech geniuses in the Bureau on the fourth floor. He called in a favor.

"Hector, Fenwick here, I need some data. Can you email a transcript of any of Mac's phone calls with a guy named 'Weathers' at the Secret Service?"

Hector didn't hesitate, "No problem, you'll have it in your email before we hang up. How's life treating ya?"

"Good, man, good. And, you, how's that movie star little boy of yours?" Jon answered.

"Couldn't be better. He is a hoot, and I don't think you're far from the truth. That little guy is a ham all the way. Give another 20 years, and you'll be seeing him in the movies." Hector's beam shown through the airwaves.

Jon laughed, "Heck, he might star in the movie they'll make on this case I'm working on, who knows."

"Sounds good, dude. He'll be ready."

"Thanks for the intel I see it in my inbox already. Talk later, I'm on a deadline."

Jon took advantage of the fact that, per Bureau rules, any business calls conducted on Bureau communication devices were available to any agent. There were ways to hide communications in cases of high security, but Jon surmised that the calls between Weathers and Mac took place without any extra security. He was correct. Every call between those two was in the email Hector sent. Jon immediately looked at the conversations between Mac and Weathers.

Fuck'n 'A', fuck'n 'A'. So, this is all about the Vice-President being a member of La Levrier! Goddamnit, the government needs this shut down because of her? What bull. And, clearly, the VP values her membership. This is wrong, dead, freak'n wrong.

With a new attitude and gusto, Jon finished his spreadsheet after plugging in details on the supplies he would need and the specific FBI personnel he would utilize. The final page of the spreadsheet was a timetable for the exact steps on the exact day that the operation was to take place. Each of the rows was broken down in 10-minute increments.

He signed his report with his coded signature and emailed it to Mac. It was 2:00 p.m. At 3:00 p.m., he received a response back from Mac. Her return email simply said, 'Fine.'

Jon opened Mac's email the minute it arrived in his inbox. *'Fine' Mac, fine. Well, I hope you are going to like Plan C because I just had a brainstorm on how to make this whole mess right.*

Jon dialed the private number of La Levrier. "Hello, Margot, may I speak to Claire?"

Margot's voice on the other end responded, "I'm not sure that she will take your call, Mr. Fenwick. Or, should I say, AGENT Fenwick."

Jon didn't even flinch at the revelation that they knew he was an agent of some sort.

"Margot, trust me, this is vitally important—maybe even life or death and that statement is not a cliché. I must talk to her immediately."

CHAPTER TWENTY-TWO

A Simple Plan

"Hey, fuckhead. What do you want?" Lieutenant Jimmy Eckhardt, assistant to the Chicago fire chief blurted over the phone.

Jon's puzzlement was immediately evident, "Nice greeting, bud." Jon chuckled.

"What's so funny?" Jimmy snapped, clearly not welcoming the call.

"Geez, bud, sorry. I thought you were kidding." Jon's tone shifted into conciliation. "I mean it's been a few years. I thought…"

"Thought what? Thought you'd check in after I had back surgery three weeks ago? A bitch of a surgery no thanks to you," Jimmy snapped bitterly.

"Come on Jimmy, that's not fair. We were kids… what, thirty years ago?" Jon demurred.

"Fuck you thirty years ago. You broke my spine." Jimmy's anger was escalating. "What? You think that shit just goes away? Like I'm a fuck'n alien, and my spine is made of rubber?"

"Geezus, every time I talk to you we go through the same shit. We were, what, 12 and we were wrestling on the

Layton's front grass." Jon's pandering evolved into matter-of-factness.

"Ya lifted me over your head and slammed me down like a fuck'n WWF guy. My fuck'n back's hurt ever since. Finally had to go under the knife because of degeneration. So, that wasn't kids play'n to me."

"Listen bud, I apologized a thousand times after that. I apologized in the ambulance that I called and saved your life. I apologized when I pulled a favor and got a buddy to sign off on your medical exam for the fire department, and I apologized when I got your son that summer job with us in that classified area two years ago. That wasn't easy, man. It's not like we go drinking and are best buds. I did that out of respect. Respect for the old days."

"We were best friends back then," Jimmy interrupted.

"And, like a lot of friends we drifted apart, went our separate ways. It happens."

"Right, shit happens. I got the T-shirt. So, now that our friendly greeting is over, why the hell are you calling me?"

"I've got a case I'm working on, and I have to coordinate some logistics with the fire department."

"OK, what ya got." Jimmy settled into a businesslike manner.

"We're going to demolish a building, and I need fire department safety back-up."

"You get a permit for that?"

"First thing I did was call Colona at the department of buildings. Called him yesterday and his people pushed it through."

"Using another childhood buddy, huh?" Jimmy was back to bitter.

Jon ignored the slam. "Don's a good guy."

"Ya, you didn't break his back."

Jon continued to ignore the bitterness. "So, here's what we're going to do. We're going to cause a measured gas leak in the building, just enough to take out the interior and make it dysfunctional. There won't be any collateral damage to the surrounding buildings, in fact, the interior walls, foundation, and roof will all be untouched. The explosion will start at the center of the basement, blast upward and collapse each floor, causing the building to be unusable for a long, long time."

"What the hell did these people do to piss off the Hoovers?" Jimmy asked.

"That I can't tell you. Let's just say this is the fastest and maybe only way to get them to stop doing what they're doing. We've explored all other options."

"OK, so give me an address and I'll have it routed to the right (fire)house."

"Sixty East Astor Street."

"Shit! An Astor Street mansion? Whaaa the fuck?" Jimmy paused. "You sure you got a permit from the city? I'll have to see it."

"Fax it right over."

"OK, so, when you going to do this?"

"Friday."

"OK." Jimmy's tone was somber. "You're not killing anybody inside this place, right?"

"Nope, in fact, I need your help- the department's that hell-bent assist in the evacuation without tipping our hand."

"Huh?"

"So, we don't involve any of your personnel, I need to borrow a couple of sets of gear to make the evacuation look real. My people will do the door knock and announce that a gas leak has been detected, get the people out of Sixty and do the same for any of the neighbors, just for safety. Once the civilians are all safe and sound, then I plan to detonate the explosives that would have been planted previously." John paused. "All my people have been drilled on what to do from there. I need your people and equipment just to be on the sidelines in case anything goes wrong, but I assure you, this is all worked out to the last detail and should go completely as planned and safe." Jon paused, then added a detail. "Oh, can you have a hook and ladder and whatever other rig you typically park outside for one of these things?"

"Sure, the responding house will take care of all that. It will look authentic." Jimmy deadpanned.

"None of your guys will get hurt or will be responsible for the damages."

"I don't really give a shit, but, I know my higher-ups are going to have a knippsion on why we couldn't have had more notice on this," Jimmy advised.

"Jimmy, sorry, this was all put in place in the last minute here as well. I will tell you that this does oddly involve national security and you and your bosses can get that confirmed by the Secret Service if you need. I can give any one of your people the channels to check this out and the other fed departments will snap on it to confirm that we're not playing here. This has to be done now."

"I may just need those confirmations, but in the meantime, I'll have everything dispatched and allocated for Friday. I'm sure you're being square with me."

"Completely. I'll email all the paperwork you need right now. Sorry about the operation. How does it feel?"

"To talk to you? Like shit," Jimmy growled.

"I meant the back," Jon snapped.

"So far, so good. Wit the shit they can do now, it actually feels better than it has since that day."

"Well, that's really good news."

"Fuck you. That doesn't leave you off the hook for anything. In fact, I have your picture in my office like you guys do, ya know that 10 most wanted list," Jimmy laughed for the first time.

"You're the number one." He chuckled some more.

"Who's the other nine?"

"Fuck you, that's for me to know or you can find out if ya ever pay me a social call here."

They ended the call with civilized 'good-byes' and hung up.

⚬⚬⚬

Thursday, 8:00 a.m.

FBI Headquarters, Chicago, a briefing meeting on La Levrier. Meeting in progress.

"Let me pass the meeting over to Jon and he will facilitate the rest of the briefing. Jon will focus on the safety of the occupants if any in the target, and on other issues relevant to his inside surveillance of the target." Mac made eye contact with Jon. "Agent Fenwick."

"Thank you, Chief. Your reports on agent safety and community safety were thorough and assured the safety of everyone involved. I will note that my final report." With a blank, businesslike expression, Jon nodded toward Mac. She stared down at the briefing manual oblivious to his gratuitous body language. Noting that her gaze cast on the paperwork in front of her, several of the agents sitting around the conference table reacted to the tete-a-tete between Jon and Mac. The years of Mac's animosity toward Jon when she was impotent to control Jon's independence was well known among all the staff at FBI headquarters. Since Jon's fuck up and Mac's constant taunting, Jon returned Mac's resentment and it was transparent throughout the building. Their compliments here were great theatre to the agents no matter how intense the briefing.

"Let me review how this is going to go down tomorrow. At 7:45 a.m. I will arrive in the basement of the target. I will place two locked and loaded, containers of Z67D gas at inconspicuous positions…"

"Those containers will not be carried into and through the target in a lethal state, correct?" Mac interrupted.

"That is correct; the containers will not be lethal until they are placed into position. Thank you for that clarification, Chief," Jon automatically agreed. Their word tango continued to entertain the group in the room.

"By eight hundred hours the containers will be ready to go. I will return to my suite in the target and wait for the next event."

A hand went up from one of that agents around the table. "Jon, ZD is volatile. I personally haven't used it so I am curious what type of detonation method are you using here?"

"Thanks, I was going to get to that later, but let me explain that now. I do have to be cautious with the gas in the tin, but I'm using tin containers precisely because of the detonators. The containers have concave bottoms so that I can attach a simple two coil heat element on the bottom of each container and yet they will still rest steady on any flat surface I find available. I will be able to fire up the heat coils from my cell phone at the specified time. The detonators will burn easily through the tin-again, that's why tin-and the gas will blow mimicking a broken household gas pipe that would pick up any small spark and ignite. The tin will be obliterated in the explosion such that there will be no trace that the blast was planned and measured. Each container will have the exact calculated amount of explosive to blow through every floor of the target and cause the entire interior of the building to crash through the lower floors and become a rubble heap in the very basement where the explosion began. There will be no damage to the interior or exterior walls, the roof or the foundation. The foundation is notable as the explosion will jet upward per the nature of the gas. It will be a nice clean event. Picture if you will a dump truck on the top floor emptying a load of super heavy material that will collapse that floor and cascade into the next and the next until all the internal contents of the building will be in a nice heap in the basement. In fact, because there will be no resulting fire, a good amount of the objects inside the building may be recovered. But, regardless, the building will be immediately and for a long time unusable."

With that, Mac smiled and nodded her head, but didn't give Jon the pleasure of an atta-boy look in his direction.

"Let me get back to details and events in order here, particularly to point out all your roles and duties." Jon took back the order of the meeting. "I left off at 800 hours. At 8:15 a.m., Williams and Rodgers in full CFD turnout gear will announce their presence at the front door of the target."

"What is this, Downton Abbey? Are we arriving for tea?" Rodgers piped in with a terrible English accent on the last phrase.

The room chuckled. Mac kept writing notes.

"Ok, wise-ass, just knock on the door or ring the bell, your choice. I didn't put either in my report so as not to take away your American inalienable right to exercise your free will." Jon smirked.

Williams couldn't resist joining the fun. "Fenwick, you're the head of this operation. You do know that in every field situation, every moment of every action is spelled out specifically for us grunts. Do we ring the bell or knock on the door OR does a place like this have a door knocker?" He snickered.

Darius Elliot, a young-looking agent that often posed as a late teen joined the ribbing. "Come on Jon, this operation can't go forward with a briefing manual like this. I mean last week I was in an operation where I was to find myself sitting between two gangbangers in the back seat of a Hummer and my briefing ordered me to sit in an exact way in case our snipers had to take out the people sitting next to me. You know agent security has to be detailed to the tiniest detail or the operation cannot be approved." Darius looked over to Mac whose head was still down and studying the briefing manual and her notes. "With all due respect, Chief."

Jon knew their jest was mainly directed at Mac and her conflicts with him. After all, no agent would deliberately throw another field agent under the bus. At some point they knew they would go into the field with each other and their lives depended on complete trust.

"Ring the damn bell like a human being, you gorilla! The CFD wouldn't barge into a house when it is coming over on suspicion of a gas leak," Jon smiled.

"So, we will ring the doorbell. Go on Fenwick," Mac said without looking up.

"So, Williams and Rodgers in full firefighter regalia RING the doorbell at 8:15 am. Most likely a staff person named Kenneth will answer the door. He is a good and reasonable fellow. Show him identification, that will be in your gear, as he will not be moved by just seeing the costumes you have on. The staff in this place has seen just about everything before. One of you will show him the evacuation order on official City of Chicago Department of Housing letterhead. It is an 8 1/2 x 11 laminated sheet."

Williams piped up, "Will that be me or Rodgers?"

Jon just gave him a stare as if to say, 'Joke time is over, Mac is not in the mood.'

"Moving on, there will undoubtedly be some discussion between you and Kenneth who will likely summon either Ted Bernardin or Claire Bernardin-or both-to come down to the main foyer. You will need to wait for either of these two to arrive, but I want you to play up the urgency of the situation. Do not let them take too much time. Make it real. And make sure you emphasize that they need to evacuate within the next 20 minutes. We don't want them to take records or personal belongings. Just get them out of the building along with any human being and animal inside."

Yvonne Darling, one of the team, asked, "Animals?"

"Yes, you will note in the addendum in your reports that there are two canines in the building. They will need to be evacuated as well," Jon answered.

"I didn't catch that. Will we need the animal control unit for this?" Yvonne continued.

"No, that would look pre-meditated. In reality, CFD would not have any idea that there would be pets in the building on an emergency evacuation. Just make note of it now," Jon responded.

Several of the team responded, "Gotcha."

"In the meantime, the rest of the team in CFD turnout gear will do a door knock on the two houses immediately next to Sixty. The neighbors will also be evacuated as a safety precaution and-of course-to keep this authentic looking." Jon paused.

"The next step that the real CFD would take is to get a head count of the occupants in the building at that time while one of the staff begins to rustle everyone out of the building. At this point, Williams and Rodgers summon the remainder of our agents in fire gear into the building to supervise the evacuation." Jon paused and looked around the room for any questions. There were none.

"Yvonne, Darius, Bill and Mark, you all immediately take the stairs and inspect the floors one-by-one to ensure all occupants exit the building. Whatever staff provides the inventory of people and pets in the building stays alongside one of you, Williams or Rodgers and you go outside and conduct a head count with that staff person to ensure no living being is in the building. We will have a bus on the street to escort all the occupants onto and detain them. There will be a separate bus for the neighbors, as we will provide them with transportation back to their homes as soon as the CFD gives us the all clear. When the head count is triple checked and the bus full, Sean, you will drive that bus to the firehouse at South Water Street and Stetson and park to await further instruction."

Jon again paused for possible questions. There were none.

"Mark, I want you to separate Claire Bernardin and Ted Bernardin and whoever they want near them to my position. Once I am escorted out of the building just like any other occupant, I will separate from the others and station myself behind the hook and ladder parked outside the building on Astor. It does not matter at this point whether anyone sees my position or not. I would like you to bring Claire, Ted and whoever to my position because after the detonation I will be bringing this group back here for interrogation." Jon ordered.

"Now the fun begins. Williams, you will text me with the 'all clear' and as soon as I have those key occupants in my area I will then use my phone to detonate the containers and the destruction will begin. Everyone stand clear of the perimeter of the building even though the damage will be contained. There is no purpose in anyone being around the mansion. The time should be approximately 9:00 a.m. I press a key and bang-we have completed our objective. It is a relatively simple operation."

Jon looked around the room. No one spoke. "Are there any other questions or issues at this point?" Heads nodded and papers shuffled, but no one had anything to say.

"Ok, simple and clean. Sean, I will text you that the building is destroyed and you will announce to the occupants of the bus that they need to make arrangements to get transportation to wherever they need to go. I have arranged with the fire house that they can go inside and make calls or such in the common room of the fire house. I would like you to stay with that group until everyone is dispersed. We have no issues with any of those people and they are free to go. You can head back here after your duties are complete. The CFD will handle the disposition of the building and seal it off per their typical protocols. That's it." Jon paused again.

"You will all report here tomorrow at 6:00 a.m. for gear and transportation to the mansion. Thank you, good luck and be safe. Our debriefing, which should be short, will take place here Friday afternoon at 4:00 p.m. I will see you all back here in this room then."

The agents filed out of the conference room. No one lingered to chit-chat. In fact, the typical muffled banter as people filed out of a room was absent. It wasn't the mood of the agents, but the simplicity of the operation. Not much to go wrong and none of them would be in harm's way.

Mac was the last to leave and she did stop to say a few words to Jon. "Don't expect me to say good job or thorough report, Agent Fenwick. This operation should have been undertaken weeks ago. Just get this done and let's find something else for you to do come Monday morning. I'm going into my office to call the Secret Service and let them know we had our final briefing and all systems are go. This will get them off my back. I think I'm going to email them your final briefing manual so they know just what is going on and how it will go down. If that's all right with you?" Mac stated.

"I guess I don't have a problem with that. Not really our standard procedure with them; but, as you say, it's a simple plan." Jon collected his materials as he responded and they both headed for the door.

Mac reached the door first and as she did she suddenly turned to Jon, almost forcing him to run into her in the process. "Oh, one last thing. I'll expect your interrogation questions for Bernardin on my desk by the end of the day and, if it fits into my schedule, I may just attend that session with her or hold it myself."

"Suit yourself. Once that building is inoperable, I could care less about the next steps. We don't have anything else on that woman and at that point we've done enough to her. I'd just as soon wash my hands of the whole thing. What, destroying a citizen's livelihood and property for no particular reason. Not something I signed up when I joined this organization." Jon pushed himself by Mac through the door jamb with an ambivalent look. Mac shot him back her 'whatever' glare and remained unruffled as he passed her.

CHAPTER TWENTY-THREE

Check Check

"Claire, are you okay?" Danielle asked as she brought a steaming mug of hot java to Claire's desk and handed it to her employer and mentor.

Claire gratefully took her first sip after a fitful sleep. The warmth of the coffee was a soothing contrast to the chill that she couldn't seem to shake. Danielle noticed Claire's hands tremble as she set her mug back down next to her computer and gave Danielle a half smile in response.

"Of course, Danielle. Everything is fine. I just didn't sleep very well last night," she stated calmly in contrast to the calamity that wrenched her gut.

"I'm sorry if I'm overstepping my bounds," Danielle began gingerly, "but you don't seem quite yourself."

Claire pulled her cream wool shawl tighter around her shoulders like a protective cocoon and tried to muster a response that would reassure her protégé that her instincts were unfounded, but she couldn't find the words. She just nodded, holding back what would surely compromise her professional dignity. Any hint of a tear would reveal weakness and contradict what she had always espoused— never let a man control your emotions.

"Does this have anything to do with Mr. Fenwick?" Danielle probed softly. "Again, I don't mean to pry…"

Claire looked up at Danielle cautiously, her eyes trying hard not to fill with tears. "I know you mean well, Danielle. This is just an… well, an unusual, situation…" she trailed.

"You love him, don't you?" Danielle nodded, placing her hand over Claire's. "It's obvious. And, to be honest, I can sense he loves you very much, too. I don't think yesterday's meeting was easy for either one of you."

"You can say that," Claire sighed, feeling a bit relieved that she could finally confide in someone other than her brother, who was anything but objective when it came to Jon Fenwick. "In all my years of running La Levrier, this was one of the toughest confrontations I've ever had, and one of the deepest betrayals I've ever felt. I never intended to fall for Jon. It's against my better business judgment to develop feelings for a client. God, I'm such a fool!"

"You're wrong on two counts," Danielle comforted. "First, you're not a fool. You're a successful, accomplished woman. Second, Mr. Fenwick is technically not a client. So, you didn't break your rules. You just followed your heart."

"Yeah, and look where it got me," Claire grunted as she raised her cup to her lips and took another sip. "How could I be so stupid not to see that he was just using me?"

"Using you or just not telling you every detail of his private life? There's a difference," Danielle countered. "How did you leave things with him after Ted and I left your office?"

"I don't know… I guess kind of open-ended. I told him that without trust, there could be no 'us.' I said I had to think about things."

"And have you?" Danielle asked.

"I can't think clearly right now. My emotions are still pretty raw," Claire confessed.

"Look, if it makes you feel any better, I know what you're going through… what it's like to fall for a guy who isn't who you thought he was. Remember what I told you about my ex? After I followed him to Chicago, I knew I had made the biggest mistake of my life. I gave up everything for him, my heart got broken and my world crumbled. But I'll never regret the good that came of our relationship—the birth of my son. I took a chance at love, and it didn't work out. But that doesn't mean your story with Mr. Fenwick has to end the same way. Jed was an ass. Mr. Fenwick seems like a good man who may be just a bit awkward at all of this 'love stuff.' Maybe he deserves another chance."

La Levrier Lobby, 2:35 p.m., Thursday

After yesterday's meeting with Claire and Ted, Jon spent the rest of the day ruminating if—and how—he could return to the La Levrier and carry out the inevitable. Was he now banned from the premises? Certainly, he had tackled tougher assignments in his FBI career, but the agony of gaining access to the property challenged his careful planning. Then, a memory struck him. As a teen, his friend, Jimmy, would procure a new baseball to play sandlot ball by strolling into the local variety store, grabbing a perfect, new hardball and just walking right out of the shop as if it was his all the while. *That's it.* Jon would merely assume that he was still welcome and walk right in.

As if Jon were expected, Kenneth was at the doorway when he rang the bell. Jon was relieved to see a familiar face welcome his arrival as Kenneth graciously beckoned him into the lobby. Jon exhaled a silent sigh of victory. His plan had worked.

"Mr. Fenwick, so nice to see you again," Kenneth smiled and gave a slight bow. "Let me take your bag and escort you to your room. I was heading up to your floor, anyway."

Before Jon could respond, Kenneth had already taken the Bric's duffel suitcase from Jon's grasp. "Are you going to be staying with us a few extra days this time?" he inquired. "Your bag feels a bit heavier than usual, unless you're packing bricks in your Bric's." Kenneth cracked a rare smile.

"No bricks in there, Kenneth," Jon mustered a chuckle, "The forecast looked a bit on the chilly side, so I packed for the weather. I'm planning a nice long run, so had to bring my jogging suit, shoes, backpack… you know, the works."

"Of course," Kenneth said as the two gentlemen entered the elevator. "I hear we're in for some crisp fall days ahead. It will be a lovely run along the lakefront, if that's your course of choice. Let's get you settled in, shall we?"

When they arrived at Jon's suite, Kenneth took his key and opened the door and then placed Jon's bag inside the doorway. "As always, I hope you enjoy your visit at La Levrier, Mr. Fenwick. How else may I be of assistance?"

"I'm all set, Kenneth. Thank you," Jon stated, trying to hide the note of impatience in his voice. For all intents and purposes, it was business as usual and this was a customary visit.

"Very well, then. I'll let Miss Bernardin know that you're here," Kenneth lowered his head and gave a slight wink. Before Jon could open his mouth, Kenneth had slipped out the door and was already on his way down the corridor.

Jon really didn't want Kenneth to flag his arrival to Claire, but it seemed that the La Levrier staff was already in on their secret—or at least Kenneth was. If Jon informed Kenneth that he did not wish to see Claire, it would have raised doubt. Yet, the mere mention of her name triggered a wave of excited apprehension in Jon's stomach. He knew he had to see Claire… in fact, Jon wanted more than anything to see her but, based on how they left things yesterday after their meeting, he wasn't sure if she wanted to see *him*. Claire's last words, "I have to think about it," left him in a suspended state, not really sure if he was a welcome guest or an uninvited intruder.

Either way, Jon had a duty to perform and he had no choice but to execute the plan he had outlined to Mac and his team. D-Day was in less than 24 hours. After that, it would be all over. With mission accomplished, he could finally escape Mac's wrath and move on to his next assignment. But things had to go perfectly for everyone— mostly Claire—to be safe, and there had to be no chance that any hint of foul play could be tied back to Jon. Maybe then, and only then, could he and Claire salvage their relationship. That is, if she wanted the same.

Claire's Office, 4:10 p.m., Thursday

"Hey, Danielle," Claire noted as she glanced up from behind her reading glasses while Danielle swept into her office to clear the coffee cups from the talk they shared earlier that day. "You know, you don't have to do that. I'll ask housekeeping to take care of it."

"I don't mind," Danielle insisted. "I'm really not here to tidy up, but to check on you."

"Me?" Claire said. "That's sweet of you, but I'm fine." The downcast note in Claire's voice told Danielle that she wasn't exactly telling the truth. "I've got to be, right? I have to meet Holden O'Keiffe this evening. He's ready to sign the dotted line for La Levrier membership. We've been courting him for the two weeks and he's finally prepared to commit. I can't miss it."

"Holden O'Keiffe?" Danielle raised her eyebrow. "Are you serious? Oh, my God! I saw his last movie, and he is totally HOT. Why would he come all the way from L.A. to Chicago? And what does he want with La Levrier? I thought he was single. He could get any girl he wants!"

"That's certainly the public perception that Mr. O'Keiffe has, isn't it? He's 33, strikingly handsome and Hollywood's golden boy…"

"I heard he might be nominated for an Oscar for his leading role in Mayhem Town. Not only is he gorgeous, he's incredibly talented. Hey, why don't you put me in charge of Membership tonight?" Danielle pleaded as they both deftly stirred the conversation away from the morning's therapy session of a chat.

Claire smiled. "I have total confidence that you could do it, but Holden O'Keiffe has to be handled with care."

"I'm a quick study!" Danielle grinned.

"Oh, I know you are," Claire assured her protégé. "But Holden is a very private man."

"…and eligible!" Danielle added.

"Not exactly," Claire countered. "That's just it. His Hollywood publicity machine would like to make young women like you believe that's the case to drive box office sales and fuel the fandom."

"Whaaaaat? He's married?" Danielle frowned jokingly.

"Not exactly that, either," Claire explained. "Believe me, you aren't the first in line at La Levrier who wants to meet Holden. Only two of my closest confidants know he's even coming tonight."

"Me and who else? I want to know my 'competition,'" Danielle smirked.

Claire paused deliberately and locked eyes with Danielle. "Teddy."

"Why would Teddy want to meet Holden?" Claire gasped.

Claire remained silent as Danielle contemplated her last statement carefully. The expression on her face morphed into the 'cat that ate the canary.'

"No, no... he can't be. Are you serious? Holden O'Keiffe likes... men?"

"Sorry to crush your dreams, my dear, but yes," Claire confirmed. "That secret, of course, stays strictly within this room and is not to leave La Levrier, you understand."

"Sure, of course," Danielle assured Claire. "Now I understand why he's so private, I guess. One leak could destroy his career."

"I knew you'd be a quick study," Claire said. "That's why his membership has to be managed so delicately. Holden O'Keiffe has to maintain his public persona as a ladies' man. While he's in Chicago, La Levrier will be taking care of him."

"Why is he in Chicago, though?" Danielle pressed.

"Because that's where Mayhem Town II is being filmed. Hollywood hasn't made that public yet, so please keep it confidential as well."

"Absolutely, you know I will," Danielle nodded. "Can I at least meet him, though?"

"Oh, Danielle, I have more plans in store for you than just an initial handshake," Claire's eyes darted mischievously. "If Holden agrees, I'd like to propose that you be his 'girlfriend' in the public spotlight. You know, dinners, plays, anything where a lovely female companion is required… that is, if you're also comfortable with that arrangement."

"Am I COMFORTABLE with that arrangement? To be Holden O'Keiffe's beard? Hell, yes!" Danielle squealed.

"It would mean that you'd have to learn how to navigate the paparazzi. It's not an easy job. I need a Levrier who is mature and trustworthy. I can't risk the media tracing anything back to La Levrier. Otherwise, Holden's career—and our cover—would be destroyed. You will need special training and coaching, which I would provide. That's why this situation is so sensitive, and why I must discuss this myself with him tonight. I need to assure Holden that we have his back," Claire stated with utmost seriousness.

"I totally get it, and I will do everything in my power to prove to you that I'm up for this assignment," Danielle replied.

"Good," Claire said. "Then I'd like for you to report the cocktail lounge at 7:00 p.m., after Holden and I have met privately first. You can have a seat at the bar, and I'll motion you over to where we're sitting to meet Holden when the time is right. Wear your Herve Leger cocktail dress. You remember, the sheer blush-colored number with the flared skirt we bought together at Saks. It looks amazing on you. I'll ask Sheldon to come to your room to do your hair. I'm thinking a half-up/half-down style might suit you best. I've been studying the types of women that

Holden is photographed with in the celebrity social media, and we want to make your look consistent. I will introduce the two of you and you'll join us for a cocktail. You will take all your cues from me," Claire instructed.

Danielle nodded diligently, absorbing every word. She knew that Claire had hand-selected her for this plum assignment, and she wasn't about to blow it. Her ability to make Holden feel comfortable at La Levrier and confident that his sexual identity would be protected were critical.

6:50 p.m., Thursday

"Don't you look lovely tonight, Danielle," Jon complimented the Levriette as she swished down the corridor in her Herve gown. She whirled around, not expecting him to be exiting his suite, let alone on the property. Danielle wondered if Claire knew he was at La Levrier, as she had not mentioned his presence during their conversation earlier that afternoon when they were discussing Holden O'Keiffe.

"Oh, thank you so much, Mr. Fenwick," Danielle purred.

"Special date this evening?" he grinned in return.

"Oh, you might say that," she smiled.

"Well, I wish you the best of luck. I hope he's a far better match that I ever was," Jon joked.

"Does Claire know that you're here?" Danielle probed, trying her best to sound conversational.

"I honestly don't know," Jon said, feeling his pulse quicken at the mention of her name. "Unless Kenneth mentioned my arrival, she certainly has not sought me out."

By this time, the two had taken the elevator to the lower level and Danielle hastened her pace. She wanted to be punctual for her appearance at 7:00 p.m., just as Claire had instructed. And, to see Holden O'Keiffe up close and personal... Danielle could barely contain her excitement.

To her surprise, Jon matched her stride as she headed toward the Greyhound Lounge. She couldn't exactly tell him not to follow her, as that would be unprofessional. Like any La Levrier guest, he was entitled to pursue every amenity he desired, and the bar was open to all.

"It was nice running into you, and I hope you enjoy the rest of your evening," Danielle smiled politely at Jon as she hurried into the stately room. Jon got the hint that she needed to tend to her obligation, although he had hoped to continue the conversation over a cocktail to gather more insights about Claire's state of mind. Or more importantly, Claire's state of heart. Time was running out, and there was so much that Jon wanted—and needed—to resolve with her before fulfilling his obligation to Mac and the FBI tomorrow. He hadn't anticipated this hiccup in their relationship, almost as much as he hadn't foreseen the progression of it from the very beginning when he was first assigned to the case.

Reflecting back to the time he first met Claire at The Drake seemed like forever ago. While his trip to Coq d'Or was carefully planned, what followed wasn't—for either one of them. Their flirtatious dialogue over sharing a bowl of salted nuts that evening had spilled into discussion months later over sharing matters of the heart. And here he was, staring at the grandiose, gleaming gold bar in a room fit for a king and he suddenly felt very diminutive. While the lounge was impressive, it seemed ironically oppressive. Unwelcome, even. Yet, it was the one place he thought he might casually run into Claire.

He sidled up to the bar top and slid onto one of the leather stools. His peripheral vision caught Danielle sitting at the other end of the bar—solo. Had she just wanted to get away from him? He recalled Claire's systematic (and failed) attempt to match him up with Danielle at Lionel Edwards' book-signing lecture hosted at La Levrier several weeks ago. Claire had been so headstrong about steering him into the arms of other potential suitors in her effort to protect herself. Maybe she had been right all along. If he had kept his wits about him, Jon could have just as easily feigned attraction to another Levrier and used her as a decoy to ride the inside track of the business without the risk of raising suspicion by falling in love with the Goddamn president, CEO, and founder!

"The usual for you, Mr. Fenwick?" Saul, La Levrier's bartender, interrupted Jon's reminiscing.

"Thanks, but this time I'll take a Kelt VSOP. I'm in the mood for something a bit… stronger," Jon replied, not his typical chatty self. He sunk into the stool, unsure of even what to say if he saw Claire this evening.

Even the vibe of the lounge felt strangely different. Instead of a pianist tinkling the Steinway ivories, piped music enveloped the room. Jon could faintly hear the tune, but there it was—Stan Kenton and his orchestra playing the renowned "Lover." *What next?* Jon thought grimly. His and Claire's mutual admiration of Stan Kenton and the evening they shared during his performance at La Levrier came tumbling back. He remembered how exquisite she looked when the sultry saxophone wailed "Body and Soul" that night. *Cut the sentimental bullshit!* Jon demanded of himself, trying to will those thoughts out of his head. Nothing, but nothing, could stand in the way of the task he needed to perform the next morning. There was no going back now. He couldn't lose both Claire AND his job.

Suddenly, a hush of silence blanketed the room as all heads turned toward the entranceway. Jon swung his stool away from the bar and craned his neck to follow the gaze. What he was about to see almost made him choke on his sip of Kelt.

It was Claire. Not the typical Claire with her platinum hair neatly coiffed in a Grace Kelly-inspired updo, but an emboldened Claire whose locks touched the top of her shoulders in loose, sexy waves. Her choice of midnight blue, body-skimming velvet sheath accentuated Claire's youthful curves and toned legs, which ended in strappy heeled pumps. Tiny rhinestones glittering from the halter neckline of her dress cast an elegant glow even across the room. Claire's radiant style and sophistication were her signatures—tasteful, yet not always predictable. Certainly, Jon could have never predicted what he saw next.

Claire's arm was linked through one of the most perfect specimens of the male species Jon had ever witnessed. Watching the couple thread their way through the gathering in the lounge, smile and shake hands make his stomach turn. The way she playfully tilted her head back and tittered at someone's insipid joke. How she subtly swayed her hips in unison with the way her companion swaggered with confidence. He towered over her, at least 6'4, boasting a strong gait and fit physique.

Jon placed the man in his mid-30s, judging from how he wore his slightly long, dark blonde hair combed back and tucked behind his ears and boasted a barely noticeable scruff along his tanned, chiseled jawline. He had a straight, Romanesque nose and perhaps his most striking feature was the unusual shade of his eyes. As he and Claire drew closer, Jon could see that they were not quite blue or green, but a pale jade. Even without opening his mouth to reveal what Jon envisioned to be a perfectly straight set of pearly whites, he instantly resented the dude.

"Who the Hell is THAT?" Jon leaned in to ask Saul.

"You mean you don't know who Holden O'Keiffe is?" the bartender gasped.

"Seriously, Man, I must be out of the loop here. Is he the guy from last season's Bachelor?" Jon snorted, pointing to his glass for a refill.

Saul chuckled as he poured another round of Kelt. "Oh, he's more famous than that, Mr. Fenwick. Surely you saw Mayhem Town in the theaters… it was all the rage this past summer. O'Keiffe was the headliner."

"Oh, shit," Jon sneered. "I must have missed his stellar performance. But I'm sure getting a taste of it now."

Claire continued to parade her date around the room like a prized pony. She obviously had wasted no time corralling her next target. The new couple slipped away from the crowd and slid into a quiet corner table across the room. Although Jon didn't want to stare, he couldn't help trying to discreetly validate his assumptions. It would just be a matter of moments before they'd be clasping hands, Claire flushed with the excitement of being in the company of a famous younger man. He never envisioned her as the cougar type but, then again, there were a lot of things about Claire that Jon never imagined.

Jon continued to survey the table as Kenton's next tune, "Eager Beaver," pumped in the background. Curiously, Danielle emerged from her coveted bar stool and strode over to join Claire and her new lover. The couple welcomed and made room for Danielle. *A threesome?* Jon was stunned by the vision of Claire engaging in such an act. There was still more he didn't know or want to know about her.

"Another," Jon mumbled under his breath as Saul poured a third round of Kelt at half the amount as the previous two servings. Jon gripped the glass and swigged it down in a single gulp, giving him instant liquid courage.

"Well, well, well," Jon greeted the three lovebirds with a manufactured smile as he sauntered over to their table. "Mr. O'Keiffe, you are one very lucky man to be in the company of these two beautiful women. May your evening be simply… bewitching."

Claire froze and looked up at Jon in shock as she had not realized he was in the Greyhound Lounge. She quickly regained her composure, cleared her throat and stated pleasantly, "Holden, I'd like to introduce you to Jon. He is a regular at La Levrier and a friend of mine."

"Ah, yes… I am a FRIEND of Claire's," Jon smirked. "Is that what you're calling us now, Baby?"

Holden interrupted any tension between the two and extended his hand to Jon. Instead of shaking it graciously, Jon grabbed a cocktail napkin from the table and stuffed it in Holden's empty palm. He then quickly fished for a Mont Blanc felt-tip pen in the breast pocket of his sport coat.

"Oh, HOLDEN," Jon exaggerated. "Could I please impose upon you for an autograph?"

Claire shot Jon a dirty look and Danielle winced. Holden noticeably blushed as he took Jon's pen and scrawled his signature on the napkin. "The pleasure is all mine," he said, handling the tissue back to Jon.

"Thank you so much," Jon sighed. "As a token of my appreciation, please keep my pen. In fact," he said, looking at Claire and Danielle, "it might even come in quite HANDY behind closed doors with both of these sexy ladies. A man can never have too many toys, you know," he gave Holden a private wink. Holden looked visibly embarrassed and an awkward moment of silence hung in the air.

"Jon," Claire interrupted. "May I please have a private word with you?"

"YOU want a private something with a FRIEND?" Jon queried playfully. "Isn't that a violation of La Levrier's code of conduct?"

"Jon," Claire stated more firmly. "Let's step aside and allow Holden and Danielle to get acquainted." She then promptly stood, excused herself and grabbed Jon's elbow.

As soon as the two were out of earshot, she hissed, "Follow me." Claire led Jon down a lengthy passageway to the back of the mansion and into a secluded study filled with top-to-bottom bookshelves lining the walls behind a rolling ladder. In the library were Marcus and Javert sleeping soundly in their cushioned canine beds on the floor. As soon as Claire entered, they stood at full attention.

"That's okay, Boys," Claire soothed. "Lay down."

"They should recognize me by now. After all, I am your FRIEND," Jon snickered.

Claire, unamused, pointed to a cream leather loveseat.

"Do you want me to lay down as well? Am I in the dog house, too?" Jon baited.

"I want you to apologize for how you just behaved," Claire stated calmly without blinking.

"I thought I was rather charming," Jon sneered. "I simply asked for Holden's autograph and gave him a good TIP."

"You know exactly how you sounded. Like a total ass, Jon. It wasn't lost on me, and I'm sure it wasn't lost on him, either. It was completely inappropriate."

"You're really beautiful when you're angry, you know?" Jon stated.

"Stop, just stop," Claire held up her hand firmly.

"Stop what, Claire?" Jon grew serious. "Loving you? Pretending that I don't care how our conversation yesterday ended? Feeling like shit that I was thrown over the very next day for another guy? A flashier, younger dude… a Hollywood star of all people? This is so cliché… SO beneath you."

"That's what you think?" Claire challenged. "If you're really an FBI agent, you ought to do a better job researching your suspects. Perhaps you'd discover that Holden O'Keiffe doesn't exactly fit your stereotypical profile."

"That's nice to hear how special he is to you, Claire. I'm really touched," Jon spat.

"Do you know what is SO beneath YOU, Jon? Your petty jealousy. For the record, Holden and I are not an item. Not even close."

"Well, then both of you are great actors, because you could have fooled me. You looked awfully cozy," Jon retorted.

"I'm glad you thought so," Claire cracked a smile. "Now it's Danielle's turn to take the reins."

Jon looked completely deflated. He searched for the right words but was at a loss. Claire took a seat next to him on the couch and didn't speak for a few minutes, either, allowing the silence between them to linger.

"I don't know what to say," Jon finally spoke.

"I told you what I wanted to hear from you when we first entered this room," Claire responded.

"I'm… sorry," he said humbly. And he meant it.

"That's better," Claire stated. "When you drop the sarcasm, you rebuild trust, as a man and as my friend."

"There you go with the FRIEND jazz again," Jon sighed. "Is that all we are now?"

"Jon, I've gone out with many men who weren't my friends. To call you a friend is a compliment and an honor," she clarified. "It's something I don't say lightly."

"I'm grateful that you consider me your friend, but you still didn't answer my question," Jon pressed.

Claire paused. "Yes, Jon, we are more than just friends. A FRIEND of mine made me fully realize that this morning."

Jon looked at her deeply in the eyes, searching for truth. "Then please forgive me. Forgive me for how I behaved tonight and in the past. It was never my intention to hurt you. There are just parts of myself that are very private. I'm not an open book, and neither are you. We have to respect that about each other and, if you can find it in your heart, move forward."

"Well, that was the most lucid thing I've heard you say all night, Jon Fenwick," Claire grinned.

"See, I can keep my sarcasm in check when necessary," Jon stated.

"Ha!" Claire laughed. "I don't want to lose that amusing aspect of your personality. And…"

"And?" Jon probed.

"And I don't want to lose you, either," Claire added softly.

She leaned in to kiss Jon with tender affection, stood up, smoothed her gown and prepared to leave. "I'll see you tomorrow, Jon. There are some matters I need to tend to now, if you'll excuse me."

With that, Claire was gone.

After Claire left Jon sat alone and chided himself. *"God damnit, what's wrong with me? Too much to drink? Too in love with her? That was not me out there, I have to get better control of myself."*

CHAPTER TWENTY-FOUR

Coitus Interruptus

La Levrier 6:30 a.m. Friday

Jon's phone alarm rang. The gentle buzz could not be heard outside his suite. Not a morning person, he leaned over to the side of the bed and let gravity pull his legs to the floor. He stood, wobbled, gained his balance, then stretched. He walked over to the bar in his suite pressed a button and fresh Intelligensia coffee began to brew from whole beans that were automatically ground to order. A half smile grew as he thought, *"This place, they had my favorite blend from day one. I'm going to miss this all."*

A leisurely trip to the bathroom and his coffee was waiting. The aroma filled the room. It was so fragrant he did become a bit concerned that its arousing scent would call attention to his activity had it escaped from his room. All his movements this morning would have to be measured and undetected. Guests and even staff were typically not up and about in this love den at such an early hour.

He walked over to the sofa and looked over the canisters of gas explosives, a black hydration backpack, his running shoes and his black and teal running suit. He had laid them all out the night before. He placed the canisters in the backpack and stood the backpack up on the back of the sofa so that the canisters would not tip. There was no reason to do that other than attention to detail as the explosives were safely enclosed in the tin no matter what position they lay.

Jon drained the coffee without hurry. He looked toward the coffee service as if to make another cup, but decided he was stimulated enough to begin this day without the second kickstart. He showered and sprayed just a light mist of his Mount Blanc cologne. He dressed, and as he strapped his Garmin running watch around his wrist, he noted the time: 7:10 a.m. "Good." He whispered to himself. Then he put the backpack around his shoulders and draped the plastic straw on his chest. He looked like he was going for a morning run.

He exited his room slowly and closed the door with both hands as to not have the antique doors creak his arrival into the hallway. Being extra stealth was second nature. Jon counted on the fact that La Levrier did not have a morning presence any more than he usually did. The stillness that blanketed the hallway on his floor patted him on the back that he would go unnoticed on this leg of his journey. His room was a short distance from both the elevator and the stairs. The stairs were the obvious choice for this duty, as the elevator would make too much noise.

He walked down the stairway making sure his steps landed on the padded carpet that adorned the middle of each stair. He didn't use the railing so as not to risk a noise from the old lacquered oak.

He arrived at the next floor without incident and descended on to another floor of suites. He looked down the hallways, and no one was about. He proceeded downward as carefully as he began.

As he approached the first floor, he paused on the stairs to remember how to get down to the lower level without taking the elevator. The only time he was in the lower level he attended the jazz concert with Claire, and he took the elevator down. Was there even a stairway to that level? There had to be, he thought.

Jon shook his head and reasoned that he need not be extra cautious on this floor as there would be nothing wrong with him walking on the first floor, especially dressed for a run at this hour, so he proceeded and took the risk that he may encounter someone on this level. He planned for this, so he kept going, now with a more normal gait.

Much to his surprise, the first floor had the same stillness that enveloped the rest of the sleepy mansion so early on a typical day. La Levrier wasn't a morning venue. He smiled, but his confidence waned as he still had the problem of finding a stairway down to the lower level or basement as he called it in his briefing manual. At the bottom of the stairs, he looked around and scanned the area for a door that opened to a stairway. A door concealing a stairway to the lower level would be the typical architecture of such a home as this, at least in his estimation. Standing in the marbled foyer, he scanned the first floor in every direction. From this vantage point he could not see the doorway he sought. There was the grand foyer where he paused, the sitting lounge with the polished black Steinway and another lounge across from it that had a copper bar that beamed a shine that bragged of not a single tarnish or smudge. The requisite mirror consumed the back wall behind the bar and Jon could see his reflection in the mirror. The remainder of the expanse had hallways that fed into this luxurious space. Now, the choice was which hallway to choose to uncover the elusive door to the lower level. It almost seemed like one of those schmaltzy game shows with the prize behind one door of many. The thought of the elevator came to his mind again because it would save time, but he couldn't remember how much noise it made as his only time in it was during a time in the mansion with the typical clatter of a busy space. There was no telling how much noise a 100-year-old elevator makes. No, it had to be the stairs for sure. He opted for silence over speed.

Having been in many investigations where he had to search through abandoned old buildings used by drug dealers and such, he contemplated the layout of a mansion like this. He made a choice and walked to the hallway to his right and just east of another hallway. When he entered the chosen hallway, there were several doors on either side immediately to his left and right.

He opened one door, and it revealed a humidor with slanted shelves each filled with cigars, pipes, pipe tobacco, packs of luxury cigarettes from around the world and vape refills. As he closed the door he was startled by a greeting, "Mr. Fenwick, may I help you?" Kenneth asked.

"Kenneth, whoa, you gave me a start I have to admit!" Jon said easily, as it was both true and embellished to advance his ruse.

"I didn't know a smoke was part of a runner's routine?" Kenneth chuckled.

"Come on Kenneth, you never saw that famous poster of the Tour de France riders all smoking on one of the legs of the race? It's classic. In fact, I'm surprised La Levrier doesn't have a copy framed in the workout room." Jon joked back.

Kenneth laughed and then offered more help, "Is there a special smoke I can help you with? It is a bit unusual for our guests to help themselves you know. I didn't even know you knew about this humidor?"

"I didn't want to disturb anyone at this hour, my friend. And, I have a confession, every now and then, after a longer run I do treat myself to a Turkish cigarette. Just one. It's a treat for a good long run." Jon looked into the shelves. "Do you have any?"

Kenneth smiled. "Actually, there are four Turkish brands here. Strong? Mild? Medium?" Kenneth reached into the humidor and nimbly grabbed four unopened packs and spread them in both of his hands.

"I don't see the brand I usually smoke. Give me one medium and a lighter. I'll bring that back," Jon answered.

Kenneth handed him the cigarette and a silver lighter with the likeness of Javert embossed on one side and Marius on the other.

"This is cool," Jon said admiring the lighter.

"With our compliments, of course. No need to return it after your run," Kenneth puffed.

Jon put the cigarette and lighter into the pocket of his running jacket. He turned to walk toward the grand entryway, then he paused. Kenneth was already walking ahead of him and into the lounge area near the Steinway.

"Kenneth, one more question. Is there a back exit? I don't feel suitable to go out and come in all sweaty, and smoky, after my run?" Jon smiled.

"Oh, that's quite fine, Mr. Fenwick, this is your place. Just use the front door," Kenneth insisted.

"All right then. But, I hope a dignitary isn't arriving as I trudge up the stairs," Jon pressed.

"All our guests are dignitaries, Mr. Fenwick. That's why you use the front door for your run, please," Kenneth retorted.

Jon strolled slowly into the lounge, through the foyer into the other lounge and toward the bar. He stopped at the bar and poured a glass of water from a crystal pitcher that was atop a silver serving tray. He looked as natural as could be and Kenneth paid no attention. Kenneth walked as if he had some duty to perform so Jon assessed he would be alone again in a matter of seconds.

"Kenneth, one more question," Jon summoned Kenneth toward him in a tone a bit above a whisper.

"Yes, sir?" Kenneth snapped.

"I don't know why this came to me right this second, but while I was sipping my water, I just had a flash memory of the cabaret on the lower level. How do I get to that? I'd love to see what that looks like empty. It was such a magnificent space." Jon brainstormed.

"I'll take you down in the elevator, sir," Kenneth answered obediently.

"No, no. I don't want to wake anyone with the clank of that old thing. And, besides, you look like you have something to attend to. What door do I go down to take the stairs? I just want to get a quick peek. I'll only be a minute."

"It's in the hallway behind you. Second door to the left." That was the opposite hallway Jon initially took in his snooping.

"Great, I'll finish my water, grab a peek of the cabaret and off to my run," Jon announced.

As Kenneth walked out of sight, he whispered, "And have the Turkish as your treat!" He chirped.

Feeling as though he dodged a bullet, Jon finished the water and as he drank his eyes darted around every corner of the room to make sure Kenneth was out of sight and to catch the possibility of any more staff or guests coming to surprise him. No one appeared, so he put the glass down and wasted no time getting to the stairs that led to the lower level. The cabaret was as good as any area to leave his deadly packages.

Jon was at the door to the cabaret within seconds. He entered and flipped the stairway light on to reveal a spectacular stainless-steel staircase. The stairs, the rail, the walls were all highly polished stainless steel. The steps had raised pimples in the metal for grip; otherwise, everything else was polished and shined with such care that it had a mirrored effect. When he reached the bottom of the stairs, the glow of the stairway and the stainless steel gave him enough light that he easily found the light switch for the cabaret. Once he flipped that switch the room came alive with the elegance he noticed when he attended the concert. The room's beauty was even more pronounced in this empty state.

"Geezus, this is one elegant space," Jon thought to himself as pursed his lips and shook his head in a 'what a shame' expression. He was consumed with a sense of loss at the grandeur of this mansion. But, he dealt with such feelings on so many other assignments when he had to take away something of value to someone, he didn't let that feeling detract him from the actions he had to take this morning. He pressed on in spite of his heavy heart. He was about to put into motion the loss of La Levrier and Claire.

He scanned the room and calculated the approximate center point. There was a table and three café chairs in that spot. It would be a perfect place to lay the canisters. He moved between the other tables and wiggled out of his backpack when he reached the spot. He put the three canisters in a grouping that surrounded the single metal stem of the table. He looked for a second, and he removed the plastic straw tube from his hydration backpack and wrapped it around the canisters. He fused the ends together with the La Levrier lighter to act as a clasp and the entire bundle sat neat and tight against the table stem. He stood up and stepped back to admire his work. It looked like it might belong there if someone was just glancing around the room. The room had enough going on to catch the eye if those tin cans had to sit there for days Jon would bet they had a good chance to go undetected.

Jon stepped back a bit more to take a final look at his handiwork and he looked at his watch.

"What the fuck are those pieces of shit you put down there?" A gun barrel poked Jon in the small of his back as the voice boomed in the empty room.

Jon recognized the voice immediately, Ted. The gun pressed into him harder. "Put your arms straight out and just freeze right here," Ted commanded.

Jon was silent. He did precisely as Ted asked.

"You didn't figure we had security cameras on every inch of the mansion? What kind of security firm genius are you? Our camera's software alerts me if any suspicious behavior is detected in any section of the building. A bit dumb on your part to come down here. A room with no traffic unless there is a party. My video picked you up immediately, Agent Fenwick." Ted pressed the gun even deeper into Jon's back.

"I oughta end this right here," Ted stated.

Jon kept silent.

"But, I want Claire to see all this first." Ted looked around the room, keeping the pistol firmly in Jon's back.

"There is no way she can deny who you are and what you are up to now."

As if planning his next move, Ted paused, holding the gun tightly against Jon's back.

"We're going to walk slowly over to that corner to the left," Ted ordered.

Jon also saw what Ted spotted. Along with some audio wire there was a full roll of duct-tape on top of a speaker. Jon guessed that Ted's planned to bind him with the tape and call Claire and others to come down to the cabaret. That couldn't happen.

Jon began to walk in minute steps and Ted didn't protest. *He's not done this before,* Jon thought, because someone with more experience puts the non-gun hand on the perpetrator's collar, grabs hold and pushes him forward at their pace. You keep the control and the balance. Besides, you don't keep a gun buried in a perp's back. You let them know it's there and hold it inches away from the bad guy for maximum effect if you have to discharge it. *"He's nervous,"* Jon surmised.

Using that knowledge, Jon turned with lightning agility and executed a spin move. Jon grabbed the gun with one continuous action and directed it away from either of them. As Jon did that, Ted reared back and landed a ferocious blow to Jon's face. The punch snapped Jon's head back, but Jon did not let go of the pistol.

Ted reached back to deliver another punch and as it came toward Jon, he blocked it with his free hand. In one motion Jon took his hand and in a straight trajectory he placed a powerful blow directly in the center of Ted's face landing to the side of his nose. The blow stunned Ted so much that it caused him to loosen his grip on the gun and Jon snapped the gun out of Ted's hand.

With his arm extended from taking the gun away from Ted, Jon instinctively whipped that arm back into the side of Ted's head and the force of his hand with the metal of the gun hitting Ted's temple. Ted fell to the floor and was knocked unconscious.

Jon looked over Ted on the ground to assess his condition and as he did he shook his head and felt his jaw where Ted struck him. "*That little bastard can punch,*" Jon said to himself.

After that brief pause he didn't waste any more time. He rushed over and grabbed the duct-tape and double wrapped a piece around Ted's mouth. He then lifted him up and sat him on one of the cafe chairs. In seconds, took the chair and dragged it across the floor to a column in the far corner of the room. He taped Ted and the chair securely to the column leaving no wiggle room for Ted to loosen the tape. This was not Jon's first rodeo at immobilizing a prisoner.

Jon flipped the lights off as he dashed out of the cabaret and up the stairs. At the top of the stairs he peeked out the door. The area was still empty although in the distance he saw a staff person in gray checked pants and white tunic walk between hallways carrying a tray. No one to worry about. He stepped out into the hallway and immediately into the grand entrance. He checked his watch, 7:49 a.m. Ten more minutes until his team arrived. He had to hurry.

On the way through the lounges he stopped and wrapped some ice in a cloth napkin and iced his jaw. "*Damn, that kid can hit.*"

"Mr. Fenwick, that was not a very long run." Kenneth surprised Jon again.

"I know, I tripped on some cold, wet pavement and whacked my jaw on a pole." Jon quickly covered his tracks with Kenneth.

"Ouch, I'll have our doctor come up to your suite," Kenneth offered.

"No… no worries. I'm fine. This ice will do the trick. I'm fine, really."

"Suit yourself. I guess no treat then after your run?" Kenneth inquired.

Jon pulled the cigarette out of his pocket and held it straight up. He frowned, then remarked, "I'm afraid not on this one. But, I'll keep it for next time."

With the clock ticking, Jon had to be polite and not arouse suspicion but he had to hustle upstairs to his room, so he bounced up the stairs and left Kenneth hanging in the conversation. Kenneth seemed to understand and Jon's deception continued to keep Kenneth at bay.

Once in his room and with the ice still on his jaw, Jon grabbed his cell phone and called Williams. "Brad, I ran into a slight alteration to the procedures here. First, I'm running a bit late, so take your time getting over here…"

Williams interrupted, "We're on the truck and on the way, probably a few blocks from Astor Street right now."

"OK, well slow down or even wait outside for a bit and give me some time to get collected here. Five minutes," Jon instructed.

"No problem," Williams blurted.

"So, that brings me to the second alteration in our plans. When you or Rodgers do your floor by floor search and evacuation, you are going to find a guy duct-taped to a chair in the lower level," Jon informed.

"OK, typical kink for that place. Go on," Williams deadpanned.

"All right smart guy. We don't have time to play here, but I get it. It's a long story. You'll get it at the debriefing.

But, anyway, cut him loose, cuff him because he's going to put up a fight, he's like a freak'n mongoose, and drape him in one of those big fire department blankets and escort him out a back door," Jon detailed.

"I don't see a back door anywhere near that lower level," Williams shot back.

"We have time, just bring him up to the next level and find a back door. Just don't bring him out the front door, OK. Not that complicated." Jon was becoming agitated and hurried.

"OK, what do you want me to do with him from there?" Williams asked, matter of factly.

"Get him in a vehicle and take him to headquarters. Do not put him in with the other evacuated people. Got that?" Jon insisted.

"Roger," Williams acknowledged.

Jon changed quickly into tan dress slacks, white button-down shirt, and a sport coat. He threw his FBI ID, his revolver and his cell phone in the jacket pockets. He packed for this visit very strategically so as not to lose any of his belongings in the rubble that was to become La Levrier. He collected himself and sat on the sofa, iced his jaw and waited for the show to start.

CHAPTER TWENTY-FIVE

Chicago Fire

Friday 8:00 a.m.

A hook and ladder truck, an ambulance and a battalion chief's red and black SUV drove up Astor street and stopped in front of 60 East Astor Street--La Levrier. To no one's surprise, they were right on time. Given Jon's instructions, all the vehicles waited in the middle of the street. Two Chicago Police squad cars blocked off any possible traffic that would come down Astor Street by parking on the east and west ends of the street. The squads turned on their emergency lights. The police officers got out of their cars and blocked the sidewalks from foot traffic as well. The stage was set.

Friday 8:03 a.m.

Jon texted Williams to let him know that he was ready to roll. With that message, Williams and Rodgers got out of the hook and ladder and with no urgency they walked up the front steps of La Levrier. They politely rang the bell and looked at each other with a smile on their faces remembering the wordplay with Jon the day before when they bantered with him about knocking or ringing the bell.

Kenneth opened the door in under a minute. "May I help you, errr, officers?" Kenneth asked.

"We're firefighters," Rodgers spoke up. "But, thanks for the promotion, not every firefighter is an officer. That's police."

"My mistake. I just am not used to fire people ringing the door in the morning," Kenneth added.

"Well, us fire people, are here on a bit of a serious purpose," Williams deadpanned. "We've been alerted by the gas company that your gas meter is showing unusual activity such that they suspect a possible leak in your pipes." Williams paused for Kenneth's reaction. Kenneth kept silent and waited for Williams' next remarks.

"So, we need to do an inspection but, with the nature of the report they received, we also need to evacuate the building as a safety precaution," Williams explained.

"I imagine we can arrange a date to do that. But, I would have to alert the owner of the building to schedule that time," Kenneth dutifully responded.

"Ahhh, I probably didn't make this crystal clear, we need this building to evacuate right now. Immediately," Williams said more forcefully.

Williams took a document from the clipboard he was holding and showed Kenneth an order and permit from the Chicago Housing Department that authorized the evacuation and inspection. The word: 'Immediate' boldly highlighted on the paper.

"That's not possible. We have guests, and I'm assuming they are not even awake yet."

Without a word, Williams lifted the clipboard to Kenneth's eye level and slightly jiggled it in front of his face.

Kenneth paused, then stated, "I have to speak to the owner. Can you wait here while I get her?" Kenneth didn't wait for an answer before he turned and rushed up the stairs.

Within minutes, Claire came down to the foyer wearing a white silk robe with pink and blue flower print and white boudoir slippers. Danielle was with her and had on a white silk robe and matching heeled slippers herself. Both Williams' and Rodgers' eyes widened at the elegance and beauty of the two when they arrived.

"Kenneth tells me we have an issue?" Claire directed to the agents.

"As I was explaining to this gentleman, the gas company has alerted us to a potentially dangerous condition at this address, and we have to inspect and evacuate the premises immediately." Williams stopped and stared at Claire. He showed her the permit and waited for her response.

Returning the stare-down in equal measure, Claire announced, "I have to call my attorney." She took the permit from William's hands and looked down at the paper.

"Ah, Ma'am, this order doesn't provide for any deliberation. This building has to be evacuated now. There is imminent danger for any and all that may be inside here. I'm sure, like us, you don't want anyone who is in this building hurt if there is an explosion?" Williams argued.

"Miss, consider this like a fire drill. Everyone steps outside for a bit while we conduct our inspection and if we find what's wrong here, and it is safe to go back in, then no harm, no foul," Rodgers spoke up.

Turning to Kenneth, Claire asked, "Have you located Teddy?"

"Not yet. I called him, but I didn't physically look for him," Kenneth answered.

"Ma'am, we don't have time to debate the logistics of all this right now. My orders are to clear out your house here. Right now. I've got a battalion chief sitting outside and the street blocked off. In fact, I can't let you all go back upstairs. I need to escort you outside immediately. Now, Mr. Kenneth here can help us go floor by floor and ask anybody who is inside to leave..." Williams started to explain.

"Brad, no, Mr. Kenneth cannot go with us. It's too risky. We'll get everyone out ourselves," Rodgers corrected.

"You're right, you're right," Williams acknowledged. "You all need to step outside immediately. There are people outside to help you." Williams insisted.

"Can we get our coats, at least?" Claire asked. Her look was a combination of alarm, disgust, and disbelief.

"We have people waiting with nice warm, comfy blankets to escort you to a heated vehicle where you can wait. I can't emphasize enough... there is no time to waste here," Williams insisted.

"Rodgers, start clearing the building. I'll escort these three out into the holding vehicle.

Claire, Danielle, and Kenneth dutifully walked with Williams out of the front door. Immediately, real firefighters and the paramedics draped them in heavy wool blankets and led them to a bus that had now arrived on the scene.

Rodgers walked up the steps of the mansion and headed to the top floors first to begin the evacuation. She knew that the prisoner was bound in the basement and planned to save that area for last. Her orders were to get the guy in the lower level out in secret.

Patrons of La Levrier began to file out of the front door within minutes. They were also escorted to the waiting bus. They all had on their own coats, being aroused from their suites. The members and staff all seemed to have a good spirit about the fuss and none protested the inconvenience. Claire, Danielle, and Kenneth each occupied a window seat and were looking out at the activity flowing from their mansion.

Inside the bus, Kenneth rose from his seat and stationed himself near the driver's seat. He greeted each of the La Levrier guests and staff and explained the situation as much as he knew of it in a comforting tone with assurances of their privacy and safety. Most of the guests stopped to also converse with Claire who added her apologies to everyone. Danielle took a lighter tone with all the arrivals and tried to paint this all as an adventure. "La Levrier always strives to provide a memorable experience that you will laugh and chat about for years," was one of her quips that she told the guests as they settled into their seats. "We'll see if we can't get some mimosas here soon," was another of her remarks. The guests all seemed to love the party tone she introduced inside the bus.

Julia, the Levriette that was the nanny for Javert and Marius walked onto the bus with the dogs on either side of her. With elegant steps that resembled a prance, both dogs climbed the steps of the bus with a burst of energy. The unfamiliar entrance to the vehicle fueled their energetic bounce up the stairs. As soon as her beloved pets reached the top steps of the bus and spotted Claire, they scampered over to her and she hugged them both. They laid on the floor of the bus next to Claire's seat from thereafter.

Swiveling her head one way to greet the guests, then back to look out the window, Claire searched for Jon to alight out the front door. He was the last one to leave and Williams, who had returned inside to help with the evacuation, was walking behind him. Jon kept the posture as if he and Williams did not know each other. Rodgers was left inside to finish the evacuation.

Rodgers finally continued her search inside with a trip to the cabaret. She immediately spotted the chair where Ted was bound. Ted was not there just the remnants of the tape dangling from the chair in shreds.

Rodgers immediately called Jon. "Jon, we've got a problem here. That guy you said was going to be downstairs is… ahh… gone."

"Shit, that little fucker is a weasel," Jon snapped. "Okay, we don't have time to worry about him. He's not in the building anywhere, right?"

"I'm sure. Listen, I'll give another search but I looked under every nook and cranny."

"Lock the doors behind you as you go through each room. Yell while you walk and announce emergency evacuation. I'll send some other people in as well. This is going to tie things up a bit, but we've got all day. Not like this place is really going to explode on its own anyway," Jon commanded.

"Gotcha," Rodgers replied while walking through the building.

The door of the battalion chief's red SUV opened and Mac stepped out dressed as if a fire lieutenant. She walked right up to Jon who was across the street from La Levrier and constantly on his phone.

Claire watched the activity from her window in the bus. With her eyes squinted like a hawk's and biting her lower lip, there was no mistaking the look of concern on her face. She turned to Danielle, now settled back into the window seat behind Claire. "Hmmm, I wonder what the fire person there is asking Jon?" Claire asked.

"She looks like a higher up. I'm guessing that because she doesn't have all the fire suit and helmet and such. And, she looks mean. She almost looks like she is yelling at Jon." Danielle observed.

"I know. And where the hell is Teddy?" Claire lamented.

"Maybe he had a date last night and didn't make it home?" Danielle wondered consolingly.

"I hope so. I guess it's not unusual he's not around 24 hours. It's just what bad timing that he's not here, for now, to help us through all of this mess." Claire paused and raised her voice for Kenneth to hear, "Kenneth, you did say you called Teddy, right?"

From his seat two rows in front of Claire, Kenneth turned around and responded, "Yes, Ms. Bernardin, as I said at the door when the fire department first arrived, I called Ted. Actually, I called for him several times and left messages as I was walking up the stairs to fetch you." Claire just stared out the window with her eyes on Jon.

The spirit of the guests and staff on the bus was festive. One of the guests even yelled out, "Danielle, when do those mimosas arrive?" another added, "Any chance of an omelet along with that?" Danielle, always deft on her feet, responded to both requests with, "As you can see, the police didn't have the foresight to allow The Peninsula to deliver our catering order that I called in earlier." The bus burst out in laughter and resumed lively conversation between the guests and their lovers.

Mac marched right up to Jon, "What's the hold-up here Fenwick?" she demanded.

"I was confronted by an employee while I was positioning the explosives. I subdued him and left him on the lower level. Rodgers or Williams was supposed to undo him and then take him out the back way, but when Rodgers arrived on the lower level, he was gone. Rodgers did report that the explosives are still in position so we are ready to go as soon as we can be assured he or no one else is in the building. It will be just a few more minutes," Jon detailed unconcerned.

"Let's just get this thing going, huh? I'm not hanging around here all day dressed in this Halloween costume." Mac thought she offered a good joke. It fell flat on Jon.

"Mac, it's not like there is a real emergency here. We don't have an egg timer on this thing. I want to make sure we have everybody out safe before I press the trigger." Jon waved his phone in Mac's face. His phone displayed the triggering app to set off the explosives.

"Goddamnit. I'm on the hook to call Washington as soon as this thing blows today. Let me remind you that they and I have been waiting for this for weeks now. Get this going. Pull the damn trigger. Your constant delays and shuffling on this case is insufferable and borders on incompetence. This goes in my report." She waved a finger in Jon's face countering his phone maneuver. Then spun around and headed back to the SUV.

Claire, Danielle, and Kenneth looked out their windows mesmerized by the body language between Mac and Jon. They couldn't tell if he was in trouble, if he knew this person from his security business, or there was another explanation for the confrontation between the two. Several times, thinking she had made eye contact with him, Claire waved Jon to join them on the bus. He didn't respond. He apparently didn't see Claire's motioning. Claire was becoming very concerned.

Friday 9:05a.m.

"Yo Jon, Brad here. There is not a living thing in this place. You are good to go anytime you want," Williams said calling Jon on his cell.

"Thanks, Brad. Get your people out of there and text me when you have your headcount and are over here in the safety zone," Jon replied.

Jon then patched in a call to all the agents and the emergency personnel. "This is Jon Fenwick. Everyone stand clear and be ready. At 9:08 I am pulling the trigger. Rescue bus, change in plans. Keep the bus with the civilians close. I want the owner to see that this is real."

Sitting in the battalion chief's SUV, Mac smiled at Jon's last statement. He recovered some points with her by making Claire Bernardin sit and watch her life literally crumble in front of her eyes. That one command dispelled any thought Mac had that all these delays had anything to do with Jon protecting this Bernardin woman. Mac whispered to herself, "Good." She then lowered her head to count down on her watch the three minutes before the building would implode.

Many of the agents in fire gear and the real fire personnel were looking at their watches as well as they stood on the sidewalk across from La Levrier.

The observant Claire noticed so many people looking at their watches. Their stances, as if waiting for a countdown, aroused her suspicions and she became more curious as to the exact nature of this whole, weird activity. She stood up to leave the bus. Javert and Marius stood along with her, but Claire motioned for Julia to keep the dog near her.

Friday 9:08 a.m.

Jon stood alone directly across the street from the front door of the mansion.

"Okay, everyone. Here we go."

CHAPTER TWENTY-SIX

Rescue

All of the fire personnel, the FBI, and the police were wide-eyed and filled with excitement to watch the big bang that was about to occur. Claire, Danielle, Kenneth, the La Levrier staff and all the guests in the buses continued to focus on everything else but the building. By that moment, Kenneth, at Claire's direction told all the staff and guests the truth as they knew it. The fire department suspected a possible leak and their inspection was routine. Kenneth ended his announcement with a lilt in his voice, "These old buildings have such quirks, God knows what shot our gas meter up." His confident, light-hearted explanation roused a chuckle out of those in the main bus. He called over to the second bus, was put on speakerphone, and made the same announcement. His inflection was a carbon copy of his first performance and everyone greeted his message with the same good-natured outpouring. The joking by the guests was lively and loud. Not a single member seemed perturbed or outraged by the inconvenience. Of course, their Levriettes did a superb job of entertaining their members as they waited for this inspection to end.

Jon stood in his spot across the street from the mansion and alternated between looking at his cell phone and La Levrier. Mac divided her attention between Jon and the mansion. Suddenly, Jon waved Mac over. She stormed over to him.

"What now?" She demanded.

"I'm concerned about that guy I tied up in the basement," Jon said with a worried look on his face."

"Goddamnit, Fenwick. Your team searched that place!" Mac barked. "There is no one in there. Now let's get this done and get back to better things to do with our time."

"Mac, I just thought of some hidden passages and doorways that they might have missed. You know how these old mansions are. Come on. We blow up a citizen; this blows up on you. I have to be sure. What's a few more minutes?"

"So…?" She cracked, perturbed.

"Let me go inside one more time and check a couple of these hiding places that might have been missed." He paused for a moment. "Here, you take the phone. I'll run out of there after my search, give you the all clear and you can pull the trigger. This way you can report to your Washington buddies that you personally made it happen."

Although she didn't acknowledge it, Jon could see in her eyes that she was elated with this idea. He handed her the phone without another word and walked toward the front entrance.

In the bus, Danielle turned to Claire and Kenneth, "What is Mr. Fenwick doing going back into the mansion? And, how is he involved?" Neither had a response and just stared at the scene while everyone else on the bus ignored what was happening and focused on other doings.

Once inside, Jon went straight into the cabaret. He walked over to the table where the explosives were strapped and bent down. As he looked closer at the canisters, a forearm wrapped around his neck and began to choke him tightly. He instinctively stood up and carried the attacker on his back. In one fluid motion, he flipped his assailant over his head releasing the head-lock and throwing the person onto the floor. Chairs and tables clanged together and the attacker slid across the immaculately polished floor.

"What the fuck, Ted?" Jon yelled down to Teddy. Piled on top of Teddy were chairs and café tables. Ted flailed his arms like windmills to throw the furniture off him and he sprung to his feet, ready to rush at Jon. Jon put a hand up and yelled, "Stop, just stop right there," Jon commanded. Jon took out his Berretta, flipped off the safety with a flick of his thumb and pointed it at Teddy. "I won't kill you, but I sure the hell will make you hurt real bad for a long time. Now stop right there."

Teddy did as commanded and stopped in his tracks. He was breathing heavy and his head was downcast and teeth clenched. He studied Jon for the slightest opening to lunge at him.

Jon knew what Teddy was capable of and could sense his attack mode, so he had only one alternative. He had to let Teddy in on his plan. "Here's the deal. I came back in to disarm these bombs. I never planned to blow up La Levrier. I love your sister and wouldn't hurt her in any way." Teddy's breathing toned down just a notch but he still looked as if he would rip Jon apart given the chance.

"Yes, I am FBI, yes, La Levrier has been under investigation. God knows who put a bug in somebody's butt and wants it shut down, but, YES, I had the orders to shut its operation down by any means necessary. And, yes,

I am not going to let that happen, and yes, you and I are going to NOT let that happen. Understand?" Jon asked.

Teddy's fury abated. He caught his breath. "Why should I believe you?" He asked.

"Well, I am certainly not going to blow up myself and you can walk out with me," Jon assured. He holstered his pistol and relaxed his stance toward Teddy. Teddy responded in kind and Jon could sense that Teddy wasn't going to rush him, at least not at that moment.

"Here's the deal. Help me defuse the canisters. You just unscrew the top, just like the top of a thermos. The detonator is under each cap. Rip it out and put it in your pocket. Hand me the contents of the canister and I'm going to replace it with a harmless gel that looks exactly like the explosive that was in there." They both knelt on the floor immediately and began the process as Jon kept reciting instructions. "We are going to walk out the front door and I'm going to give my superior the thumbs up to ignite the building. When nothing happens, all chaos will break out. We just slip away," Jon calmly stated.

"What about Claire and the others?" Teddy asked as he ripped off the detonator of the first canister.

"We are going to make an end-around and go over to the bus where they are. I'm in charge of this operation, so no one will question what I am doing with the suspects. We'll get Claire, Danielle, Kenneth and the staff and we'll get the hell outta here." Jon concentrated on a particularly difficult detonator that wouldn't rip off. "This was my plan all along until you showed up in the cabaret and wanted to take my head off."

Teddy was already finished with two canisters and handed Jon the volatile contents. "What the hell was I to think? I was just doing my job," Teddy snipped back at him.

"We'll reminisce later. Let's get this done. I've bought time with my boss out there, but too much time and she'll get even more of an itchy trigger finger." They both concentrated on the task at hand. Jon unfolded a thin, nylon backpack from his pocket, slipped the real explosives into it and strapped it on his back. He put his sport coat over the backpack so that it wouldn't be readily seen by his people once they exited the building. Teddy watched the attention to detail and then trusted that Jon was telling him the truth about not intending to go through with the explosion. Jon strapped the canisters back on the café table just how he set them up and they began to leave the cabaret level.

It took them less than a minute, and they appeared at the front entranceway of La Levrier for everyone to see them. Jon had Teddy walk in front of him. Jon had a hand on Teddy's shoulder as if he was leading him forward like a prisoner but, as if continuing to play the ruse of the fake inspection, he didn't make it look too aggressive or hostile.

As Jon and Teddy reached the last step, they turned to the left and walked a bit down the street. They began to cross the street to the opposite side. It was at this point that Jon gave a wave to Mac as if all clear. As Mac concentrated on the phone, Jon and Teddy rushed into the walkway between two houses and disappeared.

Mac waited a few minutes, looked around at where all the official personnel gathered and when she was confident that everyone was clear, she pressed the phone to detonate the explosions. Nothing happened. She fiddled with the phone. Nothing happened. She called over one of her lieutenants. They both looked over the phone. Nothing happened.

"Get Fenwick over here!" Mac yelled.

Jon and Teddy went through the yards of houses and circled the positions where Mac and the bulk of the FBI were. They approached the bus where Claire and her people were watching the activity on the street. Jon knocked on the bus doors, and they immediately opened for him. He asked for Claire and all her staff to follow him and they did without question. Jon's personal cell phone was ringing and ringing in his pocket. He ignored it.

As the group walked at a brisk pace away from Astor Street, Jon turned to Claire, "Call your garage and get enough limos to get us all into. Have them meet us at Chestnut Street. From there we'll figure out what to do."

Claire nodded to Teddy and he made the call. Chestnut Street was a short two blocks away from that spot and they all walked between buildings hidden from the view of any of the personnel on Astor Street.

Jon stopped between houses at one point and took off the backpack under his sport coat. He laid the contents on the ground. Just above it was a spout for a garden hose. He opened the lever and let water spray the clear plastic bags filled with the dangerous gas. The plastic melted once the water made contact and the gas harmlessly puddled and became inert.

Across the street from La Levrier, Mac was confused and angry, "Where the hell is goddamn Fenwick?" No one could give her that answer. She stood and stared at La Levrier straining to come up with a plan on the spot. The time was intolerable to all her agents, firefighters and police. The Chicago police and firefighters were becoming agitated and their officers approached Mac for some direction in what was going on.

A fire captain got right into Mac's face, "I want to pull my people out of here, but we can't leave this scene until we know it's safe. I'm not having my people walk in there. I'm going to call the police bomb squad over and have them inspect the charges before we do anything else," he ordered. "What kind of a half-assed operation are you conducting here?" He rhetorically added as he walked away and began to make the call. He shook his head as he got further away from Mac.

"Asshole… we've got bomb experts too," Mac muttered under her breath. Williams cautioned her, "Let it go. Let them bring their people in and then we can start over."

"What the hell, that's going to take hours. Where the fuck is FENWICK!" She demanded.

CHAPTER TWENTY-SEVEN

The Big Bang Theory

The limos arrived promptly on Chestnut Street. Jon and the administrative staff of La Levrier huddled into the black Mercedes stretch autos. Claire, Danielle, Teddy, and Jon occupied the limo first in line of the four cars that parked on the street waiting for Claire and her staff.

"Jon, what's going on here?" Claire insisted.

"It's rather complex to explain right now. The main thing is that we have to get away from here… is there any place we can all go that's safe?" Jon responded.

"Sure, we have arrangements with the Waldorf. Danielle, call ahead and arrange for some rooms." Danielle took out her phone, turned her head away from the others and made the call.

"Jon, I have an idea," Teddy interrupted. "I think we can save La Levrier. At least for the time being." Teddy looked confident as he commanded everyone's attention. It wasn't lost on Jon that his sentence began with his name as if in that minute they were now on the same side.

"How long do you think we have before your people figure out that the explosives are duds?" Teddy asked. As he said that, Claire and Danielle's heads snapped toward Jon.

"Explosives? Duds?" Claire demanded.

Teddy defended his new partner. "Claire, there is a lot to catch you up on but at another time. Right now, Jon and I have to act fast. I really think I have a way to save the building and the contents, but I have to make some calls. Time is of the essence, trust us."

In the time it took Teddy to take charge of the moment, the limos pulled into the circular entrance to the Waldorf on Walton Street. To have four black limos carrying guests all connected to the same reservation looked majestic even for the Waldorf's exclusive clientele. It certainly didn't draw suspicion that this group may be escaping from some law enforcement action.

A Waldorf attendant opened the door to Claire's limo. It hung open while the group discussed strategy. "Claire, you and Danielle check in with everyone. Make sure they are comfortable and are without any inkling of what was going on back there at Astor Street," Teddy instructed Claire. She nodded in agreement. "Danielle, start taking care of the other buses. Let's put them up somewhere temporarily, but not here. We may need to come and go freely here in the next few days without you acting as Claire Bernardin for the members right now. Let's put Danielle in charge of the quests."

Claire turned to Danielle, "I guess you just got what I might call a field promotion," Claire smiled toward Danielle.

"Ok, I have to be quick here, so both of you get out of the car and check-in everyone. Jon and I will take care of La Levrier." Teddy motioned as diplomatically as he could under the time pressure and Claire and Danielle alighted from the limo.

After they left, Teddy continued his command of the situation. "Let me make a couple of calls. Hang on, and you'll see what I have in store…"

Jon's half-smile and silence from the moment Teddy started barking logistics affirmed his approval of Teddy's quick thinking.

"Oh, like I asked before. This all hinges on how much time we might have until your friends might plan to reload those charges and continue to carry out your plan?" Teddy asked as he dialed the first number.

"Ah, how do you know this was my plan?" Jon asked.

"Just a hunch. Come on, no time for psychohistory. How much time do we have?"

"We probably have hours. My plan…" Jon tilted his head and smiled coyly. "Didn't call for any backup materials in case the first canisters didn't do the job, so it's not like they will have back-up explosives. Unless… someone thinks very fast out there and while they wait for the bomb squad and they requisition replacement material. But, quite frankly, my boss is not that snappy to take action in the field." He paused. "We have time."

"Good," Teddy agreed. He pressed a button to lower the sound-proof glass partition between the driver and them. "Jill, get us over to that parking lot over by the North Avenue Beach House." He raised the partition and continued his planning with Jon. "We'll use that as our staging area. I think you'll agree that you, especially, shouldn't be seen back there on Astor Street." Jon nodded in agreement. He continued to be impressed with Teddy's total command of the situation.

As the car drove out of the Waldorf's courtyard, Teddy furiously made some calls, but he quickly finished. "All done." He slumped back in his seat and took a deep breath.

On Astor Street, Mac was in a rage more intense than any of the FBI agents had ever seen. It was now an hour later from the time Jon went back into La Levrier to defuse the bombs under the guise of checking for Teddy.

Mac motioned for the police commander to come over, "How long before your bomb people get here?" Her tone was firm, but she controlled her fury.

"They're on the way. They react fast when called." He returned her question with a sneer, continuing to rub in her face the embarrassment of this operation now in shambles. His implied inflection communicated, 'My people are competent.' He walked away from her without a word.

As all the personnel waited for the bomb squad to arrive, many sat on the street curb, returned to vehicles or leaned against trees as if they all took a break. Mac waited a few minutes and then returned to the SUV that brought her there.

True to the police commander's statement, a gray truck that resembled an armored car pulled in front of La Levrier. Several police officers in green khakis and tees hopped out of the truck and walked toward the police commander. He immediately motioned for Mac to join the group.

The police commander instructed Mac, "Let these people know what to look for and what to expect in there." He continued the same dismissive demeanor as he had before.

Mac gave the bomb squad police the detailed rundown on where the explosives would be, the nature of the explosives and what the overall plan was initially.

The bomb squad police returned to the armored truck, assembled the equipment they would need, including the special bomb-proof turn-out gear they would wear into the building. The squad proceeded as if in no particular hurry. Their casualness infuriated Mac and, in no uncertain terms, she let her agents close to her know how impatient she was with them.

After what seemed like an eternity to Mac, two officers from the bomb squad were fully suited up and they walked into La Levier. They walked through the foyer and into the cabaret and spotted the canisters wrapped around the table leg just as Mac instructed. They looked at the canisters for a short time, snipped Jon's rubber hose and lifted one of the canisters. They carefully unscrewed the top, looked over the cap, moved away from the other canisters and placed a probe down the neck of the thermos-like bottle. They repeated the same procedure with the other canisters. When they finished, they took off their headgear, looked at each other and smirked, "Gelatin."

The bomb squad marched out of La Levrier and walked right up to their commander. Mac rushed from her SUV to join them. When she heard what the officers had to say, she stormed from the group and waved over all her FBI personnel. The police and fire trucks and cars almost immediately began to pull out from the area. It could be felt in the air that they were all saying, 'We've got better things to do.' The FBI agents were left alone to proceed without their back-up.

Once all the FBI agents were in a circle by Mac, some still dressed as Chicago firefighters, Mac addressed them, "Fuck, fuck, fuck! What's going on here? I had better not find out that Fenwick sabotaged this operation. Goddamn to shit… goddamn him… what the hell?" She took a visibly deep breath and collected her rage. "The Chicago bomb squad cleared the building. So… let's make the most of this bad situation. Let's hold our positions here. I'll get more of our people over here and we'll take over blocking the streets and keeping the neighbors safe. If things so south, we can always call the fire department to clean it up afterward. I'll call over and get some replacement explosives. The same ones that Fenwick researched. That's going to take a while, so in the meantime, we are going in there and ripping that fucking place apart. Any papers, computers, anything of value, let's confiscate. You all know the drill. I want any and everything. I'll call for a semi for storage. OK, let's go."

As Mac turned to lead the agents up to the front steps of La Levrier, she stopped in her tracks. A group of roughly 20 people sat and stood casually on the front steps leading up to the front doors of La Levrier. Mac looked dumbfounded. She paused and her agents followed her footsteps, she studied the scene for a moment and then continued to walk toward this group.

When she arrived just paces from the first step, she addressed the group, "Ah, hello. We have an emergency situation going on here with this building. You will have to leave this property," she commanded as if they were her employees.

The group was silent. They stared Mac down.

"I said, you'll have to leave this property… NOW!" Mac shouted.

The group just continued to stare at her. Then, after some time passed a large female walked out from the middle of the cluster. "I'm Attorney Willa Matthews." She pulled papers from her suit jacket. "We have a writ here that Judge Thomas signed this morning. You have no cause to enter this building."

Mac glared at Willa. "No, you're the one who is mistaken. We have an order from the city to inspect this building for a gas leak, so get off this property or I'll gladly have my people escort you away."

"Sorry, but our injunction supersedes that city bureau paper. You're the one who has to leave right now." Willa calmly stated.

Mac thought for a moment. She whispered to her agents and in unison, they placed their hands on their bodies as if indicating that they would draw their weapons if needed. Mac began to move forward toward the steps again.

As Mac and the FBI agents advanced, all 20 protesters drew weapons on the oncoming agents and Mac herself. There were small firearms, menacing looking handguns and several small automatic rifles that were small enough to be concealed under clothes. Mac just crossed her arms and looked unamused.

One of the group spoke up—a slender young man with a purple dyed hair and multiple facial piercings named Dylan Landing. "Ma'am, I suggest you and your people—whoever they are—surrender yourselves now. In addition to the writ our lawyer showed you, we have another paper here signed by one of the building's owners, Ted Bernardin, giving me and each one of these members of the LGTBQ community temporary power of attorney of ownership of this building. Under the constitution, we have a right to protect our property from intruders and use deadly force if necessary."

Mac sighed. "Do you really think your little toys and that flimsy scrap of paper can overpower the Federal Bureau of Investigation? That's right—the F.B.I.," Mac drawled slowly and deliberately. "This situation is far more serious than you realize and, if this building blows, you're all in grave danger. Now, we can either play nice, or this can get nasty. Take your pick. We don't have all day."

Dylan, unintimidated, continued. "You're right, Miss FBI. Time is of the essence for all of us. My friends and I would like nothing more than to pull the trigger on your charade and go viral on how you had a shoot-out with our community. How do you think it would look if your FBI agents got violent with us gays, lesbians and transgender citizens? The social media would gobble it right up and you'd be left with nothing but egg all over that smirk on your face."

It was becoming more transparent to Mac that she was losing the battle as the crowd refused to relent.

Willa reinforced Dylan's threat and stepped inches from Mac's face. "Now, let's play nice, shall we? It's time to head back to those little cubicles in your fancy government building and type up your reports on what happened here. File them away and move on to some other means to waste public funds or justify your existence."

Mac bit her lip indecisively and shifted her eyes away from Willa. She canvassed the scene and noticed that several of her agents began lowering their weapons despite not receiving the official command to cease and desist from their leader. Without the support of her troops, she couldn't win the war.

"Fine," she fumed. "But this isn't over. Not by a long shot. Tell your minions that if they dare set foot inside that mansion that they could not only risk losing their lives but face severe consequences for not obeying FBI orders."

"And we'll be prepared to suffer those consequences IF they manifest," Willa smiled mockingly.

Mac stormed past Willa, bumping her shoulder in the process as she waved her agents to retreat into their vehicles. As the faux firefighters and others scattered, the protesters in the LGBTQ crowd clapped, hooted and whistled. Their celebration grew even louder when Mac assumed the wheel of her SUV, flipped off the mob and screeched back to what Willa had termed her "fancy government building" to make one dreaded phone call.

Mac Owen's Office—FBI Headquarters Chicago—1:36 pm Central Time

"Chief Owens," Bill Weathers of the Secret Service greeted her after his assistant put through the call he was expecting all day. "What took you so long?"

"Hello, Bill," Mac stated flatly. "I'm sorry I didn't phone you earlier, but…"

"Well, tell me the good news. I'm waiting," Weathers interrupted.

There was silence on the other end as Mac fumbled for words.

"You shut that whorehouse down, right? The White House has been all over my ass. I just need your confirmation and we're done here."

"Well, that's the problem," Mac stammered. "We're not quite done yet."

This time it was Mac's turn to hear the silence. It grew increasingly uncomfortable as the seconds passed.

"You're shittin' me, right?" Weathers finally spoke.

"I-I wish I were, Bill," Mac muttered. "Believe me; this isn't the call I wanted to make to you today, either. We hit a snag earlier, but we're making up for lost time. I expect to give you the answer you want in the next couple of days."

"Days? DAYS?" Weathers scoffed. "I gave you weeks. Fucking WEEKS of time I didn't have and neither do you.

You let me down, you let the Secret Service down and you let the FBI down. I'm going to have to report this to your boss who, as you know, is right down the hall."

"I wouldn't do that just yet until you've heard my plan," Mac soothed.

"Our country's Executive Office is in grave danger, and we barely have minutes, let alone days," Weathers seethed. "You clearly fucked up what should have been a pretty simple assignment for someone in your rank."

"Please, Bill, let me explain…" Mac pleaded but was cut off by a sharp click, which morphed into the wail of a steady dial tone.

Desperate, Mac tried to call Weathers back, but his assistant insisted that he had left his office and his time of return was unknown. Mac then speed-dialed Fenwick. No answer. She redialed his number. Still no answer. When she finally got his voice mail, she was about to unleash a torrent of rage when her phone beeped with another call coming in.

Mac was quick to answer, "Oh, Bill, thank you for getting back to me. Allow me to…"

"This isn't Bill, Makenzie," Elliott Trost, director of the FBI, announced.

"Elliott, so good to hear from you," Mac responded, collecting herself.

"I'm sure you won't think that's the case shortly," Elliott continued. "I just received an earful from Weathers."

"Yes, Sir, I suspect Weathers gave you his side of the story," Mac acknowledged.

"And there's another side?" Elliott challenged. "All I know is the only side—the facts. You were ordered to investigate and shut down operations at La Levrier by today's deadline. As the head of our Midwest field office, I trusted you to assemble the right team, execute the right plan and get the job done right the first time. You failed."

"No, *I* didn't fail, Elliott. Agent Jon Fenwick failed. He failed miserably," Mac defended.

"Jon Fenwick reports to you," Elliott stated.

"Well, yes, but..." Mac shot back.

"Then that's all the evidence I need to relieve you of your position," he said.

"Why ME? Why not Fenwick? He's the one who put those phony explosives together and made a fool out of me, you and the entire FBI!" Mac stammered.

"That's not going to be necessary," Elliott stated. "Fenwick called me directly and resigned about 10 minutes ago. I need someone who is competent, who is dependable and who can follow the Goddamn orders of the FBI."

"That's me, Elliott, I assure you. Let me prove that I can complete this mission with a BANG," Mac appealed, grinning at her choice of words as she tried to lighten the conversation. She had known Trost for more than 12 years and wasn't about to go down without a fight.

"The only thing that will be banging is the sound of your door when I have the security guards escort you out of the building," Elliott clarified. "You have 15 minutes to gather your belongings. Effective immediately, you are officially dismissed from the FBI."

Mac heard a rap on her office door. There was no mistaking that the two figures on the other side dressed in uniform were waiting to perform their duty. With that, she had no choice but to follow orders. The final orders she would ever receive from the FBI. For Mackenzie Owens, the case was closed.

CHAPTER TWENTY-EIGHT

French Toast

Waldorf Astoria Chicago

Claire's mind drifted back to days earlier in her private Waldorf suite. Even though exhausted, she and Ted finally had a chance to connect and make sense of all the events that had so quickly transpired. Jon, it appeared, was nowhere to be found, further punctuating Claire's sense of loss amid the chaos.

"Ted, I just don't get it," Claire tried to reason with her brother. "Jon was assigned by his FBI superiors to destroy La Levrier and he knew exactly what he was doing all along. He manipulated you, me, Danielle, Kenneth, everyone, into believing his lies. At the same time, he lied to the FBI. He executed this elaborate plot of planting phony explosives, hauled us all off to safety and for what? He just skipped town like a fucking double agent!"

"Maybe he wanted to get the hell away from the FBI. God knows they're probably out for his hide, and he had to run for cover. Meanwhile, we need to figure out what to do with La Levrier."

"What do you mean?" Claire raised an eyebrow.

"Look, we can't just go back there and pretend it's business as usual. We're dead center on the FBI's radar, and it appears we have been for some time now," Ted continued. "Let's face it: we knew there was risk in accepting the Veep as a client, and it backfired. Even the Secret Service is onto us. Our asses would be in jail if it weren't for your lover boy's clever antics to derail the feds. We have no choice, Claire. We have to shut down La Levrier."

Claire sighed and lowered her face to her hands. Deep down, she knew Ted was right. It wasn't safe to return to La Levrier given the cloak of national scrutiny on its operations, its owners, its employees and even more so, its members.

Ted knew the impact of this news on his sister, who had nurtured the business since its infancy. He put his arm around her—a gesture he reserved for the rarest of occasions. "Look, Sis, I know this whole thing has taken a tremendous toll, but you and I know what has to be done. Let me handle the details. I've got my people watching our place like hawks. We haven't had any threats or break-ins, thank God, but we need to remain vigilant. Now that all of our members have returned home, it's time to communicate the reality of the situation to our staff. As Chief of Security, I've already alerted them to remain clear of the property. There will hopefully be a safe time in the near future for them to collect their belongings. But, for now, we need to consider their best interests…"

"Yes, yes, you're right, of course," Claire conceded. "I propose we keep them all on full pay for a year plus a generous severance."

"Agreed," Ted nodded. "This will ensure their cooperation and their silence. I'm sure this news would best be delivered by you personally first thing in the morning. And, may I make another suggestion?"

Claire looked up at Ted, her eyes bleary from days of lost sleep. Without waiting for a response, Ted reached into his coat pocket, pulled out an envelope and handed it to his sister.

"What's this?" Claire asked, gingerly taking it from Ted's hands.

"Something for you," Ted urged. "It's long overdue. More than ever, I think it's what you need to do. Right now."

Claire peeled the flap of the envelope carefully and lifted its contents. "I can't, I just can't, Teddy. You know it's impossible for me to do this on such short notice."

"You can, and you will. After you make the staff announcement tomorrow morning," Ted calmly instructed his sister in a loving, but firm, manner that she could not refuse.

The next morning

Claire found herself tucked in the luxurious white limo Ted had ordered for her. It swooped her up shortly after Claire called a meeting with her staff in her suite over a catered breakfast. She delivered the news softly, but swiftly, ensuring that all of her Levriettes and employees felt assured that they would be well taken care of. In exchange, she asked for their confidentiality, reminding them of the pact they had each made with La Levrier upon employment. She would always protect the reputation of her colleagues, and she expected the same in return.

Claire was struck with a wave of sadness as the limo rolled toward its destination. She would miss Danielle, Kenneth and all of her protégées who she had mentored over the years, many of them young ladies struggling to find themselves who had now transformed into beautiful and confident women. Every one of them was special to her, and now Claire had to let them go, not by choice but out of necessity. She typically would have turned to Marius and Javert for solace, but Ted had already boarded her prized Greyhounds the moment they checked into the Waldorf, to ensure their comfort and safety. Claire had been too busy in the days to care for herself, let alone her babies. Now that she had a new destination, it was just as well that they remain in the temporary care of their favorite kennel which was, in many respects, as lavishly appointed to cater to canines as was the Waldorf itself.

Claire was, alas, alone. Alone as she had always been and, it seemed, would remain now that Jon was no longer in her life. She pushed thoughts of him aside as she tried to focus on what awaited her. Claire dipped into her shoulder bag and polished her lips with a creamy coat of crimson gloss. Its boldness defied her mood but gave her a boost of confidence as she exited the limo and graciously tipped its driver who helped her with her luggage.

The next day, lunchtime

"Bonjour, Mademoiselle Bernardin. Welcome to Epicure. Chef Frechon is delighted that you are able to join us. Allow me to show you to your table," the maître d' rolled in a thick accent as he pulled a leather menu from his station.

For the occasion, Claire had donned a simple knit black turtleneck dress that hugged her hips and boasted flared long sleeves. Paired with black opaque tights, knee-high boots, and a striking silver pendant, she exuded elegance. But the crowning touch was her long, straight blonde hair clasped in ponytail that fell down the back of her grey cashmere shawl.

"Is this your first visit to Le Bristol?"

"Oui, Monsieur," Claire nodded as she canvassed the elegantly appointed, exclusive bistro that was the hotel's signature dining establishment. Although still groggy from the flight, she could not resist the charming invitation that had been personally penned and delivered to her hotel suite the evening upon her arrival. Epicure's famously celebrated chef Eric Frechon had requested her presence for lunch the next day. Claire was thrilled that she had been hand-picked for the honor of joining the chef's special table, especially because she had not eaten much since her flight arrived or in the last several days, for that matter.

The maître d' escorted her past several tables draped in ivory and vases of red roses, as her heels clicked on the cream and beige patterned marble tile. Their journey continued deeper into the room. The elaborate tray ceilings, heavy floral tapestry curtains, and stunning gilded chandeliers cooed elegance. Finally, he led Claire to a table for two at the very back of the bistro, nestled against a white shuttered window that opened to a stunning view of the hotel's famed topiary gardens.

"Please have a seat, Mademoiselle Bernardin," he said, pulling out one of the two chairs for Claire and then opening the menu before placing it in her hands. "Your guest will be joining you tout suite."

"Merci," Claire smiled. "I look forward to meeting Chef Frechon." She noticed a bottle of Moet & Chandon Dom Perignon chilling on ice in a silver bucket standing next to the table.

Claire stared at the menu before her, overwhelmed by what promised to be a lavishly delicious meal. She was sure to order Chef Frachon's famous macaroni stuffed with black truffle, artichoke, and duck foie gras as her first course.

"Pardon me, Mademoiselle," a deep voice stated behind her. "I should have given you the chef's special menu." Claire whirled around, expecting to greet her waiter.

"Mind if I join you?" he smiled.

Claire choked on her words, unable to utter a syllable.

"I assume that means yes," he stated as he pulled out the other chair and seated himself.

"Jon! What are you doing here?" Claire finally gasped.

"Waiting for you, of course," he said casually with the flip of his hand. He was dressed impeccably in freshly pressed navy trousers, a crisp white shirt open at the collar and a double-breasted wool sport coat bearing a burgundy burlap pocket square.

"But how... how did you know where I was?" she stared in disbelief.

He just smiled at her, unable to lift his eyes from her face.

"Did you honestly think I would never see you again?" he smirked playfully. "In fact, to be correct, it is you who is seeing me. I got here first."

Claire contemplated Jon's words carefully. "So, you've been in Paris all this time?"

"Yes, since Saturday. Just for the last few days until I could get things settled and have Ted convince you to take this much-needed trip," Jon replied nonchalantly, as if he knew his plans would manifest all along.

"Teddy knew about this?" Claire grilled Jon, still recovering from the shock.

"Oh, your brother more than knew about this," Jon corrected. "He was my true partner in crime."

Claire blushed, touched by the irony of his words and not sure how to respond when only hours before she thought she would never see Jon again.

"I must thank your brother for helping me to pull off the scheme of a lifetime," he added, as a huge smile broke across his face.

"Admittedly, Teddy was instrumental," Claire nodded. "He sure had me fooled. And I thought I knew my brother."

"Your brother is happily back home handling the affairs of La Levrier, while you and I have our own affair to tend to," Jon grinned. "That is, if you'll still have me."

"I'm not sure what I'll have these days," Claire whispered in return, "I'm so confused, Jon. There are so many decisions to make…"

"Maybe the chef's special menu will narrow your choices and guide you to the right decision," Jon stated, handing Claire a small, leather-bound menu.

She opened it eagerly, famished from hours of deprivation. Centered on the first page in elegant scroll was the header: "First course, second course, third course and only course." But nothing underneath.

Claire furrowed her brow. "I believe the course du jour starts on the second page," Jon urged.

She flipped to the next page where, in equally elegant, larger cursive were the words: "Veux-tu m'epouser?"

Claire squinted. "I guess I'll have to ask our waiter for a translation. I'm not sure what cuisine this refers to."

"You mean your French is getting rusty, Mademoiselle?" Jon joked. "Veux-tu m'epouser?" he repeated in a perfect Parisian dialect.

"Wow, I'm impressed!" Claire joked. "You must have been practicing."

"It's something I've been rehearsing for my entire life, Claire," he agreed in a serious tone. "But I think you'd prefer to hear the translation from me than from Garcon Alain."

Claire sat amused, waiting for Jon to continue.

"It means," he stated carefully, "will… you… marry… me?"

Claire's reaction dumbfounded him. Silence. Finally, she spoke, "Jon, I lost my business because of your precious FBI's meddling. And now you want me to marry you?"

"And for that, I'm truly sorry," Jon nodded. "But you could have lost so much more had I not done what I did to protect you, your staff and your members."

"I know you did, but…" Claire began.

"And I want you to know that I gave my notice to the FBI the day of the incident. Yes, Agent Fenwick officially resigned. I did that for us so that we could be together without any conflict of interest."

A long pause hung in the air.

"Oui, jet' epouserai!" she smiled after matching his accent with her own in perfect French.

"You knew what that meant?" Jon gasped.

"Mais bien sur," Claire smiled and squeezed Jon's hand. "I just wanted to hear you say it."

"And I've been wanting to say it since the day I fell in love with you," he confessed. "And now I have a little something for you." With that, he fished a black velvet box from his sport coat and pried open the lid, so that its contents faced Claire.

She inhaled deeply as the two-carat emerald cut diamond glinted in the light of the chandelier. Wrapped around each side of the stunning stone was a gold Greyhound. The two canines framed the diamond and their tales intertwined into a band—a custom setting created just for Claire. Jon lifted the ring, slid it on her slender finger and smiled. "Perfect, just like the lady who wears it," he declared.

As if on cue, Garcon Alain came to their table and refilled their champagne glasses with the Dom.

"Jon, I absolutely love it, and I love you," Claire stated, wiping a tear from her eye. "I never imagined I'd be here in France, let alone with you—and engaged to be married!"

"We've sure come a long way since our first encounter at Coq D'Or, haven't we? Here's to you and to us," Jon toasted, and the couple clinked glasses and kissed deeply.

"After we dine, I'd like to take you on a stroll and show you where I've been staying and where I hope you'll join me," Jon winked.

"You're not staying here at Le Bristol?" she inquired, surprised.

"Non, Mademoiselle," Jon grinned. "To be honest, these stuffy hotels aren't really my cup of tea. Overpriced tourist traps, if you ask me. I prefer to experience the local quaintness of an independent boutique inn. But, I knew from Ted that Epicure was on your wish list, and it seemed that Le Bristol would be the perfect lure. That's why he booked you here for your first night in Paris."

"Hmmmm, I'm feeling a sense of déjà vu," Claire mused. "I remember having this conversation with you when we first met and I lured YOU away from The Drake and to La Levrier."

"And you spoiled me," Jon laughed. "I've become such a hotel snob. It's my turn to spoil you now."

2:55 p.m., Paris

Following a leisurely lunch at Epicure during which Chef Frechon paid a visit to Claire and Jon's table and personally served them a celebratory dessert assortment of Bergamot, Coffee Liquorice and Lemon from Menton, the couple exited Le Bristol to take a stroll down rue du Faubourg Saint-Honore.

Jon held Claire's hand as she wrapped her shawl tighter and admired the beauty of Paris proper, with its narrow avenues and historical boutiques, some of which dated back to the late 1800s. Jon meandered confidently, promising to show Claire the famous Champs Elysees nearby, but first led her down a small, winding street which dead-ended. They stopped at a three-story, blonde brick mansion snuggled at the end of the avenue. It boasted elaborate carvings near the curved double front door and black trellises bordering the upper floor balconies, which appeared to be guest rooms.

"C'est tres belle!" Claire remarked. "However did you find this little gem?"

"I have my ways," Jon smiled. "I'm glad you like it. Let's go inside for a bit, shall we?"

Jon turned the key in the front door to unlock it and escorted Claire inside. She immediately noticed how clean, open and airy the foyer was, with its soaring archway and vaulted ceiling that welcomed the natural daylight. It carried an artsy yet elegant vibe, with soft lavender walls and bright white contrasting trim. The floor tile was traditional French black and white checkered marble, and fun Zebra-patterned benches flanked either side of the entryway. The umbrella stand, however, immediately caught her eye. It was a large sculpture of a Greyhound with an open back that housed at least three parasols.

"Charming doesn't even begin to cover it!" Claire whistled. "Whoever decorated this place has exquisite taste. I would love to meet the owner. Is she around?"

"You're looking at him," Jon beamed. "Welcome to La Levrier Paris!"

Claire laughed. "Oh, Jon, really… you're too much!"

"Too much?" he repeated jokingly. "Well, if you don't like my choice of real estate, we can always look elsewhere, but I was hoping you'd approve of your future wedding present and soon-to-be international headquarters of La Levrier. That is, if you'd be interested in resuming your business in a country under far less scrutiny."

"Are you serious? This is… OURS?" Claire said, lowering her voice as she gazed admiringly around the room.

"Every square millimeter," Jon bragged. "There's a penthouse on the top floor where I figured we would make our residence, and the lower two levels have a total of nine fully furnished suites with parlors. It was formerly the Hotel le Petit Chat, but the owner, Madame Tremont, fell ill and needed to sell… quickly, I might add. So, her realtor and I became fast friends and here we are."

"Jon, I can't think of anything more perfect," Claire cried. "Except…"

"Except?" Jon questioned, looking disappointed.

"That awful former name—little cat! How absurd," she giggled.

"And completely unfitting for our first residents," Jon added. He then disappeared down the hallway and walked toward a closed door, opening it before Claire could say another word.

"Marius and Javert!" Claire shrieked with excitement as her loves bounded out to greet her. "How did you two make it all the way to Paris?"

"Again, I have my ways," Jon smiled. "My former FBI badge came in handy when I had to pull a few strings. Marius and Javert make excellent service dogs. And, of course, Ted was a huge help. I couldn't have put all of this together without him."

"Hmmmm, now I know why he only gave me a one-way ticket to Paris!" Claire mused.

"Rest assured, Ted has everything under control in Chicago, and we can go back anytime your heart desires," Jon told Claire, pulling her close in his arms.

"What my heart desires most is you," Claire smiled and kissed him passionately. "Now, let's go check out that penthouse of ours…"